HE'D MAKE HER HIS WOMAN

Lance led her to the door. "Let's go for a buggy ride," he suggested. "I want to be alone with you."

Cassandra's heart surely skipped a beat. They went into the night air, and he helped her up into the buggy. Cassandra gazed at his virile frame as he untied the horse and drove off, around the outskirts of Abilene. When they stopped, he turned to her, looking even bigger in the moonlight, his sweet masculinity overpowering her. Their eyes held; their lips met.

This was the kiss she'd been waiting for, the kiss that said she was a woman, not a child. His lips were gentle but demanding, parting her own with expertise, lightly moving his tongue to taste her mouth as he pulled her against himself, pressing the firm, young breasts against his hard chest.

"You know I love you," whispered the impassioned girl. "Kiss me a hundred times, Lance, a thousand times. Do whatever you will. . . ."

ECSTASY'S CHAINS

F. ROSANNE BITTNER

ZEBRA BOOKS
KENSINGTON PUBLISHING CORP.

ZEBRA BOOKS

are published by

Kensington Publishing Corp.
475 Park Avenue South
New York, NY 10016

First printing: April, 1989

Printed in the United States of America

From the Author . . .

I hope you enjoy my story. I will be glad to send you a newsletter listing other books I have written, and upcoming novels, as well as personal information about myself. Simply write me in care of ZEBRA BOOKS, 475 PARK AVENUE SOUTH, NEW YORK, NEW YORK 10016. I answer all letters and enjoy hearing from my readers. Please be sure to include a self-addressed, STAMPED envelope with your letter. Thank you.

Parts of this novel refer to actual historical events involving the Cheyenne Indians, the Denver & Rio Grande Railroad and the Kansas-Pacific Railroad. Such references are based on factual printed matter available to the public. However, the characters and major events of this story are purely fictitious and the product of the author's imagination. Any resemblance of the author's fictitious characters to actual persons, living or dead, or of the author's fictitious events to any events that may have occurred at the time of this novel's setting, are purely coincidental.

The major portion of this novel takes place in what is now Kansas and Colorado.

His blood was white,
But he was raised by Indians.
He walked tall as the trees,
And was strong like the rocks.
His sun-darkened skin and eyes green as grass
Made him a part of the land.
Two women wanted him,
But only one captured his heart . . .
The other gave him a son.
And for that son he was willing
To give his very life.
They called him . . .

Rainmaker.

Chapter One

Cassandra sat on the steps of the boardinghouse where she lived and watched a buggy rattle by on the muddy street in front of her. She thought about how Abilene had changed since she first arrived four years earlier. She was only thirteen then. How could a person go from child to woman so quickly? Perhaps only from having known a man like Lance Raines.

When she first came to Abilene, it was a rough and lawless cattle town. Now that the city had its own Council and lawman, it was quieter. A year earlier, a man called "Wild Bill" Hickok had been marshal, until the local citizens removed his badge for being too quick with his gun and accidentally shooting his own deputy. But since most of the cattle and drovers now met the Atchison, Topeka & Santa Fe at Dodge City, farther to the south, Abilene's lawlessness had moved to that city with them.

The wind blew her long, blond hair over her young, pretty face, and she pushed a strand of hair out of the way with slender fingers. A bird flitted out of a bush nearby then, and she watched it fly away. It reminded her of him . . . of Lance. But she still thought of him by his Indian name . . . Rainmaker. He was free like the birds, as wild and hard to catch.

She sighed and swallowed back a lump in her throat.

Would he come back this time? Stay this time? How much longer could she wait? It was October 1872, and soon winter would set in. Surely he would come before winter. How much longer must she only dream about the moment he'd made her his woman, those days on the prairie when they had lain amid wildflowers and become one with each other and with nature. There was no point to her life without him now. She loved him desperately, and she knew he loved her. But there were some things for which a man would give up anything, even the only woman he truly loved. One of those things was his son.

The tears came then, as they did almost daily. How she prayed that somehow he could be with his son forever without having to give up his love for her. There was no way she could know what would happen now until he came back from Denver . . . if he came back at all. It seemed she'd always been looking out over the horizon for him, the beautiful man she had loved so desperately from the first moment he rescued her as a mere child from the Cheyenne. Always he had come when she needed him. Would he come now?

She sniffed and wiped at tears. He'd stolen her virginity in one moment of the most glorious ecstasy she would ever know. She belonged to him — her heart, her bones, her very blood. She belonged to Rainmaker. But who did Rainmaker belong to? He belonged to the land . . . and his son. Could he also belong to Cassandra Elliott? Oh, but he did love her. Of that she was certain.

She rose and walked up the steps to the porch swing, where she sat down and gently pushed with her feet, listening to the rhythmic squeak it made as she rocked. She leaned back and closed her eyes. Yes, she would wait for him forever, if necessary. Some day he would come riding out of the western horizon to hold her in those strong arms. He was her hero, the wonderful, strong, brave, handsome man who had risked his life among the Cheyenne to save

12

her. She worshipped him. She'd die for him.

Never would she forget the first time she saw him, and though barely thirteen then, she already knew who she loved and who would someday show her how to be a woman. It was hot that late summer of 1868, when she sat frightened and distraught inside the tipi of her Cheyenne captor, hoping and praying that somehow someone would come and rescue her. She didn't know then that a man called Rainmaker was disembarking a train at Abilene, preparing to walk into her life and steal her heart away forever. . . .

Steam exploded from the side of the monstrous black train engine just as Lance Raines stepped down from a passenger car and scanned the railroad platform full of passengers. It was late summer, 1868, and the Kansas-Pacific had only recently laid track to Abilene. Already, passenger demand was high, as people surged westward, following the rails to their last stop, absorbing the various riches and opportunities the railroad afforded them.

Lance caught the strong odor of the nearby stockyards and wrinkled his nose. He'd been around horses all his life, but the smell of a stockyard packed with thousands of cattle on a hot summer day was repugnant even to a man who had grown up around animals. Not even the herds of hundreds of horses the Indians kept smelled that bad. Such was the price of success for a booming cattle town, which Abilene had instantly become when the railroad arrived.

He pulled a worn leather hat down over his thick, dark hair, thinking perhaps he should get a haircut and go see Mattie—or maybe he'd go see Mattie first. Some things were more important than a haircut when a man had been out on the plains too long. Maybe he'd get everything he needed at Mattie's—a bath and a shave and a haircut—all at Mattie's skilled hands. A scout found little time or op-

13

portunity to tend to such things when out dodging Indians and sleeping under the stars.

He strode on long legs toward the sheriff's office, his easy gait making the fringes of his buckskins sway gracefully. Lance Raines was taller than most of the men he passed, a broad-shouldered, slim-hipped man with a commanding physique, his handsome face tanned by the western sun, the dark skin enhanced by provocative green eyes that rested behind thick, dark lashes. Few men went up against Lance Raines; those who knew him knew better, and those who didn't were usually intimidated by his size and the many weapons he sported. He was obviously a man honed hard and strong by wilderness living, a man anyone could tell was capable of using his weapons well, and a man the prostitutes welcomed with great relish.

He mounted the steps to the jailhouse, tipping his hat and nodding to a young eastern woman who was staring at him. A broad, handsome grin crossed his face when she blushed and turned away, and a sleeping hunger for a woman was awakened at the sight of her soft curves. He suddenly hoped that whatever the sheriff's news was, it would not interfere with visiting Mattie before he lit out again.

He walked through the already-open doorway, greeting a man who wore a star and was at the moment swatting angrily at flies.

"Raines!" the man exclaimed, rising and wiping at sweat on his forehead. He swatted again. "Damned pests! It's the damned cattle that bring them. All the cattle business has done for me is bring me more trouble: drunken cowboys, more saloons, gunfights." He finally set the swatter down and gave Lance a friendly smile, putting out his hand. "Glad you made it."

Lance shook his hand and sat down in a chair across from the man's desk. "I got your message. You said it was urgent, so here I am. But you're lucky you found me,

John. I was having a damned good time keeping myself hidden in the rooms above Callie's Saloon in St. Louis."

Sheriff John Goodman grinned. "I wasn't sure if you'd be in St. Louis; but I'd heard you'd been leading supply wagons from St. Louis to the railroad workers, so I figured I'd try to catch you there."

Lance fished a thin cigar from the pocket of his buckskin shirt. "I've spent the summer leading those wagons, trying to avoid Indians every mile. They're thirsty for white blood, especially anybody working for the railroad, and in some respects I hardly blame them." He stretched out his long legs and lit the cigar, taking a puff. "At any rate, I decided to hole up in St. Louis a few days and get some rest. Then that damned messenger found me, so here I am. I haven't even taken my horse off the train yet."

"Well, those Indians are the very reason I sent for you, Lance. The Cheyenne have captured a little white girl, and I want you to find her and bring her back."

Lance frowned, removing his hat and wiping his brow. "You make it sound awfully damned simple," he said sarcastically, holding the cigar in his teeth.

"Might be—for you. You know them. Hell, they half raised you. That's why you're such a good scout. I figure you'd do better going in alone than sending the damned army after her. They'd just botch things up. We've had enough trouble with Sherman and Custer storming this territory, killing at random and keeping the pot boiling. We send soldiers after that girl, and the Cheyenne are liable to kill her for spite."

Lance shrugged. "They might kill her anyway."

"Maybe. But I don't think so. You've said yourself the Cheyenne are less ruthless than some other tribes. But they'll use her for ransom—to demand food and rifles. If they don't get those things, she'll become the wife of some Cheyenne buck—or be traded to the Apaches or Comanches. You know what they would do to her. Either fate

15

would be horror for her. She's only twelve, Lance."

Lance met the man's gaze, and they exchanged a look of understanding and pity. Lance sighed and rubbed at his eyes, taking the cigar from his mouth. "Give me the details," he muttered.

Goodman took a faded picture from a desk drawer and threw it down on the other side of the desk for Lance to see. Lance stared at a lovely, blond-haired child, the cracks in the picture doing nothing to hide the girl's pretty face and eyes. She'd be a prize for any Cheyenne buck.

"Her name is Cassandra Elliott, and like the fools so many of these settlers are, her father set out on his own from Illinois to come to Kansas to homestead, totally ignorant of how bad things really are out here," the sheriff explained. "As riled as the Indians are over the railroad, I suppose maybe they thought the Elliott wagons were more railroad supply wagons. Who knows? There were two wagons, with a man-friend of Elliott's driving the second wagon. Only reason I know that much is because the friend lived long enough to get himself to town on one of their horses. The Indians hadn't stolen it because it had a limp, but the animal managed to stumble into town. By then it was so bad we had to shoot the horse, and not long after that, the man died, too. He rode all the way with an arrow in his side, and the only reason he managed that was his determination to find help for the little girl. Her parents and a brother were killed, and he saw the Indians ride off with the child."

"How do you know they were Cheyenne?"

"The arrow. It was Cheyenne all right."

Lance picked up the picture and studied it a moment, puffing on the cigar. "She's pretty. They won't harm her right away, not with that blond hair. She's better ransom bait unharmed, and if some young Cheyenne man intends to claim her, he'll probably have to fight more than one man for the honor, perhaps pay plenty of horses to the man who actually captured her in the first place. She'll be relatively safe for a while."

"Point is, she doesn't know that, and between seeing her family killed, and being dragged off by a savage to a village of strange people who to her are wild and uncivilized, she has to be terrified."

"You haven't told the soldiers?"

Goodman shook his head. "The Indians are mad enough. The railroad workers live under constant attack. You know that. Things get any worse, we'll have whole towns threatened. The damned soldiers are only making matters worse. Besides, there's something about the little girl in that picture that makes me want to be careful she doesn't get hurt. She has such a sweet innocence in those eyes."

Lance studied the picture again, puffing the cigar quietly. "Agreed," he answered with a sigh.

Goodman leaned back, folding his hands over an oversized stomach. "I don't know, Lance. I'm just so tired of all the fighting and dying. Between the Civil War and now this, I feel tired and beaten. I'd like to see this one turn out right for once — like to see the girl returned unharmed. You're the man who can do it. You know Small Beaver . . . Walking Bear . . . some of the others. You call Kicking Horse your brother, and White Eagle your father. Your Cheyenne name is Rainmaker. You understand their ways. Will you do it? There's no pay in it."

Lance removed the cigar from his mouth and laid it in an ashtray. He leaned forward then, resting his elbows on his knees and looking at the picture once more. He'd had a little sister once, long ago, before the Cheyenne found both him and the girl stranded on the prairie, their parents dead from sickness and starvation. His sister had died shortly thereafter from a strangling cough. Little five-year-old Lance had no place to go but to stay with the Cheyenne, soon forgetting his white man's name. One day during a drought he danced, mimicking the Cheyenne Medicine

17

Man's dance to bring rain, and rain had come. Thus he was called Rainmaker by the Cheyenne. He shortened the name to Raines when he reentered the white man's world a decade later, but he continued to be honored and well liked among the Cheyenne, a white man tanned nearly as dark as they by the western sun, and as skilled at warrior ways as the best of their own bucks.

It was quite possible and likely that this little girl would not be mistreated by the Cheyenne, but life was hard on the rugged plains for a white child, even if she was treated well, for Indian women worked hard and long. And what would the western sun do to this fair-skinned child? Most important, this girl had not been taken in as a child in need by friendly Indians. She had been stolen away by angry hostiles. The friendly mood of the Cheyenne had changed, and Lance did not blame them. But it was not this child's fault.

"I'll see what I can do." He rose and slipped the picture into his pocket, picking up the cigar again and putting it in his mouth. "I'm going to see Mattie Brewster first and vent some frustrations so I can think better. Then I'll look in on Kate before I leave."

Goodman rose and put out his hand. "Thanks, Lance."

Lance shook the man's hand again. "All in a day's work, I reckon. I'm supposed to report eventually to some rich railroad man in Denver by the name of Claude Françoise—big bucks I'm told—made from gold mining. Something about more scouting for the railroad. They want to take the Kansas-Pacific all the way to Denver—even talking about a railroad through the mountains. A good scout can make a lot of money working for those railroad dreamers."

Goodman grinned and Lance headed for the door. "Bring her back, Lance," Goodman spoke up.

Lance turned and met the man's eyes again. "I never make promises, John. I can only say I'll try. Where did the attack occur?"

"About eight miles east of here. We sent men out to find the wagons. They buried the dead and salvaged what they could. We're holding everything for the girl, but there isn't much."

Lance nodded and left. Sheriff Goodman walked to the entrance and watched the young, buckskin-clad man head for the train to pick up his horse and saddle, if it could be called a saddle. Lance Raines used only a small mat made of deerskin stuffed with buffalo hair and covered with a blanket, like the Indians used. It was sometimes difficult to believe the man was not himself at least half Indian. But he had been raised by them, and perhaps that was the same as being one; for the man's quiet sureness, quick skills, dress and manner were much more Indian than white.

"If anybody can con them savages into giving up that little gal, it's the Rainmaker," Goodman muttered.

Mattie stretched and pulled a sheet over her naked body, pleasantly spent after a round of heated mating with the volatile and hungry Lance Raines. She looked forward to his visits, and if she weren't a prostitute, she was sure she'd chase after the man for a husband. But men like Lance Raines did not marry whores, even though they were kind to them in bed and often considered their favorite women as friends. Lance and Mattie were good friends, and she sensed through his quickness and ensuing silence that he was troubled.

"Want to tell me now what's on your mind?" she asked.

Lance stretched his arms over his head and stared at the ceiling, his long, powerful frame taking up more than half the width of the bed and his feet hanging over the end.

"A little girl," he replied quietly. "Captured by the Cheyenne. I'm leaving today to find her, soon as I go see Kate and get me some supplies."

Mattie raised up on one elbow. "Sounds kind of danger-ous."

"Not ordinarily—at least not for me. But the Indians' mood has changed of late. They aren't as easy to dicker with as they once were. I'll have to take along plenty of food and blankets—spend my last dime on a few horses. I'll never get her without something to trade."

She sighed and traced a finger over the perfect lips in his finely-etched face, studying the square jaw and high cheek-bones, the white scar near his eye where a Pawnee knife had sliced at him in battle.

"Be careful," she said softly. "You're a hell of a man, Lance Raines, in looks and in bed. I don't want to lose my favorite customer."

He flashed a handsome grin and met her pale blue eyes, not caring that her body was growing soft from too much use and lines of a hard life were forming about her eyes. He studied the painted face of this woman who was slightly older than he. Some of that paint was smudged now. At thirty, she was almost over the hill for a prostitute, but he liked Mattie. She was patient and understanding. He could talk to her.

"You won't lose me. I'm too mean to die."

"Mmmm. You're probably right there." She bent down and met his lips, and he returned the gesture, parting his lips and grasping her hair as he pressed her against his mouth. Her huge breasts brushed against his chest, and he wrapped an arm around her waist and pulled her tight against him, rolling over and bending a knee up between her legs. "You'll be here when I get back?" he asked, moving his lips to her neck.

"Of course I'll be here."

"Whores tend to move around."

She laughed. "Whores follow the men, and now that this town is busting at the seams with cowboys herding cattle north from Texas, Abilene is the place to be. Those cattle

20

pushers get here looking to spend hard-earned money on booze, gambling and women. I'm not going anyplace."

Lance moved to her side, running a big, calloused hand over her thighs and stomach, then to her breasts, bending down to kiss them. "I like being with you, Mattie."

"Well, a handsome young man your age should be thinking about a wife and children—settling down."

He grinned and sat up, moving to the edge of the bed and picking up his underwear. "Some day. But not now. Besides, out here the pickings are rather slim. I can wait."

"Well, don't wait too long. Only thing is, I feel sorry for the little filly who chooses you. Not that you wouldn't be gentle with her, but there's only one way to break a girl into womanhood, and Lord knows the way you're built you couldn't be gentle about that no matter how you went at it."

Lance just chuckled and stood up. She studied the firm thighs and hips as he pulled on buckskin leggings, and she felt flushed and on fire again.

"I wish you had more time, Lance."

"So do I. But in this case I'd best get moving."

He finished dressing, and she lay back down to watch, drinking in his broad shoulders and hard muscles. "I hope you find that girl. But what will you do with her?"

He shrugged, sitting down and pulling on his boots. "Take her to Kate, maybe. She likes to take in strays. She took me in. If she'll take in a wild, uncivilized, fifteen-year-old boy who can hardly speak English, she'll take on a sweet little girl."

"Well, you'd best discuss it with her."

"I intend to—right now." He rose and reached for his gun, strapping it on and adjusting the huge knife that was also attached to the gunbelt. "Thanks for the shave and bath and all," he spoke up. "And especially the extra service. It was great, as usual. I'd just as soon spend the night, but like I said, I can't take that much time, Mattie."

"Sure." She smiled and pulled the covers over herself, and

21

he leaned down and kissed her lightly. "Watch yourself, Lance. I'll worry."

An easy grin spread over his face and he winked. "Just thinking about coming back here will help me survive anything."

She pushed at him and smiled. "Go lie to somebody else, you green-eyed devil."

He stood up and put on his hat, walking to the door. "Keep the bed warm, Mattie."

"My bed is always warm."

He grinned knowingly and shook his head, walking out the door and down the stairs to the saloon below, nodding to a few acquaintances on his way out. As soon as he left, a few mumbled about the white man who had been raised by Indians and about how none of them cared to get into a skirmish with Lance Raines, all wondering how many men the scout had killed in his lifetime.

Lance headed for the only person he'd been able to call family since soldiers took him from the Indians and brought him to Kate McGee, a spicy-tempered widow old enough to be his grandmother, her red hair streaked now with gray. Kate had been the only one to offer to take the wild boy with hair well past his shoulders and the scars of the Sun Dance sacrifice still fresh on his chest and arms. That was when Kate worked at Fort Kearny in Nebraska as a cook. Young Rainmaker had tried to run away five times that first year, wanting to get back to the only people he knew and loved—the Cheyenne. But always the soldiers brought him back, and twice he was jailed to hold him until Kate thought of a way to calm him again. Finally, one day she showed him a little music box—similar to one his white mother had once owned, its melody bringing back memories of another life—and from that day on, Rainmaker was calmer, more willing to relearn his English and take some reading and writing lessons. He was white, although his skin denied it, but his darkness was a sun-brown, rather than the deeper reddish-brown of his Indian friends. His eyes were the green eyes of a white man, and as he began to remember, he suddenly longed to better remember his white family.

Thus Kate McGee finally began to make headway with the wild teenage savage she had agreed to help. Kate was the kind of person who liked helping others. She gave unselfishly, taking in Rainmaker after losing a son of her own years earlier—wanting some purpose to her life that would help her feel wanted and needed again. Cooking for soldiers did not truly fill the void in her lonely heart, so young Rainmaker became to her both a companion and a challenge. Once he remembered his real first name, he shortened his Indian name of Rainmaker, was christened Lance Raines, and "officially" rejoined the white world.

That had been eleven years ago. But his heart was still Cheyenne, as well as many of his beliefs, and he still loved them and cared about them. Kate soon tired of cooking for so many men, and with her meager savings she moved south into Kansas, opening a boardinghouse in Abilene, where she knew she could see more of Lance again, who had begun scouting for the Kansas-Pacific.

Lance bounded up the steps to the house, then went through the door and into the kitchen, where he knew Kate McGee spent most of her time. She looked up from lighting her oven, then quickly shook the match to put it out.

"Lance!" she exclaimed. "You're finally back!"

He grinned. "Hi, Kate." He walked up to hug her. She patted his back, then pulled away and frowned.

"You've already been to Mattie's place!" she chided. "I can smell the cheap perfume."

"Well, a man has to take care of things, Kate," he replied, kissing a wrinkled cheek.

She moved away, closing the oven door and scowling. "You'd be better off taking care of those things with a nice wife who can give you sons, not the whores, Lance Raines!

Why don't you settle down?"

"You, too? I've heard enough about settling down for one day. What do you have to eat, Kate? I have to get a fast meal and stow up on some grub. I'm heading back out right away."

She turned in disgust, planting her hands on her hips. "You just got here!"

"I know. I'd stay, but Sheriff Goodman has asked me to go find a little white girl who's been captured by the Cheyenne. Figures I can get her back with no fuss. I'm not so sure, but I'm going to try."

The woman softened and sat down at the table, motioning for Lance to do the same. "Oh, Lance, that's a shame about the girl. Her family dead?"

Lance nodded, taking the picture from his pocket and handing it to her. "Cassandra Elliot. She's only twelve."

"Oh, my." The woman sighed. "And so pretty." She sat straighter and took his hand. "You bring that poor thing right here to me if you find her, understand?"

Lance grinned and squeezed her hand. "I was hoping you'd offer, because I was going to ask anyway. Apparently she's got no family left, but I won't know for sure till I get hold of her and can talk to her."

Kate smiled lovingly. "You brought me happiness at a time when I was very lonely, in spite of your wild and ornery ways, Lance Raines. Now you're gone nearly all the time. I need a replacement. A sweet little girl would be a nice change from the likes of you."

Lance laughed and leaned back. "I'm not so bad, Kate."

"Not now, maybe. But when you first came to me, you were a regular hellion. Fact is, when you're out from under my roof, I expect you aren't much changed—always off chasing whores and Indians. What's next after you find that girl?"

He shrugged. "More railroad work, I expect. Some man by the name of Claude Françoise in Denver wants to see me about scouting for the Kansas-Pacific to Denver and then for the Denver & Rio Grande."

"Denver! That's a way off. I wish you'd come around more, Lance, and settle down."

"There you go again." He rose and removed his hat and gunbelt. "Fix me up something, will you, Kate? I have to get moving."

The woman rose and walked over to stand in front of him, the picture in her hand. Lance thought she seemed thinner, a little more stooped. He loved her like a mother, and didn't like to see her getting older. "Fact is, I know what a big heart lies behind that devilish smile and your wayward life, Lance Raines," she told him. "Otherwise you'd not be going after this child. You're doing it for nothing, aren't you?" She handed back the picture.

His smile faded. "She makes me think about my sister, Kate, and the family I've just about forgotten. And it's like Sheriff Goodman said. There's something about her that kind of pulls at you. It bothers me to think of her out there—alone and afraid. Yet I don't even know her."

Kate patted his arm. "You wash up. I'll fix you a meal and pack some grub."

She turned away, and he looked at the picture again, trying to guess the color of the girl's eyes from the brownish photograph. Blue, he surmised, for they looked pale, and her hair was light. He felt a strange tingle, as though there was something happening he could not control, as though he was destined to find the child in the picture.

25

Chapter Two

The heat of the late afternoon sun enveloped Lance, making the vast plains seem more like a close, stuffy room. He halted his gray Appaloosa, patting its black and white spotted rump after he dismounted. He removed his leggings and underwear, then pulled a loincloth from his saddlebag and wrapped it around himself. He was already shirtless, and with the loincloth and his dark skin, most would think he was Indian. This was the way he liked to ride, half naked in the sun, no clothing to bind him and make his sweat. He tied a red kerchief around his forehead and packed all his clothes, tying the strings of his leather hat to his gear.

He grinned at the thought of how Kate would chide him if she saw him now. He could still hear the way she clucked and fussed over his near nakedness when he was first brought to her, and remembered how he fought the men who tried to get him into the hated woolen white man's pants and binding cotton shirt. Kate had finally given up and allowed him to wear his Indian buckskins, but would not allow him to parade around in a loincloth. He had worn the soft, supple skins ever since, trading supplies to his Cheyenne friends every year in exchange for newly sewn and beaded shirts, leggings, vests and moccasins. He had worn white man's clothes only rarely since he was brought to Kate, and he still hated them.

"You hot, too, Sotaju?" he asked the Appaloosa, using the Sioux name he had given the animal, meaning "Smoke." The horse's soft gray coloring reminded him of smoke, and he'd purchased it from a Sioux brave in exchange for rifles and ammunition. It was one of the best pieces of horseflesh he'd ever seen, and well worth the exchange. The Appaloosa had been a faithful and dependable mount for three years now.

He patted Sotaju's neck, and the stallion snorted and nodded his head. Lance chuckled and removed his canteen, taking a short drink before pouring some into the palm of his hand and letting the horse slurp it out. He repeated the gesture several more times, sure the animal needed a lot more water than he did, then recapped the canteen.

He scanned the horizon. He was in Cheyenne country, into the Nebraska plains now and many days north of Abilene. He knew that even for him this was dangerous. The Indian uprisings had started four years before, after the Sand Creek massacre in Colorado. He shuddered at the thought of what the Cheyenne had described as happening there, where Colonel John Chivington of the Colorado Volunteers raided Black Kettle's peaceful settlement, murdering, mutilating and plundering the surprised Cheyenne, cutting down babies with swords and shooting and carving up women, even to removing female organs and breasts. How could the Indians help but need revenge? If any of the women had been his own mother or sister or lover, he'd want blood himself. Now the railroad penetrated Indian country, its noise frightening away the buffalo, a sacred animal to the plains Indians, and their very life source. What buffalo didn't run off were shot by railroad crews and special hunters for food to sustain the hundreds of railroad workers. He'd agreed to scout for the railroad, but he couldn't bring himself to shoot the buffalo. He left that to others; for even though he was white, he, too, honored the animal, and he knew how important and necessary it was to sustaining the Indian's very life. Sometimes he was tempted to turn on his own kind and ride again with the Indian. There were plenty of whites he wouldn't mind killing himself. But he'd been with Kate too long now, and he knew a man had to be with the people of his own blood. It was natural and right.

He took hold of Sotaju's bridle. "I'll walk awhile, boy," he told the animal. "We'll head for that big stand of cottonwoods I know is not too far from here. We should reach it by nightfall."

He'd been following the faint traces of the movement of a large village, a trail he'd picked up after following tracks of a small war party that he'd found at the site of Cassandra Elliott's abduction. The men had apparently joined up with a large tribe migrating northward, probably searching for buffalo. He knew he could run into them at any time, and could only hope they were the ones with the little girl. Otherwise, he'd have to start searching all over again in another direction. He guessed those he tracked were northern Cheyenne who'd come south to hunt and now in late summer were headed back to join with the Sioux. Most of the southern Cheyenne were on a reservation in southern Kansas, although many of them strayed, none of them understanding why they had to stay on a little piece of land that did not hold enough game to sustain them, a piece of land that was hot and where many of them died of diseases. It was the Indian's way to be free and wild, to follow the buffalo, to make war. The white man was determined to change the red man, but Lance knew it would not be easily done. He headed north.

Weariness from the heat and long hours of riding and walking made Lance sleep soundly — too soundly. He awoke to the feel of cold steel against his shoulder, then quickly sat up, staring at four Cheyenne men he did not know and cursing his foolishness at not being more alert. It was rare for him to be caught off guard, and he realized he must have been more tired than he thought.

"*Voxpas!*" one of them sneered, calling Lance "White Belly."

Lance shook his head, making the sign of the Cheyenne with his hands and slowly rising. He repeated the gesture, then pointed to his scars left from the Sun Dance ritual. Already one of the Cheyenne men held Lance's rifle and gun, as well as grasping Sotaju's bridle as though to claim the animal. Lance had removed his weapons belt so he could rest better, finding a lone cottonwood tree near a dried-up creek for shade to take a short nap before going on.

"Cheyenne," Lance spoke up, continuing in the Cheyenne tongue. "I am Rainmaker, adopted son of White Eagle, brother to Kicking Horse by the mingling of our blood." He held up his hand so they could see the scar on his palm. "I was raised Cheyenne. My heart is Cheyenne." He put a fist to the middle of his chest. "I come in peace. I search for a young white girl, with sunshine hair and blue sky eyes. I can go back and bring many horses in trade for her, or guns if you like. The horses are not far. A man holds them for me right now outside Fort Kearny."

The young bucks watched in close curiosity as Lance motioned toward his horse, telling them he had something to show them. The apparent leader raised his rifle as though to warn Lance not to try some kind of trick, and Lance walked over to Sotaju, reaching into his saddlebag and pulling out his buckskin shirt. He took the picture from it and held it out.

"Do you know this girl?" he asked. "I wish to see White Eagle and see if he knows about her." He cursed himself inwardly again for allowing himself to be caught sleeping. He stood there in only his loincloth. He'd planned to rest awhile and travel more after dark when it was cooler.

The leader of the small war party snatched the picture from Lance's hand and studied it, then glanced at the others and frowned, handing the picture back to Lance and moving his dark eyes to meet Lance's.

"I do not like to hold another's spirit in my hand," he spoke up.

"It's just a picture. It's not her spirit."

"Not like. Spirit one place, girl another."

Lance's eyes lit up with eagerness. "You've seen her, then?"

The man stepped closer, looking Lance over. "I have heard White Eagle speak of his white son called Rainmaker, who has eyes the color of pale grass. You are this son?"

Lance nodded. "The girl—"

"We will take you to White Eagle," the warrior interrupted, the two of them conversing in Cheyenne. "It is his band we scout for—watching for soldiers who might follow. We travel with many bands—"

"The girl!" Lance spoke up impatiently. "You've seen her?"

The warrior grinned a little. "I have seen her. She belongs to Nimiotah."

Lance's heart fell. "Crooked Neck!" he breathed softly. "The bastard!" Crooked Neck had long been his enemy, and apparently this Cheyenne man knew it, for he was smiling now with great amusement. Lance wondered if Crooked Neck had abused the girl. Even if he hadn't, just his ornery, bearish attitude would frighten her, and because of the man's intense hatred for whites, he would enjoy frightening her.

"Damn!" he muttered, as he shoved the picture back into the pocket of his shirt, then threw the shirt into his saddlebag. "I want to go now to White Eagle," he said loudly. Inside he was wondering how he would deal with Crooked

30

Neck. He had been sure he could bargain with any of the Cheyenne for the girl; but Crooked Neck would be almost impossible to deal with, for of all whites, he hated Rainmaker the most. Still, he was happy he'd run across White Eagle's band, for it had been nearly two years since he'd seen his adoptive Indian father.

The leader of the war party nodded. "Get your things. I am Small Horse. I will take you."

Lance quickly bent down and rolled up his blanket, slinging it over his gear. He gave a challenging look to the young man who stood holding Sotaju's bridle. The warrior did not back away until Small Horse barked an order at him to let go of the horse, that it belonged to Rainmaker. The warrior backed off unwillingly, scowling as he quickly jumped up onto the back of his own horse.

Lance took hold of Sotaju's reins. "You could have whinnied or something," he muttered to the animal. The Appaloosa snorted and shook his head, and Lance frowned, easing up on the animal's back and glancing at the four Indian men, who all looked restless. These were not the kind of Cheyenne to whom he was accustomed. They had changed, and rightfully so; but it would make his job more difficult than it would have been a few years ago.

The warriors rode off, two ahead of Lance and two remaining behind, one still hanging on to Lance's rifle and gunbelt. They headed across the rolling, yellow plains of Nebraska. The color of the grass made Lance think of Cassandra Elliott's light-colored hair. He prayed to *Maheo* that the girl had not been molested or abused by Crooked Neck, and an odd feeling of possessiveness came over him.

Lance and the four Cheyenne warriors rode into White Eagle's camp amid much ado, young women glancing shyly at the handsome newcomer whose half-naked body displayed enticing masculinity. Dogs ran and barked, and children played in small groups, squealing and laughing. Strips of buffalo meat hung over rawhide lines to dry, while other pieces were slowly being smoked over many fires. The northern Cheyenne were in better shape than the southern Cheyenne—so far. But Lance knew that soon soldier harassment and the continued slaughter of the buffalo would reach these people also, and it saddened his heart. For the moment, they basked in recent victories their friends the Sioux had enjoyed over soldiers and settlers in the Dakotas and Montana, especially in the Powder River Country. Under the leadership of the great warrior Red Cloud, the Sioux and northern Cheyenne had managed to literally close all roadways into their lands, and even some forts had closed down. But Lance knew it could only be a temporary victory. Citizens and the government were crying for restitution.

A man slightly older than Lance ran forward, giving out a war cry and landing into Lance, jerking him off his horse. The four warriors who had brought Lance into camp backed off, and both men and women gathered in a circle as Lance and the man who had jumped on him wrestled heatedly. But it was soon evident that this was a friendly game, and well matched. Every time one man was thrown and stood up, they grinned at each other before landing into one another again, pitting muscle against muscle, pushing, slamming, legs and arms wound together as first one was on his back, then the other. Finally Lance was on top and held his opponent for several seconds before the opponent gave a signal of surrender.

Lance jumped up and pulled his opponent up with him. Then they both laughed and grasped wrists.

"It has been many moons, my brother!" the Indian said with affection in his voice.

"Too many, Kicking Horse," Lance replied. "How are your two sons, and Three Stars Woman?"

"They are all well. You will share our tipi tonight?"

Lance looked over at Small Horse and the other three warriors. "Well, that depends. Am I a prisoner, or a guest?" Both men spoke in the Cheyenne tongue, although Kicking Horse could speak English. Kicking Horse glanced at the four warriors, realizing then that one of them was holding Lance's weapons. He frowned.

"What is this?" he asked the others.

"We caught the white belly tracking us. Maybe he brings soldiers," Small Horse replied.

Kicking Horse turned his eyes back to Lance. "You are gone many years, Rainmaker. Some of our young warriors do not know you by looks, only by stories around our campfires. Why do you follow us? Surely you would not bring Long Hair here."

Lance shook his head. "You know better than that. I guide supply wagons for the railroad, but I would never bring soldiers into your camp. I belong to the white world now, but I do not forget my brother and father and the people that I love. I would not deceive you by bringing soldiers to surprise you and kill your women. If you would believe this, then you can no longer be my brother."

Kicking Horse looked from Lance to Small Horse, then back to Lance. "Then why were you tracking us?"

"I am looking for a young white girl, captured by the Cheyenne, perhaps one full moon ago. That is my only purpose for coming, but I am glad to find that it is your band I have been tracking. Is White Eagle with you?"

Kicking Horse nodded. "He is not well, though. He will be glad to see you."

"The girl? Do you know of her?"

Kicking Horse held his gaze. "She belongs to Crooked Neck." Lance could see by his eyes that getting the girl away from her captor would be like trying to pull the sun from the sky. Why did the thought of the young girl he didn't even know being with Crooked Neck bring such an odd jealousy and possessiveness to his soul? It made no sense,

33

for the feeling was more than just anger or simple concern over a poor girl being taken captive.

"Has he hurt her? Has he made her his wife?" he asked.

Kicking Horse frowned. "I do not think so. He has been waiting for her to flow, and she has not. His other wives say they think she is late in becoming a woman and has never flowed yet. He cannot touch her until she has had her time and is a woman. But you should know he intends to keep her."

Lance's eyes narrowed. "We'll see about that!" he answered, his voice low but angry. "Where is he? Is he in this camp? Has he beat her?"

A faint smile passed over Kicking Horse's handsome face. "You act as though she belongs to you, my green-eyed brother," he replied.

"She does!" Lance lied, suddenly realizing that to convince them Cassandra Elliott was his property was his only edge in perhaps getting her back. "I sent for her. I've never met her; I've only seen her picture. But out here white men often write back east for wives. Her parents answered the ad I put in an eastern newspaper, saying they had a fine daughter for me but she was too young. They were to bring her out here so we could meet and become friends, and I was to wait until she was of age. But Crooked Neck and some others attacked her parents' wagons, killing everyone and taking Cassandra. I've come for what is mine!"

Kicking Horse looked at the men who had brought Lance into camp. "Return his weapons!" he ordered. "This man brings no soldiers. He only searches for the little girl."

Small Horse sullenly dismounted, his long black hair blowing in the wind as he came forward and handed Lance's weapons to him. Lance took them, turning and shoving his rifle into its boot on Sotaju and slinging the belt around the horse's neck. He saw no reason to put on his weapons here.

"Crooked Neck has gone with his own camp," Kicking

Horse was telling him, as both men began walking toward a tipi painted with eagles. "He was with us only a while. We made him and his band leave us, for they make much trouble. We do not want the soldiers after us. We want only to get back north where it is safer. Your General Sherman, Long Hair Custer and a soldier named Hancock make much trouble in the south for our brothers there. If they find out about the girl, they will come after us with many bluecoats and big guns."

"I know. Hancock burned up an entire village belonging to Roman Nose, Bull Bear and Medicine Wolf. He destroyed everything. It will be a hard winter for the southern Cheyenne who choose to live free from the reservation the government has made for them. Black Kettle wants peace, but the young warriors are against it."

"The young ones are always against it. Black Kettle wants peace because he remembers Sand Creek and what happened there. He fears it will happen again."

They stopped walking. "I'm afraid it probably will, Kicking Horse," Lance told him.

Their eyes held. "It is bad everywhere," Kicking Horse said sadly. "My father knows this. I think that is why he is ill. He is dying of a broken heart, my brother. Everything has changed. The life we once knew is gone. Our land is slowly being taken from us. Our children die. The buffalo disappear. These are bad times, and they will get no better." He nodded toward a small group of young men who were passing around a bottle of whiskey. "The firewater only makes it worse. It makes our young warriors weak, even though they think it makes them strong. And it makes them do foolish things that cause trouble for the Indian."

Lance nodded. "I know." He looked toward the tipi. "How bad is he?" he asked, referring to White Eagle, the man he considered his father.

Kicking Horse sighed. "I do not think he will survive another winter. It is good you are here. You should spend a night or two with us before going on to Crooked Neck's camp. No harm will come to the girl in that short time. He pushes her around sometimes and makes her work; but she has come to no real harm, and she is still untouched."

"Then, I will see my father first. I will stay this night, but I'm not sure I can stay any longer than that."

Both men shook dirt from their hair and brushed off, grinning again over the wrestling match. The two had wrestled for years when Lance lived among them. White Eagle's son and the white boy he had taken under his wing had become fast friends and true brothers during that time, learning many things together: to hunt, to shoot the bow and arrow, to fire a rifle. Kicking Horse was two years older than Lance, and when Lance was first taken from the Cheyenne, he'd missed his friend terribly, which was part of the reason he'd kept running away. But that was many years ago, and now each man lived in his own world, but they remained fast friends.

The two men ducked inside, tiny bells wound into Kicking Horse's moccasin laces making little tinkling sounds inside, where it was more quiet. Lance nodded to Three Stars Woman, Kicking Horse's wife, and she smiled softly and looked at her lap. Three Stars Woman was pleasant to look at, a handsome woman who had married Kicking Horse five years earlier at the age of thirteen. She had given Kicking Horse two fine sons, one who played outside now and the other at her side in a cradleboard. Kicking Horse quietly gave his wife instructions to prepare some food for his brother, while Lance moved to a mat where an old man lay with his eyes closed.

Lance felt a tight grip in his chest. This could not be the proud, strong White Eagle who had raised him and who only two years ago, when he had last seen him, was still strong and healthy. His eyes teared with good memories, and he reached out and touched the man's hand. "Father," he said softly.

The old man opened bloodshot eyes and managed a quick smile. "Rainmaker!" he whispered. "My . . . green-eyed son . . . who pleases me."

Lance leaned down and touched his cheek to the old man's. "You should go out and greet the sun, my father. It will help heal you."

The old man sighed. "Perhaps. But soon the sun will be cold, and it will not matter. These are . . . bad times, Rainmaker. They are not times . . . for old men. Only for the young men . . . who have the strength . . . to run from soldiers . . . to travel longer miles to find the buffalo . . . to live through the winters with not enough warmth or food. The old ones die . . . the little ones die. It is sad. I would rather . . . leave this life now . . . than see what will happen to my son . . . and my grandchildren."

Lance blinked back heavier tears. "It is not like my father to give up so easily." He squeezed the old man's hand.

"You will understand . . . when you are this old, my white son," the man replied. He patted Lance's hand. "What brings you? Surely . . . you did not know I was ill."

Lance sat down beside the man, crossing his legs Indian style. "I did not. But I'm glad I happened to come when I did. I was brought here by some young warriors who thought I was spying for the soldiers. But I was merely trailing the village because I search for a young white girl who was taken by the Cheyenne. I am told she is kept by Crooked Neck, and I have come to take her."

The old man's eyes widened. "From Crooked Neck?"

Lance nodded. "I am not afraid of Crooked Neck. I never have been."

The old man studied him with a frown. "He has always been jealous of you . . . Rainmaker. You always beat him . . . at everything. If he knows he has . . . something you want . . . he will never give her up."

"He has no choice," Lance answered with a determined voice. "The girl is mine—promised to me when she is of age. She was on her way out here to me when she was taken. I have come for her, and Crooked Neck won't stop me."

White Eagle took his hand again. "I wish you luck, my son. She is a fair child, worth much to Crooked Neck. He waits only for her to be a woman. Then he will take her."

"He'll have to go through me first!" Lance grumbled. "And he's never beat me yet at anything!"

"I will ride with you to Crooked Neck's camp," Kicking Horse offered. "Few of them know you there. Crooked Neck might try to call you a spy and have you killed. I will go and assure them you are my trusted brother, the adopted son of White Eagle. They will listen to me. I will make sure this thing is taken care of between you and Crooked Neck, and that the others stay out of it. And I hope you get the girl away from him. Keeping her will bring us much trouble."

Lance looked over at the man. "Thank you, my brother." He glanced at Three Stars Woman again, who was bending over putting something into a kettle. He could understand why Kicking Horse had wanted her, and it seemed she had grown more beautiful, instead of fatter and uglier like some Indian women became after marriage. Watching her made him hungry again for Mattie, yet seeing her and Kicking Horse together stirred a tiny but growing desire to settle down with one woman like Kate wanted him to do.

Kicking Horse grinned. "My wife has a sister recently widowed," he told Lance. "I will take her in, but I desire only Three Stars Woman. My sister-in-law is lonely, and you are pleasant to her eyes. I saw her watching you outside. I do not think she would mind if you shared her mat tonight, if you so desired. She still sleeps in her own dwelling and weeps for her husband. You could help ease her grief."

Lance grinned. "Is she as pleasing to look at as Three Stars Woman?"

Kicking Horse laughed lightly. "Almost. But I have the prettiest."

Lance nodded and turned back to White Eagle, his concern at the moment mainly for his dying father. It if were not for the urgency of getting Cassandra Elliott away from Crooked Neck and back to safety, he'd stay here for however long his father might live. He did not like leaving the man this way. Perhaps he would never see him again. His heart was torn with memories of his two worlds, knowing that he would be just as deeply grieved when the day came that Kate McGee left this world, for she was just as much a mother to him as White Eagle was a father. He'd known two very different worlds, two very different people, and had loved them both, belonging to both yet to neither. The fact remained that his blood was white, his real parents had been white, and the white world was where he belonged. He felt refreshingly energized whenever he visited his Cheyenne friends, and he wished he could do so more often; but every year it became more difficult, for more and more of them had to resort to hiding and running, and many were becoming increasingly bitter, hating all whites for the loss of their freedom and way of life. Lance could see the gap between himself and his old life growing ever wider.

Lance entered the tipi hesitantly, and the young girl looked up at him with wide, brown eyes that were sad. She looked down bashfully when he stepped closer to her, already knowing from Kicking Horse why he'd come and acknowledging that she would like the companionship of the man's white brother for the night.

A fire burned dimly at the center of the tipi, softly lighting up the girl's beauty. She was only sixteen, but for an Indian woman that was not young. Cheyenne girls were protected and chaste until taking a husband. If widowed,

39

they became a wife to a sister's husband, if possible, for a woman needed a man to provide food and protection. Often Cheyenne men took more than one wife as a matter of practicality. Sometimes the work was too much for one wife. Sometimes the first wife could bear no more children, or could not produce a son. Children were vital to the continuation of the race; for many died young in this cruel land, and now many more were dying from white man's diseases and lack of food. Additional wives meant additional children, and without the children, the people would one day die out.

This girl would now go to Kicking Horse, unless and until she found and preferred another as her husband. And for tonight, Kicking Horse shared her with his brother, an accepted but not often used practice among the Cheyenne. They were a beautiful, gentle, loving and sharing people, and such things were allowed, with proper permission. But the young virgins were never touched and were often kept virtually hidden from the young men.

Lance sat down beside the girl on a bed of buffalo robes. He still wore only his loincloth. He touched her hair, and she met his eyes.

"Kicking Horse tells me you are lonely for your dead husband," he told her. "I'm sorry. I would like to be your companion this night, if you are willing."

Her eyes teared. "I was not long a wife," she replied, both of them using the Cheyenne tongue. "My husband . . . awakened needs in me . . . womanly needs. Now they are not satisfied."

Lance gently unlaced the shoulder of her tunic. It fell to her waist, exposing full, firm breasts. He leaned down and kissed her neck, her shoulder. "Let me satisfy them for you tonight," he whispered.

Her breathing quickened, and she closed her eyes. "It is my wish . . . to please Kicking Horse's white brother," she replied. "You are his guest . . . and have no wife."

His lips moved to her breasts, and he laid her back, tasting them as his blood began to burn for her beauty. She lay limp and willing, her breathing heavier as he pulled the tunic off and gently ran his hands over slender, dark thighs. He bent down and kissed her belly and the soft hair that hid that which ached to know a man again. She whimpered, tears slipping out of her closed eyes. She whispered a name, but it was not his.

He moved slowly back up her body, tasting, kissing, savoring each breast as his fingers explored and brought forth the moisture that meant he would be welcome. She began running slender fingers over his hard muscles and could feel he was tense with his own needs. She reached down and untied his loincloth, pulling it off. She massaged his manliness with gentle hands, opening her eyes and meeting his own.

"You are a beautiful man," she whispered. "You have much to give."·

He smiled and met her lips, kissing her white-man style and bringing out a savage desire in her soul. He moved on top of her then, and she welcomed him inside, digging her fingers into his broad shoulders. For a moment the picture of Cassandra Elliott flashed into his mind, and he wondered what he was in for trying to get her from Crooked Neck. The odd jealousy filled him again, and he took it out on the young girl who lay beneath him, thrusting deep and hard. He would worry about Crooked Neck and Cassandra Elliott tomorrow. Tonight he would enjoy this sweet hospitality.

Chapter Three

Lance approached Crooked Neck's camp with Kicking Horse riding at his side. Lance wore brightly beaded moccasins and his best leggings, tiny bells tied into them at various places throughout the fringe, determined to look as "Cheyenne" as he could, as well as put on the appearance of a proud warrior who has come courting. He wore a brightly beaded vest and a bone hair-pipe choker, a copper ornament pushed tightly over his thick-muscled upper arm and a beaded headband around his hair, which even though recently cut, still lay in thick waves around his neck. He'd never been able to bring himself to cut his hair as short as most white men cut theirs. A bright yellow stripe of paint adorned each cheek horizontally under each handsome eye, and he'd painted yellow stripes on Sotaju's rump and wound beads and bells into the horse's mane.

Few, including even some of the Cheyenne, would have thought him anything but an Indian, except for the shorter hair. The yellow stripes represented his prayer color, and he had spent a good share of the early morning praying to Maheo for the wisdom, and strength if called for, to rescue Cassandra Elliot. Crooked Neck would be stubborn, for he'd always been jealous of Rainmaker who as a white adopted son received a good share of attention from White Eagle, who was Crooked Neck's uncle and the one appointed to teach Crooked Neck the warrior ways. But when Rainmaker was adopted into the tribe, there seemed to always be competition between him and Crooked Neck, even more competition than between Rainmaker and White Eagle's own son, Kicking Horse.

As Rainmaker learned the warrior ways, it seemed he was always outdoing Crooked Neck, once taking two Pawnee scalps in a tribal war, while Crooked Neck was himself injured by the enemy. Although Crooked Neck was five years older than Rainmaker, he wasn't as strong, and he had never participated in the Sun Dance ritual, the true test of manhood among the Cheyenne. Rainmaker, on the other hand, did participate, at the tender age of fifteen, and had endured the ritual without once crying out from pain. This had brought even more admiration to White Eagle's eyes. When Rainmaker soon after rode the back of a buffalo in a daring feat of bravery, and Crooked Neck tried the same thing and took a bad spill, the final bond was sealed, as far as Crooked Neck was concerned; and the man was overjoyed when soldiers came and took Rainmaker away to his white world. Since then, Crooked Neck avoided Rainmaker when he came to visit, glad that the visits were few and far between. But he often daydreamed about how he could somehow, some day, have the upper hand over the white Indian called Rainmaker.

Lance and Kicking Horse rode boldly into the circle of tipis, while women and children stared and men watched cautiously, a few of them mounting painted ponies and riding the perimeter of the camp to make sure Lance and Kicking Horse were alone. Smoke rose lazily from evening cooking fires near tipis, and Lance's dark eyes darted around the camp in search of a child with light hair; but he saw none.

They were about a day's ride from the much larger village containing White Eagle's band and several others. Often, usually for grazing purposes, bands would split up, for the Indians traveled with hundreds of horses, and when gathered in a large tribe, there was not usually enough grass to sustain the hundreds, sometimes thousands of horses that accompanied them. This band was small, for some of them had stayed with the larger village, fearing a soldier attack on Crooked Neck's band. Lance knew there could be only one reason for that fear. Cassandra Elliott was somewhere near. It was then that Crooked Neck himself exited a tipi where a woman stood carrying on in the Cheyenne tongue about visitors.

Lance and Kicking Horse reined their mounts to a halt as Crooked Neck approached them, his eyes narrow with hatred. It had been many years since he'd seen Rainmaker, but he had not forgotten the face, and his heartbeat quickened with curiosity and defensiveness as he walked forward to greet the man, his face dark and sullen.

"Rainmaker," he spoke up in more of a sneer than a friendly greeting.

Lance nodded. "You look well, Crooked Neck."

The unusually big Indian straightened, swelling his chest and smiling proudly. "Crooked Neck is well and strong— stronger now, maybe, than Rainmaker, who has been too long in the soft white world."

Lance's chest tightened at the thought of this man threatening and frightening little Cassandra Elliott, for Crooked Neck was tall and broad, with a stomach that bordered on fat and a face that was not ugly, but always looked mean and irritated. The man already had four wives, for he had found fault with each one he had married; and he was lazy. Four wives meant much less work for himself.

Lance swung a leg over his mount and slid down, standing eye-to-eye with Crooked Neck, slimmer, harder, and he was sure, still stronger.

"There are ways to find out who is stronger," he answered the Indian.

Crooked Neck grinned more. "I have no reason to fight

you at this moment, white belly. Why do you come to my camp? Surely you did not expect a friendly welcome."

"Nor is my visit friendly," Lance sneered. "I have come for what belongs to me."

Crooked Neck's eyebrows arched. "And what do we have that belongs to you?"

Lance held the man's gaze boldly. "It's what *you* have that belongs to me — a white girl you captured about a month ago. She happens to be mine, and I have come for her."

Crooked Neck just stared at him, then smiled and began to chuckle. The chuckle led to a loud laugh that shook the man's entire huge body. The others there whispered and mumbled, a few grinning, but Lance glared at Crooked Neck, unsmiling, determined. He merely waited for Crooked Neck to finish laughing, then repeated himself.

"The girl is mine. She was promised to me," he said flatly. "You can see I dress my best, to present myself to her."

Crooked Neck's smile faded, and he folded his arms, looking Lance over the way a conqueror looks down upon the conquered. "She belongs to me!" he growled. "I led the raid on her wagons, and I took my prize! It is the Indian way and you know it! She is mine to do with as I please!"

"She is promised to me," Lance answered calmly. "Her parents were bringing her out here to me. I even have a picture they sent me." He reached into the waist of his leggings and pulled out the picture, holding it out to the man. Crooked Neck stared at it in surprise. "Now you see it is true," Lance went on. "Her name is Cassandra Elliott."

Crooked Neck stared at the picture and dropped his arms, stepping back slightly, his face dark with anger. "So, I cannot even take a captive without you interfering!" he sneered. "I thought I was rid of you, white belly! It seems I am not, but I am the victor! The girl is mine by right. I took her before she got to you, and now if you want her, the price will be high!" He grinned a little again. "In fact, I think there is no price. I choose not to bargain for her. I choose to keep her! Her skin fascinates me. Her white hair excites me! As soon as she is a woman, I choose to keep her for a wife, a fair and lovely one who will do nothing but lie in my tipi while my other wives do the work!"

Lance struggled with an urge to kill, but to do so here and now would only bring his death at the hands of the others. He knew Crooked Neck had only spoken the words to rile him.

"I wish to see the girl," he replied evenly. "I have that right."

Crooked Neck watched his eyes, enjoying the hold he finally had over Rainmaker. He finally nodded.

"All right. You may look upon that which you can never have. There are not enough horses or rifles in this land to pay for her!"

"You're a fool, Crooked Neck!" Kicking Horse put in. "Keeping the girl will only bring us trouble!"

Crooked Neck frowned at his cousin. "I see no trouble here but this bothersome white brother of yours!" He looked back at Lance. "And why is it just you who comes? Have you told the soldiers? Do you plan to betray your Indian father and brother and bring bluecoats to kill us?"

Lance gripped the handle of his huge blade in an effort to stay in control. "I have never betrayed the Cheyenne! That is the very reason I come alone. I could have told the soldiers, but I did not. They don't know yet what has happened." He spoke louder so the others could hear. "I have come here in peace, to take back what is rightfully mine! I did not bring soldiers, because I did not want to bring trouble to the people I call family. I am myself a proven Cheyenne warrior —" he turned his eyes back to Crooked Neck with a haughty pride —"who has even endured the Sun Dance torture." He saw the flicker of shame in Crooked Neck's eyes, for the man had never been brave enough to participate in the Sun Dance. "I am a friend of

46

the Cheyenne. I call White Eagle father and Kicking Horse brother. Crooked Neck has what is mine."

There was more mumbling, and Crooked Neck's jaw flexed in anger.

"Where is Thin Bear?" Kicking Horse spoke up. "He is the chief of this band."

"He hunts, but he will be back soon," one of the Cheyenne men answered.

"He cannot tell me what to do with my own captive!" Crooked Neck snarled. "She is mine to do with as I please! It is the law! The way!"

"You will bring us much trouble!" one of the others spoke up. Crooked Neck shot him a warning look, and the man backed away.

"He is right," Kicking Horse said. "We have told you this all along. Others besides Rainmaker know you have this girl. It cannot be long before the soldiers know also. Long Hair Custer has been making war on us, and others. Already our brothers in the south are herded like white man's cattle onto small pieces of land. We starve because the buffalo disappear. We need no soldiers hounding us."

There was a general mumble of agreement throughout the circle of men who had gathered, and Crooked Neck glared at Lance, his fists clenched. "Again you try to defeat me at something, white belly!" he sneered. "You will not defeat me at this! I will not give up the girl, and if soldiers come, I will kill her and scalp her. You will never get her alive!"

"Better dead than to suffer under the likes of you!" Lance shot back.

"Let him see the girl!" Kicking Horses demanded. Luckily for Lance, his Indian brother was well respected and an honored warrior, and he spoke with authority. "There is no harm in that. It is easy to see that both of you have a claim on the girl. Let Rainmaker see her and know in his heart you have brought her no harm. Then we will wait for Thin

Bear, and we will sit in council and decide what is to be done. Rainmaker is our friend, and a brother to me. The girl was promised to him. Someone must decide who is her rightful owner."

The others murmured their agreement. This should be decided by the chief, perhaps by a council of several chiefs. Many had already been against Crooked Neck keeping the girl because of the trouble white captives always brought. But Crooked Neck liked having her. It gave him importance. Many younger men had already mentioned the horses and other gifts they would give him for her, but he could not decide, for he also wanted her for himself. Now that it was Rainmaker, his hated enemy, who wanted her, he was even more determined to keep her. His hatred for Rainmaker grew, for now his presence stirred up new controversy over his white captive. He had no choice at the moment, until Thin Bear returned and could give his opinion, but to let Rainmaker see the white girl.

"It was all settled!" he growled. "There were no more arguments about the white girl until you came, white belly! Now look what you have done! You will regret this! They will all know you are a traitor. I think you have white soldiers ready to ride in and slaughter us as soon as you get the girl away!"

"I would not betray my friends that way!" Lance shot back. He was glad he had thought of the idea of claiming that the girl was promised to him. It gave him an edge in the argument, a more logical reason for coming for her and an excuse that just might convince the chiefs that the girl rightfully belonged to him. The next problem was to see the girl and make sure she went along with his story. At twelve years old, she might not even understand what he was trying to do. He must convince her not to be afraid of him. "Let me see the girl. You can stand guard around the tipi if you wish, but I want to see her — alone. I have that much right."

48

Again the crowd talked among one another and nodded. Crooked Neck pulled his knife, holding it up in front of an unflinching Lance. "Go and see her, then! But if you try a trick, try to take her without the approval of Thin Bear, or try some other trickery, you will die slowly, white belly! You will have broken the law, and not one Cheyenne will be on your side then!"

Lance pulled out his own knife, handing it handle-first to Crooked Neck. "I will try no tricks and break no laws. I wear only this knife as a weapon, and now I hand it to you as a token of my sincerity. After I have seen the girl, you will give it back to me, and we will wait for Thin Bear."

Crooked Neck yanked the knife from him and turned, storming toward his tipi. He pulled back the flap and barked some orders, and three women and several children came scurrying out, each of the women holding a baby. The fourth wife was already outside tending a fire.

"The girl is inside," he sneered at Lance.

Their eyes held in mutual hatred. Then Lance turned and ducked inside.

She sat huddled on a bed of robes, a tunic hanging loosely on her small body. Lance was surprised she was even twelve, by the looks of her tiny frame and no signs of development of any kind. Since the story was she hadn't even had her first flow, the girl was apparently a late bloomer, which also meant she probably didn't have the slightest understanding of what Crooked Neck would expect of her as soon as her first time came. Lance knew immediately he'd die before that happened, for the wide blue eyes that stared back at him were the epitome of innocence. The white-blond hair hung nearly to her waist in tangled waves, and her fair skin was sunburned. He could see that if her hair was combed and curled, and she wore her best ruffled dress, she would indeed be a most beautiful child, and she

49

would probably one day be a beautiful woman. In fact, in spite of her youth and childish frame, there was still something haunting about her eyes, something provocative about her puckered mouth that again brought an odd possessiveness to his soul that told him no man would touch her as long as Lance Raines was alive.

He stepped closer, and she cringed, her eyes quickly running over him. He realized he looked as Indian as the others, and she must wonder if he'd come to buy her or possibly harm her.

"It's all right," he told her quietly. "My name is Lance Raines. I'm white."

She blinked in amazement at his use of her own language, and she looked him over again, saying nothing. He came closer and knelt in front of her.

"I dress this way to make it easier to come here. I was raised by the Cheyenne. They're mostly good and gentle, Cassandra. Don't be afraid of them. They aren't all like Crooked Neck. That's the white name for Nimiotah, the man who keeps you here."

She frowned. "You know my name," she said in a tiny voice.

He nodded. "The friend who rode with your family made it to a town called Abilene — showed the sheriff your picture and told him you'd been taken by the Cheyenne. They sent me to get you back."

Her lips puckered more, and a tear slipped down her sunburned cheek. "They'll just . . . kill you." Her little body jerked in a sob. "Like my mommy and daddy . . . and my brother. I saw! I saw them killed!"

Her lips curled down, and she started crying, Lance reached out and put a hand to her hair, stroking downward.

"I'm sorry, Cassandra. I know how it feels," he told her quietly. "I watched my parents die, too, and a little sister. The Indians took me when I was five, but they didn't kill my family. They had already died. The Indians were kind to me. They raised me like their own. But I still remember how I felt when my white family died."

Her shoulders jerked with pitiful sobs, and he sat down beside her. "I know you need to cry, Cassandra, but right now you've got to be strong and brave and help me so I can get you away from here. You've got to stop crying and listen to me. Are you brave enough to help me fool Crooked Neck and the others?" He spoke very quietly, bending close to her ear so the Indians outside would not hear, although he doubted any of them understood English. But he had to be careful.

The girl sniffed and wiped at her eyes, looking up at him with a face now smeared with a mixture of dirt and tears. "Fool them?"

He nodded. "Listen close, Cassandra. I've told them you belong to me — that your parents were bringing you out here to marry me."

Her eyes widened, and she blinked, moving back a little. The man she was looking at was the most handsome she had ever set eyes on, his provocative manliness obvious even to an innocent child of twelve. Already in her eyes this man was some kind of hero, if he was really going to rescue her as he'd said. Yet she couldn't help but also be afraid, for he was a stranger. Even if he did get her away, would he harm her?

"I know it sounds crazy, Cassandra, but some white men do send for wives; and the only thing Indians understand about women and captives is the right of first possession. So I made up a story, telling them you belonged to me first — that Crooked Neck stole you from me when he attacked your wagons and took you away. In order for them to believe it, you must go along with me, Cassandra. You must not act afraid of me. Act like you care about me — hold my hand — and do everything I tell you to do. Can you do that? Are you good at pretending?"

She looked him over again, hardly able to believe he

really was white. But his eyes were green, and his words were like her own. "I . . . think so," she answered in her little-girl voice. "But . . . " The tears started coming again. "What will you do with me? Where will you take me? You won't really make me be your wife, will you?"

He saw the terror in her eyes, and realized from the several other beds in the tipi she'd probably seen and heard things that she'd never known about men and women, for the Indians were not shy about making love inside their tipis with children and other wives sleeping nearby.

He shook his head. "No. I won't make you be my wife. I'm going to take you to Abilene, and if you don't have any relatives back home where you want to go, you can stay in Abilene with the white woman who raised me. She's a very nice lady. Her name is Kate, and she's the kindest woman you'll ever meet. And if I know Kate, she'll treat you like her own daughter. You'd like her very much, Cassandra."

She pushed a piece of hair behind her ear. "She won't hit me, will she?"

He frowned. "Kate doesn't even like to kill flies." He ran knowing eyes over her, catching a faint bruise on the calf of her leg. "Did Crooked Neck hit you?"

She shook her head. "One of his wives doesn't like me," she answered, hanging her head. "She hits me a lot . . . with a stick . . . if I don't do my work right."

Lance sighed with repressed anger. "Nobody is going to hit you again, honey. I promise." He put out his hand. "Come outside with me. Hang on to my hand and act like my friend. I can't get you completely away from the Cheyenne yet, but I think I can at least get you out of this tipi and away from Crooked Neck's wives."

She looked at his hand, then met the gentle green eyes. "You won't . . . look at me? Promise?"

He frowned. "Look at you?"

She looked at her lap. "Nimiotah lifts my dress some-times and looks at me. Sometimes he pushes on my stomach . . . and I don't know why!" She started to cry again.

Lance reached out with both hands and put them on either side of her face. She was so small he was sure he could crush her skull between his big hands if he wanted to. But he gently forced her to look at him.

"You have to trust me, Cassandra. I've come here to help you, and I have no intention of hurting you. I promise I won't look at you. All I'm going to do is get you out of here and take you to Kate. They're even holding what's left of your things in Abilene. Some of your mother's things are there, and there's a doll. Did you have a pretty doll with a wooden face?"

More tears slipped down her face, and she nodded. "Promise, promise you won't hurt me," she sobbed.

"In God's name," he replied. "It's worth the risk, isn't it? You want to get away from here, don't you?"

She nodded. He wiped tears from her cheeks with his thumbs. "Then, do like I say, honey, and don't act afraid of me. Whatever I do—if I push you down or hold you close—whatever I do, don't act afraid. You're supposed to belong to me. Remember that. Are you smart and brave and strong enough for all that?"

She sniffed again. "I think so."

He smiled for her. "I think so, too." He looked her over again, amazed that such a child could be so provocatively beautiful when there wasn't one thing womanly about her. No wonder Crooked Neck was determined to keep her. He rose and helped her up, and to her he seemed like the tallest man in the world; for she only stood four feet ten inches tall and weighed perhaps sixty to sixty-five pounds. She quickly wiped at her face again, and his huge hand enveloped one of her own.

"Mr. Raines?" she said.

He looked down at her. "You can call me Lance, but for now call me Rainmaker. That's what the Indians know me by."

She sniffed again. "I was going to tell you to call me Cass. That's what everybody else calls me. Cassandra is a long name."

He gave her a wink. "I admit Cass is much easier. Now let's get you out of here. And remember, you belong to me. It would help if you convince them you want to be with me, not with Crooked Neck. They have to believe you were sent out here to me, and since I own you, I can take you out of here if I want. Just don't worry about anything I do or say, understand?"

She nodded. "Yes, sir."

He squeezed her hand tightly and exited the tipi, amid stares from others and a furious Crooked Neck, who stormed toward them. Cassandra cringed behind Lance.

"Why are you taking her out of there!" Crooked Neck demanded. "I only said you could talk to her and see that she is well!"

"She is not well!" Lance barked. "Your wives have beat her. I'll not allow her back in your tipi until this is settled!"

"You have no choice!"

"I have as much right to take her with me as you have to keep her here. She was mine first, and now you've had her a while. I choose to take her with me."

"Take her where? You are to wait here for Thin Bear!"

"I have decided to take her back to my own father's lodge, where she will be well treated by Kicking Horse and his wife until this is settled."

"You have no right!" Crooked Neck yelled. Cassandra could not understand the words; but she understood the tone of them, and she cringed closer behind Lance, closing her eyes in fear.

"I have every right! You risked the safety of the entire tribe when you attacked those wagons and took this girl! The chiefs are already upset about that. Now it is discovered someone else owned her first—me! The chiefs will decide what should be done with her, and no one else!"

54

He started walking away with Cassandra, and Crooked Neck grabbed her by the hair. The girl screamed at the painful jerk, and Lance whirled, his green eyes flashing with anger.

"Let her go!" he hissed

Crooked Neck grinned and tossed her aside like a sack of flour, his eyes never leaving Lance's. He slowly took Lance's knife from his own waist and held it out to him.

"Perhaps you want her bad enough to die for her!" he growled.

Lance took the knife, and Cassandra shook with fear as the two men eyed each other, huge blades in their hands, since Crooked Neck had pulled his own knife.

"Perhaps you are the one who wants to die for her," Lance replied.

Crooked Neck did not like the look in Lance's eyes. This man had beat him at everything they'd ever competed for, and he hadn't seen Lance for a long time. Perhaps he was more skilled with the knife than Crooked Neck remembered.

"You know it is wrong for you to choose how this will be solved," Lance was telling him. "The chiefs will be angry with you. They are already angry enough. Do you want to risk being banned from the tribe for disobedience? You know the law in these cases. It must go before the council. And if you kill me, you are not only in trouble with them, but you also risk the entire tribe. If I don't return, soldiers will be sent, because those who know of the girl's abduction will know something went wrong. It's your choice, Crooked Neck. I will fight you now if you wish! Or if the chiefs leave it up to a battle to the death, I will fight you then! Which shall it be?" He waved the knife menacingly, and Cassandra watched in fear and fascination. The brave stranger was actually fighting to keep her. And he seemed so skilled and sure. How strange that he would come into an Indian camp and risk his life to get her out. She moved back, brushing dirt from her tunic and rubbing at a scraped arm.

Crooked Neck backed off. "I do not fear you, Rain-maker!" he snarled. "But I do not wish to go against the council. Take her if you wish. But if you make her a woman before it is decided, I will cut off your manpart!"

Lance straightened, shoving his knife in its sheath. "If she'd been violated by you, I'd have already done the same to you!" he hissed. "And by the gods, no matter what's decided, you'll not hover your fat, stinking body over that little girl!"

Crooked Neck's face reddened with rage, and Lance boldly grabbed Cassandra up, swinging her to his side in one arm and walking to his horse, mounting up with ease still holding the girl. He perched her in front of him, chastising himself for a brief moment of desire at the sight of her shapely, slender legs. He was confused by his feelings of possessiveness and the way he kept imagining what she would be like when she was a woman, not sure why it mattered. He held her tightly about the waist, and there was not much to hang on to but skin and ribs beneath the tunic.

"Don't look back," he said to her quietly. "Look proudly ahead. If you look back, they'll think you're saying you want to stay."

She obeyed, staring straight ahead, frightened inside that this strange man might be lying and that a worst fate lay ahead for her. Yet the firm arm that embraced her and the broad chest she leaned against soon gave her a feeling of security and safety.

"When Thin Bear returns, come with him to my father's camp," Kicking Horse was telling Crooked Neck. "He and the other chiefs will decide."

The man whirled his horse and rode after Lance, galloping to catch up.

"You took a grave chance, my brother. He could have ordered you killed." Kicking Horse told Lance.

Without even thinking of what he was doing, Lance kissed the top of Cassandra Elliott's head in a fatherly fashion. "It was worth it," he answered.

Kicking Horse's eyebrows arched, and he grinned slyly. "My brother has special feelings for the girl he was sent to save," he said, realizing Lance had made up the story about sending for Cassandra to be his wife.

Lanced scowled. "I only pity her. That's all."

Chapter Four

They rode until it was too dark to go any farther, then made camp. Throughout the ride Lance kept telling Cassandra not to be afraid, that before long she would be in a whole town full of her own kind of people, and that until then he'd not let anything bad happen to her. When they stopped to make camp, he lifted her down with powerful arms, and to her relief and amazement, he didn't watch her as Crooked Neck had done when she went to the bushes to relieve herself.

While making a small fire and preparing beds, Lance and Kicking Horse talked and laughed in the Cheyenne tongue, joking about the look on Crooked Neck's face when they rode off with his white captive. Cassandra just sat and stared at them, fear rebuilding in her eyes, for she couldn't understand the Cheyenne tongue and wondered if they were joking about what they would do to her now that they had her to themselves.

Once in a while Lance would glance at her, and she could not help but notice the admiration in his eyes. Did that mean he planned to make her his wife after all? Perhaps his game of saying she belonged to him wasn't really a game at all. The little girl in her wanted nothing to do with such things, no matter how brave this man might have been in rescuing her; yet deep in the recesses of her mind was a tiny wish that she could be more of a woman, a small hope beginning to grow that the man called Rainmaker by the Cheyenne would perhaps wait for her to be a woman before he took another for a wife.

The little bells on his leggings tinkled as he walked over to her, grasping her about the waist to carry her closer to the fire. She gave out a little squeal and closed her eyes, suddenly struggling, her breathing quick and frightened. She scratched at his arms and kicked, and he had to wrap his arms tightly around her to keep her still, holding her from behind.

"You promised!" she screamed, tears coming again.

"I kept my promise!" he told her firmly, as Kicking Horse watched in amusement while he placed a freshly-killed rabbit over the fire. "I was only bringing you closer to the fire, Cass. I meant you no harm."

"You were laughing, and talking about me!"

He held her tightly. "We were only talking about Crooked Neck and the fine trick we played on him. And I was saying how proud I was of you, how brave you are. I wanted to bring you closer to the fire where it's warmer and we can talk." She kicked again and he jerked her so tightly she could barely breathe. "Stop it!" he said firmly. "I'm not going to hurt you, damn it!"

Her fighting turned to soft tears, and he sat down with her between his legs, keeping hold of her from behind and rocking her gently. "Don't cry, Cassandra," he told her quietly. "We're going to Kicking Horse's village. You'll be treated kindly there. Kicking Horse is my adopted brother, and I call his father my father. Soon this will all be settled, and I'll take you to Abilene where you'll meet Kate and see she's just as wonderful as I told you she was. Now calm down and we'll eat soon, and you can sleep."

Her little body jerked, and her tears fell onto muscular arms. "What if . . . they don't let you . . . keep me," she blubbered.

"Then I'll find a way to steal you from Crooked Neck. You won't go back to him, I promise. I'm trying to do this the Cheyenne way first. Then we won't have to worry about being chased and hunted. But if I have to steal you, then I'll steal you."

She rested her face against his arm. "I'm sorry," she whimpered.

"It's all right. Right now you have no more reason to believe me than anybody else. You just have to trust me, Cass."

She relaxed in his arms, and he lightened his hold on her but kept rocking her. By the time the rabbit was ready to eat, her head was lolling against his strong shoulder, her eyes closed in sleep.

"I guess she won't be eating. We'll save some for morning," Lance told Kicking Horse. "And save some of that corn bread Three Stars Woman made us."

Kicking Horse nodded, watching with the same sly grin as Lance picked the girl up and turned around, laying her gently on a bedroll. He pulled her tunic down over slender, girlish legs, then pulled a blanket over her, tucking it around her neck. He stared at the angelic face for a moment, again picturing her bathed and in ruffles and curls. He turned back to the fire, catching the look in Kicking Horse's eyes. Lance scowled.

"Cut me a piece of that damned rabbit!" he grumbled.

Kicking Horse laughed. "Too bad she is not a little older, is it not? Perhaps she would be more grateful for what you are doing, or perhaps you could use your handsome looks and clever ways with women to convince her you should be rewarded."

"Perhaps my brother talks too much," Lance answered, snatching a piece of rabbit. "She's just a kid. And the sooner I can get her to Kate and get myself to Denver, the better. I've got better things to do than run around risking my life for runny-nosed little girls."

60

He bit into the meat, and Kicking Horse laughed lightly as he bit into his own.

By the time they reached White Eagle's village the next day, Cassandra Elliott carried no more fear of her rescuer. By that evening she was beginning to look at him as the strongest, bravest, kindest man she'd ever known, her curiosity aroused by his Indian dress and the way he could speak the Cheyenne tongue, yet still be white. As soon as her fear vanished, the childish questions began—endless questions about himself mixed with unending jabber about what life had been like with Crooked Neck and his wives. How long did he live among the Cheyenne? Why did he have scars on his chest and arms? What was it like when the soldiers came and took him? What was Kate like? Was he married? She was relieved to learn he was not, yet didn't understand why. How old was he? Twenty-six. That sounded like eighty to her. But he certainly didn't look eighty. She was sure even at her young age that if ever there was a perfect specimen of man, it had to be Lance Raines. And he treated her with such special kindness. She wanted that special treatment forever. It made her feel good, feel safe. It had been a long time since she felt safe. An odd possessiveness began to quickly move into her heart for the man called Rainmaker. Her emotions were terribly mixed. Mostly he seemed like a big brother, sometimes like a father, and sometimes there was a different feeling, one she couldn't really explain even to herself.

Kicking Horse and his beautiful wife were kind to her. Three Stars Woman took her to a stream to bathe and gave her a clean tunic, a gift from a woman friend who had a girl about the size of Cassandra. She braided Cassandra's thick, white-blond hair into one neat braid down her back and gave her clean moccasins. When Cass came back inside the tipi that night, she noticed Lance watched her strangely, his green eyes giving her goose bumps. There was a sweet masculine scent about him that aroused something in her little heart, something brand new that made her feel flushed. The more she watched him and talked to him, the more she began almost to worship him like some kind of hero. And to her disappointment, he left the tipi that night holding the hand of a pretty young girl who he'd told her was Three Stars Woman's sister. When he didn't come back the rest of the night, Cassandra felt a pain in her chest, an odd new feeling that hurt and made her want to cry.

It was while the morning meal cooked that Lance returned, looking very happy, as did Three Stars Woman's sister. Then he came over to Cassandra, rubbing her head in a fatherly fashion.

"How is my little white captive?" he teased.

She looked up into the green eyes. "You won't go away again, will you?" she asked. "I'm scared when you go away."

He gave her a wink. "I'll stay right here. You can bet Crooked Neck and Thin Bear will come today. We'll get this all settled and be on our way."

"What will you do when we get to Abilene?"

He sat down beside her and took out his knife, rubbing it against a rock to sharpen it. "Once you get to know Kate a little, I'll be on my way to Denver. I've got a railroad job to get back to."

Her heart fell. "Oh," she muttered. She watched the strong hands and arms as he sharpened the knife, wanting to cry at the thought of Lance Raines ever being out of her sight.

Crooked Neck arrived in the late afternoon, with three other warriors and his chief, Thin Bear. Eight bands were represented in the huge tribe that was headed north, and the eight chiefs gathered in council, as well as Crooked Neck, Kicking Horse and Rainmaker. White Eagle, ill

62

though he was, was determined to sit in his place at the meeting, for he loved Rainmaker like a son and wanted to be sure he was fairly represented. He could not sit up straight like the others, but had to lie on a reclining back rest made of willow reeds.

As in all such meetings, the pipe of peace and prayer was first passed from man to man, each man offering the pipe toward the sky, to *Heammawihio;* then to the earth, to *Ahktunowihio;* then to the four directions in thanksgiving to the gods who provided them with all their needs from the land and the animals. Cassandra watched from the shadows, standing beside Three Stars Woman and the hundreds who had gathered to see what would happen. Lance's arrival and claim on Crooked Neck's white captive had provided interesting excitement among the tribe, the problem made more complicated by the fact that although raised by White Eagle, Lance Raines, to them Rainmaker, was still a white man.

The circle of sober, dark faces was lit up by the fire at the center of their circle. Each man wore his best regalia, and Rainmaker was dressed completely in bleached buckskins, their nearly white color accenting the beautiful colors of the beads and paintings that decorated the shirt, leggings and moccasins. When Cassandra first saw him exit the tipi to go to the council meeting, her eyes widened with admiration. If a man could be beautiful, then Lance Raines was a beautiful man, and he was doing all of this for her. Never had she noticed anything different about a man like she did about him. Never before had a man made her chest hurt like it hurt when she looked at him.

Now she waited nervously with the others, realizing that at some point she would probably have to go forward and say or do something. The talking had begun, and she could only guess at what was being said. Crooked Neck was ranting and red in the face, whereas Lance only sat quietly and calm, letting Crooked Neck carry on. The man looked as though he was bragging, probably about his attack on her parents' wagons and his capture of the white girl, which made her by rights his property. The memory of the attack brought back the horror of seeing her beloved parents and little brother killed, and tears welled in her eyes again. She squeezed her eyes shut, praying for Lance, praying that he wouldn't be hurt like her parents had been, praying he really would be able to take her back to a place where she could be among people like herself.

Crooked Neck finally seemed to be finished. Then one of the chiefs nodded to Lance, who rose and spoke calmly in the Cheyenne tongue.

"Just because Crooked Neck took Cassandra Elliott in a raid does not mean she belongs to him," he told them. "She came out here so we could get to know each other, and when she was of age, she was to become my wife. I sent for her. Many white men do this who live out here, because there are not enough white women."

"There are plenty in your towns," one of the chiefs spoke up.

"Not the kind a man marries. Those are the loose ones who take money to please men. I wanted a virgin, as any of you wants when you marry, so that she is just yours. Many of you know me. You know I speak the truth. And you know that just because my blood is white does not mean my heart cannot be Indian. I lived among you once—proved myself through the Sun Dance ritual—took two Pawnee scalps. I am as much Cheyenne as the next man, and because of that I have a right to speak my rights and claim Cassandra Elliott. She belongs to me."

"It is a trick!" Crooked Neck interrupted. "The white people sent him to get the girl back—for nothing! She is worth much in ransom—many rifles, much whiskey!"

"It is not a trick!" Lance shot back. "I came myself because the girl belongs to me! And I offered you many horses—and rifles. But you refused! You said you wanted to keep her, even though you know you risk having the soldiers come!"

"If the soldiers have not come by now, they will not come at all," one of the chiefs stated.

"They will! When I discovered Cassandra's wagons had been raided, I told friends where I was going. They vowed to say nothing, unless I am too long in returning. Then the soldiers will come looking!"

"Perhaps they are already in waiting, because you have brought them!" Crooked Neck snarled.

"I brought no soldiers. Nor will I speak of this to them if I can leave with my woman. That's all I ask of you—as a friend—as a son of White Eagle and brother to Kicking Horse. I could have brought many soldiers, but I did not, because I care about the Cheyenne and do not want to bring them harm!"

"No white man is our friend any longer!" Crooked Neck shouted. "Once we called the white man friend, but white men have betrayed us too many times. Once this white man was one of us, but now he lives in his white world. We know he is a scout for the hated railroad. He leads their supply trains. We should put him to death as an example of what happens to traitors!"

Some of the younger warriors raised weapons and gave out war cries in agreement as Crooked Neck stood pointing at Lance. Cassandra's heart seemed to freeze and her eyes teared. Were they going to kill him after all?

"Kill me and keep the girl, and you'll have more trouble than you can handle!" Lance retorted. The crowd quieted again. "All of you know what has happened to the southern Cheyenne," Lance went on, turning to face each of them. "Long Hair Custer rides even now, harassing the camps of those who choose not to live on reservations. There is no peace for them—no rest. They are hounded and hunted. Many are killed for no reason. All of you know about Sand Creek. Some of you were there to see what happened! The soldiers need little reason to do the same again and again. Why give them reason, when things are already bad enough? Your children sometimes go hungry because the buffalo are disappearing. Why risk more trouble over one little white girl when I can take her right now and leave and no one would be bothered?"

"Why do you scout for the railroad?" one of the chiefs asked.

Lance met his eyes. "Because in my world a man does what he knows best to earn a living. You go out and hunt—take what you need from the land. I prefer your way, but that doesn't work in the white man's world. White men get what they need with money, and money must be earned. I know this land and love it. So I earn my money by scouting. I only lead the wagons. I don't look for Indians to kill, nor do I hunt and kill the buffalo. I have refused to do that."

"And if Indians attacked you, you would kill them?" another asked.

There was a long moment of silence before Lance answered the delicate question. He spoke quietly. "All of you forget that I couldn't help what happened to me when I was a child. I was white. You took me in and raised me to be something it was not in my blood to be. Then I was taken back to the white world. This has made my life difficult, my heart torn. None of it was of my choosing. I cannot help what I am, any more than you can. If someone took you as a small boy and raised you among whites, you would have feelings for them—love them—yet your heart would yearn to be what you truly are—Indian. And if you went back with the Indians and were forced to fight the white man, you would kill the white man. It is the same with me. If I am fighting for my life, I will kill any man—Indian or white. But if I kill an Indian, it does not mean I have stopped loving them. Always in my heart there will be a special place for the Cheyenne, and I will never deliberately betray my red brothers. If I wanted to do that, I would have already done so."

There was a quiet mumbling among the chiefs, and Lance sat back down. "Bring the girl forward," one of the chiefs finally spoke up.

Kicking Horse walked over to Cassandra, who stared at him with frightened eyes, her whole body shivering as she was brought forward to stand in the circle of men who to her all looked like terrible savages, their faces painted, their heads adorned with war bonnets of many feathers. She looked straight at Lance and felt calmer.

"Tell her in her own tongue, Rainmaker, that we intend to kill you and allow Crooked Neck to keep her," one of the chiefs demanded.

Lance frowned in confusion, and White Eagle raised up slightly. "No! He is my son! I love him as a son. He has not betrayed us, and the girl belongs to him!"

"Tell her!" the first chief snapped.

Lance sensed some kind of test, and told himself not to pull any weapons yet and risk Cassandra's life. He looked up at her, his eyes sincere. "I want you to be brave and obedient so Crooked Neck never hurts you," he told her. "You are to be given to Crooked Neck. I am to be killed."

Her eyes widened, and she looked around frantically at all of them, her breathing coming in quick gasps. She shook her head. "No! " she screamed at them. She ran to Lance, flinging her arms tightly around his neck. "They can't kill you!" she wailed. "No! No! I'll die, too. Tell them to kill me, too. I don't want to go back to Crooked Neck! Tell them! Tell them I'll find a way to kill myself! Don't let them kill you, Rainmaker! Don't let them!"

She broke into miserable sobbing, and he embraced her. The chiefs all looked at each other and nodded.

"We can see you mean much to the girl, and she to you," the first one said. "Surely your story is true that she belongs to you. We come to the last test, then. Are you willing to die for this girl, Rainmaker?"

Lance held her close. "I am."

The chief turned to Crooked Neck. "If you also are willing to die for her, then you and Rainmaker shall fight for her—to the death. This hatred between you will end tonight in death, or you will willingly give the girl to Rainmaker and go your way, Crooked Neck."

Crooked Neck glared at Lance. "I do not give her willingly! I will fight for her, if the white belly is not afraid!"

"I am not afraid," Lance answered. He gently pulled Cassandra's arms from around his neck. "It's all right," he told her in English. "They just wanted to see how much you cared about me." He kissed her cheek. "You were perfect. Now go back with Three Stars Woman. I am afraid I have to fight Crooked Neck if I want to keep you now."

"No!" She sniffled. "Don't fight him!"

"I have no choice, Cass. Go on back with Three Stars Woman and be a brave girl. I won't lose, I promise. All I have to do is think of Crooked Neck touching you, and there is no way I can lose."

He pried her away from him and gently pushed her toward Three Stars Woman, who reached out and grasped her arm. Cassandra could not stop the tears from flowing as she watched Lance remove his shirt, jewelry and moccasins. He stripped off his leggings and stood in the middle of the huge circle of Indians, wearing only his loincloth, as did Crooked Neck, both men big, but Lance much leaner and harder. The look on Crooked Neck's face would have frightened most men to death without even a fight, but Lance just watched him calmly.

"A knife at your waist in its sheath," the primary chief intoned. "And a tomahawk in your hands. Those are the only two weapons you will use, and this fight will not end until one of you is dead."

Crooked Neck grinned. "This will be a good day for me!" he growled as a warrior put a tomahawk into his hand.

"First I will kill you—then I will claim my prize. I will make her my woman tonight whether she is ready or not!"

Lance crouched in a defensive position. "You'll never touch her!" he hissed.

Cassandra watched wide-eyed as Crooked Neck came at Lance, swinging his tomahawk hard. Lance leaped backward, and the missed swing made a singing sound in the night air. The fight was on, and the men crowded around to watch. Cassandra ran to a clump of young cottonwoods and scrambled up into one of them to see better, her light weight causing no problem for the young branch she sat on. She climbed up so fast her legs were scratched and bleeding, but she didn't care. All she cared about was that Lance Raines would not be hurt.

The two men were circling and slashing, and Cassandra could see a deep cut on Crooked Neck's left arm.

"Please don't get hurt!" she whimpered, watching Lance, who looked every bit as Indian as the rest of them, and fought just as well.

They went at each other again, each catching the other's right arm with his own left, then standing pitted and pushing, muscle against muscle, both men straining wildly. Finally Lance managed to push Crooked Neck backward so hard that the man fell to the ground. Lance came at him, swinging downward with his tomahawk, but Crooked Neck kicked up, sending dirt into Lance's eyes, then pushing his feet into Lance's stomach and heaving him up and over his head.

Cassandra screamed as Lance flipped over Crooked Neck onto his back, rubbing at his eyes because he could not see well. Crooked Neck was up again, and he raised his tomahawk. More by sense than sight, Lance quickly rolled away, and the tomahawk came down into the dirt. Lance took a moment to shake his head and wipe at his eyes while Crooked Neck yanked his tomahawk out of the hard earth and got back to his feet.

The two men circled again, gripping their weapons tightly, first Crooked Neck swinging, then Lance, then Crooked Neck; and this time Crooked Neck managed to cut a slash across Lance's stomach. Cassandra put a hand to her mouth and gasped as blood immediately began running in several drips from the cut. Her chest hurt with fear for him as Crooked Neck kept swinging at the startled Rainmaker until his tomahawk cut right into the handle of Lance's and chopped off the iron head so that his tomahawk was useless.

The crowd of warriors around them went wild, some cheering for Crooked Neck, others for Rainmaker. Cassandra started crying as Crooked Neck stood staring at Lance with a wild grin on his face, sure he had the upper hand now. Lance threw down the useless handle of his tomahawk and yanked out his knife.

"This fight isn't over yet!" he hissed at Crooked Neck. Blood ran down his stomach and over his loincloth, but Crooked Neck's left arm also bled badly.

"I have the better weapon," Crooked Neck snarled. "It is over for you, my white-bellied friend!"

He started slashing again, and Lance kept backing away, waiting for the right moment. The crowd moved with them as Crooked Neck kept pushing Lance farther back until they were almost directly beside the tree where Cassandra sat watching. Men cheered and gave out war whoops, and Cassandra watched in aching fear. One of the warriors noticed her then and reached up, pulling at her legs, shouting about the grand prize that would go to the winner. Cassandra screamed as the man pulled her from the tree and began passing her around. One warrior held her up in the air for Crooked Neck and Lance to see.

The sight of her terrified eyes put new life into Lance, who was weakening from loss of blood. Crooked Neck came at him again, and gauging the man's swings, Lance made a dive at Crooked Neck's legs as soon as the man's arm came back from a swing with the tomahawk. He sank his blade into Crooked Neck's thigh, and the man cried out as Lance sliced downward. The pain of it caused Crooked Neck to drop his tomahawk, and Lance pushed the man backward and kicked the weapon out of the way.

"Now we are even!" he growled. "Take out your knife, you fat-bellied coward!"

Crooked Neck was purple with rage. He whipped out his blade, but had trouble standing back up. He lunged at Lance but stumbled on the wounded leg, his knife slicing a piece of skin off Lance's calf as he went down. Lance paid no attention to the new wound. He immediately grasped Crooked Neck's hair and lifted, cutting off most of its length. Then he pushed the man onto his back and put a foot on the wrist of the hand that held the knife. He pushed hard, holding the warrior's hand against the ground with his foot and waving Crooked Neck's own hair before his eyes, enjoying the shame such a thing brought to the man's face.

"Now who is the better man?" Lance sneered, looking as savage as the rest of them. "One who would rape a half-grown girl is not a man at all!" He knelt down, pressing his knee into the man's chest, then quickly slashed his blade deeply across Crooked Neck's throat.

The crowd quieted, and Cassandra watched in wide-eyed horror. Lance stood up and threw Crooked Neck's hair down at his face, then turned to face the crowd as a warrior slowly set Cassandra on her feet. Lance walked up to her, and he looked frightening even to her, for he'd just slashed a man's throat. His eyes were wild, while blood dripped from his wounds and from his own knife. He grasped her braid, and she squinted as he held it tightly.

"It is settled!" he growled at the others. "She belongs to me. Does anyone else want to try to claim her?"

No one replied, and Lance turned to the chief who had proclaimed the fight. "It is over now. A fight to the death, you said. I can take her away with me, and by your own honor, the Cheyenne cannot try to stop me!"

The chief nodded. "You have won her back. Go to your father's tipi now and tend to your wounds, Rainmaker. You may leave whenever you feel you are ready."

Lance pulled on Cassandra's braid as he walked over to Crooked Neck, bending down and wiping off his knife on the man's loincloth. He stood up and shoved it into its sheath, then stumbled into the crowd, where Kicking Horse put an arm around his waist, shouting orders for others to help White Eagle back into the tipi and for Three Stars Woman to prepare some herbs and bandages. Lance had finally let go of Cassandra's braid, and she followed behind them into the tipi, where Lance collapsed onto a bed of robes. Cassandra just stared at his near-naked body a moment, watching the hard muscle of his stomach move as he breathed heavily. He was covered with dirt and sweat, and his eyes were closed. Three Stars Woman and her pretty sister hurriedly came inside, both women fussing over him then, the pretty sister touching his face with gentle hands and a cool cloth and speaking to him softly in Cheyenne.

In that instant Cassandra hated the pretty sister. She wanted to be the one to put the cool cloth to his head, to nurse him and make him better. But the other women had taken over, and she couldn't even go to him and thank him or do anything to make him feel better. Lance Raines had just nearly sacrificed his life for her, and now she could only sit in the shadows and watch as others tended to his wounds. He grunted when Three Stars Woman poured whiskey over the wound on his stomach. Her sister began gently bathing off dried blood, removing the soiled and bloodied loincloth. Cassandra's eyes widened in curiosity then, and she could not help but stare at that which made a man a man. She still was not totally sure what happened between a man and a woman, even though she'd seen Crooked Neck moving strangely in the shadows of the night

72

with each of his wives. She was not sure the sounds they made were from pain or pleasure, but she could not help but think it had to be pain. She wished she understood such things better, wondering if a man could just be good friends with a woman and belong to her without having to do embarrassing and painful things together. She would like to be friends like that with Lance Raines. She would like him to belong just to her, for he was a fine man, strong and brave and beautiful, her hero in every way. But to look at him naked frightened her. Yet he had spent the night with the pretty sister, and the sister seemed pleased and happy the next morning. Perhaps they had talked and had not even slept together.

Now the pretty sister was putting a clean loincloth on Lance, and his stomach wound was wrapped. The pretty sister cooed and clucked and washed his face again, bending down and lightly kissing him. Cassandra's chest raged with pain again at the sight. Then she heard her name murmured.

Her heart leaped, for it was Lance who had spoken her name. The pretty sister turned to her with a smile, motioning that she should go to his side. Cassandra wiped at tears on her cheeks and moved closer to him. His eyes were open, and he reached up with one hand and touched her face.

"Sorry I pulled you hair," he told her in a weak voice. ". . . had to . . . show them you were . . . my property. You okay?"

She nodded and sniffed.

"I'll have you . . . out of here in a couple of days," he added. "Soon as . . . I can travel."

"I'm glad you won," she whimpered through puckered lips.

"Hell, I told you . . . I would," he replied, trying to smile.

She leaned down and touched her cheek to his. "I love

you, Rainmaker," she whispered. "I'll be your friend forever."

She quickly rose and ran out of the tipi then, embarrassed at what she had said, her heart swelled with childish affection and magnified feelings because of what he had done. Her words echoed in his mind, almost like a vision. He could see a beautiful woman, with blond hair and gentle curves, telling him the same thing. She was reaching out for him, but for some reason something held him back from going to her. There were tears on her face, and she spoke the words again in his strange dream. "I love you, Rainmaker. I'll be your friend forever."

Chapter Five

"Will you miss him a lot, Rainmaker?" Cassandra rode in front of Lance on Sotaju. The large camp of White Eagle and the others had disappeared behind them several hours earlier. It had been five days before Lance was able to travel, for the location of the cut on his stomach made it break open again with practically every movement. Finally it sealed well, but he still suffered extreme soreness. In spite of it, he insisted on being on his way and getting Cassandra to Abilene. Lance had spoken little as they rode, and Cassandra felt awkward; for now they would be alone together, and she'd felt bashful and had stayed away from him as much as possible during those five days of recovery, still embarrassed over what she had told him the day he was wounded. Now she was desperate to be easy friends again and to be sure he wasn't laughing at her, or perhaps angry with her.

She had been thinking sadly about the tender parting between Lance and his Indian father, White Eagle, and could think of no other way to get him to talk to her.

"I will miss him," he replied quietly. "I think perhaps I'll never see him again. He's dying."

A gentle wind blew the yellow grass of the prairie as they rode, and Lance looked down at her yellow hair, thinking how it matched the grass. Never in his life had he had such odd feelings. He knew it wasn't right to envision being her first man; for she was just a child, and in reality he would never touch her. Yet he kept picturing her grown, and could not get the dream out of his mind that he'd had the day he was wounded. She was sweet and beautiful, but far from being a woman, and he chided himself for his ridiculous feelings. He was getting more and more anxious to drop her off at Kate's and be on his way, after a visit to Mattie, who would remind him what a real woman was. He grinned at the memory of Three Stars Woman's sister. His two nights with her had been pleasing indeed. There, too, was a real woman, and he didn't doubt that Kicking Horse would not be long in making her his second wife.

"What was your white father like?" Cassandra was asking.

Her question brought him back to reality, and he shook away all foolish thoughts of her. She simply had a childish crush on him. That was obvious by her words when he was wounded and the way he'd caught her looking at him since then. The sooner he was away from her, the better for her, for he had no time for such silliness and felt awkward about the whole thing. Surely she felt embarrassed herself, and it was his responsibility as the older and wiser one of the pair to set things straight and relieve the awkward situation.

"I have little memory of him now," he told her. "I do remember he was dark. I'm not even sure why he and my mother were coming out here. But my father got sick and died, and my mother was stranded. I remember her a little more clearly. She had kind of red hair, and my sister was blond, like you. Mother did what she could to keep us alive, but she wasn't much good at driving a team or shooting a rifle, and she didn't even know where she was going. I remember hearing her cry at night."

He stopped talking and swallowed, his heart always hurting at the memory. "I'll never forget that," he continued. "I wanted so badly to help her, but I was just too little to be of any use. I guess that's maybe why after she and my sister died, the Indians found me, I was determined to be the strongest, most skilled warrior among them. I was angry because I'd been too little to help my mother and sister. I vowed when I grew up I'd be able to take care of myself and my loved ones better than most men."

Her heart ached at the words. His loved ones. He'd valiantly saved her, hadn't he? Did he love her? "You mean—like if you had a wife and children?"

"Yup. But so far all I've had is Kate to care about, and she's such a fiesty woman I don't much worry about her. Kate is the independent sort, and she can handle a rifle. And she lives right in town, so there's not too much to worry about there. So until the day comes I settle, which probably won't be for a long time, I use my skills in other ways—leading wagon trains and such." He reached up and tugged at a piece of her hair. "And sometimes rescuing little girls."

She giggled, relieved that he didn't seem angry with her and was apparently not going to say anything about what she'd said the day he was wounded.

"And now you know that not all Indians are bad," he added. "There was a time when no Cheyenne would consider attacking white people, Cass. But some bad things have been done to them by whites, especially, in the case of the Cheyenne, by the Colorado Volunteers. At Sand Creek three years ago, several hundred Volunteers attacked a peaceful Cheyenne camp, doing terrible things to the women and little children. There was no reason for it at all. The camp that was attacked was Black Kettle's, probably the most peaceful of all the Cheyenne chiefs. The Indian can't forget things like that, Cass, nor all the broken promises and treaties, and other attacks on them similar to Sand Creek. Some of them have become very rebellious, wanting to do everything they can to hurt the whites, and I can't always blame them. They're dying, Cass—all of them—

slowly but surely. The whites are chasing out or killing off all the buffalo, and without the buffalo the Indian is dead. It makes my heart very sad."

"But they could just live like us, couldn't they? We live okay without the buffalo. They could have houses and farms and work."

They rode on in silence for several minutes, as the wind whispered over the prairie grass.

"You hear that wind, Cass?"

She nodded.

"When I hear it, I hear voices—the voices of Indians all over this land. The Indian is like the wind, Cass—always moving, wild and free. You can't catch and hold an Indian any more than you can catch and hold the wind. It's impossible for the Indian to live like the white man. I don't know how to explain it, I just know that's how it is. There is something about the Indian that no white man will ever understand in a thousand years. But then most of them won't try to understand anyway."

"You really care about them, don't you?"

"I love them."

She frowned, looking down at the dark, strong hands that held the reins of his horse. "Are you like the wind, too, Rainmaker?"

He grinned a little. "I suppose I am. Kate's always after me to settle down. I probably will some day, but after eleven years away from the Cheyenne, I still don't have all that wildness out of me. No sane, proper woman would want me the way I am right now. But like every man, I want sons, so some day I'm going to have to make up my mind to stay in one place. Not many white women want to live their lives wandering all over the place. They want a house they can fix nice—a garden—a fireplace. That's the way it is with women. But men, even a lot of white men, like to wander. It's hard for a man to stay in one place— stay with one woman."

She felt the raging pain in her chest again at the thought of him with other women. He probably had women friends everyplace he went, for he was a fine-looking man. She supposed a lot of women would like to catch him for keeps, and wondered if one would before she was old enough to try to catch him herself.

The sun was falling behind the Rockies far in the distance, and he halted Sotaju. "I think we'll make camp early tonight," he told her. "My stomach is damned sore, and I'm not feeling too good."

He grunted with pain as he dismounted, and Cassandra was overwhelmed with guilt and fear. If not for her, he'd not be wounded. And what if he got sick? She wouldn't know what to do. What if he died? Would the Cheyenne find her and take her back to Crooked Neck? And how would she go on living knowing Rainmaker was dead? He was her best and only friend in the whole world now, and more than that, she loved him.

He laid out two bedrolls and lay down on one of them, mumbling to her that she should build the fire and could eat some of the dried buffalo meat Kicking Horse had given them. She quickly rummaged up some dry cottonwood branches that had fallen from the trees near the stream where he had stopped, stripping off some of the bark and laying it in front of Sotaju. She was proud that she had learned a few things from the Indians, including the fact that horses liked cottonwood bark. She got a fire going, then walked over to Lance, hesitantly putting a hand on his shoulder.

"Rainmaker? Are you hungry? Or do you want a drink of water or something?"

He rolled onto his back, and his face was wet with perspiration. He rubbed at his stomach. "Just a little water." He wore only a vest, and she noticed the bandage at his stomach had some blood on it. She felt weak with fear.

"Rainmaker, it's bleeding again. We left too soon! You

79

should have listened to Three Stars Woman."

He rubbed at his eyes. ". . . probably right," he muttered. "Dump some whiskey on it . . . put a new bandage on. I'll be all right. Get me some water."

She hurriedly got the water and helped lift his head, worried that he felt worse again but glad she was the only one around to nurse him. She took a bottle of whiskey and clean bandages from his gear and hurried back to him again, taking his own knife from its sheath at his waist and cutting off the old bandage. She carefully removed it, trying to ignore the odd feelings it gave her to touch the bare, hard-muscled stomach; the memory of seeing him naked bringing the flushed curiosity about how a man used that part of himself to mate with woman. In spite of the fear that thought planted in her soul, she knew instinctively that some day she wanted no other man but Lance Raines to show her.

She wrapped new bandages around the wound, and he had to sit up in order for her to do so. He watched her with the same mixed emotions, realizing that she was innocent and untouchable, feeling guilty over his thoughts as he smelled the light scent of her, studied the silken sheen to the golden hair, and noticed the cute little curves about her that would one day be beautiful. She stopped wrapping and tied the bandage, then straightened and met his hypnotic green eyes. She was at once flushed and nervous again at the way he looked at her, until he flashed the handsome smile and took her hand.

"You're a good little nurse," he told her, lying back down but still holding her hand. "And a good friend." He sighed deeply. "Don't be . . . afraid, Cass. I'll be all right. Just . . . let me sleep. I'll know if . . . trouble comes. I can handle it. You eat . . . sleep."

She blinked back tears of fear and gently covered him, then crouched between him and the fire. She couldn't eat. She wasn't hungry now, not knowing if something bad might have happened inside of him and he was dying. She closed her eyes and prayed.

The sky was red in the east when Lance awoke. The first day's ride after being wounded had been harder on him than he had figured it would be, and he'd slept more soundly than he normally would. His first thought was of Cassandra. Someone could have . . .

He stirred, and it was then he realized the girl lay right beside him, her arm around his neck. Either out of fear, or perhaps in an effort to keep him warm, she'd curled up beside him under the blanket and now lay there sleeping soundly.

He turned his face just enough to look at hers. A piece of blond hair blew softly against a pink cheek, and in sleep she was more a child than ever. It struck him full force then that at times she still held the shadows of a very little girl, a baby-soft puffiness to her face and hands. She was in the difficult transition time of girl to teen to woman. He felt more of a fool than ever to visualize her as a grown woman. That time was far away. He'd let his pity for her, his infatuation with her unusual beauty, carry his imagination to ridiculous thoughts.

Enough was enough. He lifted the small arm from his neck and sat up. The movement woke her and she gasped, quickly standing up and straightening her tunic, her cheeks more pink.

"I . . . I was afraid you were too cold," she told him.

He grimaced as he stood up. "Thank you," he mumbled. He walked behind some trees, and she quickly stirred left-over coals and added some sticks to them. She knew by the look on his face that he thought her a silly child, and she probably was. Lance Raines was a big, grown man, with places to go and things to do and plenty of women wherever he went. There was no chance in the world that he would wait for years while she grew up, and even if he did, why did she think he'd be interested in her? She didn't really want him the way a woman wants a man, for she didn't even understand all of that. She only knew that he was the most wonderful man in the whole world, and that she loved him and wanted him to be her friend forever. She couldn't bear the thought of another woman having him for keeps. It seemed he should belong to Cassandra Elliott, for he was her hero. He'd fought to keep her, hadn't he?

She threw some buffalo meat and sliced potatoes into a black frying pan that she set over the fire, after first putting some lard into it. She could at least show him that she could cook. She'd cooked things since she was six years old. The thought of it made her think of her mother, who had patiently taught her such things back in Illinois on their little farm. Why had they left? She wished she could go back there, go back to the green grass and big trees, the swing in the backyard. That was all gone now, as were mother and father and brother—everything. And to think that Lance Raines could ever care about her was stupid. It all hit her in one sweeping emotion, and she burst into tears.

They needed to come. And once they did, they would not stop. Lance returned to see her crouched on her knees and crying. He hurried to her side and grasped her shoulders.

"Hey, what's this?"

"I want my mother!" she sobbed. "I want to go back to our farm!"

He petted her hair. "Do you want me to take you there? Do you have other relatives there?"

She sniffed and shook her head. "There's nobody. And Daddy sold the farm." She cried harder, and he held her close. "What will I do, Rainmaker?" she wailed.

He patted her back. "You'll go to Kate, like I said. In time you'll feel better, Cass. I know it hurts. It hurts real bad, and the hurt never really goes away. But it does get better. And Kate will love you like a mother."

He sat and held her for several minutes while she released all her pent-up grief, then gently set her aside to stir the meat and potatoes.

"I was going to fix you a nice breakfast," she sniffled.

"You did. After all, you started it, didn't you? I'm just stirring it so nothing burns. Go fill that old coffeepot at the creek, will you? I'll throw in some coffee, and you'll find out what truly bad cooking is."

He grinned at her, and she could not help but smile. "Do you feel better?"

He rose to get the coffeepot, hiding his pain. "Much better, thanks to your good care." He held open his buckskin vest. "See? No blood stains. But I'm afraid we won't make as many miles today. I've got to keep myself healthy if I'm to get you to Abilene. I wouldn't want you to be left out here stranded."

She wiped at her eyes. "I was afraid last night. You looked awful sick, Rainmaker."

"Well, I felt awful sick." He handed her the coffeepot. "But I feel good this morning. Here. Fill this thing. We've got to get going."

She stood up and took the coffeepot, looking up at him with her wide blue eyes. The sun she'd been exposed to was creating new freckles over her nose and cheeks, making her look even younger. "Did I ever thank you, Rainmaker?"

He grinned and touched her nose. "Not in words. But you didn't need to. I knew."

"I'll always be your friend. Anything you want me to do, just tell me." She sniffed again. "And if anything real bad ever happens to you, I'd take care of you the rest of my life — like if Indians cut off your legs or something awful like that."

He laughed lightly. "Well, it's nice to know somebody would care about me if I didn't have any legs." He turned to get out a sack of coffee. When he turned around again, she was watching him, blinking back tears.

"Don't laugh at me, Rainmaker. I really meant it."

He tossled her hair. "I know you did. I wasn't laughing at you, Cass. That was a very nice thing to say. It's just that Indians don't generally go around cutting off men's legs. They either let you go or kill you, depending on the mood they're in. Now go get the water. We're leaving late enough as it is."

She turned and ran off to the stream, and he laughed again. Seeing her in the morning light only accented even more what a child she was. It would be a relief to get her to Kate and go see Mattie.

The third day of their journey they approached a soddy settled in the side of a yellow hill, two corrals and a log building with a sod roof nearby.

"Fort Kearny isn't far from here, but I don't want the soldiers to see you," Lance told her. "A trader lives here — a half-blood who runs messages between the soldiers and the Indians. He was holding horses here for me that I would have come to get in trade for you if I needed them."

A short, heavy-set man appeared at the doorway of the soddy, his dark hair hanging in two braids, his face round and his skin looking pitted. He waved at Lance and called out a greeting in an Indian tongue. Lance answered. "Don't be afraid of him," he told Cassandra, realizing the man was rather ugly and had a mean look to him, even though he was not mean at all. "He's part Sioux and part French."

They rode closer and the man smiled, one tooth missing in front. Lance did not dismount. Cassandra noticed several horses in the two corrals, but her curiosity was interrupted by a hand on her calf. She gave out a little squeal when she looked to see the half-breed feeling her leg. Lance held her tighter against him.

"So, you found her, my friend!" the half-breed said.

"I did, Round Face," Lance replied, both men speaking in English now. "And I don't need the horses after all. I came to pay you for holding them for me. I intended to buy several if I needed them to get her back, but I got her back without them."

Round Face frowned, looking her over. "How did you do that?"

"I fought for her."

The man's eyebrows arched, and he grinned. "Ah, she must be quite a prize for you to risk your life. There is only one way to fight for such a prize—to the death."

Lance nodded, and Round Face laughed. "You are a good fighter, Rainmaker! I wish I could have seen it!"

Lance just grinned, reaching into his pouch that hung on his weapons belt. "Is five dollars enough, Round Face?"

The man squinted, looking Cassandra over again. "How about I give you five horses for the girl, and you pay me nothing? I like her yellow hair."

Cassandra's heart pounded. Would Rainmaker betray her after all?

"No" came the firm reply. "I didn't go through a fight to the death just to sell her for five lousy horses. I'm keeping her."

Round Face rubbed his chin, then shrugged. "She is too skinny and young anyway." He grinned again. "Hey, Rainmaker, you better be careful. If you try to make that little thing a woman, you will kill her." He laughed hard then while Lance took some gold coins from the pouch. He handed them out.

"Five dollars, Round Face," he told the man with a sober face. Cass cringed close to him, afraid of the ugly half-breed. "And remember your promise not to tell the soldiers. I promised my father and Kicking Horse I would not tell the soldiers so they wouldn't be chased. If you betray that promise, I'll kill you. Understand?"

Round Face sobered then himself and took the money. "Round Face understands. Rainmaker speaks only the truth. I will not tell."

"Good. And I'm sure you won't have any trouble selling your fine horses to the soldiers at Fort Kearny. I am grateful that you waited first for me to come back."

Round Face nodded. "If you had come back, and I had no horses, you would have been angry with me. Round Face does not like for Rainmaker to be angry."

Lance backed his horse. "Thank you, my friend. I will see you again when I come this way." He turned the horse and trotted off, and Cass closed her eyes tightly, sure the ugly Round Face would shoot Lance in the back so he could steal her for himself. But nothing happened, and when she opened her eyes again, they had crested a hill and the soddy was out of sight. She breathed a little easier then.

"Weren't you afraid he'd shoot you?" she asked.

Lance halted his horse and took a thin cigar from his pocket and lit it, careful to hold it away from Cassandra. "No. Round Face just thought you were pretty—thought he'd try talking me into a trade. But he's not dishonest or a murderer. There are a lot of men who look nice and talk nice who'd double-cross you a lot quicker than that one. You have to learn to judge a man, Cass—and not by looks." He puffed the cigar. "I'll go slow so you can stay on without me holding you for a ways. I need a smoke, and I only have two hands."

He urged Sotaju ahead at a slow walk.

"Rainmaker?"

"Hmmm?"

"What did Round Face mean?"

"About what?"

"About if you made me a woman, you'd kill me. How would you make me a woman? And why would you kill me? Don't you like me?"

He didn't know whether to laugh or be angry, realizing

86

he had no right to be either. She didn't know what she was talking about, and he didn't know how to explain it.

"Do me a favor and ask Kate some day," he answered. "And of course I like you."

"But why would you kill me?"

He rolled his eyes, taking another puff on the cigar. "It was only a figure of speech, Cass. He just meant . . . he meant you're too young and immature to be a wife, and if a man made you his wife, he'd probably hurt you. Now don't ask me any more questions."

She thought for a moment, putting together the reply, remembering the nights in Crooked Neck's tipi. She began to redded with shame. Did it hurt that much, whatever it was the man did? Was it so bad that it could kill a girl? Surely not if the man was Rainmaker. Rainmaker would never hurt her, let alone kill her. But now she wished she could crawl away and hide for asking such a stupid question.

Lance rubbed the cigar against a thick leather strap to put it out, then threw it down. He put his arm back around her, giving her a light hug that told her everything was all right, then urged Sotaju into a faster gait.

The next several days were spent in almost constant conversation, as Cassandra peppered Lance with questions as they headed for Abilene, learning what she could about Kate McGee and Abilene, about the Cheyenne and Lance's life with them. She often talked about her life back in Illinois, sometimes falling into tears again at the memories. A few nights she woke up screaming with a nightmare about the day of the attack, and Lance Raines was always there to hold her until the dream faded enough that she could go back to sleep. She helped Lance change his bandages twice more, and the wound was healing nicely.

Three times Lance found water deep enough that she

could take a bath — once in the Republican River. She never worried that he would look at her or do that awful thing to her that might kill her. They became good friends, talked a lot, laughed together. Often he walked so she could learn to ride, and although Sotaju was a restless stallion, he always seemed to sense that he must be gentle with the little girl.

The days passed, and Cassandra knew soon they would be in Abilene, and Lance Raines would go away then to the place called Denver. Perhaps he would meet a pretty woman there and never come back. She didn't want their trip to end. She wanted to be alone with him forever. She wanted Lance Raines to be just her friend and no one else's. Her little heart worshipped him, loved him, exalted him to the mountaintops as her hero forever; the nicest, gentlest, strongest, bravest, most handsome man who ever walked. How could she tell him how she felt? He would only laugh, for Lance Raines was a full-grown man who had been everywhere and done everything and knew all about grown women. She knew nothing about men or the world or even how a girl became a woman. And once Lance Raines got her to Abilene, he would go away and forget her, and she'd probably never see him again. The thought hurt her chest so badly she sometimes put a hand to her heart to try to make it stop hurting. Her only consolation was that he would take her to the white woman he thought of as his mother. At least if she stayed with the woman called Kate, she had a chance of seeing him once in a while, and maybe, if she prayed real hard, he would not find some other woman to settle with until Cassandra Elliott was old enough for such things.

Chapter Six

The sun was setting when they rode into Abilene, and already the streets were becoming unruly. Before returning from St. Louis over a month earlier, Lance had not seen much of Abilene since it began to boom from the cattle business. The Kansas-Pacific had not long had its tracks to that point. When Kate had asked him two years earlier where she could do a good business with a boardinghouse, he'd suggested Abilene, knowing its population would grow, especially with men on the move who would need a room when the railroad hit that town, which was then hardly a town at all. But Lance had underestimated the kind of growth the town would enjoy, and with that growth came a growing lawlessness.

Piano music and laughter floated out from saloons that were already busy and would stay busy all night. Here and there a painted woman stood on the boardwalk, hanging on a cowboy. The smell of cattle stung his nostrils again, as thousands more waited in pens not far from town for their journey east. Soon they would all be gone for the season, and so would the cowboys, but while they were there, law and order was becoming unheard of. Lance frowned angrily as two men rode by, liquored up and shooting their guns carelessly into the air. As soon as they spotted the pretty girl perched in front of Lance they sobered slightly, riding on but holstering their guns and looking at each other with grins, then circling around behind him.

A moment later the two men were on either side of Lance, and he slowed Sotaju, pulling the animal back so that the cowboys were slightly ahead of him. They turned their horses to face him.

"Looks like the Indian has himself a little white captive," one of them said with a grin. "You lookin' to get hanged, Indian?"

"I'm not an Indian," he answered calmly. "I just rescued this child from the Cheyenne, and I'm taking her to a woman who can help her. Now get out of my way!"

They moved their horses closer together, directly in Lance's path, and Cassandra's heart beat hard with fear.

"Get your dirty Indian hands off that girl and hand her over," the other man told Lance. "You do that, and we'll let you go. Otherwise, this whole town will string you up."

The other man grinned. "Besides, we can take the little girl to some ladies who can make her rich." His eyes ran over Cass. "Put a pretty dress on that little thing and she'd be a sight."

Lance's sidegun was out so fast both men were startled when they realized he was pointing it at them. "This little girl stays with me, you white-eyed sons-of-bitches! Now get out of my way before I blow your guts out!"

The two men straightened and glanced at each other, then back to Lance. "Indians don't pull guns on white men and get away with it," one sneered.

"I'd say I'm getting away with it right now!" Lance barked in reply.

"What's going on here!" a woman's voice spoke up. She hurried up to Lance, touching his leg. "Lance! You just get back?"

Cassandra's heart turned instantly from fear to jealousy. The painted lady knew him well. She was one of his women.

"This is some welcome for a man who's been out risking his life to save a little girl," he replied coldly, his eyes still on the two men.

Mattie Brewster turned to the cowboys, her hands on her hips, her huge breasts bulging from a pink satin dress. "You two idiots or something? This is Lance Raines. He's as white as you and I. He's a scout—raised by Indians but on our side now. Go get your jollies someplace else, you worthless bastards!"

They stared another moment, then Cassandra jumped and screamed when Lance's gun fired, knocking the hat off one of the men. The men's eyes widened, and both turned and rode off.

Lance slowly put his gun back in its holster while Mattie turned her eyes to a shaking, wide-eyed Cassandra Elliott. "So, this is what you went after," she commented, looking the girl over.

Lance's cold anger began to melt away. "This is Cassandra Elliott, Mattie. I had to fight a death duel to get her, but I was damned if the big son-of-a-bitch who captured her was going to keep her."

She turned her eyes to Lance again with concern. "You all right, honey?"

Cassandra's heart raged, and tears came to her eyes. "I'm all right now," he was answering. "Took a little tomahawk wound to the stomach."

"Oh, Lance!" She lightly patted his buckskin shirt at the stomach. Then she moved her eyes to Cassandra again, and in spite of Cass's instant jealousy of the woman, she could not deny the gentle concern in Mattie's eyes, and it made her feel guilty. "And how about you, honey?" she was asking. "Those redskins didn't do anything terrible to you, did they?" She looked at Lance again. "Does she need a woman to talk to? Did something terrible happen?"

Lance grinned a little. "No. She's just been badly frightened, and she's not over the death of her family. I'm taking her to Kate."

"Oh, I'm glad she's all right." Their eyes held. "You'll come

91

back to my place tonight, won't you? I won't take any customers if you're coming."

After weeks of being around a charming little girl he couldn't touch, the invitation was not necessary. "You bet I'll be over, Mattie."

She patted his thigh, and Cassandra fought harder not to burst into tears. There was so much she did not understand, yet she knew instinctively Lance and the woman called Mattie would do man and woman things—like Lance and the pretty Indian woman, and Crooked Neck and his wives. Never had her childish love for him seemed so hopeless. A tear slipped down her cheek.

"Oh, poor thing! She's starting to cry, Lance. You'd better get her to Kate."

Lance gave her a hug, oblivious to the real reason for her tears. "She's been through a lot. Those damned cowboys didn't help any. What the hell has happened to this town? Where's Sheriff Goodman?"

Mattie's face fell. "He's dead, Lance. A gambler shot him. Right now there really is no law and order in Abilene, but you know there wasn't that much in the first place. Goodman was just a volunteer, and not that good. Since the cowboys hit town, everything has gone to hell, and I think it will get worse."

Two men came flying out of a nearby saloon and started fist-fighting in the street. Cassandra watched in surprise, wrinkling her nose at the awful sight, more tears coming. Everything had changed now. She and Lance weren't alone on the prairie anymore. That lovely episode in her life was over. Now they were in a town strange to her, a lawless, frightening town, and she was going to a strange woman to be cared for. Then Lance would go to Mattie's arms and on to Denver, and she would lose him—lose him forever! Her sobbing increased. She felt more scared and lonely than ever.

"Well, they'd better get another damned sheriff!" Lance was saying.

"Nobody else will volunteer," Mattie answered in a louder voice. Men had gathered around the two fighting men and were cheering them on. "And till we declare ourselves a town and elect some true officials and get out from under county control, there's not much that can be done." She grinned a little. "You knew this was a lawless town when you left. How come you act like you're just now noticing?"

He shook his head. "I don't know. It never seemed to matter before."

She looked at Cassandra, then back at Lance with a knowing smile. "And now it does?"

Lance scowled. "Never mind. You get yourself back inside, and I'll be around later."

She ran a hand over his thigh. "I'll be waiting impatiently. I was worried about you, Lance. I'm glad as hell to see you're back."

He backed his horse a little. "I'm just sorry I can't tell Goodman I found the girl. He's the one who sent me. I'm sorry he's dead. He was a good man."

Mattie nodded. "I agree." She took Cassandra's hand. "Don't cry, honey. You're a lucky girl this man here was the one sent after you. And you'll just love Kate. You'll see. Pretty soon you won't have anything to cry about anymore. Don't let these ruffians scare you. You're safe at Kate's."

How could she tell the painted woman her real reason for crying? She wasn't afraid, not as long as she was with Rainmaker. She was never afraid with Rainmaker.

Lance turned his horse and edged around the cheering men, the two fighters still going at it. It irritated him that he hadn't thought before about how lawless Abilene was. He'd talk to Kate about never leaving Cassandra alone or allowing the girl to go into town alone. He headed for the other end of town, where the familiar white-washed, two-story boarding-house stood with roses blooming around its porch.

Cassandra watched the slender, aging woman who exited the back kitchen door as Lance dismounted and tied Sotaju. She walked briskly, her arms outstretched to Lance, who swept her up and whirled her around, kissing her cheek as he set her down. Nothing was said at first. There were just smiles, and when Lance let go of the woman, Cassandra saw that she was crying. She lifted an apron to dab at blue eyes. Her red hair was piled into a not-so-neat bun, and she pushed a piece of it behind her ear.

"I was so worried, Lance," she told him. "The Indians have been causing so much trouble. It's not like when you used to go out. And trying to get a white captive away from them —"

She looked up at Cassandra then and gasped. "Oh, Lance, such a child!"

Lance reached up and lifted her down. "Kate, this is Cassandra Elliott, and she's been through hell the last few weeks. But at least the bastard who took her decided not to make a wife out of her right away, if you know what I mean. But it was still a bad experience, and the man's wives beat her." He squeezed Cassandra's shoulder. "Cass, this is Kate, the lady I told you about."

Cassandra nodded slightly, her face still smeared from recent tears. "Hello, ma'am."

"Ma'am! Oh, call me Kate," the woman fussed. She touched Cassandra's hair. "My, aren't you a beautiful child! You poor thing. Don't you fret one more minute. If you have family, Lance will take you to them. If not, you can live right here with me, which I would dearly love." She embraced the child, and Cass closed her eyes, breathing in the scent of lilacs. She liked Kate right away, feeling the genuine love that eminated from the woman's smile and arms.

"She has no family, Kate. Apparently she's here to stay, unless someone comes along to claim her."

Kate patted her shoulder and began leading the girl toward the door. "Then, it's my ward she'll be — a real daughter, no doubt. Oh, and look at you child — still wearing a tunic! I'll buy you some new clothes right away, and you can take a bath and we'll fix your pretty hair. . . . " The woman carried on, clucking and cajoling as they went through the door. But Cassandra stopped, turning doleful eyes back to Lance.

"You're coming in, aren't you?" she called out. "Don't go away yet."

Lance grinned. "I'm coming in. I'm just getting a few things off my horse. Go on inside. It's okay."

Their eyes held a moment, and Kate frowned, quickly surmising by her keen instincts how the child must feel about the man who had rescued her. Cassandra looked up at the woman then, a relieved look on her face.

"Rainmaker fought the man who captured me," she said proudly. "It was a fight to the death. That was the only way they would let me go."

Kate's eyebrows arched. "Is that so?" She looked at Lance again. Yes, what a hero he must be to this little girl. "You have any wounds I should tend to?" she called out to him.

"Healing fine, Kate," he replied, unstrapping some supplies. "Kicking Horse's wife and her sister took good care of me." He looked at Cassandra and winked. "And Cass kept me going after we left."

Kate sighed and looked at Cassandra. "Was he hurt badly?"

The girl had to literally tear her eyes from Lance to reply. "Yes, ma'am. I mean—yes, Kate, He got a bad cut on his stomach. But he's fine now, just like he said." She smiled. "I bet nobody can kill Rainmaker. He's the strongest, bravest man I've ever seen."

Kate suppressed a grin, "He is, is he? Well, I suppose he's all of that, but he's a devil sometimes, too. You come inside now, and we'll get you all cleaned up. You hungry?"

"Not much. I'm mostly tired."

"Of course you are." Kate whisked her the rest of the way inside, into a neat, large kitchen that was obviously used often. "I've kept a big kettle of hot water going every day the past week, hoping every day you would show up and knowing when you did you'd want a nice bath and all. I have an old housecoat that will do you for tonight, and you can stay in your room in the morning until I find you something. I just hope I can find decent clothes for such a child in this wild, uncivilized place. There are a lot of farmers living outside of town. I might have to go to those with children and see about a couple of temporary dresses until I can make you some more." The woman rattled as she led Cassandra up a back stairway from the kitchen to the floor above. "I have two washrooms in this house," she explained, taking Cassandra into a small room where an old iron tub sat beside a stand with a washbowl on it. A chamber pot sat in the corner. "This is the one you will use, honey. And right across the hall from this door is the room you can use. It will mean I can take one less boarder, but that doesn't matter to me. Right now all my boarders are out. You don't have to worry about any of them. I only let the better ones stay here, and I keep a good watch. If you stay in the end room there at the head of the stairs and use those stairs up and down from the kitchen, you'll seldom even run into the boarders. And I'll make this washroom off-limits so nobody disturbs you."

"Oh, but that would be a lot of trouble for you."

"No trouble." She patted the girl's shoulder. "I'll be right back up with the hot water, and then we'll pour in some cold water to mix it some. Do you want some help washing your hair?"

Cassandra folded her arms, not ready for anyone to look at her yet, not even a nice old woman like Kate. "No. I can do it."

"Whatever you say, child." The woman turned and pointed to the door across the hall. "That's the room you'll use. I've been keeping it vacant, hoping Lance would show up with you. The housecoat is on the bed. I usually rent the room while Lance is gone, but I didn't this time. It's Lance's room

96

whenever he's home, but I suspect I know where he'll be staying the next couple of nights; and after that, I think he'll be heading for Denver, so you might as well take it yourself."

Cassandra's heart fell at the words, and Kate hurried back down the stairs. Cassandra stared at the door to what was sometimes Lance Raines's room. She walked across the hall to it, opening and peeking inside. The room was small, containing an iron bed and one wooden dresser.

She walked to the bed, running her hand over it. Lance slept here sometimes. Now she would have his room. She was glad. She would at least have that much of him — sleep in the bed he'd used — walk where he'd walked. She sat down on the bed, crying once again. He was leaving! And what did Kate mean about suspecting where he'd be the next couple of nights? The woman called Mattie? Of course. He'd stay with that painted lady and do things with her that he couldn't do with little girls. After all, men saw nothing interesting in little girls. They were just something to be teased and laughed at, and rescued when necessary. She lay down on the bed and cried quietly.

Kate came back up the stairs and dumped a pot of hot water into the tub, the pot and water looking much too heavy for such a frail woman. But Kate's size belied her strength. She walked back out, noticing the door open to the bedroom, and peeked inside to see Cassandra lying on the bed. She set down the iron pot and walked inside, bending over the girl.

"Are you all right, honey?"

Cass sat up quickly, as though startled. She wiped at her eyes. "Yes, ma'am. I mean, Kate. I'm fine."

Kate patted her head. "Soon you'll be all settled here, and the past will fade; and all you've been through won't hurt so much," she assured the girl.

Cassandra nodded. "Is he . . . is Rainmaker still here?"

Kate eyed her closely. "He's still here. He's downstairs, eating me out of house and home as usual."

"Will you tell him to . . . to stay . . . until I've had my

bath?"

Kate frowned and wiped at the tears on the girl's pink cheeks, thinking what a child she was. "I'll tell him. You can come down the back stairs when you're finished and eat in the kitchen. No one will see you. But you'll only have my old housecoat to wear. What about Lance?"

"It doesn't matter. Not with him. We're good friends. He can see me in a housecoat."

Kate pursed her lips. "Mmm-hmm." She rose. "Don't get too attached to that wild animal," she warned the girl gently. "He's here today and gone tomorrow. I see admiration in your eyes, child. Lance Raines is a grown man, and as hard to hold as the wind. You'll be making friends with the farmers' children before long, and you'll see Lance for what he really is — a man who saved you from the Indians — that's all. He's not the kind a twelve-year-old girl can be close friends with. A wolf is a closer friend of that one than anything human."

She turned to leave again. "But I'm not twelve!" Cassandra spoke up quickly, wondering herself why it even mattered.

Kate turned. "The sheriff said you were."

"I was when I was captured. But it was almost my birthday then — August twenty-ninth. It's past that, isn't it?"

Kate nodded, trying not to laugh. "So, you're thirteen. Well, that still leaves you a girl, but not so little, I guess. A whole thirteen years! Why, I'll have to bake you a cake, Cassandra Elliott. Would you like to help me decorate a cake?"

The girl's eyes lit up. "Oh, yes! I've baked lots of cakes. My mother and I —" Her smile faded. "We baked a lot."

Kate walked back to her and squeezed her shoulders. "I know, child. It hurts so much. Your problem is you've lost all your loved ones, and then along comes Lance Raines and saves you from a fate worse than death. He was your savior, your first real friend. You've put all your trust in him, turned all your sorrow over to him, and right now to you he's all you have. You shouldn't think of him that way, honey. He'll be gone soon and might be away for a long, long time. That's the way Lance is. He lived with those Indians too long — put a wild streak in him. Mix that with his white blood and you've got a roaming man who's sometimes violent and who has a woman waiting for him wherever he lands. If he wasn't so big, I'd take a stick to him and cage him up for a while."

Cassandra hung her head. "But he is wonderful, isn't he?"

Kate pulled her close and gave her a hug. "Yes, I guess in his own way he is wonderful, child. I love him like a son myself. You take your bath now and you'll feel all better. I'll make that wild animal downstairs stay around awhile."

"Thank you, Kate."

Kate picked up the robe and walked with her to the washroom. "Let me go get a bucket of cold water to cool off that hot water," she said. She hurried back downstairs and set a bucket in her sink, pumping water into it with a hand pump. Lance sat at the table, eating half a pie.

"You sure know how to bake, Kate. It's a wonder I didn't get fat when I was living with you all the time."

"Men who never sit still for five minutes don't get fat," she said, irritation in her voice.

He looked up at her curiously. "What did I do now?"

She sighed and lifted the bucket from the sink, setting it on the floor and facing him. "Nothing, I suppose. But that little girl up there thinks you're the greatest thing that ever walked. You . . . you didn't do something foolish out there on the plains, did you, Lance?"

His eyebrows arched, and he burst into laughter. For several seconds he couldn't talk at all. "Jesus, Kate!" he finally managed to say. "You know me better than that. I might not be the holiest thing that ever walked, but I don't go around forcing myself on little girls." He scooped up the last bite of pie.

"Well, I fear for her part it wouldn't be force, and you know just what I mean. That little girl worships the ground you walk on. And she told me with all kinds of hope in her eyes that she's thirteen, not twelve, as though that makes her a woman."

Lanced swallowed the pie and sobered. "Kate," he said with a sigh, "damn it, you know better. I'd never touch a child like that. What kind of a man do you take me for?"

She smiled a little. "A damned good one, underneath that wild exterior of yours. Yes, I know better. I was just testing you out. But you are a fine-looking man, and in her eyes a hero. You're all that girl has right now."

"Which is why I plan to stay away the next couple of days at Mattie's," he answered, pulling out a thin cigar and lighting it. "Then I'll be on my way to Denver; and she'll make new friends, and it will all blow over. You know that."

"I don't suppose going to Mattie's has anything to do with having to be with that pretty little girl all this time?"

Lance scowled. "Nothing at all. And for your information, she hasn't even had her first—" he pushed the pie plate away— ". . . you know . . . her first time of month yet. That's the only thing that saved her when she was with the Cheyenne. They won't touch one that's not flowed yet, and good God, neither would I."

She held his gaze. "She did get to you, though, didn't she?"

He shrugged. "If you mean feeling sorry for someone."

Kate nodded. "Then, feel sorry for her a little longer. Don't leave till she comes back downstairs. I promised her you'd still be here."

"Kate McGee, you know I'm anxious to get over to Mattie's. It's already getting dark."

"I don't care. Don't you budge from that table. You're that girl's only security at the moment. You can't just dump her off here and disappear."

It was spoken as an order, rather humorous considering her size, but the woman had a way of making Lance do what she said with just the inflection of her voice. By now he obeyed merely out of respect and love.

"Let me take that bucket to the top of the stairs for you," he told her. "You got away from me on the last one. You know you shouldn't be carrying these."

He rose and took the bucket from her, taking two stairs at a time as he carried it for her. He set it at the top, where Cassandra stood waiting, clinging to the housecoat. He met the blue eyes and was instantly full of pity again.

"You'll stay a little while, won't you?"

He sighed. "I'll stay a little while. Just don't dawdle in the bathtub." He gave her a wink and she smiled. He turned and scowled chidingly at Kate, then bounded back down the stairs, going outside to brush down Sotaju. "Sometimes I wish I could be like you, old friend," he told the animal, brushing vigorously, perturbed by Kate's remarks. "You can take your women with no feelings. Sometimes I even have feelings for Mattie." He stopped and sighed. "But not the same as the goddamned, crazy feelings I've felt for that damned kid in there. All of a sudden I feel like I have no control over my future, and I'm heading out of here just as soon as I can; so you rest up good the next day or two."

He led the horse to one of several stalls kept behind the house for boarders, then fed and watered the animal. When he went back inside, it was almost completely dark, and night insects were singing. He wondered how long it would be before the snows came down from the Rockies and inundated the prairie for the winter, realizing he'd better be getting to Denver soon.

Inside, Cassandra sat at the kitchen table eating soup. Her hair was damp but brushed out long and clean. She wore Kate's robe, much too big for her, and she looked up at Lance with devoted blue eyes, her young face freckled and sunburned. Lance squinted and came closer, studying her closely.

"You the same girl I brought here an hour or so ago?"

She smiled. "You know I am."

He shook his head and stood straighter. "Must have been

101

more dirt on you than I thought." He sat down across from her. "How are you feeling?"

"Better since my bath. Will you take one, too, pretty soon?"

Lance suppressed an urge to laugh. "I expect so. But it won't be here." He leaned back, envisioning Mattie's expert hands sudsing him down. Cassandra lost her smile and looked at her soup.

"You're going to that painted lady's place, aren't you?"

He watched her a moment, wondering what she understood and what she didn't. "Yes. But that doesn't mean we can't be friends, does it?"

She looked up at him. "No." She pressed her lips together and blinked. "Will you always be my friend, Rainmaker?"

He winked again. "Always. Just like you said you'd always be mine."

She reddened and looked down again. "I . . . didn't know for sure if you heard me then," she said quietly.

"I heard, and I remembered. There's nothing wrong with loving me, Cass. I think it's very nice, and it's natural for you to feel that way. You love me like you'd love any good friend. I risked my life for you, and I'd do it again. But only because you were a helpless little girl in trouble. Do you understand that?"

She nodded quietly.

"I'll be leaving for Denver soon. I could be gone a couple of years for all I know. Kate will get you into school. I hear they're building one for the settlers' children in the area. You'll make friends with them, and in time you'll feel at home here and be happy again."

Kate came into the kitchen after tending to a new boarder. "Full house tonight," she commented. She patted Cassandra's shoulder. "You get a good night's sleep tonight, honey. I'll look in on you often. My room is right next to yours, and there's a door between. I'll leave it open. If you want anything at all, you just holler. I run a quiet house here. Nobody will

102

bother you, in spite of the rowdy town we're in."

Lance rose. "You watch her good, Kate. I don't like what's happening to Abilene when all those cattlemen are around. I was really upset when I heard John Goodman was killed. I don't like the looks of things. Don't let her go into town alone."

"You think I'm that stupid? Of course I won't let her go alone. She'll be right here with me. And I carry my own handgun when I go into town. Anybody bothers that sweet child, they'll answer to me."

Lance grinned, happy to see that even Cassandra was smiling at the remark.

"Didn't I tell you Kate could take care of herself?" he joked with the girl.

Cassandra nodded, watching him with eyes full of love.

"Well, if I couldn't, I sure never would have took on the likes of you, Lance Raines. You did everything you could to discourage me from keeping you when they first brought you to me. But you didn't scare me any, no sir. I knew if I kept at it long enough, I'd get enough of the wild Indian out of you to make you at least halfway civilized. I accomplished that much."

She set a basket of eggs on the table and got out a large bowl to begin preparing dough for biscuits in the morning. "The work never ends when you run a boardinghouse," she grumbled.

"You love it," Lance answered. "And let Cass help. It will help her get her mind off the last few weeks, and she'll get to know you better."

"Tomorrow is soon enough. Right now she'd better get some sleep in a real bed."

She began breaking eggs into a bowl, and Lance crouched beside Cassandra, taking her hand. "You'll be fine here, and I meant it about being friends. I'll be gone a couple of days, but I'll see you before I leave for Denver."

"Will you write to me after you go away?"

"When I can. But I'm not very good at writing or with words. Kate taught me what she could, but I could never sit still long enough to learn much."

"I don't care. I wouldn't laugh or anything. I just want to know you're okay and everything."

He nodded. "I'll write, then. But I might not get your return letters very fast. I move around a lot."

He rose then, fighting an urge to kiss her small, sweet mouth. "I'll see you two later," he told them, leaving quickly and suddenly. The screen door slammed before Kate could even turn around and say good-bye.

For two days neither Kate nor Cassandra heard from Lance. He spend his time with whiskey, cards and Mattie Brewster, not always in that order. He did everything he could to get Cassandra Elliott out of his mind. If it wasn't for the dream he'd had, he knew he wouldn't feel so strange about the whole affair. But visions meant a lot to Indians, and through his upbringing, they meant a lot to Lance. Still, in the vision Cassandra was a woman. She was just a child now. So what did the vision mean? Perhaps it meant nothing, for the vision had come when he was badly wounded. A man's mind played strange things on him when he was in pain.

Whatever was wrong, Mattie didn't mind his sexual urgency. Lance Raines had always been a lot to handle, even for a woman like herself. To have him be almost violent at times only excited her more. She suspected the reason, but worried she'd anger him if she mentioned it, realizing how guilty and confused he must feel. She knew Lance Raines well, knew that down under that outer wildness lay a very tender-hearted man who respected women, even those like herself. If that was the case, how must he feel about a young, untouched girl? She gladly let him vent his feelings on her, including holding him once while he quietly wept for White

104

Eagle. Yes, there were things about Lance Raines not everyone understood, maybe not even Kate, for he didn't always tell Kate his deepest feelings.

On his third night, Lance insisted he'd better go sleep at Kate's and stay there one more day and a night to please the woman, before heading for Denver. Mattie urged him to stay just the night with her again, for it was already late and he was full of whiskey. He didn't drink often, but had drunk almost constantly since returning. Mattie knew he was deeply troubled and shouldn't go back to Kate's without a clear mind.

"My mind is plenty clear," he argued. "I've got to see Kate some before I go. I should have gone home yesterday."

He planted a long, hard kiss on Mattie. "I might be gone a long time, Mattie. Will you be here when I come back?"

She laughed. "You always ask me that. Who knows? Just follow the cowboys and you'll find me, Rainmaker." She sobered. "Take care of yourself. I'll miss you."

He kissed her again. "I'll miss you, too." Their eyes held.

"I'll keep an eye out for her," she told him, knowing exactly what he was thinking. "And your feelings are natural, honey. Right now you don't know if that kid is a friend or a sister or a daughter . . . or what. And she's a kid, so you feel like a rat, right?"

He grinned, but there was a sadness in his eyes. "You understand everything, Mattie." He gave her a hug.

"You're not a rat," she spoke in his ear. "You're a good man, Lance Raines. Get yourself to Denver and you'll be all right."

She patted his back, and he pulled away from her and left without another word. His mind swam with mixed feelings as he walked to Kate's house, unaware of the people and things around him. He was so full of whiskey, he wasn't even sure how he got to Kate's, and he automatically unlocked the kitchen door with a hidden key and went up the stairs to the room he always used when he was home.

He quietly walked inside, not wanting to disturb Kate, moving with the near silence of an Indian. He removed his gunbelt and moccasins, then the rest of his clothing, the room only dimly lit from moonlight. If not for the whiskey, his keen senses would have detected another presence. But they did not this time, and he pulled back the covers and crawled into the bed. Someone gasped and moved in the bed, and he frowned and sat up, fumbling for a lamp while someone got out of the bed, squeaking "who are you?" Lance cussed when he couldn't find the lamp.

"Who the hell are you!" he grumbled in reply.

"Rainmaker?"

He recognized the voice then. In his anger he was tempted to pull her back into the bed and show her what men did to women. Maybe if he scared the hell out of her, she'd get all romantic notions out of her head forever, and would hate him besides, which would be better than the way she usually looked at him. But the evil side of him couldn't win out over his true nature.

"What the hell are you doing in my bed?" he grumbled.

"Kate gave it to me to sleep in. I . . . we didn't know you'd come home at this hour. And I thought — " He heard a sniffle. "I thought you were one of the guests come to hurt me."

He sighed. "Well, I'm not. Go on into Kate's room and sleep with her. She won't mind." He finally found the lamp and lit it, turning it up a little. Her eyes widened at part of a bare hip, exposed when the blankets fell awkwardly away, and she backed up, realizing a naked Lance Raines had crawled into her bed. She felt overwhelmed with the reality of it, for fantasizing about him and actually being with a man that way were two very different things. When she met his green eyes, he was looking at her strangely, and she realized he must know she was naked beneath the nightgown. He stared at her long, disheveled blond hair, and the whiskey in him made him think things better left alone.

"Get the hell out of here," he told her.

106

She blinked back tears and turned and ran into Kate's room. He flopped down on his pillow, glad for the whiskey that would help him go right to sleep. He'd leave in the morning. No doubt about it. He'd not stay an extra day and night, even though Kate would be very disappointed. He'd leave in the morning, and that was that.

Chapter Seven

Lance halted Sotaju at the crest of a hill overlooking Denver from the southeast. Below him lay a sprawling, growing city, one that had survived a terrible fire in '63, followed by a devastating flood in '64. Now Cherry Creek quietly drifted its course amid the sounds of busy city life and the hammering sounds of constant building.

He opened a pouch and took out a wad of tobacco, laying it into paper also kept in the pouch. He licked and sealed the cigarette, then lit it and relaxed in his saddle, studying the size and movement of Denver. He'd never been here before, in spite of all his travels. His youth and his scouting had kept him in the plains east of the Rockies, and when he had lived with the Cheyenne, they had always avoided the white man's cities when going to the mountains.

He still did not like such places much himself. The small town of Abilene was to him enough civilization for his liking. But Denver was much bigger, boasting a population of nearly five thousand, an almost unheard-of figure for western towns which were mostly here today and gone tomorrow. Only cities like San Francisco in the far west could speak of any sizeable population. But there were wealthy men who believed in Denver and backed it, men like John Evans and Dennis Sheedy. The man Lance was going to see was another such man. Claude Françoise was a Frenchman who had been in America some thirty years and who had earned his initial wealth by questionable means. That was all Lance knew about the man, other than that now he resided in Denver, an owner of several gold mines and investor in more, as well as a railroad investor. He held a great deal of stock in the Kansas-Pacific, and the only reason Lance knew that much was through talk among local work crews and masters of supply wagons he'd scouted for as the Kansas-Pacific progressed westward.

"I'd accept the invitation," one of the men told him the day Lance received a note from Françoise himself, asking him to come to Denver when convenient.

Lance was skeptical. In spite of being white himself, he'd been raised by the Cheyenne not to trust too many white men, especially the wealthy ones. He knew that John Evans himself, governor of Colorado Territory at the time, had appointed the hated Chivington to head the Colorado Volunteers who had massacred so many Cheyenne women and children at Sand Creek four years earlier. That only verified the Indians' wariness of powerful white men, and planted more caution in Lance's own heart, even though he'd reentered the white man's world.

He found it difficult to imagine what Claude Françoise could want with him, and if not for Cassandra, he might have said to hell with the trip. But he needed a reason to leave Abilene and Cassandra Elliott; Claude Françoise gave him a perfect excuse. Leaving Cass behind him had not helped get her out of his mind, and that was the hell of it. Maybe if he'd not been raised by Indians, he wouldn't have such a strong belief in visions. He tried to forget the vision he'd had of Cass being a grown woman, reaching for him and he not being able to get to her.

He smoked quietly, the thought of some other man or worse, an inexperienced boy, some day claiming Cassandra Elliott again burning at his guts. Why did that bother him so? A man his age couldn't exactly say he was in love with a thirteen-year-old child, yet neither did he like the thought of any other man being her first. Perhaps that, too, was the fault of his Indian upbringing. In the eyes of an Indian man, thirteen was certainly not an unheard-of age to marry, as long as the girl had menstruated and was able to bear children. Yet he'd been with Kate long enough to know deep inside that such an age was simply too young for love, too dangerous for bearing children.

He sighed and took a last drag on the cigarette. He hoped Françoise had a time-consuming project in mind that would keep him out of Abilene for a good, long time. That was the only answer—time. He wished he hadn't been forced to be a part of two such different worlds. If he could have known nothing but one or the other, he could be happy, but knowing both so well, his mind and heart seemed constantly at battle over his wants and beliefs. His wild side fought his civilized side. His thirst for freedom fought his better sense that a white man should settle with one woman and have children.

He urged Sotaju into motion again. Yes, he'd settle some day. That was part of the reason he'd come here. It was time he at least set aside a nest egg toward whatever his future held for him. If he was to take a woman some day, he must have white man's money to use toward buying a farm or getting into ranching. Perhaps he'd raise horses. That was what he knew best. Or he could start up his own freight business, hauling supplies from railroad stops to outlying settlers, ranchers and miners. He knew the land well, could dicker with Indians, and had friends from all walks of life. He'd scouted for the Union Army during the war and had friends and acquaintances all over the Great Plains. Actually he had lived quite a full life for his twenty-six years. He was independent, his own man. But now, of all things, he was disturbed and frustrated by the vision of one blue-eyed little girl with hair the color of yellow grass.

He kicked his mount into a faster gallop, angry at his inability to deal with Cassandra Elliott. All he could see now was her face as he departed several days ago: the wide, blue eyes, the salty tears on her cheeks, the worshipful way she looked at him as he mounted up. He probably could have at least given her a hug, maybe a kiss on the forehead, something to soothe her sad heart. But he'd left deliberately and quickly, with hardly a good-bye, more angry with himself than with her. Perhaps if she knew what had gone through his mind the night he came home drunk and found her in his bed, she'd have no feelings for him at all. It would probably be easy to break down the resistance of a moon-eyed girl that age, but he didn't have the heart to use her or hurt her. He felt guilty even thinking such a thing, let alone doing it. It was better this way. Maybe by leaving so quickly she'd be angry with him and quit looking at him in that certain way that messed up all his logical thinking.

He headed into town. Surely there were lots of free women in a place like Denver. He'd get a feel of the city first, visit a few saloons, find out where the best prostitutes stayed and then in a day or two he'd look up Françoise.

Cass clung to Kate's hand as they walked along the boardwalks that lined the dusty main street of Abilene. They both pressed against the side of a building as another herd of cattle came rumbling through town, creating a stink and a cloud of choking dust that nearly hid the cowboys who herded them along. The men gave out hoots and yelps that reminded Cass of the Indians, and she clung more tightly to Kate's hand, remembering Lance's warnings about the cowboys.

"Danged, no-goods," Kate mumbled, pulling Cass into a dry-goods store. Cass blinked and rubbed her eyes, trying to get sand and dust from them. "We'll find us some nice material to make you some more dresses," Kate told her, leading her to a counter where several bolts of cloth lay. A gawdily-dressed woman also standing there turned to look at them, and Cassandra's heart immediately took a leap of hatred. It was the painted lady Lance had slept with!

Kate gave the woman a scowl. "Afternoon, Mattie."

Mattie nodded. Cassandra sensed there was not a lot of love shared by the two women, but Kate McGee was not the type to be totally unkind to anyone. Decent women didn't often speak to women like Mattie Brewster, but Kate knew this woman was a friend to Lance, in spite of the other things she was to him.

Mattie looked down at Cassandra, and Cass stared back at her. The woman broke into a sly grin. "My, my. The way you look at me, child, I should be dead. Whatever did I do to you?"

Cassandra reddened and looked at the floor, while Kate picked up a bolt of cloth and carried it over to a clerk. For several minutes Cassandra nervously fingered various materials, while Kate dickered with the clerk and Mattie watched Cassandra in amusement. Then the woman moved closer to the girl.

"Don't worry, honey," she said quietly to Cassandra. "I don't mean anything to that wild stallion but a good ride."

Cassandra looked up at her, frowning. "What do you mean?"

The woman laughed lightly. "Forget it. You think a lot of Rainmaker, don't you?"

Cassandra shrugged, embarrassed to confide such things with this painted woman who knew Lance Raines intimately. "Will he write to you?"

Mattie grinned. "No. He never writes me. Men don't write to women like me."

"Oh." Cassandra turned away. "I think he'll be gone a long, long time. Maybe he'll never come back."

Mattie touched her shoulder. "Sure he'll come back. And you'll be older and more . . . filled out. Maybe every time he comes back it will be harder for him to go away again."

The words brought hope to Cassandra's little heart, and she began to like the painted lady a little. Kate returned then, and Mattie lost her smile. "I don't suppose if you hear from Lance that you could find a way to let me know?"

Kate gave her a reproving look. "I'll get word to you."

Mattie's eyes softened. "Thanks, Kate." She looked at Cassandra again. "You sure are a pretty thing. You'll make a fine-looking young woman some day, little girl." She winked and walked to a different counter.

Kate hoisted the bolt of bright blue cloth under her arm and led Cassandra back outside. "What did that hussie say to you, child?"

Cassandra tried to quell her joy at what Mattie had said. If Mattie said it would be harder for him to leave every time he came back because of the way she would "fill out," then surely it must be true. Women like Mattie knew about those things.

"Nothing much," she replied. "She just wanted to know if we had heard from Rainmaker."

"Well, I'm still mad at him for leaving so quick. He close to broke my heart doing that."

Cassandra looked up at her. "I'm sorry, Kate."

Kate stopped walking and studied her. She suspected this child was the reason Lance had left so quickly, and was surprised that Cassandra understood that.

"Lord knows it's not your fault, child." She smiled. "Besides, I'm used to that wildcat darting off like that. Now, let's get you off these streets and make you a new dress. School starts tomorrow, and you'll need to be going." She started walking again. "I'm amazed they manage to keep a school going in this town, and if they don't do something about those drunken cowboys, some child will get injured by a stray bullet some day. If it wasn't for the farmers and settlers outside of town, there'd be no kind of law or education or religion at all around here, not that there's much of

113

it now."

Cassandra was already accustomed to Kate's almost constant fussing about things, realizing the woman's heart was gold in spite of the tough outer skin she showed. Even when she seemed angry she was usually just teasing. She liked Kate. The things that had happened to her recently would not have been bearable without her. The memory of her family still burned her heart at night when she could see so vividly their massacre, remember the awful Crooked Neck yanking her up by the hair and riding away with her. But then the memory of Rainmaker coming to her rescue would soothe her remembered terror.

Rainmaker. Surely she'd see him again. Surely by staying with Kate she'd have to see him again. He loved Kate. He'd come back. Maybe it was better that he didn't come back for a while. It would give her time to "fill out," as Mattie had said. Yes, maybe it was better that way. But she'd have to pray hard that he'd not find some other woman before that time came. Surely he'd meet all kinds of fancy women in that place called Denver. He'd forget her quick enough, that was sure. But maybe not.

The arguments swam in her head almost constantly: hope and despair, joy and sorrow. Waiting for him would seem forever.

Lance considered wearing a suit, but he had never liked white man's clothing, no more today than he'd liked them the first time soldiers tried to dress him after taking him from the Indians. Besides, he didn't like pretending to be something he was not. If Claude Françoise had an aversion to buckskins, then he would simply leave.

He finished donning his best bleached and beaded buckskins and studied his clean-shaven face. He was humble and unappreciative of his own handsomeness, for he'd learned from the Indians it wasn't looks that made the man but rather strength and wisdom, courage and honesty.

He combed his hair and tied a red headband around his forehead, then strapped on the leather belt that held his hunting knife in a colorfully beaded sheath. He would leave his gunbelt behind in his room. Perhaps Françoise wouldn't like weapons being worn in his house, especially since Lance was going by invitation. He left the room and walked out of the hotel to the livery, where he picked up a restless Sotaju and rode out of town a short way to a hill southeast of town, on which two grand-looking mansions were perched in the distance, shrouded by a misty evening fog. He'd been told Françoise lived in the red brick mansion the farthest south, and he headed that way.

As he approached the three-story structure, he was struck by the realization that civilization had indeed come west to stay. He could not help but contrast the ostentatious structure, with its pillared porch and decorated chimney stack, with the common tipi of the Cheyenne, or the sod huts some settlers still used. Since the discovery of gold, the big money had moved in, and most of it seemed to be centered in Denver, which would probably also become a railroad hub. He felt out of place as he came closer to the manicured splendor of the house and grounds, and with the rumors that Colorado's heydays of gold were fading, he wondered what would keep Denver going once the gold played out.

He halted Sotaju and dismounted, tying him to a hitching post shaped like a horse, then mounted perfectly molded cement steps to the large oak front door, banging the brass knocker.

Moments later a woman wearing a white apron answered, her eyebrows arching at the sight of him, for if not for the green eyes, one who knew little about Indians would surely think Lance Raines was one. "Can I help you?" She watched him apprehensively.

"I'm here to see Claude Françoise," Lance answered,

surprising the woman with the English. "Is he in?"

"Who is it, Marian?" came a woman's lilting voice.

The woman called Marian turned to someone. "I'm not sure. He looks like an Indian — says he's here to see your husband."

A woman peered around Marian, and Lance was struck by her dark beauty. It was obvious she was in turn just as struck by the man she saw. Her eyes widened in admiration for a moment, running over him with an instant desire Lance read well. He'd been around women long enough to know that look, and he flashed a handsome smile, bowing slightly, reminding himself inwardly that this was apparently the wife of the wealthy Claude Françoise, and therefore dangerous territory. She came closer, full breasts displayed nicely by a deep-red velvet dress that fit her perfectly, with darts in just the right places. The tight-fitting bodice led to a small waist and sash, opening to a full, rustling skirt.

"Who are you?" she asked.

"My name is Lance Raines. I've been working as a scout for the Kansas-Pacific. My promised duty is over, but I got a message from your husband that he'd like to see me."

She smiled softly, through full, sensuous lips. She was beautiful, and Lance figured her to be just about his age, perhaps slightly younger. She had a bright smile and dancing dark eyes, and she reminded him a little of Three Stars Woman's sister. She had a dark beauty about her like the prettiest Indian maidens, and he could not help but wonder if she had Indian blood, deciding that even a wealthy man like Claude Françoise probably wouldn't care considering her beauty.

"I see," she was saying. "Won't you come into the parlor? I'll get my husband."

She turned, walking with a gentle, seductive sway he suspected was just for him. He watched appreciatively, as any man would do, then felt irritated with himself when

Cassandra suddenly popped into his mind. Here was a definite example of a real woman, and yet his mind snapped immediately to little Cass. He scowled at his thoughts and concentrated on the thick, dark hair ahead of him, done up in perfect curls. He could not help but wonder how it would look all undone, falling over dark, naked shoulders. But he reminded himself that this was another man's wife and he had no right thinking any such thoughts. It seemed lately he had a habit of thinking about women he couldn't have, and it irritated him.

"Go and get Claude, Marian," she was saying, as she led Lance over polished hardwood floors and through a double-door entrance into a warmly lighted room with a fire burning quietly in a marble fireplace. The woman walked to a glass coffee table and picked up a polished ebony box. "Do you smoke, Mr. Raines?" she asked, turning and opening the box to display several thin cigars.

Their eyes held for a moment, and he told himself to be careful, for she seemed a sorceress with her eyes. The look in them was practically equal to her standing there and removing her clothes, and he wondered if she greeted all strange men this way. He decided Claude Françoise must have his hands full keeping his wife out of other men's beds.

"Thank you," he replied, reaching out and taking a cigar.

"I'll help you light it." She walked to the fireplace, removing a long, slender stick from a vase and holding the end of it in the fire. She walked to Lance, holding it out, and he lit the cigar. She blew out the little flame and smiled. "So, you're the scout. Are you part Indian, Mr. Raines?"

He puffed the cigar for a moment, enjoying its rich flavor. "No Indian blood," he answered, sitting down in a velvet chair she offered. His big frame seemed too big and rugged for the chair. "I was raised by them from five years old to about fifteen, when the soldiers decided I belonged in the white world. I'd just as soon they'd have left me alone. I was enjoying myself."

She laughed lightly. "You mean you'd have preferred to live among them?"

"Sure. The Indians know how to relax and enjoy life. They don't get all wrapped up in money and power and houses and other burdensome things."

Her eyebrows arched, and she looked around the room. "Oh, but money and power are such nice conveniences," she answered. "I don't find them burdensome at all. I can relax and enjoy life to the fullest."

Their eyes held again, and he wondered just what all she did to "enjoy life."

"I'm sure you can," he replied. "But most folks spend their whole lives struggling and fighting to get what you've got, and they never get it. I say why go through all that hell? A man doesn't need much to get by."

Her eyes ran over him again as she sat in a love seat, spreading out the full skirt of her dress. "Well, there are ways to be rich and powerful without the struggle," she answered, casting him a sly look. "A man like yourself, for instance, would merely have to find himself a rich woman."

Again he felt an inner warning. "Or a woman would merely have to find herself a rich man," he countered.

She laughed again, a lilting, provocative laugh, throwing her head back slightly so that he could envision her throwing it back in ecstacy rather than laughter. "Exactly!" She leaned forward. "Tell me, Mr. Raines, what Indians did you live with?"

"Cheyenne."

She grinned. "Cheyenne. I don't believe there are many left in Colorado, are there?"

He sobered, not liking the flippant way she said it. "Not many. John Chivington wiped out a lot of them at Sand Creek—took a few private parts from women and scalps from children as souvenirs."

She sobered then. "I'm sorry, Mr. Raines. I've made you angry."

"It's easy to do. I happen to be very fond of the Cheyenne, ma'am, so why don't we talk about something else, like why I'm even here. And you haven't told me your first name, unless you don't care to."

She folded her hands in her lap. "It's Jessica, but since I've just met you, you'd better call me Mrs. Françoise, at least in front of my husband. And I haven't the slightest idea why Claude sent for you." She rose then, putting on a smile he suspected was fake this time. "Claude, darling. A Mr. Lance Raines is here to see you."

She looked past Lance, and he rose, setting the cigar in an ashtray and turning to see a man perhaps in his late forties, with dark but heavily graying hair, a trim mustache and wearing a handsome smoking jacket. He was not a big man, hardly taller than his wife, and slender. He gave her a rather dark look before meeting Lance's eyes. He smiled then, putting out his hand.

"How do you do? I'm Claude Françoise."

Lance shook his hand, thinking how small it seemed compared to his own. "I'm Lance Raines. A lot of men on the crews just call me Rainmaker, my Indian name."

"Well, I shall call you Lance, if that's all right. But I would prefer you call me Mr. Françoise. It keeps our relationship in its proper perspective."

Françoise walked toward the fireplace, and Lance swallowed an urge to tell the man he'd call him whatever he wanted to call him. "Do you like good whiskey, Mr. Raines?"

Lance grinned. "What red-blooded man doesn't?"

Françoise frowned, looking him over. "Any Indian blood? Indians and whiskey don't mix, you know."

Lance's eyes turned colder. "No Indian blood. But I lived with them a number of years, and if you're going to insult them and me, maybe I should leave right now."

Françoise grinned a little. "Don't be angry, and don't leave. My apologies." He looked at Jessica. "Pour us a

119

couple of bourbons, would you, love?"

The man's speech carried an obvious French accent, but it was long faded after many years in America. He looked at Lance again. "What do you think of Denver, Lance?" He motioned that Lance could sit back down, so he sprawled in the velvet chair again. Françoise sat in the love seat where Jessica had been sitting. Lance forced himself not to watch the woman as she went to a buffet to pour the drinks, suspecting Françoise would not like him looking at her.

"A big town for these parts—too much civilization for me."

Françoise laughed. "I suppose it is! But it will get much bigger, you know. I predict that in twenty years this will be a city of well over a hundred thousand people."

Lance frowned, finding the figure amazing. He shook his head. "I don't see how. The gold is playing out."

Jessica brought the drinks, touching Lance's fingers lightly as he took the glass and giving him another teasing look. She handed the other drink to her husband, kissing him lightly on the forehead and sitting down beside him.

"Ah, but there is something new on the horizon, Lance," Françoise replied. He leaned forward and almost whispered the word. "Silver."

Lance sipped his drink, enjoying the smooth whiskey. He looked from Françoise to Jessica and back to her husband. "Silver?"

"Don't say that too loudly yet, Lance, although the news is already spreading. It seems that a great deal of the muck and rock the gold miners have been throwing aside is full of silver. A new smelting process is under way, something developed in Europe. I just came from there myself. With this new process, it's easy to get the silver ore, and Colorado will boom all over again just like during the gold rush. Denver will continue to prosper. Gold was just the beginning, Lance. Silver will take over, and I don't doubt more gold will be found in some overlooked area some day.

Then, of course, there is the railroad—more than one—heading right for Denver. We'll be the central depot of the West. There is a lot of money behind Denver, Lance, a lot of money. This city will live and grow forever. You'll see."

Lance shrugged. "So it lives and grows. What does that have to do with me?"

The Frenchman laughed lightly. "Not so much. I just like to talk about Denver, Lance. I'm proud of this city, excited about it. And the only reason you're here is because I asked my management out in the field to give me the names of the best people I have working for me. I'm a big shareholder in the Kansas-Pacific, you know. We have plans to bring it all the way to Denver now, and I want to filter out those who aren't doing their jobs and are costing me money, and keep my better people. I just decided I wanted to meet the better ones, know who is working for me, give them a little bonus and ask them to stay on with the KP all the way to Denver. After that there will be more if the good men want it. I am also taking part in the plans for a railroad from Denver north to Cheyenne, and south to Santa Fe—maybe even rails into the mountains."

Lance frowned. "The mountains? How are you going to lay a line over the Rockies?"

Françoise held up his drink. "Where there's a will, there's a way." He sipped more, closing his eyes as he did so. Lance used the opportunity to glance at Jessica, who was watching him like a hungry cat, her eyes full of warm admiration and desire. He quickly looked away and sipped his own drink.

"So—will you continue with the KP?" Françoise asked. "I'm told you're a magnificent scout, and you look it. I admire your Indian garb. I take it you prefer buckskin to a woolen suit?"

"Any day," Lance replied. He sipped more whiskey, then set the glass down. "So, what's the pay, and how long a project are we talking about?"

"We'll probably be about two years getting to Denver,"

Françoise answered. "I have investors out buying up right-of-way property right now. Of course, some people don't know how much their property will be worth some day when the railroad comes through, and we don't bother telling them. Some day that property will pay me great dividends. A man has to be clever and hardworking to build his wealth, Lance. I am both. And I admire other men who are both. You are clever in your knowledge of the land. And I'm told you put in a good day's work when necessary. I like to reward such men who work for me. So—I am giving you a bonus of one thousand dollars, and will pay you five hundred a month until you reach Denver, after which we will talk more about future building. Perhaps by then you'll have earned a leg up into a more lucrative job with the railroad."

Lance shifted, feeling uncomfortable in the small chair. "That's a lot of money. I'm not sure I'm worth all that much."

"Oh, but you are. You're worth it because you're also single and unattached, which means you won't have to be running home to a wife all the time. You can concentrate on your work."

Lance struggled not to look at Jessica again, but he could feel her pleasure at learning he was unattached. "That's true. Fact is, I don't really have anything better to do for the moment. And I have been telling myself it's time to build some kind of nest egg and decide what the hell I'm going to do with myself. There's no way I can live with the Indians any more. They're being shoved onto reservations, and I'm not really Indian myself." He sighed, meeting Françoise's eyes. "A man has to think about what he's going to do with his life. I guess I can't just wander forever. Some day I'll settle. I'll need money when I do that, although I'm not so fond of the importance white men put on it."

"Oh, but money is very important, Lance. You're just beginning to understand that. At any rate, there is no one

122

special at the moment, is there? You're a free man?"

Lance thought of Cassandra again, envisioning her grown, reaching out to him. "No. No one special," he answered quietly, reaching for his drink. He downed the whiskey. "I see no reason for not continuing with the KP," he added. "I sure as hell don't have anything else in particular going at the moment."

"Fine. I don't need any details about you yourself. My men do a good deal of checking. I know quite a bit about you, Lance, including the fact that your home base is Abilene, with an old woman who raised you after soldiers took you from the Indians—Kate McGee, I believe her name is?"

Lance set his glass down, staring at Françoise in surprise and a grain of anger. He didn't like people checking on him, nor did he like the inflection in the man's voice, as though he was warning Lance he could put his hands on anyone at any time. The man liked control and power, that was obvious.

"That's right. She's like a mother to me. But why do you care about her?"

"Oh, I don't care in the least!" Françoise replied with a smile. "I simply like to know everything about my people, you see. I'm a careful man, Lance. After all, a man in my position always has people out to get him in one way or another, and of course there will be those from other railroads who might try to trick you or those you know into giving away some of our own plans for the future. But my investigations tell me you're a smart man, and loyal once you choose which way you will go."

Lance wondered, if the man was so careful, why he hadn't been more careful about choosing a wife. Surely she was not loyal to her husband.

"I'll take the job, Mr. Françoise," he told the man. "But I won't be taken apart and investigated behind my back. I don't like it. You have any more questions about me and

123

my business, ask me straight on."

Their eyes met boldly, and Françoise nodded. "Fine. I have no questions, though. I want you to know I have every confidence in you, Lance. You probably won't even see me again, at least not until this project is finished. We're at Hays City now, and I need a man like you who knows Kansas and the eastern plains of Colorado. I want you to guide my men over the firmest terrain, the best places to bridge over the Smokey Hill, things like that. You'll lead supply trains from the end of completed rails to work crews far ahead, and help greenhorn surveyors and the like so they don't perish from their ignorance of the land. It's mostly what you've been doing all along. It's just that I want this job done well, and done quickly. I'm filtering out those who cost me time and keeping those who will make the completion of the KP timely and successful. And I think it helps to meet my workers face to face. Gives them more incentive, and gives me some reassurance that I have good men working for me."

Lance rose. "I've always done my best. But I'm not much on taking orders. I do a job right without anyone having to tell me."

The man nodded. "I'm sure you do. When you leave Denver, just head right to Hays City and see a man called Jim Beck. He's managing the stretch from there to Denver. We've bought up plenty of land north and south, so we can be somewhat versatile in where to lay the tracks. Of course, you're free to visit Abilene once more before you begin, if you choose."

Lance shook his head, thinking again of Cass. He didn't want to see her for a while. "Thanks, but I'll go right to Hays City. Besides, winter will be hitting the plains soon. I hope you realize that part of our progress depends on the kind of winter we have. They can get mean on the plains, and we could be buried for days with one good blizzard."

"I understand. I know you'll do your best." He rose

himself, smiling. "There's a great future for the railroad and for Denver, Lance. By next spring the Transcontinental Railroad should be completed. We'll have a railroad coming south into Denver from there, and we'll end up connecting with every major railroad in the country. Denver will be a center of trade and travel. Our only competition is the Atchison, Topeka and Santa Fe, and they're progressing much more slowly, although they'll probably be in Dodge City in three years or so. They're south of the KP, so we'll lose a lot of the cattle business. The cattlemen will use the AT&SF because they'll hit those lines first. But it won't matter by then. We'll be connected with Denver, and we'll be reaping the rewards of this central city, and the very lucrative business of hauling gold and silver out, as well as hauling supplies in to miners." He led Lance through the double doors and toward the front door. "I'm honored to have met you, Lance Raines," he added, putting out his hand.

Lance shook it again, thinking how easy it would be to break the man's arm. He'd take the job, only because Kate was after him all the time to save some money and think about a future and settling down. He didn't like Claude Françoise, but as long as he didn't have to associate daily with the man it didn't matter.

"I guess I should thank you," he told the man. "What about that bonus?"

"There is a draft for one thousand dollars in your name at the First National Bank. You may go and cash it, or leave it there to collect interest, whichever you prefer. It's yours whenever you want it."

Lance thought a moment, as Jessica moved quietly up beside her husband, taking his arm. "Could you have it transferred to Abilene somehow? I'd like Kate McGee to have it, to help take care of a little girl I sort of turned over to her care. I rescued the girl from the Cheyenne, and her family is dead."

Jessica's eyebrows arched again in admiration, her blood stirred by the picture of the overpowering man who was Lance Raines valiantly rescuing a little girl. Françoise nodded.

"Whatever you wish. I'll have it sent to a bank in Abilene with a wire to inform Mrs. McGee about the money and where it came from."

Lance nodded. "Thanks." He glanced at Jessica. "Nice to meet you, Mrs. Françoise."

She nodded. "And you," she answered softly.

Lance glanced at Françoise once more, then turned and left, visions of two women teasing him now: one a mere child, with blond hair and blue eyes; the other all woman, with dark hair and eyes. And he had no rights to either of them. He decided it was a good thing he had this job to keep him busy for a while. The best thing he could do was stay away from both little Cass and Mrs. Claude Françoise, and stick to the whores who followed the train crews.

Chapter Eight

Lance headed out of the supply store and back to his hotel. A rooster crowed in the distance, and the sun was just beginning to cast a pink light on the ridge of mountains that loomed on Denver's western border. It would be a good day for riding, cool and crisp, a bright blue sky. With the sun just waking, so was the city of Denver, and Lance wondered if Jessica Françoise was also just arising. He grinned at the thought of how lovely she must look in the mornings, her hair tangled, her body warm.

Again he chided himself for his thoughts as he entered the hotel and went to his room. It was a good thing he'd be leaving right away. He'd already seen to having his bonus money wired to Kate. There was nothing to do now but be on his way. He reached the top of the stairs that led to his room, then stopped, shifting his package of supplies. Jessica Françoise stood at his doorway, dressed in a burgundy and gray striped taffeta day dress, with elegant burgundy ruffles flowing in layers around the bottom of the full skirt, equally deep ruffles gracing the full, pagoda sleeves. Again, the bodice was well fit to the waist. She carried an umbrella that matched the dress, and wore a burgundy lace puff bonnet. She smiled a beautiful smile through full lips, and Lance could not help the teasing desire she stirred in him. Again, she looked at him with the look he understood, and again he reminded himself she was married to someone else — someone rich and powerful, and his own employer at that.

"Good morning," she greeted in her rich, soft voice.

Lance nodded, scowling slightly, annoyed with her for baiting and teasing him the way she was doing now. He approached his door and pulled a key from a small pocket at the waist of his buckskin pants.

"I didn't know rich people got up this early," he said, unlocking his door.

"It depends on whether or not they have reason."

He stayed outside his room, pushing the door open but not moving. "And your reason?"

Her dark eyes ran over him hungrily. "I just wanted to have a chance to talk to you again before you left."

He sighed and leaned against the doorjamb. She had a way of making him feel as though he'd always known her, and he suddenly realized that it was already understood that some day he would share her bed. The look in her eyes told him so, and the natural man in him would not argue it.

"Why do you need to talk to me? My business is with your husband. You do have one, you know, Mrs. Françoise."

She smiled more, strolling into his room. "There are all kinds of reasons for having husbands, Mr. Raines." She turned and faced him again, and Lance remained in the doorway. "May I call you Lance?"

He watched her cautiously while moving inside and laying his package down. "I suppose."

"Good. And you may call me Jess." She turned again, walking in the rustling dress to the window to look out at the street below. "Since you lived with Indians once, I suppose I can tell you I have Indian blood myself. My mother was a Seminole."

She turned to face him again, and his eyes ran over her

128

appreciatively.

"You're not surprised?"

"No," he replied. "I suspected right away."

She shrugged and sauntered to stand at the foot of the iron bed, unmade and rumpled from his night's sleep. She looked it over, then met his eyes.

"The Seminoles are from Florida, you know."

"I know." He folded his arms. "And how did a half-Seminole woman end up with a man like Claude Françoise?"

She smiled seductively. "Let's just say I . . . 'worked' my way up to the top."

Their eyes held, and he realized she had the air of a prostitute about her. He was fast losing his concern over whether or not she was married.

"Worked your way up from what?"

She laughed lightly. "I'll let you wonder . . . for now." She sauntered closer. "I suppose you're leaving this morning?"

"You suppose right." He lowered his arms and moved away from her to finish packing some things into his saddlebags. "You never really said why you're here, Mrs. Françoise."

"I said you could call me Jess."

"I know what you said. I prefer to call you Mrs. Françoise. But you can still call me Lance. And I'd like to know what you want." He strapped shut the bags and straightened to face her.

She took a deep breath, coming closer again, studying the green eyes.

"You," she answered softly. "Just you. You're the most beautiful man I've ever laid eyes on."

He slung the bags over his shoulder, almost angry with her literally torturing him with her deliberate wantonness. "Thanks for the compliment, but married women can't go around having any man they want."

She smiled slyly. "Married women can do anything they

want—if they're clever about it."

He moved past her to take his gunbelt from where it hung over a bedpost. "And what was your excuse to your husband for leaving the house so early?"

"I didn't need one. He was out riding, and I often come into town early to shop. I don't like crowds."

He slung the gunbelt over his shoulder. "I don't understand you, Mrs. Françoise. You hardly know me."

"Why do I need to know you any more than I do? I know that you're a man in every way, and that you are single. There is nothing else to know."

He frowned, studying the dark eyes. "Even so, you move awfully fast. How do you know I won't go to your husband and tell him you've been here?"

She came closer again, encircling him with her arms. "You won't. You won't because you want to decide first whether or not you'd like to have an affair with me." She pressed her breasts against his broad chest and looked up at him, and he could not resist bending down to meet her lips. She answered the kiss with a whimper, parting her mouth in heated desire. He knew women, and this one knew exactly what to do with a man. He could not help but suspect she had been a prostitute, or at least promiscuous enough that she might as well have been. The kiss was long and hungry, and when she felt his hardness against her belly, her breathing quickened and she left his mouth, kissing at his neck. "Surely you don't have to leave so quickly," she whispered.

He pulled away then, the warning voice still telling him to beware. His green eyes flashed with anger that she should bring on the pain of desire for someone he could not have.

"You're a witch, Jessica Françoise." His voice was husky with desire. "I don't know what you're up to, but I don't play games this early in the morning, and not with some other man's wife. I can't imagine why you would throw yourself at a man you hardly know. We talked all of five minutes last night."

"But I had longer than that to look at you," she answered before he was finished, her own eyes glinting with anger. "Long enough to know you could be the man my husband is not!" Her gaze dropped to the obvious evidence that she had aroused him, and she smiled a little, meeting his eyes again. "The moment you walked into my house you wanted me," she added. "And I wanted you. Those things just happen sometimes. Eyes meet, and there is nothing that can be done about the feelings . . . the desires. It doesn't even have to be love. It's an animal instinct as old as the beginning of time, Mr. Lance Raines." She stepped closer again. "Think about it while you're out there on the lonely plains, love. Think about Jessica Françoise . . . and satin sheets. You will know when you return in the spring for your pay what you must do to keep from going crazy."

She whirled then, the rustling skirts creating a little draft that moved the fringes on his buckskin pants. She walked out without another word, and he stared after her, his emotions mixed. He wondered if perhaps she was slightly demented. How often did she throw herself at near strangers this way? Did Françoise know about her activities? Was she one of those women who couldn't get enough of men? Some women were worse than prostitutes. They needed men, and they didn't even take money. Was that the kind of woman Jessica was?

Whatever she was, she had ruined his morning. If she were not married to his own employer, if he knew more about her first, maybe he'd have prolonged his departure and shared his bed with her. He had no doubt it would be one of the most delightful such encounters he'd had in a long time, maybe even better than Mattie. But for now he'd get while the getting was good before he offended someone or fell into her spider's web.

He quickly left the room himself, glancing around as he

went out but seeing her nowhere. Yet he felt she was watching him, and it made him uneasy. He headed for the livery, where he saddled and packed Sotaju, his mind reeling with the generous offer he had just passed up. How many red-blooded men said no to something like Jessica? Was he being too conscious of right and wrong? What did it matter with a woman like Jessica Françoise?

He paid the boy who tended the horses and eased himself up onto Sotaju. "Let's get the hell out of this damned town," he told the animal, kicking its sides. He headed out, mud flying from beneath Sotaju's hooves.

Jessica stood in the doorway of a hat store just as he rode by. She'd been watching the livery. Once he rode past, she stepped out to watch, her body aching for him. She smiled, happy that by being clever she could have the best of two worlds; a rich husband and now and then a man of her chosing with whom to share her bed. It wasn't often just the right man came along for what she wanted. Lance Raines was one of them—perfect in every way. She needed a perfect man for her particular purposes. And she didn't doubt that at the same time Lance Raines could carry her to heights of ecstasy she had never before visited. Her nerve endings screamed to know what he was like in bed. She was so sure that very morning she would have found out. But she had moved too quickly, and there wasn't time enough to seduce him fully. But he would be back, and she smiled at the thought of it. Surely Lance Raines's nights would be very restless now, until he saw her again.

Kate opened the wire the messenger had brought her, while Cassandra looked on, her eyes wide with fear that something had happened to Lance. Kate smiled then.

"That worthless, no-good has deposited a thousand dollars in the local bank by wire—a bonus he got from the railroad. I'm to use it to help take care of you." She looked at Cassandra. "How about that?"

Cassandra smiled. "A whole thousand dollars? That's a fortune!"

Kate laughed lightly. "Well, not a fortune, but it is an awful lot of money. That's Lance for you. One minute I'd like to knock him right up the side of the head, and the next I love him to death. He's got a good heart, Cass."

"I know that," the girl said quietly, her own heart bursting with love for Rainmaker. "He pretends that he doesn't, but I know he does."

They sat down at the kitchen table, and Cassandra rubbed at her stomach. This was her first time, and with it had come pain. At first she'd been surprised and frightened, but kind and patient Kate had explained it all to her. Now she didn't mind the pain, because what was happening to her meant she was finally becoming a woman, and it couldn't happen fast enough as far as she was concerned. The sooner she was a woman, the sooner Rainmaker would look at her like a woman. And he had sent money! He was still thinking about her, planning for her! Even though they hadn't yet received a real letter from him, at least they were on his mind, and they knew they could get messages to him through Hays City.

"I want to write him a letter right away," Cassandra announced.

Kate looked up from shucking peas into a pan she had put on her lap. "Give him a little time, child. He might not even be to Hays City yet. That was just a wire from Denver, not a letter. Wires travel fast over telegraph lines."

"Oh," The girl's face fell and she sighed. "Do you think he'll answer my letters when I do send them?"

Kate picked up another handful of peas. "I reckon he will, in his own time. Don't be expecting too much of that one, Cass. He might answer the first letter and then not answer the rest. Depends on the mood he's in and how busy he is. Like I said, he's got a good heart, but his mind wanders from writing letters to chasing buffalo. Between the two, he'd rather chase buffalo. Sometimes I wonder if he'll ever be dependable, but at least he's taken this new job; so I expect maybe at last he's considering the future. Who knows? Lord, I'd love to see that man with a wife and child before I die."

Cassandra's blood felt hot at the words. She wondered if anyone would ever love Lance Raines like she loved him. How she worried that he would find someone else. What would she do? How would she go on living? How she longed to be the wife Lance Raines someday chose, in spite of her fear of what a wife had to do to get babies. But surely with Rainmaker, that wouldn't be so bad. He'd be nice to her and patient with her. He'd never be mean and in a hurry.

Kate glanced at the girl, seeing her face was flushed. Cassandra was staring at the checkered tablecloth.

"I hate to be an old crab, child, but you must stop thinking about Lance Raines the way I know you're thinking," the woman said kindly. "He's too much man for the likes of you, and he's thirteen years older. I'm worried about you. You're headed for a lot of hurt."

Cassandra met the woman's blue eyes, then looked away, reddening even more. "Rainmaker would never hurt me. Some day I'll be all grown up. Then it won't matter that he's older." Her eyes teared and she looked at Kate. "He's the most wonderful man in the whole world, Kate. Some day he'll belong just to me—just me and nobody else. You'll see. Those dumb boys at school aren't anything compared to Rainmaker. They're stupid and they're cowards. And Rainmaker looks at me sometimes like he likes me a lot. I think sometimes he even wanted to kiss me."

Kate scowled. "You stop that talk. Of course he wanted to kiss you. He's a man, isn't he? And you're a pretty little girl. He admires your sweetness. Lance is good and he appreciates your own good heart. But you're just a child to him. Just because he looked at you that way doesn't mean he loves you like a man loves a woman. It doesn't mean anything at all. You have a lot to learn about men, Cassandra Elliott. And you'd better be careful while learning it. Men are easily tempted, and you don't know what you're about."

The girl's eyes teared again. "Am I bad, Kate?"

The woman sighed and met her eyes. "Of course you aren't bad. You're a sweet little girl who doesn't know the difference yet between the married kind of love and infatuation. How can you be bad when you don't even understand men yet? Now, I explained a lot of things to you a couple of days ago when your time came. What's happening to you is just the beginning of learning a lot of things. I just don't want you thinking things in your heart that aren't so, honey." She grabbed another handful of peas. "I don't want you to be disappointed. You shouldn't concentrate all your thoughts on Lance, because that's something that can probably never be, child. When you're older, you'll see that. In the meantime, don't waste these growing up years pining away for a grown man who's reckless with women and never around and hardly ready to settle. That's foolish. Have fun while you're young, and don't be looking to someone who's bound to break your heart in a thousand pieces. And it won't be his fault if he does. It will be yours for thinking things that can't be and expecting too much from a man who doesn't owe you such things."

The girl's lips puckered. "I can't help it, Kate. We got to be good friends after he took me away from the Cheyenne. I like being around him and talking to him. And what he did for me, fighting like that and everything, I just know it means we're supposed to be together some day. I just know it."

"You just get your mind and heart on school and your young friends right here."

"But I don't like them. I only like Susan. She's nice to

135

me. But the other girls and most of the boys aren't real friendly to me."

Kate frowned, setting aside the pan of peas. "Why?"

Cassandra shrugged. "I guess because Indians took me. The boys call me squaw girl." She said the words quietly, her head hanging.

Kate knew what the parents of the other children must have been telling them. They must suspect Cassandra's Indian captors had raped her. Even if they had, those people had no right making it look as though poor little Cassandra was anything but an innocent child, as worthy and good as their own children, probably more so.

"Don't you listen to them folks," she told Cassandra. "Those boys don't know what they're about. Most of them probably don't even know the meaning of squaw girl. I'd like to bare their behinds and lay a strap to them!"

Cassandra looked up at the woman with watery eyes. "What does it mean, Kate?"

The woman sighed and wiped her hands on her apron. "It's just an expression. It's just a way some white folks have of talking about Indian women and about white women who've been captured and returned. None of them folks know what it's like or understand the terror of it. They're cruel, unkind, unChristian people, and most of them go to church every Sunday and pretend they're kind and loving. I'd like to take a stick to all of them! I had problems with that kind when I took in Lance. But I talked right back to them, and I didn't let them bother me one whit. That's what you've got to do, Cass. You hold your head up and don't let them make you act like you're ashamed of anything, because you've got nothing to be ashamed of. You just be yourself, and in no time most of them will be your friends." She reached out and took the girl's hand. "I know it's all been hard for you, child. But you haven't been here all that long. Time will take care of a lot of things. It will heal your wounds from losing your folks, and it will make the others forget and just like you for you. And in time you'll have lots of friends, and you'll see you don't need to put so much importance on Lance. He's important now because of what he did for you, and because he was your first real friend after all that terror. But that's all he is and probably all he ever will be, and you've got to face that and grow up some, Cassandra." She squeezed the girl's hand. "Do you understand what I'm saying?"

Cassandra nodded. But a tear slipped down her cheek. "I can't help it, Kate. I can't help how I feel. I don't care about anybody else but Rainmaker." Her chest shook in a sob. "It hurts so bad sometimes."

Kate sighed and rose, coming around to put her hands on the girl's shoulders. "I know it hurts. I remember the first time I thought I was in love. It was a young neighbor man who was always nice to me. But then I got older, and I fell in love with somebody else — real love, not child's love. And I married Mr. McGee, rest his soul."

Cassandra picked up a peapod and twisted it in her fingers. "But what about the neighbor man you thought you loved? You never really forgot him, did you?" Cassandra asked curiously. "Don't you sometimes still think of him and wonder about him, still love him a little bit?"

She sniffed and wiped at her eyes while Kate's face went melancholy. "Yes. I still think of him now and again, although Lord knows he's probably not even alive any more. When I think of him, I picture him the way he was then, young and strong and sweet."

Cassandra turned around and looked up at Kate. "Maybe if you hadn't met Mr. McGee, and you got older and that man asked you to marry him, maybe you would have always been with him, Kate. Maybe you just didn't wait long enough."

Kate studied the hope in the girl's pretty blue eyes. She didn't have the heart to tell her that first man had married someone else before she was a real woman. That was

137

probably what would happen with Lance, if he ever married at all. She just shook her head and patted Cassandra's head.

"Maybe I didn't," she answered. "But a girl can waste a lot of happy years waiting for a dream, Cass. Let yourself be a child while you are one. There are plenty of years ahead to be a woman, and believe me, that brings a lot of heartache and pain sometimes. I've lost a husband and a son, so I know what I'm talking about. Don't burden yourself with things that needn't be a burden right now. And be patient. Time takes care of a lot of things."

Cassandra sniffed again, getting out of her chair. "Can I start a letter anyway, Kate? I won't mail it for a couple of weeks. But I could make it kind of a diary, putting down each day and telling Rainmaker what I did—and you, too."

Kate laughed lightly and waved her off. "Go on with you, then. You're hopeless. Start your letter."

The girl grinned and hugged her. "Thank you. I'll be down in a while to help you with the supper."

"You be sure you are. I have a full house, and they're all men with big appetites. I'll start these peas soon."

Cassandra ran to the stairs. "Thank you, Kate!"

The older woman watched her bound up the stairs, and she shook her head. Cassandra was a good girl, nice company to have around in her aging years. It angered her that some of the children ridiculed her for something she couldn't help, and thought things that were not even true.

"I've a mind to go down to that school and give them all a piece of my mind!" she mumbled. "Or maybe I should visit each one of those farm families." She retrieved a big kettle and set it on the stove. "Probably wouldn't do any good," she went on, talking to the stove. "People are going to think what they want no matter what anybody else says. They've got their minds made up. But I'll bet they'd not say it in front of Lance Raines! I'd like them to try. Squaw girl! Those no-goods! Those mothers ought to get captured

138

themselves — get a taste of what that poor child went through. Then they'd understand! Doggoned gossips!"

A light pain jabbed at her chest again, a new pain that had been giving her trouble of late, making it difficult to breathe sometimes. She squinted and put a hand to her chest, standing still while she caught her breath. After a moment it went away, and she returned to her cooking.

Jessica Françoise settled into a soft chair across from where her husband sat smoking a pipe and studying the latest edition of the *Rocky Mountain News*. She sipped at some tea and watched a fire in the stone fireplace. Outside, cold December winds blew against their fortress of a house, and windows rattled. She shivered, pulling a shawl closer around her and wondering what it was like for Lance Raines out on the plains, where there was nothing to stop the wind, no shelter, just wide open land that never ended.

She had slept with many men. But never had she desired one quite as keenly as she had desired Lance Raines, and although nearly three months had passed, she could not get him off her mind.

"A penny for your thoughts, my love," her husband's voice spoke up.

She drew her dark eyes from the fire to look to him. Claude Françoise was far from an ugly man. He was quite handsome, for his age and size. But he was not a Lance Raines, and she was quite certain that in bed there was probably no comparison at all.

"I am just thinking about how cold it must be for your railroad men out on the plains."

He watched her closely. "Any particular man you're worried about?"

She dropped her gaze. "Of course not."

He smoked quietly for a moment. "I married you for many reasons, Jessica: your beauty, your charm, the way you make me crazy with the want of you . . . and because you're a healthy woman in her prime child-bearing years. I thought you the perfect woman to give me a fine son, an heir to my fortune. That's very important to me. I didn't want some pampered, fainting ninny who whines around the house and gives birth to spindlings, even if she might be rich. I don't need another woman's money. So I chose you, Jessica Lake, a young half-breed girl I found in a brothel and turned into a lady. It's been a fascinating task, and I think I did well. You're everything a wealthy man's wife should be. You've been perfect in every way, except that I still don't have a son."

She met his eyes again, and the fear returned that if she didn't get pregnant soon he'd divorce her and find someone else. Never had she known such riches. She didn't love him; but she loved her lifestyle, and she would not give it up if she had to die to keep it.

"You know how hard we've tried," she told him. "Perhaps it's . . . " She swallowed. "Perhaps it's you, Claude."

His face grew dark with anger. "How dare you suggest such a thing!"

She closed her eyes and sighed. "It's just a thought."

"Then, think again! Maybe you can't even have children! When you were a whore you never got pregnant!"

Her eyes widened then, flashing with irritation. "You never fail to remind me what I was when you're angry, do you? I suppose you intend to use that over my head for the rest of our lives!" She set her cup down and rose, walking to the fireplace.

"I'm sorry, Jessica," he said quietly. "I just get anxious."

She whirled. "Well, when I was a whore, as you keep reminding me, I had ways of avoiding pregnancy. I never really tried like I am doing now. Maybe if you would just quit harping about it all the time, I could relax more, and I would get pregnant easier."

"Maybe," he answered, looking her up and down. "And

maybe you turn to other men because you think your childlessness is my fault. Maybe you think some other man can get you pregnant, and therefore you can always share the vast Françoise fortune."

She glared boldly at him, and sometimes he could clearly see all the Indian in her. "I promised you when you proposed that I would be true to you," she replied. "I love this life. I will not break that promise," she lied. She had to lie, for if she didn't take up with other men, how could she hope to get pregnant? Yet in her position, it was a difficult situation. She had to be discreet, and that narrowed down her chances of being with a man often enough to take his seed and have it hold. It was easy for her to be untrue, for she enjoyed men, and since setting eyes on Lance Raines, there was one in particular she wanted above all others.

"See that you don't break that promise," he warned. "We have an agreement, Jessica. I give you a beautiful home, prestige, respect; you are true to me and you give me a child—more than one if possible. I'm not certain you've been true, and I still have no children. Your purpose for being here is not being fulfilled."

She floated to a buffet and poured herself a small glass of whiskey. "I don't suppose you've had any feelings of love, my darling Claude?"

He grinned. "No more than you have. But we get along quite well otherwise. I've treated you well. If you give me a child, it's possible I could have feelings for you, simply because you are my child's mother. In all other ways I am very pleased with you, Jessica, and in spite of not truly loving you, I do feel an unexpected jealousy when I imagine you with another man. You belong to me, legally. I hope you will remember that. An heir should be of my own blood. I'll not hand my fortune over to some other man's bastard."

Jessica swallowed some whiskey, keeping her back to him and thinking of Lance Raines. "Don't worry, love. When I have a child, he will be yours." She turned to face him. "And then I can be your wife for always?"

He rose from his chair, setting his pipe into an ashtray. "Of course. That's what I promised." He walked up to her, taking the glass from her hand. "Why don't we go and try again? That's another reason I married you, Jessica. You enjoy a man—no excuses for not sharing your bed as often as your husband likes. Women from my circle all too often come up with headaches." He laughed lightly, his gaze dropping to her bosom.

"Some of the wealthier ladies of Denver think I'm not worthy to be in their circles, you know," she told him, pouting. "I think it's because I am so dark. They suspect I am of a nationality they . . . are not fond of."

He scowled. "I've told my friends you are French and Spanish. That is acceptable."

"And Indian is not?"

He laughed lightly. "Of course not."

She smiled almost sadly. "White men have strange values, strange judgments. But it matters little to me now. As an Indian, I was poor and spit on, making my living by groveling with every man who came along." The words were sneered, but then she sauntered up to her husband, putting her arms around his neck. "But as the French and Spanish wife of Claude Françoise, I am a respected woman. Perhaps you will say something to your friends again. Perhaps if their wives do not stop snubbing me, you will cut off your contributions to their various causes?"

His eyes were getting glassy with desire. "I'll see what I can do."

She kissed him then, in the way she had of making him weak and unable to resist her. He was a man of power, until Jessica worked her witch's spells on him, using all her expertise to make him want her even though he didn't love her. Maybe this time his life would take hold inside of her and grow into an heir.

She took his hand, leading him toward the stairway to their bedroom, wondering how long she could keep convincing him to keep trying and not send her away. She had only her own skills at teasing a man into wanting her to rely on. He did not love her. Her only hope was to convince him that surely she would get pregnant any time. But that hope was dwindling. In another year or two, she would lose this wonderful life she had found if she did not get pregnant. She wished she had had time to spend with Lance Raines. There was a potent man, a virile man who surely carried good seed. But she had failed to seduce him into staying longer, and it frustrated her. The thought of lying beneath such a man made her blood run hot, in spite of her own experience.

But one could always write. She would remind him through discreet letters that she still wanted him, convince him to come back to Denver in the spring. That would be a good time. And there would be good reason—to report to her husband, to collect his wages and bonus. Yes, she would tell him what some of the good excuses would be to come back to Denver in the spring. Even without any letters, she was sure he would come anyway. For surely she had given him some exciting things to think about.

There would be other men until then, but few. She had to be very careful in this town where everyone knew her husband. It was becoming more and more difficult to be discreet. That worried her, for she was inwardly convinced it was Claude's fault she was not getting pregnant. Surely something was wrong with his seed. But he would not believe it, and to please him she must somehow get pregnant and tell him it was his child. Lance Raines would have been the perfect man, but he had gotten away from her. She must get him back, for she wanted him out of pure desire, for the beautiful man that he was. No matter what else happened, her harlot's heart was determined to know Lance Raines intimately. She would write, or find some other way to get him back to Denver. And he would come. She was sure of it. When he came he would not be able to resist her bed, for that would be the very reason he would come. And she would take his seed — over and over she would take it, willingly, joyously, thrilling in the man. She had a good feeling about Lance Raines, an odd premonition. Maybe it was the Indian in her. But he was the one. She was sure of it. He was the man who would plant life in her belly so that she could present Claude with a son . . . and keep the Françoise fortune and lifestyle for herself.

Chapter Nine

Lance drew his buffalo-skin coat closer around his neck against the bitter wind, pulling the large collar up around his head and tying it with a woolen scarf. He nudged Sotaju into a slow walk, circling and studying the travois marks and hoof prints in the thin layer of snow that had blanketed the plains the day before. Far behind him, a railroad crew carried on with the laying of rails, some of the men suffering frostbitten fingers from the cold steel they worked with.

He looked out over the horizon, seeing nothing. But he knew that the marks of unshod ponies he had studied belonged to Indians, most likely Cheyenne, and he was curious. Neither the northern nor the southern Cheyenne did much moving around in the winter. Since a couple of travois were being used, it could not be a war party. Yet he didn't want to bet on it. The year of 1868 had been a restless, warring year for the red men of the plains—frightened and angry. Hope for peace had been smashed at Sand Creek. The Cheyenne would not forget, and they proved this at a small island on the Republican River in the past September, where, according to newspaper accounts and talk along the railroad, Cheyenne Indians held a large party of scouts at bay for nine days, the men nearly starving to death before the Indians finally left them and soldiers arrived to help them. The scouts had been sent out to locate the hostile

145

Cheyenne and entreat them to return to the reservation in Oklahoma. The hostiles had given their answer. They would not go back. But the battle had cost lives of good men on both sides: a Lieutenant Beecher, some damned good scouts, all of whom Lance had known, and a settler who had gone along for vengeance because the Cheyenne had killed his wife. The great Cheyenne leader, Roman Nose, had also lost his life in that battle.

Lance could not help but wonder how he would have reacted if he had been one of the scouts. It was hard for men like himself who knew the Indians well, liked them, understood them. They were men walking a fine line between two worlds, understanding both sides. It was even harder for Lance, for he'd lived among the Cheyenne and called them family.

Now soldiers worked feverishly to hunt down the hostiles. General Sheridan himself was in charge of stopping the Indian raids and getting all the Cheyenne into one place. Lance knew that would not be easy, and it irritated him that Long Hair Custer was one of the officers out campaigning against the Cheyenne. He'd met George Custer and didn't like the man. He was obviously arrogant and itching to make a name for himself, no matter how many Indian lives that might cost, whether they be men, women or children. And what bothered Lance at the moment was that the tracks he saw had come up from the south. Why would any southern Cheyenne head north in December? They should be down on the Cimarrón or the Washita.

The wind blew his hair in his face, and the sound of it made him feel lonely . . . lonely in many ways. The railroad was progressing through Indian country, changing the land forever. The Indian was a dying race. He could already see it happening. The buffalo were also dying, and without the great beast of the plains, the Indian could not survive, let alone what white men's diseases did to them. Then there was the loneliness in his own heart, a loneliness he did not fully understand. He'd been on his own all his life and had never felt lonely. Yet ever since the letter from Cassandra, he had been unable to reconcile his feelings for her, let alone the fact that the memory of Jessica Françoise tormented his nights.

He leaned into the high collar, sheltering himself from the wind as he halted Sotaju again to roll and light a cigarette. It seemed lately there was too much to think about. Until this time in his life, he had lived without much concern for anything or anyone in particular, other than caring about the Cheyenne and about Kate. But his life was independent and of his own choosing. Now, suddenly, he was hit hard by what was happening to the Cheyenne, and that Kate seemed older and thinner when last he saw her; and there was the matter of Jessica's offer, a tempting one indeed; and last but not least, Cassandra. Why did the memory of her pull at him?

He removed the letter from his pocket again, turning so that his body sheltered it from the wind, and holding the cigarette in the corner of his mouth as he read the letter for the fourth or fifth time. For some reason it made him feel good, warmer, happier.

"Dear Rainmaker," she wrote. *"I guess I will always call you Rainmaker, because that is what I called you first, and that is how I think of you. I hope this letter finds you well and not in any trouble with Indians or something like that. I get afraid sometimes that something bad will happen to you. If it does, remember that I said I would always be your friend. Kate worries about you, too. She fusses all the time. I used to think it was because she was mad at me about something, but now I know she isn't. She just likes to fuss."*

Lance grinned again at the remark. He could easily picture it, and had long ago learned to take Kate McGee's clucking and chiding in stride, just grinning at her and knowing that only made her more angry and scolding. He enjoyed playing those games with her and missed it sometimes.

"I am worried about Kate," the letter continued. *"Sometimes she acts like she doesn't feel good; but she doesn't say anything, and I think*

147

she tries to hide it. I think you should come and see her in the spring if you can stop what you are doing for a little while. And we both miss you anyway.

"I am in school now. It's okay, and I have some new friends. But some of the kids, especially some of the boys, I don't like very much. They say things to me about being captured by Indians, untrue things. It makes me want to cry sometimes. Kate says those kids and their folks just don't understand and they aren't good Christians. She said I should hold my head up and not act ashamed of anything. She even talked to one of the mothers when she saw her in town, and she really gave that woman a good tongue-lashing. I almost started to giggle right there, but it still hurts when I think about some of the things those people think."

That part of the letter irritated Lance. He didn't like the thought of people thinking anything bad about Cassandra Elliott. More perfect innocence could not be found in Abilene, he was sure, and he'd shake out a few tails himself the next time he went home.

He shifted in his saddle, the thought of that very innocence again stirring unwarranted desires. He wanted to protect her from all outside danger, to some day be her first man. But such thoughts meant he must love her. How could he say or even think that he could love a girl that age?

It was the same problem over and over. She haunted his nights, tempting him with her innocence, while Jessica pulled at purely animal instincts. It was as though perhaps his body could belong to one, and his heart to another. He tried to ignore both thoughts, but his mind and emotions would not let him. He took a deep drag on the cigarette and finished the letter.

"The cattle and cowboys are finally gone from Abilene for the winter. We are all glad, for it seems like every day somebody gets killed in an argument or something. Kate fusses about that, too, and threatens to move to some other town. But I don't think she will. She says that some day the cattleman will move to another town, when the railroad gets farther west, and she says there is a railroad being built south of us, too; and they'll get to that railroad before they get to the Kansas-Pacific, so

then Abilene won't have to worry about the cattlemen any more.

"I do real good in school, and sometimes Kate helps me study. I really like Kate. You were right about her. Sometimes I still miss my parents and my brother so much that I cry again, and I wonder if I will ever forget that awful day they were killed. Sometimes I wonder why God lets things happen, and then I think maybe there was a reason. There had to be one. At least I like to think so. Maybe the reason was so you could come and find me and we would meet. Maybe God meant for me to meet you, and you to meet me, and we should be good friends for always. Do you think that could be true? I think about it a lot, and I think about you. I will never forget that you might have died saving me from the Cheyenne, and I will always be ever so grateful for that. You will always be special to me, Rainmaker. I know it probably sounds silly, but I can't help it. Kate says you're wild and undependable; but I know inside you're good, and I know you're brave and that you help people. You're the nicest man I've ever met.

"I hope you can come home in the spring. If you do, I'll bake you some apple pie. Do you like apple pie? I make it real good. Kate says I make it better than she does. But she told me I would have to make a lot of them for you because when you eat pie you eat a whole half at once, and sometimes a whole pie! I laughed when she told me that. No wonder you're so big. It's a good thing you are tall, or you would be fat. But Kate says you move around too much to get fat.

"Before I say good-bye, I want to thank you for sending the money to Kate to help take care of me. See? That's how I know you're good inside and not always wild and undependable. I know Kate doesn't mean anything she says about you, and when she got the wire about the money, she had tears in her eyes.

"I hope you will write back to me, even if it isn't a long letter. That's okay. Just tell us if you are well, and what you are doing now, and where you are. And tell us if you will come home soon. If you do, you will be surprised when you see me. I got a little bit taller, and I am starting to look more grown up.

"I pray for you every day. We heard what happened to the scouts last fall, and you're a scout, too. I'm glad you know some of the Cheyenne, but some of them who don't know you any more might kill you. I don't

149

know what I would do if that happened. I think I would want to die myself, for you are my best friend. Please write to me, Rainmaker.

"Sincerely, Cass."

He folded the letter and put it back into his pocket. He wondered if by looking more "grown up" she was trying to tell him she was filling out in a womanly way but didn't know how to put it into words. The thought was interesting and teased his curiosity. Yet he suspected he'd be better off not to go home in the spring. He shouldn't see her yet. If he waited another full year, her thoughts would have faded more, as would his own thoughts of her. He didn't like how he felt, and didn't like the thought of settling, either. Why did he think of settling when he thought of Cassandra Elliott? He wasn't ready for that. Besides, what good would it do to go home to a child? It would be the same situation he'd left, and it was foolish and ridiculous. He was angry with himself again for even considering Cassandra Elliott as anything but a little girl he'd rescued. Yet the letter had brought to mind her pretty face and golden hair, and the feel of her against him when she rode in front of him on Sotaju.

He sighed and urged the horse into motion again, studying the Indian signs more. He'd be better off thinking about Jessica Françoise, and going to Denver in the spring to see if she still wanted him in her bed. At least a woman like that couldn't be hurt like Cassandra could be. What did it matter if a man toyed with the feelings of someone like Jessica, who he suspected had had many other men before he came along. Jessica was the kind of woman a man could have a delightful time in bed with, without feelings and responsibilities. After all, she was already someone else's wife, although she didn't act it. He would never willingly even consider touching another man's wife, and he never had. But Jessica Françoise might as well not be a wife at all, and considering the fact that he was surely one of many, what did it matter? A single man with no cares didn't pass up such opportunities. She was ravishing, and hungry for him. He had no doubt that if he

150

returned to Denver in the spring and the opportunity arose to meet her alone again, she would show him as good a time as any prostitute could. And by then, he'd not be able to pass up the opportunity, for a long winter on the prairie with a bunch of men and the cold wind constantly at his back made a man hungry for a warm bed with a woman in it. That was one area where his appetite was also very hardy. He was not a man to go long without enjoying female companionship, and the bewitching charms of Jessica Françoise were tempting indeed. He would have to consider it strongly, but still wondered if she had some kind of devious plans for him. Maybe she liked getting men into trouble. Maybe she used men to make her husband jealous for some strange reason. Who could know with a woman like that? Whatever her reasons, it could not be all bad for him. She was the kind of woman a man could have a good time with but not the kind a man married, and why Claude Françoise had married her, he could not imagine. If and when he ever got married himself, it would be someone like Cass, someone sweet and innocent and untouched, someone . . .

He turned Sotaju back toward the railroad camp. He was doing it again, thinking about Cass in ways he had no right to think of her. No. He would not go back in the spring. But he would certainly consider going to Denver.

Outside, the winter winds of a building blizzard regaled the sides of the boxcar in which Lance sat with several surveyors playing cards in front of a pot-bellied stove. This was their winter home, crude as it was. Other men in the work crews stayed in other boxcars, all waiting for an engine to come and take them a few miles east to the closest town, where they would wait out the storm. But the storm had come hard and fast, and Lance suspected it would be a while before help came. He wondered how long he could stand sitting boxed up with complaining greenhorns, who hated

151

the inconveniences of life on the lonely plains and who longed for their cities.

"I'm going nuts!" one of them complained, making a scraping noise as he scooted back his chair and rose. "Count me out. I'm going for a walk or something, snow or no snow."

"I'd think twice about that," Lance told him. "You can get lost real easy out there."

The man scowled and pulled on some boots. "I'm tired of taking orders from you, Raines. What the hell is an educated man like myself doing taking orders from an uneducated, half-savage plainsman who's never seen the inside of a school or any place of culture?"

Lance watched him darkly, taking a drag on a cigarette. "I may not know much about schooling, Thomas; but by God I've been to the school of survival, and I'm telling you that if you go out there your ass might be lost for good. Out here people come up missing in blizzards and are found the next spring lying ten feet from their houses. But if you want to die that way, be my guest. I'll not miss you."

A couple of the other men at the table chuckled, including Jim Beck, supervisor of the project and the man Françoise had told Lance to report to. Paul Thomas scowled, rising and pulling on his fur coat.

"I wouldn't expect you to miss me, Raines," he muttered. "I suppose if you found my body, you'd take my scalp and claim it as a souvenir."

Lance carefully put out his cigarette and laid down his cards, then rose, his stature even more overbearing inside the boxcar. "I'm tired of your insults, Thomas," he told the man, his voice cold. "I get along real well with everybody else here. You're the only one who complains all the time. Who the hell do you think you are, anyway? If you think you're better than me, then prove it—the man's way."

He wrapped his hand around the handle of his knife, and Thomas swallowed. He backed up a little as he buttoned his coat. "It's just this damned useless land getting to me," he told

152

Lance, his voice more subdued. "I'm going crazy looking at all of you every day, listening to the damned wind that never stops, seeing nothing on the horizon but more nothingness!"

"You think it's any easier for the rest of us?" Jim Beck asked. "We don't exactly love looking at your mug, either, Thomas." He looked up at Lance. "Don't get your dander up, Raines. He isn't worth it. We don't need any killings out here in the middle of nowhere; and you're a damned good scout, so I don't want to lose you over something like this."

Lance just glared at Thomas, a small man with beady eyes and a haughty air about him. He hadn't liked the man from the moment he met him. He walked around the table toward the man, who reminded him of a weasle, and the others just watched, not about to try to stop Lance Raines if he was truly angry. Lance grabbed Thomas by the collar of his fur coat.

"Lay off, Thomas, or I'll take one of your sharpest surveying instruments and shove it right up your ass! In the kind of school I attended, I got real good at such things. You understand that, educated boy?"

The man paled visibly, his cold, gray eyes wide and bulging. He held up his chin. "I understand."

Lance grinned. "Good." He let go of the young man with a shove. "Now, you go for that walk, Thomas. But you put a rope around your waist and tie the other end to this railroad car, then you walk just the length of the rope so you don't get lost. You got all that?"

The man took a deep breath. "I've got it."

Lance walked to the end of the car and grabbed a long rope that hung wrapped around a hook. He threw the heavy cord to Thomas. "Use that," he told the man. "Personally, I'd just as soon you went out there and froze your ass and never returned. But considering that I'm your scout and your advisor on survival out here, I guess I have to do my advising proper and earn my money. But once we're through and I'm paid, if I ever see you in civilian life again, maybe we can finish this little question of who is the better man. And I

153

don't think education does it. Not out here!"

They glared at one another for a moment. Then Thomas tied the rope around his waist and pulled a beaver-skin hat over his head. He picked up some gloves and slid open the door. A howling wind blew snow inside the car. He jumped out and slammed the door closed, and the men at the table breathed easier, having been worried they were about to witness a murder, for Lance Raines had murder in his eyes when he looked at Thomas.

All of them wondered how many men the man had actually killed. They had had enough time talking over meals and cards to know his background, even that he had ridden with Indians against other Indians. He was fascinating to know, and they felt good having him around. In spite of his wild look and buckskin attire and his powerful size, they trusted him. He had already proven his expertise by helping a sick railroad man with special Indian herbs, and by his quick and effective treatment of another man who had accidentally shot himself in the hand. He could spot a snake several yards away in high grass and could smell a rainstorm coming before the clouds made an appearance. His sure shot netted the workers plenty of fresh meat, but when he shot a buffalo, he refused to take just the meat and leave everything else. He carefully stripped off the skin, stretching it over the tops of the boxcars to dry and intending to keep it for himself and later give it to the Cheyenne, along with a gunny sack full of bones he knew they could use for utensils. The animal was becoming more and more scarce, and Lance refused to waste any of it, sure the people he loved would be grateful for the skin and bones, even if there was no meat to go with it.

And he knew the land well. With his help the surveyors spotted the lay of the rail through places where Lance knew there was least likelihood of flooding in spring, as well as places he knew there was the least problem with mud. Besides his skills and knowledge of the land, Lance was entertaining, full of stories of his days with the Cheyenne when he rode as a young warrior. He had learned his skill at telling spell-binding stories from the Indians, for telling stories was a favorite pastime among the red men of the plains, especially in winter tipis when families had to sit huddled next to fires and it was too cold for children to run and play.

But no matter how much Lance explained to them about the Indians and their way of life, it did not alleviate their fear of attack; for the Cheyenne, Arapaho and Comanches still played havoc with the railroad crews, and soldiers roamed the plains searching for hostiles all that winter.

Lance sat back down and picked up his cards. "I know something that would be a hell of a lot more fun than these cards right now," he muttered, fanning the cards in his hand.

"What's that?" one of the others asked.

"A pretty and grateful woman."

There was a moment of silence, then a light laugh from Jim Beck, soon joined by the others.

"Can't argue that," another offered.

"Say, Raines," Beck put in. "It's obvious you're a fine-looking man to the ladies. Surely you've had both — Indian and white. Which is best?"

Lance sighed, throwing down two cards and asking for two more. He thought about Three Stars Woman's sister — and Mattie. He wondered about Jessica Françoise — and Cassandra. "Whichever one you're with at the time is the best," he answered.

They all laughed. "What a diplomat!" one of them guffawed. "Perfect answer."

Lance grinned himself. "Actually, there is one who stands out in my mind. She was Arapaho." He sighed again. "I saved her from the hands of a Pawnee warrior about to carry her away for himself. She was very grateful . . . and damned beautiful to boot."

Jim Beck chuckled more and handed him the two cards. "Yeah, there are usually one or two who stand out the most. That reminds me. You ever meet the boss's wife — Jessica

Françoise?"

Lance studied his cards, realizing he'd better be careful with his words. How well did Jim Beck know Claude Françoise? What did he know about the man's wife? Maybe he's been with her himself.

"I've met her. A lovely lady."

"Mmm-hmm." Beck studied his own cards. "Lovely is an understatement, but I don't know about the 'lady' part of it."

Lance met the man's eyes then. "Oh? She seemed like a lady to me."

Beck returned Lance's gaze and nodded. "Sure."

Lance knew by the man's eyes that Jessica Françoise had used her bewitching skills on Beck at one time. He nodded then, while the other two men watched curiously. "Fine woman," he said carefully. "I only saw her once — in her own home when I visited Françoise." He caught a hint of jealousy in Beck's eyes, along with a hopelessness.

They all made their bets, and Beck threw in his cards. "Yeah, it's strange how some women can get to a man and torture his emotions without even trying," he half grumbled. "All they have to do is smile, use their eyes a certain way, maybe not even that much. And sometimes you're with a woman you think will mean nothing to you, and she shouldn't anyway, but you end up—"

He stopped short and glanced at Lance again. Lance wondered even more what Jessica must be like. Maybe it was better if he stayed away from her altogether. It was amazing the way women could turn a man's thoughts upside down, and his were in an even worse turmoil. Apparently Jessica Françoise had won in her efforts with Jim Beck, a middle-aged widower and a handsome man in his own right. But Beck had apparently been unable to keep feelings out of the picture.

All thoughts of women were interrupted when Thomas pounded on the door and slung it open, scrambling inside.

"Indians!" he said excitedly, standing up and untying the

rope from his waist. "A hundred of them right outside! They just rode out of the snow like ghosts—sitting there on horses staring at me!" He looked at Lance. "Do something! They'll kill us all!"

Lance slowly rose, walking to a corner where he kept his rifle. He put on his buffalo jacket and picked up the rifle, checking to be sure it was loaded while the others watched, wondering why he wasn't more excited.

"You going out there?" one of them asked.

Lance glanced at him, then back at the rifle, cocking it to get a cartridge into the chamber. "Of course I'm going out there. That's my job, isn't it?" He looked at Thomas then. "Were there women with them?

"How the hell do I know? They're all wrapped up, and they all look the same—dark savages, all of them!"

Lance just shook his head and walked to the door, sliding it open. A cold wind stung his face, and the others hurried to the door, closing it to a crack when Lance jumped out, some of them running to crude windows that had been installed in the boxcar.

At first no Indians could be seen in the blinding snow. Lance looked down the railway at the other six boxcars full of men. The snow was so thick, he guessed some of them hadn't even noticed the Indians yet, but the door of the car directly behind their own suddenly slid open.

"We saw some Indians out there!" someone shouted. "Be careful, Raines."

Lance shouted through the wind. "Keep that door closed and don't show your weapons. Don't do a damned thing unless I come running and fire a signal. No Indian comes through a blizzard to make war. I don't think it's anything to be worried about. Stay inside."

His heart was heavy. Not only was he certain Thomas had exaggerated about the number of Indians he'd seen, but he knew that if they were really out there, they were in a bad way. Indians didn't travel around in this kind of weather.

157

They camped in sheltered places and stayed inside their tipis. Spring and summer were a time for making war, not winter. Only white soldiers attacked in winter, for it was the best time to catch the Indians off guard, their ponies hungry and weak.

He stepped farther into the snow, and the wind calmed for a moment. It was then he caught sight of a handful of men on ponies not thirty feet away.

A pain pierced his heart at the sight of their gaunt faces and hollow eyes. The wind blew at their worn buffalo robes and ponies' manes, and the ponies themselves looked as starved as their owners.

Lance stepped toward them, making the sign for Cheyenne and calling out to them in their own tongue, for he knew from first glimpse that was what they were. One man rode forward.

"What is it you want?" Lance asked, yelling to be heard above the wind.

"You have food?" the apparent leader asked. Lance guessed the man to be about forty, but he could tell he was not any kind of chief or even a dog soldier. These were stragglers from something . . . somewhere.

"How many are with you?" he called to the man.

"Only twelve of us: three small ones, one old woman, three young women and five men. We are on our way to join the northern Cheyenne, but the storm has made us lost. The little ones and old one will die without food."

"And without warmth," Lance shouted back. "Come inside the train car. It is warm inside. I will get some food together."

The man frowned and shook his head. "Cannot come inside. We would become prisoners of the white men."

Lance shook his head. "No. I give you my word. I lived among the Cheyenne once. I call White Eagle my father and Kicking Horse my brother. Do you know them?"

The man nodded. "In the summer I see them at the Sun Dance. White Eagle was not well. You are the white adopted son of White Eagle, the one they call Rainmaker?"

Lance nodded. "You can trust me. Get your people inside for the night. In the morning maybe the wind will go down and you can leave. We will give you food to take along."

The man put up his hand as a signal to wait, then disappeared into the blowing snow. Moments later he reappeared with seven other horses, some of them carrying two people, children and the old woman among them.

"Wait there and I will explain to the men," Lance told them. He hurried to the boxcar, and Jim Beck slid the door open to let him inside. Lance set his rifle aside. "I've told them they can come inside for the night to get warm," he announced. "And we will give them food. I'll give them those buffalo robes—"

"Like hell they'll come inside!" Thomas interrupted loudly. "You looking to get us all killed?"

Lance glared at him. "There are only twelve of them, and only five of those are men. They're starving and freezing and lost, Thomas, and I'm going to let them in and put their ponies in that empty boxcar down the line to get them out of the wind. For God's sake, if you white men want to make peace with the Indians some day, it has to begin someplace! They need help!"

"And if you leave them out there, they'll die and we'll be rid of a few more Indians!" Thomas shot back. "It's simple. You go out there and tell them to leave! We'll not help those lice-infested bastards!"

Lance lunged at him, looking to Thomas like a huge bear with the buffalo robe around his shoulders. He grasped Thomas around the throat, shoving him against the wall and squeezing until the man's face started to turn purple. The helpless man's arms flailed as he made gagging sounds, and the other men pulled at Lance's arms to no avail, for in his anger he was too strong for them.

"Raines, for God's sake, you're killing him!" Beck shouted. "Let go of the man or you'll be hanged for murder!"

Lance finally released his grip, and Thomas sank to the floor. He turned to Beck, and to the man's surprise he was sure there were tears in Lance Raines's eyes.

"I'm letting them inside," he said coldly. "If anybody in here doesn't like it, they can go to another car; and if anybody brings them harm, I'll kill him! And I'm giving them some food. If I lose my job over it, then that's the way it will have to be!"

Beck sighed. "All right. Bring them in." He looked at the other men. "You two get Thomas to a different car, and tell the other men to set their rifles down and not stir up any trouble."

The two men nodded, glancing warily at Lance and deciding not to argue with him. They helped Thomas to his feet and half carried the man out of the boxcar. Lance started to follow.

"Raines!" Beck called to him. Lance turned. "I could fire you for what you did."

"So? Go ahead. I don't need the money so bad that I'll turn these people away. They're like my own."

"And if we're attacked by that same kind?"

"That's different. I'll help fight them; and I know how they fight, so I'd be better than most at knowing what to do. But these people can hardly stand on their feet, let alone fight a battle with healthy men who outnumber them and have better weapons."

He jumped down and disappeared then, returning shortly with an old woman in his arms. He handed her to Beck, who took her with a scowl.

"The railroad will have our assess for this," he grumbled.

"Makes life more exciting, Beck," Lance answered. "Just think. Maybe you'll get called to Claude Françoise's presence, and you'd have to see his wife again. That can't be all bad."

Beck took the woman. "Can't it? Take my advice and stay away from that one, Raines. She only wants one thing, but she gets in your blood." He turned away, and Lance left again. This time several Indians were outside when Beck came back to the door. Lance lifted three children, one by one, into the boxcar. The women entered next, looking around with frightened eyes, then the men, gripping worn-out weapons. They were all thin and coated with ice and snow, and all fell gratefully to sitting positions in front of the wood-burning stove.

"I'll put your ponies in an empty boxcar," Lance told them in the Cheyenne tongue, repeating in English to Beck what he was doing. "I'll be right back."

He disappeared again, and Jim Beck sat down at the table, his handgun near his hand. He watched the tattered people who sat shivering near the stove and could not himself keep from pitying them, in spite of the fact of what some of their kind had done to railroad workers in vicious attacks to stop the railroad. By why shouldn't they try to stop it? Its presence brought more whites and chased away the buffalo.

Lance loaded up the ponies, then went to a car where his own horse was kept along with a few others owned by the railroad and picked up a bag of feed, taking it to the Indian ponies and scattering it for them. He left that car and returned to his own, ignoring shouts and curses from men in other cars for helping Indians. He reentered his own car, and Beck was the only other white man there. The other two had not come back and probably would not. Beck looked relieved when he saw Lance.

Lance slid the door shut and went to a crate, taking out some bread and handing it out among the twelve people, who accepted it humbly.

"We have nothing to give you in return for this gift," their leader told him. "It is not good that we accept this, but we have no choice when our children are starving."

Lance nodded. "What's your name? Why are you out here?"

"I am called One Cloud. We are all of the northern Cheyenne, but we had decided to stay among the southern Cheyenne this year because many are our relatives. Then a few suns ago, while we were camped on the Washita with Black Kettle's band, the soldiers came, led by Long Hair."

"Custer? He attacked your camp?"

Beck became more alert at the sound of the name. The rest was spoken in Cheyenne, and he could not understand it. "What is it?" he asked.

"In a minute," Lance replied, his eyes on the old man.

One Cloud was nodding sadly. "It was bad," he said to Lance. "Many women and children were killed by the soldiers. And Black Kettle, the great peace chief of the southern Cheyenne, is also dead."

Lance rubbed at his eyes. "Damn," he muttered. Black Kettle. He had once been given a peace medal by President Lincoln, and he flew an American Flag above his tipi.

"Many were taken prisoner, some escaped. We had no time to organize, for it was a surprise attack," One Cloud continued. "One group of soldiers, I think, was killed to the last man, though, but not Long Hair Custer. We just fled north to go to our brothers there, but then the snow came. There was not time to grab food and extra clothing and ponies. Everyone took what they could take quickly. Many died in the snows. We left behind many saddles and robes, lodge skins, powder and lead revolvers, hatchets and bows and quivers, many blankets, and a whole winter's supply of buffalo meat. I am sure by now Long Hair has burned everything, and as we fled, the soldiers were shooting all of our horses. We were lucky to get hold of the sorry ponies we have with us."

Lance clenched his fists and paced. "A surprise attack in the dead of winter on the most peaceful band of the Cheyenne," he muttered. He wished he'd never been taken by the Cheyenne, never learned to love them. It seemed his heart had been ripped in half. He looked at Beck then, picking up a bottle of whiskey on the table and taking a slug. "It seems the illustrious George Armstrong Custer has got himself another great Indian defeat to brag about," he told the man, setting the bottle back down. "It sounds like Sand Creek all over again. Help me fix up some stew or something for these people, and I'll tell you what happened."

"You see trouble on the spring horizon?"

Lance slammed a sack of potatoes on the table. "Plenty. I'll have my job cut out for me as soon as warm weather hits. We'll probably have to have soldier protection. But if the damned soldiers and people in charge would show the Indian some fairness and talk with a straight tongue, we wouldn't have any of these problems."

One of the Indian women began wailing then, rocking the old woman in her arms. She was dead.

Lance watched them in silence, his hand going to the breast pocket where Cassandra's letter lay folded. Why did he suddenly want to talk to her? Why did he think she'd understand in spite of what she herself had been through as a captive of these people? She would understand because she'd want to understand—simply because Lance Raines loved them. He knew instinctively she would love anything that he loved, and suddenly that was important. It was odd how he thought of her at the strangest moments.

He shook the thought away and began preparing a stew, realizing that come spring he'd probably not be able to go to Abilene, nor would he go to Denver right away, something he'd planned to do first, to take care of a little matter called Jessica Françoise and get her out of his system. It was probably better he saw neither Jessica nor Cass.

"Finish this stew, will you?" he asked Beck. "I'm going to try to dig a grave for the old woman."

"But the ground is frozen."

"I'll use a pick or something. I'll find a way. I'll not leave her lying in the snow like an old log."

Beck took a potato from him. "If the men know I'm cooking like an old woman for a bunch of Indians, they'll lose their respect for me. This is ridiculous, Raines."

Lance laced his buffalo robe closer around his neck. "Yeah, well, if anybody gives you a hard time, you just remind them that these people will tell their friends in the north that we helped them. They'll remember. Indians repay a favor for a favor."

"And a death for a death?" Beck added.

Lance grinned a little. "That, too."

He pulled the collar around the back of his head and told One Cloud in Cheyenne tongue he would go to dig a grave for the old woman. One Cloud's eyes teared and he nodded.

"I would help you, my friend, but I am weak. I would be no good to you."

"I know. Don't worry about it. You just sit there and get warmed up." He looked at Beck. "Don't worry. Your scalp is safe. Besides, this breaks the monotany, doesn't it?"

Beck nodded his head. "That it does." He met Lance's eyes. "Say, Raines, one last thing about that Jessica Françoise thing. I probably said too much in front of those men, and I'll not talk to you about her again. But if you haven't already fallen under her spell, I'd advise you to stay away from her. She's up to something. I never did figure out what it was, and I decided to get out while the getting was good, before Françoise found out. He's a powerful man. Remember that."

Lance grinned. "I'll try. Besides, there's somebody else who's on my mind a lot, but she's just a kid. I think I'm better off staying away from both of them, and from the looks of things around here, I won't have any trouble doing that."

He left, thinking he should answer Cassandra's letter soon. He'd put Jessica out of his mind. Beck was right. The woman was dangerous territory, and mystery surrounded her promiscuity. Such women could only get a man in trouble. That was what Kate would tell him.

Chapter Ten

Cassandra headed home from school, carrying the little music box that had once been her mother's, a remnant from the burned-out wagon the Cheyenne had left after killing her family. It was May, 1869, and this had been the last day of school until the next fall. Everyone was to bring something and talk about something exciting that had happened to him or her. Cassandra's story was exciting, but not in the way that others were. Some told of their first horse, or a new baby in the household. Cassandra's story of Indian attack and capture, then her rescue, had them all enthralled, and some of the children cried, all but the three boys who had given her trouble all year and constantly made remarks about her captivity.

Most of the children had been kind and understanding, and now Cass had friends among many of them. But contrary to what Kate had told her, having new friends and the passing of time had not made her forget Rainmaker. If anything, she loved him more. He had written only twice, once in the winter, telling her about the poor, starving Cheyenne he had helped, and a letter she'd received just days ago. Both letters worried her, for there was much trouble with the Indians; and the saddest part was that he said he couldn't get to Abilene for a visit for a long time. The thought of not seeing him for weeks, perhaps even months, brought the ache to her chest again, and it seemed like every little thing made her cry. Now all she wanted to do was hurry home and put the music box away safely and write Lance Raines a new letter.

She walked alone toward the other end of town. The large herds and the cattlemen who accompanied them had not started coming in yet, for spring roundups were not finished. Between that and the fact that Kate had not been feeling well, Cassandra had assured the woman she could walk to and from school by herself, as long as the town was still relatively quiet. Until three weeks ago, Kate had walked to school with the girl, and had met her there afternoons to walk her back home, determined no harm would come to Cassandra. The woman didn't mind the walk, muttering that old women needed exercise to keep them going. But lately she seemed too tired for it; and that worried Cassandra, for it wasn't like Kate McGee to admit to being too tired for anything. She wasn't certain if she should tell Lance or not. Perhaps it would only worry him, but then again, perhaps it would make him come home sooner.

She hurried down the street, clutching the music box, heading straight home as she always did; but just as she passed a supply store, three boys ran out from an alley, making hooting noises like Indians on the warpath. They stood in her way, grinning, and Cassandra's heart froze. She hated these boys, the three who had teased her all year. They were older, big and overbearing, their minds and mouths always thinking and saying bad things. She glared at them with hate in her eyes, especially for the biggest one, Huey Brown, nearly six feet tall and not yet fifteen, a pimpled, ugly boy, with dark dirty hair and hands that were never clean.

"You boys get out of my way!" she scowled, turning to walk around them. But they only moved over, following her again when she moved in the other direction. The boys all laughed, and Cassandra's face reddened with rage. "Why don't you leave me alone?"

"Because we're curious, squaw girl. What's it like, being took by an Indian?" Huey sneered.

Cassandra blinked back tears, clinging to the music box. "You leave me alone, or you'll be sorry! I'll send Rainmaker after you!"

They all laughed, holding hands and dancing in a circle around her. "Rainmaker! Rainmaker!" they chanted. They laughed again. "Who is Rainmaker?" Huey goaded. "An Indian buck who lifted your dress to see a white girl's bottom?"

More tears came, and Cassandra ducked down to scoot under their arms to get away. Huey reached down and grabbed her dress and slips, flinging them over her head and exposing ruffled pantaloons. He planted a foot on her rear and pushed her into the mud.

"Hey, she does wear things under her dress!" he laughed. "I thought Indian squaws were naked under their clothes!"

"Stop it!" Cassandra screamed, on fire with rage and embarrassment. She struggled to get away, getting mud on her music box.

"Let her up!" a woman's voice demanded.

"Why?" Huey sneered defiantly. The other two boys, a slim blond, fifteen-year-old called Johnny Sorrell and a quieter but equally vicious sixteen-year-old called Richard Gobles, just laughed.

"Let her up, or I'll tell every one of your folks that you boys have been to see me!" the woman answered. "By God that ought to be cause for taking you to the woodshed and doubling your chores, you little sons-of-bitches! Now let her up or I'll be visiting your houses tonight and let your parents know what you've been up to!"

Cassandra turned her head to see Mattie Brewster standing there in a red checkered dress, her hands on her hips in a commanding stance, her painted face colored with anger.

"But we've never—"

167

"They'll believe it when I tell them!" Mattie interrupted.

Huey's foot left Cassandra's bottom, and she scrambled to her feet, shaking and crying, brushing mud from her dress.

"Bitch!" Huey sneered at Mattie.

"I'd rather be a whoring bitch than an ugly, pimple-faced, ignorant, clumsy fool like you!" she shot back. "Now you and your friends get out of here. And if you ever bother this girl again, I'll do what I said I'd do! Your folks wouldn't be too pleased!"

The three boys turned away and left in a huff, and in the next moment, Mattie's arm was around Cassandra's shoulders. "You okay, honey?"

Cassandra nodded and sniffed, brushing dirt from the music box. "I don't know what I'll do . . . if it's broke," she whimpered. "It was . . . my mother's."

Mattie took the box and brushed it off more, winding it and opening the lid. The music tinkled and she smiled. "There. See? It's all right. Come on. I'll walk you to Kate's place."

She helped brush off Cassandra, and the girl was glad the street had been quiet during the incident. Still, there had been a few people around. The fact that they did not help her only accented how lawless Abilene was. It seemed odd that the person who had helped her had been what the others would have called unChristian, yet no one else had come to her aid.

Cassandra smiled and closed the lid to the box. "Thank you."

Mattie patted her shoulder. "Any friend of Lance's is a friend of mine. Lance sure would have given those boys what for, wouldn't he? I'd love to see the looks on their faces if he'd come along."

Cassandra smiled more. "So would I." They started walking, and the girl wondered what people would think of her walking with a prostitute. Her feelings about Mattie Brewster were mixed, for she'd been determined to hate the woman. After all, this was Rainmaker's favorite painted lady, whom he slept with whenever he was in Abilene. Cassandra didn't like him being with any woman, even though she was not herself ready to be a woman for him. It hurt her heart to think of him being with others, yet frightened her to think of being his woman herself. And to think she could ever be his woman was probably futile.

She wiped at tears on her muddy face, and Mattie handed her a handkerchief that had been folded into the sash at the waist of her dress. "Here. Blow your nose and wipe off that face. I hope Kate isn't too upset when she sees you."

"So do I. She hasn't felt well lately."

"Oh? Does Lance know?"

"I'm going to write him a letter. But I hate to worry him. He's so busy with his scouting job, and there is a lot of trouble with Indians, he says."

Mattie nodded. "I've heard. I hope he'll be all right."

They stopped walking, and Cassandra faced the woman. "Why did you help me, Mattie?"

The woman smiled softly. "I told you. Any friend of Lance's is a friend of mine."

Cassandra could not control new tears from coming at the thought of him; for Huey Brown's words still stung her ears when he'd chanted Rainmaker's name, and she still shook from the humiliating experience. Mattie reached out and pulled her to herself, patting her back.

"Don't you listen to those ignorant farm boys," she told the girl. "What do they know? Some people believe what they want, no matter what. They don't understand what you've been through, and they take it for granted that just because you're a pretty little girl, some Indian man or men abused you. That's because they also don't understand about Indians. They just take things for granted."

"I hate them!" Cassandra wept, pulling away and wiping at her face again. "The Indians didn't do those bad things to me. Rainmaker came and took me away before they could."

Her body shook in another sob. "I wish Rainmaker would come home. He'd make everything all right."

Mattie smiled sadly. "That he would." She took the girl's arm and began walking her toward Kate's again. "Surely you do have friends among the other children, Cassandra. You're a sweet girl. And you have Kate. Things aren't all bad."

Cassandra blew her nose. "But all I want is Rainmaker. Kate said I would forget about him after a while and after I made new friends." She wiped at her eyes. "But I'll never forget him." She stopped and turned to Mattie again. "You know all about men and such things." She sniffed and swallowed to keep from crying more. "Could somebody like Rainmaker ever love somebody like me, Mattie? I know it sounds silly—" she sniffed in another sob "—but I love him. I know I do! I know it!"

Mattie sighed, looking her over and noticing that she'd grown a lot in the past year, taller, budding young breasts beginning to fill out her dresses. How could she speak for Lance, other than knowing he'd talked about the girl before leaving, mentioning she disturbed his thoughts.

"You shouldn't set your sites on a man like Lance," she told the girl gently. "Sure, I suppose he could love you some day. But considering your age and his, and the fact that you'll hardly ever see him, how can you expect anything to happen? Maybe you're just mixing grateful friendship up with love. I know how you must feel, him saving you like he did and all. But, honey, that isn't always love. And Lance, he's a roamer, with lots of women. You have to face reality, Cass. Hell, I expect in a way I love that green-eyed devil myself. But I can face the reality that he'd never love a woman like me, not the marrying kind of love, anyway. I can live with that. I have for a long time."

Cassandra turned away. "At least you get to sleep with him."

Mattie's eyebrows arched in surprise at the remark. "Well, as you can see, sleeping with him hasn't won his heart. I hope

170

you aren't thinking that will do it."

Cassandra shrugged. "I've wondered sometimes, if I saw him again, maybe if I told him he could sleep with me—"

"Don't talk foolish, child," Mattie interrupted. "If that man ever loves you, it will be because you *didn't* sleep with him. You have a lot to learn about men, Cass, and the best way to hold on to a man like that is to keep his respect. Besides, what do you know about sleeping with men? You don't even know what you're asking. Lance Raines is a lot of man. And I know he'd never touch a child like you. And besides that, he'd not be ready to do you right, and he'd just break your heart even worse. Don't be considering foolish things like that, Cass." Cassandra sniffed and wiped at her eyes and nose again. "Look, honey," Mattie continued, petting her hair. "You have a lot of growing up to do yet. Give yourself some time. Some day you'll be a woman, and you'll marry some nice man and have babies and all of it. Maybe that man will be Lance Raines. Maybe it will be somebody else. But let things happen naturally, child."

"It has to be him," the girl whimpered. "I don't want it to ever be anybody else. It will be Rainmaker. I know it will."

Mattie sighed. "If it makes you feel better to believe that for now, then believe it. I can't say you're wrong. But don't waste your growing-up years over that wild Indian."

Cassandra met the woman's eyes again. "Please don't steal him from me, Mattie. He might marry you some day."

The woman laughed through painted lips. "Not likely!" she chuckled. "We're just good friends, that's all. Fact is, I'd like to see him settle with some nice, sweet thing, except I'd not get to enjoy his company any more."

Cassandra looked at the ground. "How can you do that?" she asked. "How can you sleep with men like that, without loving them?" The question came before she thought, and there was a moment of silence. She looked at Mattie Brewster, whose eyes were watery. "I'm sorry, Mattie. I . . . I didn't mean it as an insult. I just wanted to know. I don't understand those things."

The woman smiled sadly. "It takes some living to understand," she answered. "Some day you'll understand better. But part of it is how we're brought up, Cass. My pa was selling me to men by the time I was ten years old, so it's all I ever knew. By the time I realized things weren't supposed to be that way and that I wanted to be respectable and married, I was too soiled to ever consider it. And a woman has to survive, so I survived doing what I already new best."

Cassandra looked away. "I'm sorry. I guess . . . I guess there are worse things even than your parents being killed."

"There are. At least yours were good to you while you had them. Cherish the memory, Cassandra, and you stay the sweet, innocent young lady that you are and let things happen the way they're supposed to happen."

Cassandra faced her then. "Thank you, Mattie. I . . . I always wanted to hate you, but I never could. I don't think Kate hates you, either. She just wants Rainmaker to settle down. She worries about him."

Mattie smiled. "We all do. Has he said when he'll be back for a visit?"

Cassandra sighed. "Not for a long time yet. I got a letter from him, a special one addressed just to me." Her face brightened. "Do you think that means anything?"

Mattie laughed lightly. "You never stop hoping, do you?"

Cassandra shook her head. "Never."

"What did it say?"

They began walking again.

"It wasn't very long, but he doesn't write long letters. He just said he was glad I was doing good in school, and he looked forward to seeing how I've changed. And he asked about Kate. He said the Indians are giving the railroad a lot of trouble. I think it's hard for him to do what he does, Mattie, because he cares about the Cheyenne. He lives in two worlds, and I feel sorry for him."

Mattie nodded. "That's always been a problem for him."

She stopped walking. "So, he said he looked forward to seeing how you've changed."

The woman chuckled and shook her head, and the stopped in front of Kate's house. Cassandra frowned. "Do you think that's good?"

Mattie looked her over. A beautiful, budding young woman and already a tempting sight for any red-blooded man. "Knowing Lance, it probably is. I'm sure he's curious to see what kind of woman you'll turn out to be."

Cassandra smiled, forgetting the incident with Huey Brown. It didn't matter. Nothing mattered! Mattie had given her a tiny bit of hope. "Do you think so, Mattie? Do you think he'll wait awhile and not marry somebody else?"

"Now, don't go getting all lathered up. Like I said, take things as they come, girl. And right now, I don't know of any particular woman that roamer is interested in. So maybe there's at least time for you to grow up a little."

The girl hugged her quickly, then ran up the steps. "Thank you, Mattie!" She darted inside, and Mattie shook her head, walking back into town, wondering what kind of woman she might have been if not for her father. How she envied young innocent girls like Cassandra Elliott. How lucky they were.

The surveyors worked diligently and quickly, constant fear of attack from the Cheyenne in their hearts. Just days before, Cheyenne warriors armed with rifles had attacked seven track repairmen in that very area. As the railroad men pumped their way madly by handcar back toward the Fossil Creek Station for safety, two of them were shot down and four more wounded. When they finally reached the station dugout, the Indians kept them trapped there while some of the warriors tore up newly laid track. During the night, an oncoming train hit the destroyed rails and overturned.

Now surveyors worked ahead of the destroyed rails, while crews were already repairing the track and a wrecking crew had righted the overturned engine. In the attack on the repairmen earlier, Lance Raines had ridden outside the attacking Indians and had risked his life trying to distract them. All knew that if not for Lance, more of their men would have lost their lives that day.

Lance rode the perimeter of the project. The surveyors felt safer with Lance watching the horizon for them; but all of them hoped the soldiers they had requested would arrive soon, for it seemed the Kansas-Pacific would not be completed until they had soldier protection. Still Lance realized these attacks were simply a last futile effort on the part of the Cheyenne. He could not forget the gaunt, sad faces of the northern Cheyenne the day they left in the bitter cold that past December, headed for home on pitiful ponies and with a meager supply of food and blankets. He wondered if all of them had made it safely, and he knew it was a sign of the beginning of the end. Washita might have boosted their anger and wish to fight, but he knew that in the long run it would break their spirit. Long Hair Custer had hunted and harassed the southern Cheyenne all winter, destroying and burning villages, taking prisoners, shooting horses, destroying food supplies.

It could not be long before the Cheyenne's only hope for survival would be to go to Camp Supply on the reservation set up for them and stay there to collect government rations. It was a sorry thing for them, a loss of pride and honor. He knew no Indian could live reservation life and be happy with it. Many would die of broken hearts and broken spirits. They would long for their true homeland, the great plains of Nebraska and Kansas and Colorado. But that land was being taken from them in the name of progress, by white men who had decided that the land rightfully belonged to them and that the Indians were the intruders. Indians were not even considered American citizens, and if it were not so sad and wrong, it would be almost humorous when considering the backward thoughts of lustful white men.

Land. Land and gold. They were a savage craze for the white man, just as savage as the Indian's desire to keep what was rightfully his own. Treaty after treaty had been broken and changed, as soon as the white man found some new wealth on Indian land. And so it would continue, until there was nothing left for the Indian but a tiny plot of land that was totally worthless. The buffalo would be gone. Freedom would be gone. And Lance's sad heart knew that that whole part of his life was gone. He could not go back to it, but neither could he blame the Indians for clinging to hope and continuing to fight back, even though it meant he had to fight them himself.

It was mid-June, and Lance was anxious to find some way to get to Abilene soon and see about Kate. He avoided thoughts of Cassandra, not allowing himself to admit he wanted to go home to see what she was like now. She was still too young for him to think such thoughts.

The surveyors, called "point men" by some, were spread out far apart now, some a half mile and even a mile apart. Lance urged Sotaju farther ahead of the last man, roaming the rolling hills and alert for a sign of Indians or soldiers. He saw neither at first. Then the horizon of a distant hill changed shape, as though tall grass was moving. He watched the change quietly for a moment, and his keen eyes and knowledge of Indians told him what it was.

He turned Sotaju. "Hopo! Hopo!" he commanded in the Cheyenne tongue, urging the animal to make haste. Man and horse rode hard, Sotaju's tail flying out behind him. Sod flew as Lance headed over a hill toward the closest surveyor, which happened to be Paul Thomas. He would just as soon leave the man to the Indians, for he still disliked him. But his job was to protect these men.

"Pick up your instruments!" he shouted. "Indians!"

He flew past Thomas, who stared at him wide-eyed and grabbed his equipment, quickly loading it into a wooden case and locking the case. He ran to his own mount, slinging the case over the saddle horn, and began to mount up. But the horse shied in response to Thomas's alarmed state, and Thomas was unable to get his foot in the stirrup.

"Hold still, you ass!" the man cursed at the horse, and the animal again shied sideways, whinnying and tossing its head. Thomas picked up a rock and threw it at the animal in anger, and the horse reared and ran off. "Come back here!" Thomas shouted.

Lance was himself already over the next hill, warning the next surveyor, who immediately mounted up, not even taking his instruments. He rode hard, but could not catch up with the sleek, muscled Appaloosa Lance rode. Lance went on to warn a third man, then circled around to check the first two.

The second man was coming over the rise and riding hard. "Get back to base and barricade yourselves in the boxcars!" Lance shouted. He knew without riding out to meet them that the oncoming Indians were out for blood and there was no use in trying to reason with them. He didn't care to ride right in their direction, for he could already hear their hoots and war cries; but he saw no sign of Thomas. It was then he spotted Thomas's horse, running toward him but riderless.

"What the hell!" he muttered. He urged Sotaju forward and over the rise to see Thomas running, flailing his arms, the Indians approaching behind him.

"Help! Somebody help me!" the man was shouting.

Lance scowled. It would serve the man right to let the warriors ride down on him and scalp him, and he hesitated for a moment, contemplating leaving the man behind. But he knew the sight of even a man like Thomas screaming for help would probably haunt his mind, and he realized then just how "civilized" he had become.

"Damn you, Kate McGee," he muttered. "Damn the white man inside of me." He rode down the hill toward Thomas.

He could see already the timing would be close. He well knew the speed of Cheyenne horses and the agility of their riders. But Sotaju was as fast as any Indian's pony, and Lance Raines had been taught how to ride by the very Cheyenne who were coming now. Sotaju's muscles rippled as Lance forced the animal into full gallop toward Thomas, who stood waiting and reaching for horse and rider. Lance came close and held out an arm, and Thomas grabbed it. Lance literally lifted the man with his arm onto the back of his horse, for Thomas had no skills in leaping onto a mount without stirrup or support.

Sotaju whirled, and they were off again, Lance leaning forward and urging the horse to run like the wind. Thomas hung on for dear life, sure a bullet or an arrow would pierce his back at any moment. Shots were being fired then, and the thunder of the Indians' horses was behind them. Lance prayed Sotaju could keep up the pace, for now he carried extra weight and was already tired. He could hear the animal's rhythmic, heavy breathing, knew the lather was building. He loved Sotaju and didn't want to run him to death. But neither could he stop now.

Minutes seemed like hours as they crested hill after hill, thundering down the other side again. Finally the end of the tracks were in sights, and farther down, the boxcars. Lance felt the brush of an arrow as it sang dangerously close past the side of his face. A gunshot ripped right through his saddlebag and Sotaju whinnied and faltered, then regained his pace.

The boxcars were close now, and Lance could see men shouting and waving them in.

"Hurry up! Hurry up!" Thomas was shouting. "They'll murder me! Scalp me!"

"Shut up!" Lance roared back at him. He thundered up to the boxcars and drew Sotaju to a quick halt, the animal's hooves digging into the earth. Thomas jumped down and climbed immediately into one of the boxcars, while Sotaju whinnied and pranced and tossed his head.

Lance dismounted, yanking his Winchester from its boot.

It was then he noticed blood on Sotaju's rump, but there was not time to check any further. The Indians, Cheyenne, were circling the boxcars now, yipping and yelping, firing at random. Lance ducked between two cars, hanging on to Sotaju's reins, sure one of the warriors would try to steal his grand horse.

He quickly tied the horse to a car hitch and began firing at the marauding Indians. Men inside the boxcar also fired, while one brave soul crouched beside a telegraph pole, sending a message with the telegraph box at the base of the pole back to Hays City. Lance guessed at least thirty warriors surrounded them, more than their match, for there were only twenty of their own men, many of them poor shots. But the Indians did not have the best rifles, nor did every brave carry one. And their arrows were useless against the boxcars. Lance saw one warrior ride hard toward the train cars with a flaming torch in his hand. He took aim and fired, knocking man and torch from the horse. It would be important now to watch for others who would try to do the same and burn the men out of the cars. He hoped the men inside had sense enough to use their ammunition carefully and not waste it, for if help did not come, the Indians could keep the men trapped in the cars for hours, even days if they chose to do so. The heat inside would be unbearable after a while, for this mid-June had turned hot and humid.

He couldn't be sure how long the siege continued before the warriors suddenly dropped away, disappearing over a western hill. There was a sudden silence, and after a few minutes men began exiting the boxcars.

Lance moved out from between the two cars where he'd taken shelter. Six Indians lay dead or wounded nearby. "Anybody hurt?" he called out.

"We're all fine," Thomas replied. Lance noticed he carried no gun, nor did the man offer a thank-you for the fact that Lance had saved his skin. He simply turned and began talking to some of the others. Lanced charged toward him, grabbing his shoulder and turning the man forcefully.

"Where's your gun, Thomas?" he growled.

Thomas sobered. "I . . . I can't shoot a gun."

Lance drew an arm back and landed a big fist into the smaller man's face, sending him sprawling onto his back with a split lip and blood spattering his nose and cheeks. Everyone stopped talking and stared at Lance, who walked to Thomas and jerked him up. "Thanks to your being a coward, and ignorant, I might have lost the best horse I've ever had!" he stormed. "You'd better hope my mount doesn't die after that hard ride I gave him saving your hide! And I don't remember hearing you say thanks, you scrawny bastard!"

He threw Thomas back down and turned to go to Sotaju.

"Raines!" Beck called out. Lance turned. "Will they be back?"

Lance nodded, his eyes cold. "They'll be back. I've got to see to my horse. Have some of your men see if any of those Indians are alive. We'll save them for the soldiers, if and when they come. And dress their wounds like you'd do for any man."

Some of them began checking bodies, while Lance went to Sotaju. The animal pranced and whinnied as Lance quickly removed all gear from him.

"I know you want a drink, boy, but I can't let you have one till you cool down. Water's no good for a lathered horse." He inspected the blood on the animal's rump, which appeared to be only a flesh wound. He poured water over it from his canteen, then retrieved a special salve and smeared it on the wound.

Yips and calls came again, and men took cover, dragging wounded Indians inside the boxcars. Again the Indians came over the rise and circled. This time two of them headed for the boxcars with flaming torches. Lance hit one, but the other managed to throw a torch on top of one of the cars.

Lance scrambled up a steel ladder to the top of the car and crawled to the torch, throwing it to the ground and pounding out flames with his hand, lying low to keep from being hit. It was then he heard the whistle of a train. It didn't seem that enough time had passed for help to come, but in such situations, two hours could go by quickly. The Indians headed for a string of railroad horses tied to a long rope nearby. One brave warrior hung over the side of his mount for protection and rode along the horses, deftly cutting the rawhide reins and loosening the mounts. He then whooped and yipped and urged the horses into motion, herding them away from the cars. The acrobatics he used to keep from being shot were almost entertaining, and familiar to Lance, for the Cheyenne were the best horsemen on the plains. Lance let him go, not having the heart to shoot the warrior's horse from under him. His Indian upbringing had instilled in him too deep a love for fine mounts, and the one the warrior road was fine indeed. Besides that, more Indians came to his assistance then, helping herd the horses over the hill as the train full of soldiers and volunteers from Hays City approached, but too late to save the horses.

Lance moved back to the ladder and climbed down, his hand red and blistering. He picked up his canteen and poured cool water over it as men exited boxcars to greet those who had come to help them. Lance stayed back, smearing some of the same salve he'd put on Sotaju on his burned hand, trying to ignore the pain. Men talked and joked and were already exaggerating about the fight. Several minutes later Jim Beck approached Lance, carrying an envelope in his hand. Lance was smearing more salve on his wound.

"What happened?" Beck asked.

"Had to put out a little fire on top of your boxcar," Lance replied.

Beck frowned. "I'm sorry. I didn't know. Any other wounds? You were out here the whole time."

"No other wounds."

"Well, I'm sorry about the horse, too, you having to ride him so hard. Do you think he'll be all right?"

Lance patted Sotaju's neck. "Hard to say yet. If he gets through the night, he'll probably be all right. But I don't dare ride him hard for a good long time now. I hope I don't have to run from any more Indians for a while."

"There are a couple of wounded ones in our boxcar if you want to talk to them before the soldiers here take them."

Lance nodded. "I'd like to find out if anything instigated this besides plain old hatred of the railroad."

Beck handed him the envelope. "One of the men from Hays City brought this along for you." Lance took the envelope. "It's from Denver," Beck added.

Their eyes met and Lance frowned, putting the envelope into a pocket. "I'll talk to the Cheyenne men first." He walked around to the open door of the boxcar, climbing inside and approaching the lesser wounded of the two warriors, a young man of perhaps only twenty, his arm bandaged but still bleeding. The young warrior looked at him darkly, until Lance knelt in front of him and spoke to him in Cheyenne. The young man answered angrily, waving his good arm, his eyes sparking, his teeth gritted. Lance said something more and the young man quieted and suddenly saddened. Lance gripped the young man's shoulder for a moment, then stood up, his own eyes sad.

"One of their most honored warriors, Dull Knife, and another, Curly Hair, were both shot down by guards while prisoners at Fort Hays a few weeks ago," Lance told Beck in a low but angry voice.

Beck shrugged. "Were they resisting?"

Lance's jaw flexed in anger. "Dull Knife was eighty years old! Curly Hair was fifty! Does that sound threatening to you — old, unarmed men inside a stockade?"

He turned and jumped down from the car. "Make sure those prisoners are treated with respect!" he shouted, walking away from the cars and the men. He didn't want to talk to any of them at the moment. How could they blame the Indians for their desperate attempts to keep the white men

181

out, when the coming of the white man meant total destruction of the Indian?

He breathed deeply for self-control, then took the envelope from his pocket, studying the address. He had no doubt it was from the Françoise residence. He opened the envelope carefully to avoid getting salve on it from his wounded hand, then removed and unfolded the letter.

"Mr. Raines,

"Request your presence forthwith. Have Beck hire a temporary scout to replace you. I will expect you in Denver at whatever speed your horse can bring you.
"Sincerely,
Claude Françoise."

He closed his eyes and sighed, stuffing the letter back into his pocket. He turned to look toward the east. Not far away was Abilene—Kate and Cass. Why was he so afraid to see Cass yet? He knew why. He was afraid he would like what he saw, afraid the same strange urges would still nudge him. But she was still a child. He looked for any excuse to avoid seeing her again, and in spite of being worried about Kate, Claude Françoise had given him that excuse. He would go to Denver first. Why Françoise wanted to see him so urgently, he couldn't imagine.

Chapter Eleven

Lance approached the massive brick Françoise residence, stopping at the gate just to look for a moment and wondering why he did not turn away. Maybe he should just forget the railroad and scouting and settle like Kate wanted him to do. But he still could not forget the vision of Cassandra reaching out to him. His Indian senses told him he must wait before choosing a woman, wait to see what the vision meant. Until Cassandra was older, he could not make any decision but to do what he did best, and he continued to chide himself for the fact that he still thought about the girl at all. He should have gone to see Kate before coming here and said to hell with Françoise. But seeing Kate meant seeing Cassandra, and he wondered what kind of fool he was to be shying away from a mere child. He'd had all kinds of women, and none of them had teased his thoughts the way Cassandra had over the past year, yet he had never touched her.

He urged Sotaju forward. The normally two-week trip had taken over three weeks. It was already July tenth. But he had refused to overwork Sotaju for any reason, even for the prominent Claude Françoise. The horse was more valuable to him than anything Françoise would have to say, and the animal was not yet ready to be ridden hard again.

He rode up to the front steps, dismounting and tying

Sotaju. He could not ignore the other reason he'd answered Françoise's request. He was still curious about Jessica Françoise. What were her motives for cheating on her husband? Simply to make him jealous? For some reason he didn't believe that. She had only to flirt or to have other men looking at her to make him jealous, and other men looked at her often. How could they not admire such beauty? She certainly didn't need to find a richer man. And surely Françoise provided her with everything her whims could ask. The man was himself handsome and mannered. What more could a woman want? He could only come to the conclusion that she was some kind of hopeless harlot at heart, and any healthy, red-blooded man would be a fool not to take advantage of her offers, except for the fact that she was married to Claude Françoise. The fact remained that he'd turned her down himself. Was he a fool? Or was he smart? There was something about her he didn't trust. But now it had been a long time since he'd been with a woman, and he wasn't so sure his natural urges would allow him to turn her away again if she offered herself as freely as she had the first time he'd met her. He remembered Jim Beck's words about staying away from her. Beck also didn't trust her motives, but neither man could come up with what those motives might be.

He climbed the steps, then banged the knocker. It was dusk, and the Rocky Mountains to the west were dark and shadowed, for the sun was setting behind them now. The same small woman in an apron answered the door, only this time she frowned for just a moment, then smiled.

"Weren't you here a few months ago, sir?"

Lance nodded. "Lance Raines. I'm here to see Mr. Françoise. He sent for me."

The woman smiled and stood aside. Lance entered the cool, hardwood-floored entrance, his eyes scanning the Oriental vases of plants that lined the walls. The maid left, and moments later Jessica Françoise glided into the hallway, her

184

eyes literally glittering with joy at the sight of him. He'd worn the bleached buckskins again, and she drew in her breath when their eyes met.

Lance was at once struck again with her beauty, and all logic left him. Neither said a word at first, as he remembered that morning he'd left Denver and this woman who had offered herself so willingly. Her eyes ran over him quietly now, drinking in the beautiful man that he was. The glorious white buckskins only made his tanned skin seem darker. He was lean and hard, beautifully etched lips set in a handsome face with high cheekbones, and lovely green eyes framed by dark lashes and nicely shaped eyebrows. Manliness filled the very air around him, and his eyes watched her carefully as she came closer, her own dark eyes literally glazed with desire and appreciation for the man she saw.

Her look now was not haughty or cleverly sure, but totally submissive and loving. He wondered if this was some new trick to break down his resistance, and reminded himself that Jim Beck agreed she was a witch in the way she could manipulate men. But at that moment he wouldn't mind being manipulated. He hadn't seen anything better than horses and railroad crews for months. She was like a breath of fresh air. And what better way to get his mind off little Cass? It was too bad she had to be married to Claude Françoise.

"Lance!" she finally said softly. "I didn't think I'd ever see you again."

He frowned and nodded. "Didn't your husband tell you he'd sent for me?"

Her eyebrows knitted in thought. "No. And Claude has left for Pueblo for a few days. When were you supposed to arrive?"

Their eyes held. Her husband was out of town. It was all said in a look, and his own manly urges began to awaken. "He probably expected me several days ago. But my horse

185

was wounded and ridden right into the ground in an Indian attack. I've been favoring him—took it easy all the way here."

Her eyes moved over him again, then she looked around to be sure no one was looking, before stepping closer and reaching up to touch his thick, dark hair with slender fingers, tracing down to where his hair curled fetchingly around his neck.

"Well, I'm afraid you've missed him. If you stay in Denver a few days, he'll be back, and you can find out what it was he wanted."

Her dark gaze captivated him, and he felt as though he were falling into a deep pit. "And what would a man like me do in a place like Denver for that long?"

She smiled softly. "We could think of something. I often entertain Claude's clients and workers, show them around Denver, have them for dinner. Surely you can stay. Come into the parlor and I'll give you a drink."

Before he could reply she turned and walked toward the parlor, her hips swaying beneath a summer yellow linen dress. He followed. It was easy to imagine how she "entertained" her husband's clients. His better sense told him to turn and walk right back out the door. But his manly needs would not let him. He entered the parlor, and she poured him a glass of whiskey.

She turned and handed him the drink, and he let his fingers linger on hers when he took it. She felt fire rush through her blood at his touch, and the way he looked at her with those searching green eyes unnerved her. She was usually the temptress, the one in control, but she could see that Lance Raines would use her just as readily as she intended to use him. He would not whine to her and beg her to leave her husband for him as others had done. Lance Raines was all man, his own man. He'd turned her down the last time he was in Denver. That was something unheard of, and it had frustrated her ever since. Now he was here again—and Claude was away.

"Where is your husband?" Lance was asking.

She blinked as though just recovering from a dream. "My husband? Oh! As I said, he's in Pueblo—more railroad business. They'll be starting soon on a railroad from Denver south, eventually into the mountains. I think it will be one of those narrow gauge things—you know, skinny tracks or something like that."

She turned to pour herself a drink.

"The rails are closer together," he informed her. "Such a train can carry just as much, but narrower tracks are more convenient when building through the mountains. The engines and cars are lighter weight, designed for steep grades."

She turned with a drink in her hand. "You railroad men. You love to talk about such things."

He took a swallow of whiskey. "Not me. I'm not even sure I want to stay with the railroad. That's why I was anxious to talk to your husband and see what he wanted. I'm not a railroad man—just a scout. And I don't know if I have a few days to wait. I should have gone home first to see some people who are more important to me. This will make me even later in getting there."

She sauntered closer. "And where is home? Who are the people?"

She had a musky, hungry smell about her, one that brought out all the animal side of him. In a way she was a lot like Mattie Brewster, yet strangely he had more respect for Mattie, even more feelings. At least Mattie truly cared about him, and she admitted what she was. She wasn't cheating on a husband. Jessica Françoise was the worst kind of woman, yet at the moment it mattered little to him. He'd been too long without one, and the only woman he really cared anything about was not even a woman yet and could not satisfy his present needs.

Their eyes held, saying other things while he spoke in

reply. "Home for the moment is Abilene, where the woman lives who has been a mother to me. Her name is Kate. She runs a boardinghouse there. The girl I rescued from the Cheyenne last year lives with her. She's a nice kid. I'd like to see how she's doing."

Her eyebrows arched. "Is she pretty?"

He grinned and slugged down the rest of his whiskey. "More than pretty. But she's also still a child. I'm just interested in her welfare. I risked a lot getting her away from the Cheyenne. That makes her special."

She sipped her drink and licked her lips seductively. "It must be nice to be thought of as special by someone like you."

He set down his glass. "I wouldn't know about that. And I guess I'd better leave."

"Please, not yet!" she said quickly, gliding to a love seat. She sat down, patting the spot beside her as an indication he should join her. "Tell me, how was life on the plains?"

"Hot. Miserable. Dangerous and boring," he replied. He came to sit beside her as she laughed at his reply.

"And did you fight savage Indians?"

He sobered slightly. "I did."

She sighed then. "I forgot. I'm not to joke about Indians. I'm sorry—truly."

He put a hand across the back of the love seat, and she felt weak. "It's all right. I don't expect people like you and your husband to understand. You have to know them, and people like you don't take the time to know them and you don't care."

Her eyebrows arched. "Don't tell me you're going to give me a long speech about Indians! I *am* one, you know."

He looked at her then and flashed an unnerving smile. "No. I just get a little irritated. I've heard some news about a couple of old Cheyenne warriors that upset me, that's all. And then there was that attack by Custer at Washita that killed old Black Kettle."

188

"Yes. That was even in the Denver papers. Of course they dressed it up as a glorious soldier victory, as they always do."

Lance sighed and leaned forward, resting his elbows on his knees. "I know how they do. The soldiers shoot down and cut up women and children, after attacking a village by surprise in the middle of winter, then call it a victory." He turned his head to look at her again. "Let's talk about why I'm here. How long will I have to wait?"

"Five days, perhaps, maybe six. Surely you can afford that much. I'd make sure you weren't bored."

She reached out then, touching the handsome face.

"Please do wait," she said softly. "Don't run away again."

For several seconds he just studied her. "You have a husband."

Her hand moved down to rub over his chest. "And I have my reasons for what I do. What do you care? You're a single man. . . ." She breathed deeply then. "And all man. You have nothing to worry about. All you have to do is give me your room number and hotel, and I'll come in the back way—tonight yet, if you wish. I have all kinds of excuses for going out. No one ever questions. And with Claude gone, who cares?"

He grabbed her hand, pushing it away. "What's your angle, Jessica? What are you after?"

Her eyes actually teared, and he wondered if it was real or just an act. He could not forget Jim Beck's words about her seductive ways. "What does it matter to you? Why do you ask so many questions, Lance Raines?" She took his hand and pressed it against her breast. "Give it up, Lance. So you have five or six days with the wife of Claude Françoise. So what? Surely you need a woman, after all those lonely months on the plains."

He was not going to be a fool twice and turn down what this woman had to offer, no strings attached. Besides, maybe he could get a lot out of his system before going back and seeing Cass again. He leaned down to meet her lips.

Jessica wondered if there truly had been an explosion nearby, for she thought she heard one the moment his sweet, beautiful lips touched her own. She'd had many men, but this one would top them all, she was certain. Hot passion ripped through her bones and blood, and she returned the kiss wildly, encircling her arms about his neck. She used her own lips and tongue to break down his untrusting resistance, until she felt him falling, falling into her spell just as she fell into his. It was purely animal instinct and purely pleasure, and the kiss lingered hungrily, their breathing heavy and warm, until he gently pulled away. Both of them shivered with the excitement of it.

"I must be a fool," he uttered in a husky voice. He rose and walked to the doors, then turned. "I'm at the Denver Inn, room twelve."

He turned and left, and she looked around the parlor, studying its expensive decorations. She put a hand to her stomach. "Maybe this time," she said quietly. She hurried to a window to watch Lance Raines ride away. Yes. She would go to him tonight. This time it wasn't just her scheme that mattered, but the man. She'd never met one like Lance Raines, never wanted one with such passion. She'd not wait another moment to glory in lying beneath such a perfect man, giving him pleasure and taking her own. She had never wanted a man physically like she wanted Lance Raines, wanted him the first moment she'd ever set eyes on him. He moved with an animal grace, and his power and sureness brought alive every womanly instinct she possessed. She hurried out and upstairs to her room. She must get ready. She must go to him. This time he would not turn her away.

Kate folded the letter and looked at a hopeful Cassandra.

"He's not coming yet, honey," she told the girl. "He got called back to Denver first."

The girl's face fell. "Denver? But . . . but he'd come here first, wouldn't he? To see you?"

Kate sighed, her own disappointment showing. She never expected to see much of Lance anymore. But this time she'd had her hopes up, for she knew inwardly she wasn't well, and she wanted to see him again. But she could bear her own disappointments. It was Cass she cared about now. The girl looked ready to cry.

"I'm sure he'll come here before he goes back to whatever he'll be doing next, child. Don't you fret. He'll be here within a month. I know my Lance. He's careless and sometimes not timely. But he'll come. He's got a big heart."

Cassandra nodded, saying nothing. She rose and walked out of the kitchen. It wasn't so bad that she'd have to wait a little longer, but he'd written Kate to tell them, instead of writing to her. She'd expected one more letter, a sign that he still thought about her. But then why should he? Maybe he had a lady in Denver. Yes. That was probably it. He had a lady in Denver and maybe he'd even come home married.

She blinked back tears, walking out onto the porch. It was a warm, sunny day, and suddenly the house seemed too confining. Being outside and looking at the big sky and the endless horizons of Kansas made her think of Rainmaker, for he was like the land, big and wild and uncatchable as the wind. She looked to the west, toward where the city called Denver lay. She suddenly wondered if she would spend the rest of her life waiting like this, hoping to see a man on a spotted horse come riding out of the horizon. Why did she think he would ever come riding back from his exciting life to be with a child?

Maybe Kate and Mattie were right. Maybe she was wasting her time. She descended the steps and began walking, with no place in particular in mind to go. It was either

191

walk, or lie in her room and weep. Rainmaker. How she loved the name. How she loved the thought of him. How she worshipped the brave, handsome, skilled man who had rescued her. He was more than a man to her. He was a god. The life she'd once known in Illinois, a life of parents and family, was gone. All her hopes and dreams and love had been channeled into one man, her first friend after her abduction, that kind, understanding, beautiful man called Rainmaker. She knew she loved him. She could not envision the sexual part of that kind of relationship, and the thought was both exciting and frightening, for he knew everything and she knew nothing. But she could envision at least the feel of his arms around her. She could imagine telling him she loved him, for she'd already told him once, and she was glad. Would he always remember her words? Would he really wait, like Mattie said he might?

She walked toward town, paying no attention to her surroundings, or to the new herd of cattle being herded her way by whooping, yipping cowboys ready for a wild night on the town. People moved out of the way, but Cassandra ambled absentmindedly, her thoughts totally absorbed with Lance Raines and her love for him. Her heart was heavy, her mind far away. By the time she realized cattle were thundering up behind her, it was too late to get out of the way.

She turned and screamed as a snorting longhorn rammed into her, knocking her over. After that, all was pain and blackness as hooves battered into her, tossing her around and stamping her into the muddy street. By the time the last cow thundered past, Cassandra Elliott lay still and unconscious, and seemingly lifeless.

Lance stretched, then turned and pulled Jessica close, her back to him. He wasn't sure how many times he'd been with her over the past five days, but each encounter had been an experience even for a man of many women like himself. He pressed a hand against her belly and nuzzled her neck.

"Good morning," he whispered.

She moaned and turned to him, and he moved a leg over her, pulling her close and kissing her throat. "How do you get away with this?" he asked, running a hand over her bare hips. "You've been gone all night."

She smiled. "I have a lot of prominent friends. I simply tell the help I'm staying at 'so-and-so's' house because I'm lonely for Claude."

He moved down to taste the full breasts he'd tasted often of late. "This is probably our last day. You'd better go home and stay there after this morning. Your husband will be showing up."

She sighed, running a hand through his thick hair. "God, I'll miss you, Lance. I didn't want any feelings to be involved. But you're such a beautiful man. I've never been with anybody like you."

He moved back up, grasping her hair and kissing her cheek and ear. "It's been good, Jess. Maybe when I come back next year . . ."

"Maybe. I'll think about you a lot."

He kissed her hair, her forehead, moving on top of her. "Tell me more about yourself, Jess. And why you're really here in my bed."

She kissed his chest. "Make love to me again first."

She opened slender legs invitingly and he gladly obliged. She'd said nothing about her own past or what her reasons might be for being with him. All they had done was meet and make love. It was understood that it was natural. It must happen. It could not be stopped. There were no ties other than animal attraction. Lance Raines had never been serious about a woman before, and he doubted Jessica Françoise had ever been serious about a man. Each was experienced at pleasing the other, and the end result was a sharing of bodies that took each of them to heights of glorious sexual pleasure.

He moved rhythmically, wanting to devour her, wanting to please her as no other man had done. She gloried in his bronze body, the hard muscle of it, the gentleness of his touch, the size of him that made her cry out with intense pleasure. Yes, she would miss this man of men. He was sweet and beautiful, and above all, he was the perfect mate to give her a healthy child. Surely after sleeping with him so many times she would get pregnant, for he was so much man. Surely his life was good. And he had planted it deep. She had taken it with much relish, hoping, hoping each time that this man's virility would plant a seed in her that would take good hold. It must! She must give Claude Françoise a child! All she had to do now was sleep often with Claude as soon as he got home. Then if she was pregnant, the timing would make sense. It would all work out beautifully — if only.

Lance grasped her hips and thrust deep, just as she felt the shuddering explosion of pleasure he always brought her. He groaned with the pleasure of her sweet moistness and her own rhythmic arching to greet him. Moments later his life spilled into her again, life she'd already assured him would come to nothing, for she'd told him she was barren. It made the whole affair even easier. It mattered little to him that such a loose woman was married. If a woman wanted to sell herself for a smile, he was willing. He had no ties, and he had a healthy appetite for women.

Still, to his irritation, little Cassandra had often flashed into his mind over these past days, sad, blue eyes begging him to come home. Cass. She was the kind he'd settle with if ever he settled. It wouldn't be a woman like Mattie or Jessica. It would be someone innocent, someone who would belong only to Lance Raines. At twenty-seven, he thought about it more lately, about settling. But he couldn't do to Cassandra Elliott what he was doing now to Jessica Françoise. He would wait.

He rolled off the woman, lying limp and exhausted as she got up to wash. Jessica pulled on a robe and poured some water from a pitcher into a bowl.

"So tell me," Lance spoke up, pulling himself up better onto the pillow and reaching for a pre-rolled cigarette. "Why are you doing this? How did Claude Françoise get so rich, and how did you end up with him?" He lit the cigarette and looked away as she quickly washed.

She waited a moment. She was not about to tell him Françoise married her because she looked like healthy material for having babies. "I told you I'm part Indian," she answered, powdering herself and tying her robe. She turned, running her fingers through tangled hair. "For a good many years I was a prostitute, a common way for a half-breed girl to make her living. That probably doesn't surprise you."

He met her eyes. "It doesn't. I suspected."

She smiled a crooked smile. "Claude was one of my customers. That was in New Orleans. He was already wealthy — made his money in slave trading."

Lance frowned in disapproval. "He ran a slave ship from Africa?"

"That and other things. He got very rich, until the war ended slavery. By then he was quite wealthy anyway — grubstaked some gold mines that paid off very well — invested in the railroad because he sees a great future for it. He's a smart man. I don't know much about his early life myself, and I never asked. I really don't care. He liked me. I was his favorite, and before long he became my exclusive customer. He didn't want other men touching me. His possessiveness turned to love, I guess. He asked me to stop what I was doing, to marry him and come west with him — said I looked strong and hardy enough to live out here in this desolation." She sat down on the bed, leaning back on the pillow beside him. "Of course I agreed. Why not give it a try? I'd be rich." She looked at him then with eyes suddenly cold. "And I intend to stay rich and remain Claude Françoise's wife forever. I'll never give up this life."

He watched her carefully. It was as though she was trying to warn him about something.

"Why should I care?"

She shrugged. "I don't know. I just make sure my men don't get any ideas of something permanent."

He took a drag on his cigarette. "It was the last thing on my mind. But how in hell do you intend to stay Mrs. Claude Françoise forever if you keep seeing other men? And why risk it in the first place, if your new life is so important to you?"

She refused to meet his eyes. It irritated her that he was prying. None of the others had cared. She felt an odd premonition that she might have made a mistake picking a man like Lance Raines. He was afraid of no one, nor of power and money. What if she did get pregnant? And what if he found out? Would he make trouble?

"Let's just say I never got over my lust for men," she replied. "I like men. It's just the way I am. I think Claude suspects sometimes, but he doesn't say anything. He wants me to be happy."

Lance frowned. None of it made sense. No man would put up with such a thing. But then there were all kinds of people in the world.

"Well, if he made you quit the business, he sure wouldn't like the idea of you seeing men after he married you. It doesn't make sense, Jess. What are you leaving out?"

"Nothing!" she snapped. "Why should you care anyway? After today—" Her eyes softened. "After today . . . it won't matter. You'll be gone."

Their eyes held and he leaned over and kissed her. He didn't care now that she was Françoise's wife. He had no use for a man who dealt in slavery. The Françoises were an odd couple indeed, and the sooner he was away, the better.

Jim Beck was right. There was a lingering mystery about Jessica Françoise, and he already knew it would bother him.

"You'd better get dressed," he told her. "I left a message at the stage station that when Claude arrived he should be told I'm in town and get word to me so I can see him right away. I want to get back to Abilene."

She smiled then. "No rush. Claude didn't send that letter. I did. Claude is really in San Francisco."

His eyes changed from gentle to angry. "What?"

"I sent the letter." She sighed and patted his cheek. "Oh, Lance, don't be angry. I just couldn't bear going any longer without seeing you, being with you. You drove me crazy, the way you left here last time."

He turned and got out of the bed, tying a loincloth around himself. "Get the hell out of here!" he ordered.

She frowned, getting off the bed. "Lance, so what?"

"I was needed out there! Besides that, Kate hasn't been well, and she's been waiting for me to come and see her. The message from Françoise sounded urgent, so I came here first; and on top of that I made my lame horse travel a lot of extra miles—all because of your lie—all because you wanted to go to bed with me? What the hell kind of a woman are you, anyway?"

"Well, I just thought—"

"You don't think at all! I don't like games like that, Jess! I'll sleep with you if it pleases you, and get my own pleasure in return, but I'll not be lied to and tricked! I don't like it! I came in reply to an urgent message just to find out I've been bedding you while Kate might need me." He pulled on his buckskin pants. "I ought to hit you!"

Someone tapped on the door, and they looked at each other. Lance motioned for her to get away from where she could be seen through the door, then went to the door and opened it a crack. "Yes?"

"I have a telegraph message for you, sir. It's from Abilene" came a man's voice.

"Thanks." Lance took an envelope and closed the door. He ripped open the envelope, his face visibly paling as he read. "My God!" he whispered.

"What is it?" Jessica asked.

He met her eyes. "Little Cass. She was trampled under cattle. They don't think she'll live." His eyes widened then, and the color came back into his face as his anger grew. "It happened just a few days ago. I'd have been there if I hadn't come here first! Maybe it wouldn't have happened at all if I'd been in Abilene!"

Jessica swallowed, afraid of the look on his face. "Does she . . . mean that much to you?"

He wadded the message and threw it on the floor. "If not for your damned lying letter, I'd have been there!" he growled. "Or at least working on the KP and close enough to get there quickly! She could die before I ever get there now!" He walked up to her and she backed away, but he reached out and grasped her hair. "Damn you!" He threw her on the bed. "Jim Beck was right! You're a witch!"

He turned away and quickly finished dressing. He began throwing personal items into saddlebags, practically ransacking the room to be sure he had everything. Then he headed for the door.

"Lance, will I see you again?"

"Not if I can help it! Thanks for the good time, Mrs. Françoise!"

"Lance, I'm sorry! Truly I am! How could I have known? And what good will it do for you to be there, anyway? She's just a little girl you rescued once. You hardly know her."

A pain pierced his heart. Kate's message had said to please come quickly, for Cassandra cried for him in her pain. He suddenly realized how special she'd become to him. What if he didn't get there in time?

"She isn't just a little girl. She's sweet and afraid and has nobody but Kate and me. And you'd better hope she doesn't die, or I just might come back here and kill you with my bare hands!"

He turned and left, and she put a hand to her chest to quell an urgent pounding of her heart. She'd gone and picked a man who cared about things most people didn't care about—a stupid little girl, Indians. That could only mean one thing. Surely he'd care about his own child. If he'd made her pregnant and ever found out . . .

She shivered.

Chapter Twelve

Lance had no choice now but to ride Sotaju hard and hope the animal was ready for it. He'd had a good rest, but Lance still could not run the Appaloosa stallion full out. He kept a fast, steady pace for several minutes, then slowed to a trot, then a walk, then back to a gentle run again. For the first time he agreed that trains would be welcome in this land. In emergencies like this, it would be wonderful just to board a train and get to Cassandra in a couple of days.

Poor Cass. What a terrible way to die. He wouldn't let her die. If he could get there in time he'd make her live. He felt crazy with anxiety. He slept restlessly at night, staring at the stars and praying to *Maheo* to let Cassandra Elliott live and not be crippled. He could not forget his vision. Did it mean she was reaching out to him in death? But in the vision she was a woman, not a child. That gave him hope that she would not die. But visions could mean a lot of things. The worst part was that if he hadn't gone to Denver he'd have been in Abilene, or close enough to get there quickly. In all his life he'd not done such a stupid thing, and he wondered if the spirits were angry with him. Jessica was most definitely a witch, and he'd fallen into her trap. He wanted nothing more to do with her, if possible. If Cass died before he got there, he'd never forgive himself. He vowed he'd make a blood sacrifice for her in the Cheyenne way, and somehow he would make Jessica suffer for tricking him away from Abilene.

Day and night he envisioned the wide, blue eyes, remembering how she looked at him that first time he entered Crooked Neck's tipi to take her away. He could feel her shaking with fear when he touched her, could feel the soft brush of her long blond hair as it blew in the wind when she rode in front of him on Sotaju. He didn't care any more that he thought of her fondly. He knew in good conscience he'd never touch her wrongly, that he would wait to see the kind of woman she became. After all, grown Indian men often waited for mere babies to come of age for marriage. Surely he could wait two or three years.

He halted Sotaju for a rest and realized he'd used the word "marriage" in his thoughts. He had never considered it before. Why did thinking about Cass make him think about marriage and settling? It was as though his entire future was mapped out for him by fate. But he couldn't worry about that now. He would take a day at a time. For now he had to get to Cass. Maybe she'd feel better if she saw him. Maybe his presence would help make her want to live. She still depended on him, still looked to him as a friend. Somehow his rescue of her had made her look to him for help in every other way. He was her only security. The poor girl had suffered so much in the last year; she didn't deserve this new catastrophe. And it must be hard on Kate.

Suddenly his responsibilities had come full around to stand boldy before him. Somehow Cass made them more vivid to him. He had raided and killed with Indians, and had wandered at trapping and scouting since his return to the white world, with no real purpose to his life. He guessed Kate was right. A man had to settle sometime. And he'd thought often about what it would be like to have children, especially a son. Sons were cherished treasures to the Cheyenne. He'd never thought seriously about any of those things until finding Cassandra Elliott. Perhaps it was the fact that he'd already declared to the Cheyenne that she belonged to him that he'd actually started feeling that way. He didn't really want her yet himself, not as a woman, but neither did he care for the thought of her belonging to anyone else.

But it was possible none of his thoughts would matter. She might be dead or crippled, and he felt it was partly his fault for not acting on his first instinct to go home before going to Denver. He wasn't sure now what he would do about his job. He'd stop and report to Jim Beck on the way and tell him it was impossible to say when he'd be back on the job. He would not go back until he knew Cass was all right. And he'd have to explain to Jim about the note. Jim would understand, for he understood Jessica Françoise's witchcraft and tricks. Beck would have to report to Françoise that Lance had gone home because of an emergency, and that he'd report back to work as soon as he could. Françoise didn't need to know any more than that. He didn't even need to know Lance had been to Denver. Lance would decide later if he wanted to continue working for the railroad, and if Françoise didn't want him any more, that was fine, too. Nothing mattered now. Nothing but Cass. Every time he thought of it, a pain shot through his chest. His fear of not getting to her in time was overwhelming. He pushed Sotaju harder and prayed for the best. Getting to Denver had not been worth losing his treasured steed over. But getting to Cassandra was.

"Hang on, boy," he told the horse. "You'll get a good long rest in Abilene."

Lance approached the house slowly, fear building over what he might find. More than two weeks was a long time after the kind of accident Cassandra had suffered. He tied Sotaju at the back door and dismounted. He would unload the animal later, much as he needed it right away. But first things first. He strode to the back steps and went inside to find the kitchen empty. The house was quiet. It was mid-afternoon. Was Cass dead and Kate at her funeral? Then he heard a creak on the back stairway.

"Kate?"

Someone descended the rest of the stairs rapidly, and in the next moment Kate came around the corner, looking haggard and even thinner, her eyes red and tired. She put a hand to her face. "Lance! Thank God, you came!"

She looked as though she might pass out, and he rushed to her side, grabbing her into his arms as she broke into tears.

"My God, Kate. Please don't tell me she's dead."

He squeezed her tightly as she regained her composure. "No," she managed to mutter. "But it was . . . so terrible."

"Come on and sit down," he told her gently, leading her to a chair.

"I haven't been . . . taking any boarders," she sniffed as he helped her into a chair. "I just couldn't keep up . . . taking care of poor little Cass all the time like I've had to do. I've prayed and prayed for you to get here. I was so afraid . . . you never even got my message."

He rubbed her shoulders gently. "Well, I'm here now. Tell me all of it, Kate. And then you get yourself to bed. You look terrible, and I know you haven't been well yourself. We'll talk about that later. You tell me about Cass first, and I'll tend to her myself the rest of the night."

"Oh, she'll be so happy to see you, Lance. She cried for you . . . so often. I really think the only reason . . . she kept hanging on . . . was to see you again. I told her . . . I'd send for you, and she said she'd not close her eyes in death . . . till she saw your face again. And she said if she could just see you again . . . she knew she'd not die at all."

He rubbed her neck. "You want some tea or something?"

"Oh, I'd like that." She reached up and patted his hand. "Thank you, Lance. I feel better already having you here."

He left her to put a pot of water on the stove. "Well, I'm here to stay until Cass is out of danger. You'll not bear this burden alone. I've shunned responsibility too long now. Once this is settled, I'll probably go back to work for the railroad, Kate, but just long enough to get a good nest egg built up so I can settle." He sat down across the table from her to wait for the water to heat. "I've thought more on all those things lately, Kate, and you're right. And when I get settled, you're going to live with me and quit this boardinghouse business. You'll never work again, not like you do now."

She wiped at her eyes and looked at him closely. "What brought all this on?"

He shrugged. "A lot of things—things that happened out there on the plains—the things that are happening to the Cheyenne—something that happened in Denver. I'll tell you about it later. How about Cass? Should I go up right now?"

The woman sighed. "I just got her to sleep. You can wait awhile." She shook her head. "It was so terrible, Lance. The men herding the cattle felt real bad about it. They said they shouted to her, but I think—" she sighed again, watching him with sad eyes—"I think she was thinking about you, Lance. I had just read her that letter saying you were going to Denver instead of coming home first. I'd had it for a couple of weeks, putting off telling her. But when you still didn't show up, I thought I should tell her. I expect you were in Denver by then. She'd been waiting—asking about you. When I told her you'd gone to Denver, she was real sad. She just left the house. I didn't even know she'd gone into town. The next thing I knew, a bunch of men were carrying her to the house. Somebody told them where she lived. They said a herd of their cattle ran her down in the street."

Her voice choked, and she blew her nose on a handkerchief from her apron pocket. Lance gritted his teeth, rising then and turning away from her. "Damn!" he hissed. "I knew it! I knew I should have come here first! My God, Kate, this is all my fault."

"No, it isn't, honey," the woman answered. "I didn't tell you that to make you feel bad. How could you know? I only told you so you'd understand what that little girl thinks of you. After all this time, you're all she talks about. She worships the air you breathe, Lance. I don't know what to tell you to do about it. I just think you should know so you're prepared."

He sighed deeply as the water started to steam, then took a cup from the cupboard, filling a small tea strainer with tea leaves from the bin where Kate kept them, thinking how organized good old Kate was. Everything was where he always remembered it to be. He poured water over the leaves and let the strainer rest in the cup as he carried it over to the woman, sitting down again himself.

"I'm damned sorry, Kate. I don't know what else to say. And I don't know what to do about Cass, either. Sometimes I think about her all grown up, but at fourteen, what the hell can I tell her? I can't even tell her to wait for me. Who says I'll love her just because she's sixteen or seventeen, or that she'll even feel the same about me? I can't talk about love or even think it at this age, and she's too young to know what she really feels."

"I know all that. But for now, just go and be with her. That's all she needs — just your friendship — to know you care about her." She sipped at the tea. "Besides, you do care about her, more than you let on. I know you, Lance Raines. Right now you're just doing what's proper, and that's as it should be. You're right to do that. To make promises to a child like that, or to take advantage of her, would only hurt her more, and she's been hurt enough. Lord knows you're man enough to understand all that. I don't need to tell you those things."

He rubbed at his eyes. "How bad are her injuries?"

The woman shook her head. "She was so broken up inside it was hard for the doctor to even tell, Lance. She was in awful pain. And of course the doctor in this town isn't any expert. There wasn't a lot he could do besides set a broken leg and two broken arms the best he could. She had some broken ribs, too, and her body was just covered with awful bruises, from head to toe — still is. Every movement, every breath brings her pain."

He rose again, feeling restless and angry. "Is she in any

more danger of dying?"

Kate put her head in her hands. "Hard to say. At first we were sure she'd die. She even stopped breathing a couple of times. The doctor said it was probably a collapsed lung. Once we got her to breathing right, the rest was a matter of waiting to see. God only knows what was injured on her insides. Her bladder and bowels seem to be working now, but at first there was blood. I suppose she's out of the worst danger; but just today she got a bad fever, and there's a funny bump on her left side. The doctor says it's just a rib that didn't heal right, but I don't think he knows everything. Sometimes I wonder out here if some of the doctors that hit these towns are really doctors at all."

He ran a hand through his hair as he paced, then he removed his weapons belt. "I'm going up there to check her over myself. When you live with Indians, you learn a lot about treating your own injuries. I don't like the sound of her being fevered. She's probably got some kind of infection inside."

"That's the way I figured. But I don't know what to do, Lance."

He headed for the stairs. "I'm going up, asleep or not. And I want you to sit there and finish that tea. Then take a hot bath or something and get some sleep. If you want a bath, let me carry up the hot water."

She looked at him with weary eyes. "I'm so glad you're here, Lance."

Their eyes held. "So am I. I just wish the circumstances were different. I'm damned sorry, Kate. I placed a great burden on you."

"It wasn't any burden. She's a sweet girl, a good helper and wonderful company. I've grown to love her. She's not been any burden at all."

He turned and went on up the stairs, entering Cassandra's room quietly on moccasined feet. The room was warm, and a gentle breeze coming through the windows did little to cool it. He walked quietly to the end of the bed, standing and studying her for a moment, struck by how she had changed. Her hair seemed a little wavier, and a prettier gold than he had remembered. Her freckles were gone, as well as some of the babylike roundness to her face. The blankets were turned down to her waist, and he could tell that beneath the cotton gown she wore, young breasts were blooming into womanhood. The gown's material was thin because of the hot room, and he could just barely make out the small pink nipples as her chest moved up and down slowly in labored breathing. There was a raspiness to her breathing that worried him, and his heart ached at the sight of her; for her face still had purple bruises on it, as well as her neck. Both her arms lay at her sides, wrapped tightly into splints, and one hand looked swollen.

He quietly went around the side of the bed and pulled back the blankets to see a splinted right leg. Her gown was crumpled to mid-thigh, and he could not help but take note of the slender beauty of her legs in spite of her condition. The left leg was badly bruised and scraped.

Still, none of the obvious injuries were enough to kill her. It was the possible internal injuries or infection that worried him, for her face and hair were wet with perspiration. He lightly touched a hand, which was burning up, a sure sign that the perspiration was not just from the heat of the room. He wanted to examine her more closely, but he didn't want to startle her. He leaned over her, bracing himself with one hand on the bed rail over her head and gently stroking her forehead with his other hand.

"Cass?"

She stirred slightly, groaning when she did so. He stroked some hair back from her face.

"Cass? It's me—Rainmaker. Will you wake up for me so I can take a look at you?"

She stirred again, blinking open the lovely blue eyes he remembered so well. There was a different look to them now, the small spark of a woman behind them. She looked up at him with an almost blank expression at first, then the eyes teared.

"Rainmaker!" she whispered. "You came!"

"Sure I came. Did you think I wouldn't? I was all the way to Denver—"

She burst into sobbing and groaning at the same time. "I was so scared . . . you wouldn't come," she choked out, followed by a groan. "It hurts . . . to cry . . . but I can't stop."

He sat down carefully on the edge of the bed, placing both big hands on either side of her face and gently wiping at her tears with his thumbs. "Calm down, Cass. Please. Everything will be all right now, and you shouldn't cry. You'll just make everything hurt more."

"Don't go away! Don't go away!" she whimpered.

"I'm not going anywhere till I know you're going to be well." He reached over and took a handkerchief from a dressing table beside the bed. He gently wiped tears from her eyes and wiped her nose for her. "You've got to stop crying, *Kseé.*"

Her body jerked in another sob. "What's . . . that mean?"

"It means 'young girl' in Cheyenne." He leaned down and kissed her forehead, and in spite of her injuries her joy knew no bounds. Rainmaker had come! He was sitting right here beside her, his big, gentle hands had touched her face; he'd kissed her! And how beautiful he was! More beautiful than she remembered.

"Will you stay a long time? And teach me more Cheyenne words?" she sniffled.

He smiled the brilliant smile that made her sick with love for him. "Sure I will. But right now the important thing is your injuries. I want to look them over myself, if you'll let me. I don't trust that doctor."

Another sob made her shudder. "I don't like him much, Rainmaker. I don't like how he looks at me. Kate says she's not sure he's a real doctor at all." She sniffed and swallowed. "But I trust you. You can . . . fix anything. I don't care if you look at me . . . but everything hurts so bad . . . and I'm so hot."

"I know." He stood up. "That's why I want to see that lump at your side Kate said you had. She said the doctor said it was just a rib that didn't heal right, but I don't like the sound of it."

He pulled the blankets past her small feet, studying the splinted and bandaged right leg. "The sad part is if he didn't set your bones right there's nothing much I can do about it now. I just hope they heal right. Now you lie real still." He unbuttoned her gown and ran his hands gently over her collarbone. "You tell me what hurts. How do you feel? Can you eat?"

She closed her eyes in a mixture of ecstasy and embarrassment as he moved his hands down over her breasts and ribs. She didn't care. This was Rainmaker, not that ugly doctor. Rainmaker wouldn't look at her bad or touch her wrong or hurt her any more than he had to.

"I eat a little, mostly soup," she answered.

"Does it hurt to breathe?"

"Not as bad as it did."

He frowned, taking his hands from inside her gown and running them outside of it down her ribs. "It feels to me like your ribs are in place."

She suddenly cried out when he moved a hand farther down her left side. "That's the place . . . that hurts bad," she whimpered.

He sighed and gently pushed up her gown, forcing himself not to look at soft blond hairs that hid secret places he was more and more determined would be discovered only by Lance Raines. She kept her eyes tightly closed as he carefully pushed the gown up past her waist to expose the swollen spot. He ran his fingers around it and she cried out again.

"Hang on," he told her, pressing on the lump itself. She screamed when he touched it and started crying again, and he pulled a light blanket over her and leaned close, kissing her forehead.

"I'm sorry, Cass. I had to do that."

"What is it?" she asked, her eyes looking frightened.

He picked up the handkerchief and wiped at tears that were starting to run into her ears. "It's an infection from some injury inside. It's got to be lanced and drained, Cass, or it will kill you. Do you understand?"

She sniffed and studied the gentle green eyes. "Will it hurt bad?"

He nodded. "I'm afraid so."

"Will you do it?"

"If you'll let me."

She managed a slight smile. "Only if it's you and nobody else. I don't want . . . that doctor to do it."

He grinned back. "I won't even let him come up here any more."

"Promise?"

"Promise."

"When will you do it?"

He frowned then. "I'm afraid the sooner the better, Cass. Right now wouldn't be any too soon. Every minute we let it go, the more danger there is of the infection getting into your whole system and killing you. We don't want that to happen. But Kate is pretty worn out, and I'll need help. I'm worried about Kate, and I want her to rest. So I'm going to go and get Mattie Brewster to come and help me. All right?"

Her eyes showed their disappointment. "I guess so. But . . . you'll stay afterward, won't you? You won't go back . . . with Mattie? You'll stay with me?"

To her surprise he leaned down and kissed her lips lightly. He knew of no other way at the moment to boost her courage and make her feel better. She stared at him wide-eyed, feeling faint from the touch of his lips rather than the pain.

"I'll stay. I won't go back with Mattie," he promised.

Their eyes held. "How do you say . . . 'I love you' . . . in Cheyenne, Rainmaker?"

He studied her for several seconds, a strange, sad look in his eyes. *"Nemehotatse,"* he replied.

"Nemehotatse," she repeated.

He studied her lovingly. Again he could see the vision, and he pulled back. "I'll be back in just a little while. I'm going to see that Kate gets into a hot bath, then I'll go and get Mattie. You rest, Cass. I'll see if that worthless doctor at least has some laudanum for your pain. We'll get you all fixed up."

"I know you will," she replied, her voice still young and high. "You can do anything. Thank you for coming back."

He frowned. "I'm sorry, Cass. This was partly my fault, and I'll never forgive myself."

Her eyes teared again. "It's all right. You didn't do anything wrong. It was all my fault. But now that you're here . . . I'm not afraid any more."

Their eyes held a moment longer, then he turned and quietly left to get Mattie.

Lance washed shaking hands in a bowl on the nightstand, while Cassandra finally lay in a peaceful, sedated sleep. He was not a man easily shaken, but Cassandra's awful screams while he cut away at her had been almost more than he could bear. At least he'd had some laudanum to numb some of the pain, and Mattie had been there to literally hold the girl down while Lance pushed and squeezed out as much of the infection as he could before dousing it with alcohol and stitching and wrapping it. There was nothing to do now but wait and hope more infection did not appear.

Mattie folded her arms and studied him with an amused grin. "I do believe this little ordeal shook those calm, cool nerves of yours, Lance Raines."

"Don't joke about it, Mattie. I hated hurting her like that."

She shook her head, patting his back. "Well, it had to be done, so don't feel so bad about it." She pulled a thin cigar from her handbag and lit it. "Tell me, big boy, if you're so

211

afraid of hurting her, how in hell are you going to bring yourself to make love to her for the first time? That should bring a few screams."

He scowled at her. "Cut it out. Besides, who says I'll ever make love to her?"

"I do. And you know it's true. Oh, it might be a couple of years away, but it will happen. That little innocent girl has you wrapped right around her finger." She laughed lightly. "I love it."

He threw down the towel. "No woman has me wrapped around her finger."

"That's true. But she's not a woman yet. No woman can get to you, but a little girl can. It's written all over your face, you big dope."

He sighed and ran a hand through his hair. "I don't want to talk about it. Right now the important thing is that she gets well."

Mattie puffed on the little cigar. "Agreed. But you'd better keep in mind how she's growing. Every year she'll be prettier and more tempting to some young man who might be willing to offer her security and marriage and children — all the things you aren't ready to offer anybody."

He leaned against a wall, lighting a cigarette he had rolled earlier. "I have to take one thing at a time. She's still a kid, so forget that talk." He puffed on the cigarette. "Thanks for helping me, Mattie."

"Any time. And I'm sorry to poke fun, Lance. But you know I'm right. And I like the kid. She's about sick with love for you, you know. She's a nice little girl, good to Kate, but she's always lonely without you around. By the way, did Kate tell you about those farm boys?"

He drew his eyes from watching Cassandra to meet Mattie's eyes. "What farm boys?"

"Oh, there's about three of them. They gave her a hard time during school — calling her squaw girl and such. They seem to think that just because she was an Indian captive she became some buck's woman. You know how people talk."

His face grew darker. "She wasn't touched by the Cheyenne that way!"

"Simmer down, love. I caught them giving her a bad time in the street one day, pushing her around, making her fall down. I proceeded to tell them all that if they ever bothered her again, I'd go to their parents and tell them those boys had been to see me and my girls. That put the fear in them, let me tell you. They haven't bothered her since."

Lance smiled, looking her over. "Clever idea. Thanks, Mattie." His eyes saddened again. "But I don't like anybody thinking bad things about her. She's as innocent as a newborn."

Mattie smiled slyly. "Well, as soon as she's well, you'd better hightail it back to the railroad, or she won't be innocent for long, not from the look in those eyes. You remember her age, love."

He frowned and walked up to the woman, pulling her close, the cigarette dangling from his mouth. "There are ways of remembering the differences between women and children," he answered, pressing her close against himself.

She smiled. "You coming tonight?"

He took the cigarette from his mouth and bent to kiss her cheek. "No. I promised Cass I'd not leave her side until she's much better."

"Mmm-hmm. Just as I thought." She gave him a squeeze and a disappointed smile. "I hope she'll be all right, Lance. I really do. She's a nice little girl. And from what I could see, you do good work, Dr. Raines."

He grinned. "When you learn to use your knife as deftly as an Indian, you're as good at slicing open a wound as you are at removing a scalp. The same expert technique applies to both."

She frowned and pushed at him. "Go on with you, you savage." She sighed and picked up a shawl. "I can see I'll not be enjoying your company for a while. Go ahead and baby-sit. I understand."

She brushed past him, and he felt a longing for a woman. But he'd made a promise, and he realized it was the first time he'd passed up the company of a good woman for something that meant responsibility. The only other time was when he'd left Mattie's bed before he wanted, in order to go and rescue Cassandra. It seemed the girl had a way of making him do things extraordinary for Lance Raines.

"Mattie," he called after the woman. She turned and met his eyes. "Thanks for coming."

She sighed. "You will come and see me before you leave Abilene, won't you?"

His eyes moved over her, but she knew that in the not-too-distant future, Lance Raines would not grace her doorway again. "Sure I will," he answered.

"I'll look forward to it. You're changing, you know. I don't have much time left with the old Lance."

He drew on the cigarette and shook his head, glancing again at Cassandra. "You've got plenty of time." He looked back at Mattie. "I'll be over. I might be several days, but I'll be over."

She gave him a wink. "I'll be waiting—anxiously." She opened the door. "And you keep me posted on how she's doing, will you? If you need me again, just holler."

He nodded and she left. Lance walked closer to Cassandra, touching her forehead and cheeks lightly to check for fever. She was cooler and seemed to be resting well. He closed his eyes and thanked *Maheo*.

He heard footsteps behind him then and turned to see Kate coming into the room, her graying hair disheveled. She was tying her robe as she came inside.

"You're supposed to be in bed yourself," Lance chided, turning away from Cassandra.

"I was just waiting for that woman to leave. You should have let me help, too, Lance." She walked up to Cassandra to study the girl closely. "I heard her screams. Poor child. Is she

214

all right now?"

"As far as I know. Time will tell. And I didn't want you in here because you've been through enough strain. Mattie did fine, and you shouldn't look down on her so much, Kate. She's a good woman at heart. She had a hell of a life as a child."

Kate smoothed back Cassandra's hair. "I don't look down on her, and I talk to her often. It's just that little girls like Cass shouldn't be talking to her too much. It looks bad, no matter how nice the woman might be. Mattie would know what I mean."

She straightened and looked at him. "I'm grateful she came." She looked him over. "You look pretty terrible yourself. Do you realize you haven't stopped to rest once since you got here? It's dark outside, and your poor horse is still tied out there loaded down. You must have ridden for hours before you even got here. You get your horse and yourself bedded down soon, Lance."

He walked to the end of the bed, leaning on the rail and watching Cassandra. "I'm going to sleep on my bedroll on the floor right in here. I promised her I'd be here when she woke up. I just hope I did everything right. And I hope to hell that doctor set those bones right."

"He seemed to do a pretty decent job. But Cass didn't like him. I wasn't too crazy about him myself. I'm glad you came. She probably would have died if you hadn't drained that infection. Word is we're getting a new doctor in town soon, supposedly a real good one. I hope it's true."

Lance nodded, still watching Cassandra. "It won't be long before the cattle business moves farther south and west," he told her. "Pretty soon the Archison, Topeka and Santa Fe will reach across southern Kansas, and Abilene will be rid of most of its cattle and drovers."

"And good riddance, I say. This town is a mess." The woman moved closer to him, looking up and studying his tired eyes. "You're different, Lance. What's happened?"

He looked down at her with a frown. "I don't even know. I guess I just got a good lesson in accepting some responsibility. I feel like this thing is my fault. I'd have been here weeks ago if I hadn't gotten a letter to go to Denver. I thought it was from my boss, in which case I still should have come here to see you two first. But I went running to Denver, and to top it off, I found out days later my boss never sent the letter. His wife sent it."

Her eyebrows arched. "His wife? Why!"

He smiled sadly. "Why do you think? Her husband was out of town."

She blinked and thought for a moment, then scowled the way he knew she would, looking him up and down and folding her arms. "Lance Raines! Your own boss's wife!"

He walked to look out a window. "You don't know what she's like. She's a witch—a sorceress."

"Lance Raines, it's bad enough she was some man's wife, but your boss. You said this man you're working for is extremely rich. That means power and influence. Don't you know what he could do to you if he found out?"

Lance shrugged. "I'm not afraid of that kind of man. Besides, he'd have to do the same thing to twenty other men, maybe more. Who knows? The woman is worse than Mattie, Kate. She sees a man she wants and she takes him. At any rate, she tricked me into going to Denver, then offered herself like a free meal. I took her up on the offer. I'd been out on the plains too long to have much resistance." He turned to face her. "The strange thing is, that isn't what bothers me. I can't even put my finger on what bothers me. It's as though she had some kind of plan, some motive for what she was doing that she wouldn't tell me. I was using her, yet I felt like I was being used, for something else. And I don't know what. It keeps eating at me."

"Well it should. Messing with a woman like that will only lead you to trouble, Lance Raines. You need somebody like little Cass here. Give her a couple of years and—"

"I can't say for sure about something like that, Kate."

"Can't you?"

Their eyes held for several seconds before he turned to look out the window again. "Maybe I can. But I feel like this thing with Jessica isn't over yet, and yet I don't know why I feel that way. I have no feelings for the woman, especially now. It's her fault I got here so late. Maybe none of this would have happened at all if I'd come to Abilene first." He swallowed. "I feel so responsible, Kate. That's what I mean about beginning to see what is and is not important in life, and it made me start thinking about settling some day."

"Well, at least you've accomplished that much."

He sighed deeply. "As soon as Cass is better, I'll probably finish out my job with the railroad. It pays good and I can save up a lot — maybe buy myself a lot of land for a horse ranch, something like that. It will all take a couple more years. Maybe by then . . ."

She frowned. "By then, what? Maybe Cass will be old enough for you?"

He shrugged. "Maybe," he answered quietly. "Right now I don't know how I feel about anything. I've never been so mixed up inside before. I've been living in this crazy white man's world too long, I guess. I should go back and live with the Cheyenne for a while and get my thoughts together. But I can't do that, either. Most of them are on reservations, and the rest are at war. And for all I know my Cheyenne father is dead by now. He wasn't very well the last time I saw him, and that was a year ago. It bothers me not knowing. I'll probably not see him again, and I guess that part of my life is over. It makes me sad."

She patted his arm. "You get your horse unloaded and get yourself bedded down and sleep on it. You're just too tired to be thinking on these things tonight. Personally, I'm just glad you got here and that I'll have some help with Cass. By the way, there are some cotton strips of cloth in the drawer there that I use at night to wrap around her bottom kind of like a diaper. She can't get up to go to the bathroom, you know. You'd better put one on her, unless you want me to do it."

He rubbed at his neck. "You go back to bed. I'll do it."

She patted his arm again. "We'll talk in the morning. I'm sorry about White Eagle, Lance. I know you loved him. Maybe you'll see him again after all. You do like I say for tonight and get some rest. Taking care of our little girl takes a lot out of a person. You want to be rested by morning."

He nodded and Kate left, walking slowly back to her room. Lance watched her, seeing death also in the old woman who had raised him. It seemed he was losing all the people he loved most. He went to the drawer and took out two pieces of square cotton cloth, then uncovered Cassandra, careful not to disturb her too much. He gently worked the cloth underneath her, feeling oddly possessive of secret places as he drew a corner of the cloth up between her legs and two more corners around her hips to tie them together. He could not resist gently pressing the small, flat belly, wondering if she would ever be woman enough to hold a child between such narrow hip bones, or even woman enough to take a man in order to get pregnant in the first place. The thought stirred him, and that made him angry with himself. He covered her then and bent down to kiss her forehead.

"Sleep tight, *Kseé*," he said softly.

He left the room, and Cassandra tried to answer, but she was too drugged. She had sensed his touch, heard his words, even heard him talking about some woman in Denver, yet she couldn't seem to open her eyes or make a sound.

Chapter Thirteen

Cassandra awoke to the dim light of an early morning sun. A rooster crowed somewhere in the distance, and the room was cooler. She lay there quietly for a moment, gathering her thoughts after a night of drugged sleep. It came back to her then, the awful pain of Rainmaker's knife, Mattie's hands holding her down, Rainmaker's gentle words of reassurance, telling her to hang on, that soon it would be over. And finally it was over. She remembered him telling her he'd be there when she woke up.

She turned her head slightly, and smiled with love and joy when she saw him lying on the floor a few feet from the bed. He was stretched out on his back on a thin bedroll, and wore only a loincloth because of the heat of the room the night before. She could not help but take the opportunity to just stare at him while he slept, still hardly able to believe he had really come.

How tired he must be, riding all that way and then having to take care of her after he arrived. But how beautiful he looked lying there now, more man than she had remembered, the thick, wavy hair now tangled around his face and neck; his handsome face looked peaceful in sleep, in spite of the violence he had known. She moved her gaze down his body, wanting to remember every part of him, for she knew in her heart he would probably go away again.

She tried to imagine what it must have been like for him to go through the Sun Dance ritual, and she winced at the sight of the scars on his chest and upper arms from that test of manhood. His shoulders were broad and powerful, his skin dark from riding half naked in the sun. His stomach was flat, hardly moving in his deep sleep. She stared then in wonder and curiosity at the loincloth, remembering the day Three Stars Woman and her sister had stripped the bloody one off him after his fight to keep her. She remembered what she had seen then, and as often happens with men in early morning sleep, that part of him was swollen from warm, deep dreams. To think of ever being with him that way filled her with fear and embarrassment, mingled with keen curiosity and an intense desire to be the woman who pleased him more than any woman he had ever been with. She hoped he hadn't left with Mattie the night before, and somehow knew he had not. He had promised her, and Rainmaker didn't break promises. She studied the muscles of his powerful legs, and the perfect masculine form of them.

Such a beautiful man he was! If only he could be hers. Was it possible? He'd seemed so concerned the night before, and now he'd seen her naked, had touched her. Even though it was out of necessity because of her injuries, it still made him special. No other boy or man had seen her that way, except the doctor, and he didn't count. This was Rainmaker, her beloved, and she didn't even mind. His touch was kind, his eyes respectful, his concern genuine. And hadn't he kissed her? Yes! She blinked back tears. He had! She remembered now! Rainmaker had kissed her, right on the lips! And he'd told her the Cheyenne word for "I love you." What was it? To her frustration she couldn't remember it. But when he told it to her, he'd looked right at her with those green eyes and had said it as though he truly meant it. And he'd seemed so worried she might die, so concerned, so sweet and gentle. Surely he was thinking perhaps he loved her, perhaps he'd wait for her. Why, oh why, did she have to be so young? In her heart she was old enough, she was sure of it. But Rainmaker would never think she was old enough to be his woman. How could she be sure he'd wait?

She could not stop looking at him, and could not help but look again at the loincloth, wondering if she would ever know all the things it took to please a man.

"Good morning" came his voice then, husky with sleep.

She reddened instantly, her eyes darting to his to see him smiling and watching her.

"You look pretty bright-eyed for the rough night you had."

She averted her gaze, wondering if he'd caught her staring at things she shouldn't be staring at. He embarrassed her so easily, with all his manliness and worldly knowledge. She felt like a stupid child, which she surely was.

"I feel better," she said quietly. "I'm thirsty."

He was up in an instant, moving about the room on quiet, bare feet. He dipped a cup into a bucket of water and brought it to her, bending over and gently lifting her head slightly. She sipped the water as he put the cup to her lips, then met his eyes as she finished. Their eyes held as he lowered her head to the pillow again. He set the cup aside, then put his hands to her face and neck.

"Your fever is gone. That's good news," he told her. He pulled the covers off her, and now that she was much more awake and alert, she was more embarrassed when he pushed up her gown. He studied the bandages around her, seeing no blood, then gently pressed around the area where he'd cut her. "How does it feel?"

"Sore. But not the kind like before. Just sore like a cut."

He ran his hand all around the area, pressing, waiting for a reaction. But she apparently felt no pain.

"By God, I think we did it, *Kseé*." He looked at her and smiled, and she smiled back at him.

"Thank you, Rainmaker," she said quietly.

"You should hate me," he answered, untying the diaperlike cloth. She reddened deeply. "It's partly my fault this happened. I'm damned sorry, Cass."

He removed the damp diaper and dropped it in a bucket of soapy water beside the bed Kate kept there for soiled things. He took another cloth from the drawer then, and she was so embarrassed she couldn't say anything as he wrapped the new one around her; yet he didn't seem to stare at anything, never touched her wrongly. His every movement was careful and gentle. When he finished he pulled down the gown and covered her again, looking up to see her face crimson and quiet tears running from her eyes.

He leaned over her then, wiping at the tears with his fingers. "Don't worry about it," he told her, kissing her forehead and making her weak with love. "You're a sick little girl, and I want to help you, and give Kate some relief." He frowned, studying her intently and pursing his lips. "By God, you've changed, Cassandra Elliott. I do believe your freckles are gone, and a tiny bit of woman is showing through those pretty eyes. Could it be you're growing up?"

She sniffed and smiled. "I grew five inches this year. I'm five feet one inch now." She sniffed again. "Kate gets mad because she says every time she makes me a dress, two weeks later it's too short."

He laughed lightly. "That would be discouraging, and I can just hear Kate fussing about it."

She smiled more. How she loved him, standing there smiling and handsome in all his manly glory. "Will you stay until I'm well, Rainmaker?"

He nodded. "I said I would, didn't I?"

"Yes. But that was yesterday, and I was sicker. I was afraid I didn't hear you right."

"Well, you did. And I bet you'd like to get out of that bed and get some fresh air."

Her eyes brightened. "I would. I have sores from lying here, and it gets lonely."

"Well, I'm going to wash and dress, and then I'll come back here and give you a sponge bath and put a clean gown on you. And then, Miss Elliott, I will carry you right out of here and down the stairs and outside. You need some sun and fresh air."

Her heart pounded at the thought of him giving her a bath. Could this really be? How would she live through the embarrassment of it? Yet the thought of it gave her shivers. And the thought of being moved . . .

"Won't it hurt? I'm scared to move," she told him.

"Well, it can't hurt to at least try, can it? I'll be as gentle as a baby kitten. But you've got to get some air and some sun. You're shriveling into a pale skeleton up here. And I want you to start eating better."

"I'll do whatever you tell me if you'll stay awhile."

Their eyes held again, and he felt almost guilty at the look of love in her own. He knew that if not for the injuries, and in spite of any fears, she'd let him do whatever he wanted with her this very moment. It would be easy to take advantage of her worshipful puppy love, if he were a lesser man. But he knew she would give herself to him out of innocent affection and desire to please him, not because she was a wanton woman. Not Cassandra. She was special, and if she got up and danced naked in front of him this very moment, he'd not touch her. It was strange how he could think of one day making her his own, yet found it easy at the moment not to touch her at all, or even to allow manly desires to take over when he saw and touched places he hoped to see and touch again, for different reasons. Only then, when she was older and ready, could he allow himself to look at her with any desire. He could wait. He knew it now.

He walked over and rolled up his blankets. "Well, you can start by eating better. You just lie still there, and I'll go wash and then bring you some breakfast. I want to check on Kate, too." He straightened and frowned. "How sick is she, Cass?"

The girl sighed. "I'm not sure. She goes on like she always does. She just seems more tired, and sometimes she holds her chest like it hurts. But she never says much. I'm glad you came, Rainmaker, to help her. She's missed you." She swallowed. "I missed you, too."

He winked. "And I missed both of you. I had business in Denver, or I'd have come here first. I still feel bad about that, Cass. I'm sorry."

"It's all right." She thought about his conversation the night before. Had she dreamed it, or was there some woman in Denver? Her heart sank. Of course there was a woman in Denver. Lance Raines had a woman wherever he went. Would she ever be his woman? And could she ever make him love her enough to be his only woman? What did it take to keep such a man all her own? She wanted to ask him about the woman, but felt too young and inexperienced to ask. Maybe it would make him angry. After all, it wasn't really her business.

He walked past her and squeezed a toe as he left. She was almost asleep again when he returned, carrying a tray of food, which he fed to her himself, telling her some of his adventures on the plains, including the hard ride to outrun the Indians with Paul Thomas sharing his horse. He left again and returned with a bucket of clean, soapy water and Kate, who helped him undress her and wash her. Cassandra closed her eyes against her embarrassment and prayed Rainmaker would like what he saw and it would make him want to wait for her. She breathed in his manly scent when he gently pulled her to him and held her carefully while Kate washed her back and powdered it. When they were completely through, the two of them gently massaged a sweet-smelling cream on her sore skin and put a fresh gown on her. Then Lance wrapped a light blanket around her

ACCEPT YOUR FREE GIFT
AND EXPERIENCE MORE OF
THE PASSION AND ADVENTURE
YOU LIKE IN A
HISTORICAL ROMANCE

Zebra Romances are the finest novels of their kind and are written with the adult woman in mind. All of our books are written by authors who really know how to weave tales of romantic adventure in the historical settings you love.

Because our readers tell us these books sell out very fast in the stores, Zebra has made arrangements for you to receive at home the four newest titles published each month. You'll never miss a title and home delivery is so convenient. With your first shipment we'll even send you a FREE Zebra Historical Romance as our gift just for trying our home subscription service. No obligation.

BIG SAVINGS
AND FREE HOME DELIVERY

Each month, the Zebra Home Subscription Service will send you the four newest titles as soon as they are published. (We ship these books to our subscribers even before we send them to the stores.) You may preview them *Free* for 10 days. If you like them as much as we think you will, you'll pay just $3.50 each and *save $1.80 each month* off the cover price. *AND you'll also get FREE HOME DELIVERY*. There is never a charge for shipping, handling or postage and there is no minimum you must buy. If you decide not to keep any shipment, simply return it within 10 days, no questions asked, and owe nothing.

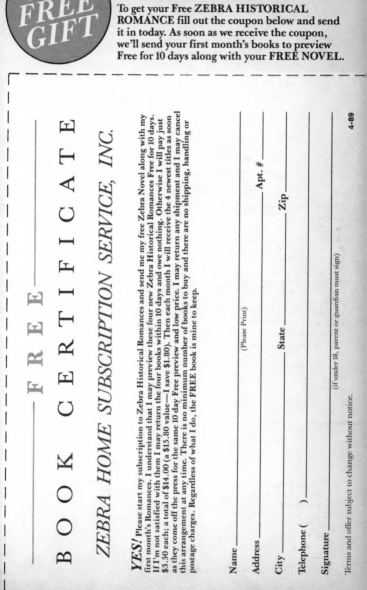

GET FREE GIFT

MAIL IN THE COUPON BELOW TODAY

To get your Free ZEBRA HISTORICAL ROMANCE fill out the coupon below and send it in today. As soon as we receive the coupon, we'll send your first month's books to preview Free for 10 days along with your **FREE NOVEL.**

—— F R E E ——

BOOK CERTIFICATE

ZEBRA HOME SUBSCRIPTION SERVICE, INC.

YES! Please start my subscription to Zebra Historical Romances and send me my free Zebra Novel along with my first month's Romances. I understand that I may preview these four new Zebra Historical Romances Free for 10 days. If I'm not satisfied with them I may return the four books within 10 days and owe nothing. Otherwise I will pay just $3.50 each; a total of $14.00 (a $15.80 value—I save $1.80). Then each month I will receive the 4 newest titles as soon as they come off the press for the same 10 day Free preview and low price. I may return any shipment and I may cancel this arrangement at any time. There is no minimum number of books to buy and there are no shipping, handling or postage charges. Regardless of what I do, the FREE book is mine to keep.

4-89

Name _____
           (Please Print)

Address _____ Apt. # _____

City _____ State _____ Zip _____

Telephone ( ) _____

Signature _____
           (if under 18, parent or guardian must sign)

Terms and offer subject to change without notice.

Get a Free
Zebra
Historical
Romance

*a $3.95
value*

and carefully lifted her.

Her weight was like nothing to him, and she relished being held in his strong arms, her head resting on the bare, muscular shoulder. He wore only leggings and a vest against the warm day. She ignored her pain, for she was afraid if she complained too much he'd lay her back down and she wouldn't be in his arms anymore.

"I'm taking her outside, Kate. Can you change the bed while I've got her out of it?"

"Of course I will," the woman answered. "You take our little Cass out for some fresh air. It will be good for her." She breathed deeply. "Oh, it's good to have you here, Lance. I feel so much better."

"Well, I'll expect a few pies for this, old woman."

She waved him off. "I should refuse to bake for you until you start dressing like a white man is supposed to dress."

"Then I'll have to forget about ever eating pie again," he answered, going through the door with Cassandra. He looked down at her. "Am I hurting you?"

She closed her eyes against the pain. "Some. But don't take me back, Rainmaker. I want to go outside."

He took care in going down the steps and through the kitchen, pushing open the door with his foot and stepping outside. "Just a little farther," he told her, going down the steps to one of the few cottonwood trees in the whole town that provided any decent shade. It was in Kate's backyard, and Kate often sat under it herself at the end of the day.

Lance went to his knees then, very carefully laying Cassandra on two blankets that covered a bed of straw, which he had already made up. She could do little with her arms to help him, and she looked pale.

"Damn it. Maybe I shouldn't have done this yet," he muttered, fluffing a pillow under her head.

"It's all right," she answered, looking around at the sky and the grass. "This is wonderful. It feels so good to be outside again."

225

He smiled then, sitting down beside her and sticking a weed in his mouth, chewing on it while he looked out at the horizon. She studied him as a breeze ruffled his hair. Yes, he was just like that wind.

"What do you think about when you watch the horizon?" she asked him.

He didn't answer right away, thinking a moment before replying, as wise Indians often did. He thought about how long it sometimes took White Eagle to answer his many questions when he was young.

"Lately I think mostly about my own future, what it will be," he finally answered. "I want to be with the Cheyenne, but I can't. Not anymore. And I think about them—what's happening to them. I think about Dull Knife and Black Kettle—the cruel way they died. They're running and afraid—starving. I don't blame them a bit for fighting to hold on to what should be theirs." He sighed deeply. "And I wonder about White Eagle. I have good memories of my boyhood days—riding free—hunting buffalo." He swallowed back emotions, and his voice was husky. "I'll never have the kind of peace in this life that I had then. I pretend I don't care, but I do."

She watched him quietly, feeling his hurt. "I was afraid of them, until I met you—and Kicking Horse," she confessed. "Now I understand better, and I feel sad for you. Peace comes from inside, Rainmaker. You just don't know inside what you want to do, what you want to be." She took a deep breath for courage to express her feelings. "Rainmaker . . . if I die . . . I hope I'm beside you like this. I would die in peace then."

He turned to look at her, and to her relief he didn't look angry, nor was he laughing. He looked worried, and he put a hand to the side of her face. "You won't die. I won't let you."

She looked into his eyes. "Why?"

He rubbed at her cheek gently, and she felt dizzy at his

226

touch. "Because you're too good to die. Sweet little girls like you aren't supposed to die. Worthless bastards like myself should be the ones to die."

"Don't say that, Rainmaker. You aren't worthless. You're the most wonderful man who ever lived."

He grinned bashfully then and took his hand away, chewing on the weed and looking out over the horizon. "I'm not always so wonderful, *Kseé*."

She swallowed for courage. "You mean like . . . like when you were with that married lady in Denver?"

He frowned then, looking back down at her. "How do you know about that?"

"I remember . . . I heard it last night. It was like I dreamed it, but I heard you talking."

He looked away again, and her heart felt shattered. So, she'd not dreamed it.

"You won't . . . go back to her, will you?"

He shrugged. "I doubt it. She's no good. Her kind is worse than Mattie. I just have this strange feeling she isn't out of my life yet. It's been bothering me."

She struggled to keep from crying. "Do you . . . love her? Or Mattie?"

He laughed lightly. "No. A man doesn't love that kind — not like he loves a wife."

She wondered where she got her courage. "Will you stop seeing painted ladies like Mattie . . . when you do have a wife?"

"Sure I will. I wouldn't need them any more." He chewed on the weed for a moment, then looked down at her blushing face. "You're sure full of personal questions about things you don't know much about."

She reddened more. "I'm sorry."

He leaned down beside her on one elbow, grinning, the weed in his teeth. "It's all right. I didn't realize until I left here what good friends we were. I guess you can ask me anything you want. I like talking to you."

"You do?" Her eyes lit up.

"Sure I do. Kids are more honest than grown-ups."

How she wished she wasn't injured, so she could wear a pretty dress for him and stand up and show him how tall she was now; she would even wear an undergarment that would accent how her breasts had grown. She could walk pretty for him, flirt with him. But all she could do now was just lie there practically helpless. But at least it gave her reason to be touched and bathed and held.

"I'm not so much of a kid, Rainmaker."

His eyes moved over her, and a brand new urgent feeling swept through her, something she'd never felt before. It made her hot all over. It made her want to be his woman.

"I know that. But you aren't grown up, either."

Their eyes held. "Why did you kiss me last night?"

He frowned. "I don't know. For courage, I guess—to show you I cared. I didn't want you to be afraid." He sighed deeply and studied the blue eyes. "Don't get ideas, Cass. Not now, anyway. I risked my life for you. That makes you special."

Her eyes teared. "I know you think I'm just a dumb little girl," she whimpered. "But I don't care. I still love you, Rainmaker. I tried to stop, but I couldn't. I think about you every minute, and I pray for you, and—"

"Stop it, Cass!" he said quickly, sitting up again. "I didn't bring you out here for that. I brought you out here for fresh air and because I care about you as a friend. Think of me as your big brother or something. That's the more natural way to think."

Her crying grew worse, until it became a mixture of tears of sorrow and of pain, for all her insides began to ache. Her body shook with the sobs, and Lance pulled the weed from his mouth and threw it down. "Damn!" he muttered.

He turned then, resting on one elbow and pulling her into the crook of his arm. "Don't cry, Cass."

"I . . . can't . . . help it," she blubbered. "I know . . . what you think . . . of me . . . and now I . . . made you mad . . . and you'll go away."

He sighed and leaned down to kiss her hair. "I'm not mad at you. I'm mad at me." He stroked her face gently. "You make me feel things I shouldn't feel for a girl your age, that's all. Don't make it so hard on me, Cass, and on yourself. Let yourself grow up. For now I'm your good friend, like a brother. When you're older, you might feel differently. Maybe I will, too. But we'll always be friends, no matter what. Agreed?"

"I'm . . . sorry. I shouldn't have . . . said all those things. Please stay till I'm well, Rainmaker."

"I already promised that. And don't be sorry. You make me feel . . . good . . . honored . . . like a proud young warrior who has found out the beautiful daughter of the chief has eyes for him."

"Truly?" She looked up at him, her face wet with tears. He took a corner of a blanket and wiped them off gently, being careful of all the bruises.

"Truly. And I know when a person is in pain, they get upset easily, and say anything that comes to mind. You're hurt and you're depressed. It's all right to let your feelings out. Let's not talk about it any more. Let's just get you well and enjoy each other's company until I leave. I'll teach you more Indian words, and you can read to me and show me what you've learned in school. Let time take care of things, Cass. And let me take care of you like I did when I got you away from the Cheyenne."

She sniffed. "You've saved my life twice now. Maybe that's some kind of sign."

He thought about the vision. "Maybe." He put her head back on the pillow and sat up again. "What's this Mattie tells me about some farm boys poking fun at you?"

Her eyes clouded. "They pushed me down. They think the Indians did bad things to me—made me a squaw. I

229

think I know what they mean, and it makes me embarrassed; and it isn't true. Mattie caught them teasing me one day, and she helped me. I like Mattie, except Kate says I shouldn't be seen talking to her in public."

He took tobacco and paper from a pouch at his waist. "Well, she's probably right there. Have the boys bothered you since?"

"No. But school has been out. I don't see them when I'm not in school."

"Good." He lit his cigarette and took a drag. "How do you feel? You want to go back inside?"

"Not yet. I like it out here under this tree. The pain is still bad, but not like yesterday when I had that lump. I know I was dying. I was so scared I'd die without seeing you again. Kate kept promising you'd come."

"I came as soon as I got the message. It's just that I was pretty far away."

"In Denver."

He nodded, smoking and staring at the horizon again, and she knew he was thinking of the mysterious Jessica. "Yeah. In Denver." Her heart burned with a jealousy she had never felt before. He brightened then and turned to face her. "I'm making good money, though. I've been thinking about settling down like Kate wants me to do. But a man has to have money for things like that, so while I'm deciding about my life, I'll keep stashing away my pay."

She watched him lovingly. "And you'll wait a couple of years?"

He laughed lightly then and shook his head. "Yes, I'll wait a couple of years."

She grinned. "Good. And you'll stay this time, really and truly, until I'm well?"

"Well, maybe not all the way until every bone is healed, but at least until you're out of danger. If I stay away too long, I might lose my job." He held the cigarette in his mouth, getting on his knees beside her and grasping one

230

arm. "Let's see how you're healing. You should at least be able to move these arms. You want to try?"

"As long as it's you helping me."

He grinned and gently bent her arm, then straightened it, watching the pain on her face, "Can you make a fist?"

She tried, but was not successful. "It hurts too much."

"Don't worry about it." He leaned over her and tried the other arm. She could bend it up, but when he went to straighten it, she screamed for him to stop.

He frowned, gently feeling around her elbow. "That's all the farther you can straighten it?"

"Yes," she whimpered.

"That quack bastard probably set it wrong!" he grumbled. He pulled the blanket away from her and ran his hand along the splint on her leg and ankle. Her right food was puffy and pink. "In another couple of weeks we'll stand you up and start exercising this leg lightly—very lightly. You've got to build up the muscles soon or they'll be useless."

"Will I be crippled, Rainmaker?"

He saw the fear in her eyes. "I can't say, Cass."

New tears came. "If I'm crippled . . . I won't be pretty."

He grinned and covered her, his pity for her bringing an ache to his heart. He leaned close to her and touched her cheek. "Something tells me you'll be pretty whether you're crippled or not. A man can't look at that golden hair or into those big, blue eyes without forgetting a simple thing like a limp."

"Really and truly?"

Their eyes held again. "Really and truly."

If there was any more wonderful man in all the world, Cassandra Elliott would argue there was not. For her, there was only Rainmaker.

Days turned into weeks, and those first few days took

231

Cassandra close to and away from death again several times, the infection returning, forcing Lance to cut and drain it again. Finally it seemed she would stay on the road to recovery; but still the left arm would not straighten, and there was no movement in the right ankle. A new doctor arrived in town, and upon examination declared the only solution was to rebreak the bones and set them right. It was Lance who cautiously told the girl the bad news, but to his surprise she did not panic or cry.

"If he doesn't fix them, will I be crippled?" Cassandra asked, watching him with trusting eyes.

Lance frowned, touching her hair. "I'm afraid so, Cass."

How she loved him! How she wanted to be perfect for him. "I don't want to be crippled, Rainmaker. I want him to fix me."

Lance studied the blue eyes. "You sure? You'll go through the pain all over again, Cass."

"I don't care. I can stand it if you . . . if you stay with me."

Lance sighed deeply, taking her hand in his own. "If that's what you want, I'll stay with you." He leaned closer, kissing her hair. "You're a very brave girl, Cassandra Elliott." He was touched by her courage, surprised by her strength of will. There was surely a strong woman in the making in the person of Cassandra Elliott, the kind of woman a man in such a land needed. He studied her carefully, holding her eyes with his own hypnotic gaze.

"Cass, don't do this just for me. You'd still be able to walk, but with a limp. You couldn't straighten your arm completely, but you'd still be able to use it. You don't have to go through this."

"No. I don't want to limp and have a crippled arm. And I don't want you to always feel sorry for me. Tell him I want him to do it."

He smiled sadly. "I'll be right here the whole time."

"I know you will." She blinked back tears. "See how

232

grown up I am, Rainmaker?"

He nodded, smiling at the childlike hope in her eyes. "Yes, you are." He patted her cheek. "You rest. I'll go talk to the doctor."

It was done the same day, and Lance and Kate could only thank God that the new doctor had a supply of the blessed ether that was coming to be used more and more now to put people to sleep so they were spared the pain of injuries and operations. But the fact remained that Cassandra would be in pain all over again once the ether wore off.

When the doctor finished and left, Lance remained beside the girl, watching her sleep, his feelings torn.

"She did it for you, you know," Kate told him, coming back into the room.

Lance turned to look at her. "I know. And the hell of it is I can't even promise her anything, Kate." He got up and went to the door. "I'm going to Mattie's place to get a drink. That damned kid has me so confused my head hurts."

He started out. "Lance."

He turned back to look at Kate. "What?"

"The doctor said she'd wake up in a couple of hours. You promised you'd be here."

Their eyes held. "I'll be here."

Kate's eyes had tears in them. "Underneath all that wildness and devilishness you're a darned nice young man, you know."

He almost winced at the words, snickering and shaking his head. "Keep wishing, Kate." He disappeared then, and moments later she heard the door close downstairs.

Lance's heart ached at the new pain and swelling Cassandra suffered, admiring the fact that she tried to be big about it, never complaining, seldom crying, bravely weathering the awful sickness that came when the ether wore off, followed by those first days of painful mending. Lance was there every day, helping her in every way he could. Cassandra grew to love him more and more, became accustomed to his seeing her when he bathed her, grew to trust and depend on him. She felt she belonged to him; and Lance in turn felt more and more that he owned her, felt his curiosity growing about how she would look the next year or two when he came home again, maybe for good. To see her as a woman, touch her as a woman, brought restless dreams, and still the vision haunted him.

Cass read to him when she felt better, and he told her Indian stories and taught her Indian words. The girl could not have been happier, except for the knowledge that every evening he left, and sometimes did not return until the afternoon of the next day. She knew where he went every night, but she forced back her jealousy, wanting to understand, reminding herself that Lance Raines was a full-grown man with needs she could not possibly fulfill. Her only hope was to show him how mature she was becoming, to show him how strong she was, how brave and uncomplaining. But it hurt. Oh, how it hurt, to think of him with that Mattie woman, to think of someone else giving him love and pleasure.

"He doesn't love that woman, does he, Kate?" It was three weeks since her operation, but she still didn't have much of an appetite, not when she envisioned her Rainmaker with Mattie Brewster. She picked at a breakfast of biscuits and gravy, and Kate fluffed her pillow.

"Mattie's just a good friend, Cass. Men don't love women like that, not in the way you mean. And I expect some day when you're older, you won't have to worry about it."

Cass met her eyes. "Do you really think so?"

"With you all better, and looking prettier than he thought you would?" She smiled. "I've seen how he looks at you when he thinks we don't notice. You've got his mind a-whirl, child. That's a fact I'm sure of."

Cassandra sniffed. "Oh, Kate, sometimes when I look at

him I think my heart will just explode. And then sometimes it scares me to think of—"she blushed—"to think of . . . being with him . . . like Mattie. I wouldn't know what to do."

Kate chuckled. "I doubt you'd have to know. He'd show you quick enough. But he's a man of good conscience, Cass. So don't push him to do things he knows it isn't the right time to do. Leave him be, girl. No man likes being pushed, especially not a man like Lance." She patted the girl's arm. "I'm going to get some water for your morning bath."

Cassandra watched her leave, then picked up an Indian blanket that Lance had given her from the foot of the bed. She hugged it close, unable to stop the jealous tears.

Too soon came the day Cassandra dreaded. Although she was still bandaged, she could walk around on her own with the use of crutches, and everything was healing perfectly. Already the air was cold with coming winter, and it was winter in her heart, for Lance said he had to leave. Kate was better and taking boarders again. Lance had to get back to the railroad.

"They'll be in Colorado by now," he was telling Kate. "They'll reach Denver by next spring, I expect."

The three of them ate pie alone in the kitchen while the boarders finished their supper in the dining room. Cassandra felt her heart tighten at the mention of Denver. Would he go and see the woman called Jessica when he got there?

"For all I know I'm out of a job by now," he was saying. Cassandra hoped it would be true. If so, he'd come back to Abilene. He wouldn't go and see that woman.

"You mind yourself, Lance Raines," Kate was telling him. "You know what I'm talking about. You'll get yourself in a pack of trouble."

Lance drank some coffee, glancing at Cassandra, who sat

staring at her plate and looking ready to cry.

"I can take care of myself," he answered, turning his eyes back to Kate. "I think I'll leave in the morning. You well enough to go on your own for a while?"

She took a deep breath. "I feel much better. This is the longest you've stayed in years, Lance. It's been nice having you here."

He reached over and squeezed her arm. "You sure? Don't lie to me, Kate."

She smiled and patted his hand. "I'm fine. Old women get aches and pains all the time. But then you wouldn't know much about that, would you, a young man like yourself, running with the young, pretty ones. Some day you'll slow down, too, Lance Raines."

He laughed lightly and turned his eyes back to Cassandra, who still stared at her plate. "Think you can get along without me now, *Kseé?*"

She only swallowed and nodded. He got up and took her arm, urging her out of her chair. "Come on outside a minute," he told her in a gentle command. He glanced at Kate as Cassandra got up, and Kate cast him a warning look to remember she was a child. He frowned and winked teasingly, leading Cass through the door, walking slowly with her as she walked lightly on the healing ankle.

He helped her down the steps, then led her around the side of the house and up against the wall, placing a hand on each side of her as though to trap her. She looked up and met the gentle eyes in the moonlight.

"Wait for me, Cass," he said quietly.

It was all she needed to hear. Her heart burst with joy, and her eyes teared. "I'd wait for you forever."

He sighed. "Some young man might come along who makes me look a hundred years old. He might offer you all the things a young girl wants—all the things I can't offer yet—things I can't even promise yet. You should consider what he offers, and let yourself look at young men. Just don't . . . don't go giving yourself to anyone. I know it sounds selfish for me to ask you to wait and choose. I'm probably dead wrong, but—"

"There's no man I'd even look at twice. My heart is full of you, and you know it. I didn't know how you felt, Rainmaker. I thought you didn't care that way at all. I thought . . ."

Flames shot through her when he placed his hands on either side of her face, squeezing lightly to stop her talking. He bent close then, meeting her lips gently, drinking in the taste of her virgin lips in a long, slow kiss that told him of the woman she could be.

But she was only fourteen. Again his better senses took over, and he trembled as he released the kiss. "Go on inside, Cass. I'm going riding for a while, and I'll be leaving at daybreak. I probably won't see you again, but I'll write."

He turned away, quickly disappearing into the darkness. "Rainmaker?" she called out. But there was no reply. She touched her fingers to her lips, a golden warmth spreading through her body. She ran her tongue over her lips. She would remember that kiss. Forever and forever she would remember.

In the morning Cassandra awoke with the sensation that someone had been in her room She sat up quickly. Dawn was breaking. Rainmaker! She pulled on her robe and walked to the window when she heard the kitchen door close downstairs. Sotaju was saddled outside, and now she could see him walking to the horse.

"Rainmaker!" she called out.

He looked up at the window. "Don't be walking the streets in a daydream any more," he yelled. "You be careful, Cass."

"Don't go yet!"

237

"It's best I do." He eased onto the horse with no effort.

"Tell me the word again," she called.

"What word?"

"The Cheyenne word for . . . for I love you."

He stared at her for a moment. *"Nemehotatse."*

Her eyes teared. Was he saying it to her? Didn't Indian men his age often marry very young girls? Wasn't it possible he could love her? He'd asked her to wait. He'd kissed her—that beautiful kiss she would remember forever.

"Nemehotatse," she called down to him.

He watched her a moment longer, studying the long, loose hair that fell in golden waves over her shoulders, thinking how warm and sweet she must be in the mornings.

"Take care of yourself, Cass." He turned his horse and headed west. Kate watched from the kitchen door, her own eyes wet with tears.

"You take care of yourself, Lance Raines," she muttered. "And you stay away from that woman in Denver."

Chapter Fourteen

Claude Françoise folded his napkin and leaned back in the chair, watching his beautiful wife, the two of them looking small sitting at the grand dining table all alone.

"So, you said you wanted to dine alone and celebrate something," he told the woman. "You haven't told me yet what we are celebrating. By the way, remind me to thank Rose for the fine roast. She did a marvelous job, as usual."

Jessica smiled. "It's a good thing we have her. I was never much of a cook, dear husband." She rang a little bell, and a maid came through the door from the kitchen. "Get that bottle of chilled wine I told you I'd want after dinner, Marian."

The maid bowed slightly. "Yes, ma'am."

"Actually, I have some celebrating to do myself, Jessica," Claude was telling her. "I've been staying in constant touch with William Palmer. He's that fellow who I told you is striving to build a railroad from Denver southward, all the way to Santa Fe, with branches into the mountains to reach the mining towns. The man has a great dream, and I think he can do it. I've gone in with him on buying up as much land as quickly and quietly as we can before anyone discovers what we intend to do with it. He has several other wealthy investors behind him. By the time the Kansas-Pacific reaches Denver next summer, we'll be ready to break ground for the Denver and Rio Grande." His eyes glittered with excitement. "We'll build north to Cheyenne and connect with the Union Pacific, and we'll build south as far as we can go! Denver will be the hub of transportation, its banks the central depositors, its businesses the center of trade. With the coming of the railroad, Denver's future as a great city is guaranteed!"

Marian brought the wine and carefully poured it as he spoke, and when she left, Jessica raised her glass. "To Denver," she said softly.

They touched glasses and sipped some wine.

Claude grinned. "And to the hope of more investors. Palmer will be getting married late next summer, and then will be traveling to Europe to talk to some very wealthy men there who are interested in our idea. It's all so exciting, Jessica!"

She nodded. "Then I will add to your joy, my love." She raised her glass again. "To our son—or daughter. Hopefully, a son."

His smile faded and he was visibly shaken. He just stared at her a moment before finally finding his voice. "You're . . . pregnant?"

She laughed lightly. "Why do you look so surprised? We have been diligent in mating for this very purpose, have we not? Isn't that why you married me—because I was a healthy woman who could enjoy her man and therefore work harder at giving him a child? You finally have your wish, Claude."

His eyes actually teared, to her surprise, and he touched her glass. They quietly sipped some wine.

"When?" he asked then.

"Around March, if I've guessed it right. I'm over four months along now, according to my calculations." She held his eyes steadily, refusing to give him any room to wonder if the child was really his. "It must have happened those first couple of days after you came back from San Francisco.

240

Remember how excited you were with all your railroad talk—how happy we were? We made love often."

She tried to accent the fact, knowing deep inside the child was not her husband's at all. It only made sense by her timing that the child belonged to Lance Raines, but the timing was close enough that she knew she could convince her husband it was his own.

"But . . . we've made love that way many times," Claude told her, his voice husky with overwhelming joy. "How . . . how did it finally happen this time?"

She laughed and sipped more wine. "Oh, Claude, how would I know? Who can say why these things happen?" She had to remain happy and teasing. She must not let him consider the fact that she was alone for several weeks before his return. He must think the child was his. "I suppose God knows when the time is right," she added, setting her glass down. She took his hand. "And now I can always be Mrs. Claude Françoise and share this house and this happiness? You will keep me?"

He picked up her hand and kissed it. "Of course I'll keep you, Jessica. In fact I . . . I think perhaps I'm falling in love with you after all."

She smiled through the deceiving, seductive lips. "And I am learning to love you," she replied. "I am so proud to be your wife, Claude. And mostly I am proud that I will be a mother. There was a time when I never dreamed I could have such a life. I will love this child so very much."

That part was spoken from the heart, for her motherly instincts were already taking over; and she could only pray nothing would happen to destroy that part of her happiness. Would Lance Raines figure it all out? Perhaps he would never even see her again. That would be best. Yet the thought of him brought the same hot desires he'd instilled in her the first moment she set eyes on him. This child was a part of that beautiful man. Surely the child would be beautiful, too. She would present Claude Françoise with a fine, healthy child with all the strengths and beauty his or her father possessed. The memory of those five days with Lance Raines brought a warm yearning to share his body again. But it would be best now that she never even saw him. She had told him she could have no children. What would he think of this? Surely he would put it all together and realize she had tricked him, realize that the child was his. And he was a proud, possessive man, a man with deep concern for those he considered his own. That was evident by his anger and urgency when he got the message about the little girl he'd rescued being hurt. If he was that concerned over a little girl who did not even belong to him, how would he be about a son or daughter of his own blood?

It was the only black cloud that spoiled her present joy, and her feelings were torn. On one hand she almost hoped something would happen to Lance Raines. Perhaps he would be killed by Indians, or perhaps he would quit the railroad and stay in Abilene with the old woman and the girl he was so fond of. But on the other hand, she did not totally relish the thought of never seeing him again, never being possessed by him again, never enjoying the ecstasy of being one with the beautiful piece of man who was Lance Raines. Yet the most important thing now was the baby. Not even Lance Raines could make her give up this wealth, this lifestyle, this prestige. The baby guaranteed all of that for her, guaranteed that Claude Françoise would keep her as his wife, for she would mother the man's heir and would therefore have a permanent hold on him. Claude must never, never suspect this child was not his own.

"How are you feeling?" he was asking her. "Have you seen a doctor?"

"I'm fine, Claude. But perhaps . . . perhaps we should move back east, where there are better doctors, for me and the child's sake."

"Nonsense! Denver has good doctors now. And I love this country. I want my son to be born in the mountains, to

242

grow up here where America's future lies. And look at you, so beautiful and strong and healthy. Surely everything will work out fine." He rose from his chair, pacing in his excitement. "March! What perfect timing! By May the Kansas-Pacific should reach Denver. We'll have one grand celebration, perhaps a tremendous barbecue right here on the estate, with the best beef from Texas. We'll invite the whole damned crew who have been building the K.P. We'll celebrate reaching Denver, and celebrate the birth of my son as well!"

She struggled not to pale. If he invited the entire crew, that would include Lance Raines. Would Lance come? Of course he would—out of meanness because she had tricked him with the note; and perhaps even out of a desire to find a way to bed her again. After all, the two of them had had a glorious time together. Claude turned to look at her, grinning from ear to ear. "And all the men will look with envy upon my beautiful wife and son."

She masked her concern with a smile. "How can you be so sure it will be a son?" she asked.

He came over and grasped her arms, pulling her up. "I feel it. After all of this waiting, surely it will be a son. Julien Pierre Françoise. You see? I have even been thinking of a name all this time. It will be a son!"

She puckered her lips and stepped closer, putting her arms about his waist. "If it's a daughter, will you throw me out?"

He laughed lightly and hugged her close, kissing her hair. "Of course not. We will simply try again. Perhaps now that you are pregnant, it will be easier the next time to get pregnant again." He gave her a squeeze. "Do I dare hug you tightly?"

"Of course. It won't hurt anything." She leaned back, and he bent down to kiss her hungrily, gratefully. He left her lips and rubbed his hands over her back. "From here on you do nothing but sit or lie down."

"I'll be fat!" she objected. "i'm going to gain enough weight as it is. The doctor said I should go on about my business as I have always done."

"I don't care what he said. You have an easy life here, and lots of help. Take advantage of it, Jessica. Don't do anything to risk losing this baby. He or she means everything now."

She rested her head against his chest, hiding her worry, not about the baby and the birth, but about Lance Raines. Yes, this baby did mean everything, not just to her husband, but to her own future. What would it mean to Lance Raines?

Lance hunched under his blanket as a spring rain drenched him and Sotaju. He spread the blanket around him, protecting his rifle and handgun, and pulled his leather hat lower over his forehead. The surveyor he guarded waved that he was ready to move forward, and Lance waited for him to mount up with his equipment, then headed Sotaju over the next hill, scanning the horizon when he did so.

The long, cold winter had diminished any Indian threat, and Lance guessed that the northern Cheyenne were suffering from too much hunger and too busy keeping settlers out of the northern area to give them much trouble. Word was, they and the Sioux had joined in attacking the Union Pacific and settlers in areas even farther north. The southern Cheyenne were becoming resigned to reservation life, although there was always the threat of roaming, nomadic bands who opposed the treaty and continued to live as they pleased. And there was always the chance that both northern and southern tribes might roam the land hunting for buffalo, which were becoming more and more scarce.

He saw no sign of Indians, and he signaled the surveyor to go on about his work. The man dismounted and got out his equipment again. Lance got along better with this new crew. A few originals were still with the crew, but since he'd left and returned, a few had resigned, including Paul Thomas. That was fine with Lance. If he never saw the man again, he'd be satisfied.

He looked at the western horizon. They were close now, very close. Soon they would reach Denver. Should he go and see Claude Françoise, or just have his pay sent to him? His better sense told him to stay away all together, but an inner voice pulled at him, telling him he must see Jessica.

Why? He couldn't understand an almost urgent feeling about it. It had nothing to do with wanting to see the woman, or even wanting to bed her again, although he sensed that if he could be alone with her again, he'd do just that, out of sheer manly hunger, just as he had done the first time. But as long as she was not in his sight, he didn't even want her physically. It was something else that called to him, made him feel drawn to Denver. It was almost as strong and haunting as the vision he'd had about Cassandra.

He smiled to himself. Cassandra. When he thought of Jessica, his insides felt cold and animalistic. When he thought of Cassandra, he felt instantly warm and loved. It was odd how he wanted her so badly yet did not find it really difficult to wait for her. He almost savored the thought of it, the anticipation, as much as he knew he'd savor the real thing. But there were too many things in the way of claiming her now. He was too unsettled, and there was this damned, unwanted desire to go to Denver. Besides, he still didn't have enough money saved, and Cassandra was still too young.

But the memory of her satin, lily-white skin brought sweet urgencies to his loins. He'd seen the firm, young breasts, but could not taste them. He'd seen the soft blond hairs that hid the most womanly part about her, but he could not touch or invade such special places until the time

245

was right. He'd seen the woman she could be—some day. Yet there had been so much about her that was still child, and he wondered how such a small thing could ever make room for him; how such narrow hips could ever hold a child between them; how such small breasts could ever grow to nourish a baby.

He shifted uncomfortably on his horse. He realized he needed a woman. It had been a long time since he left Mattie's bed, and in that time he'd been teased by memories of Cassandra. He'd come back to the railroad to find there was still room for him. The scout who had replaced him was getting anxious to head south before winter penetrated the plains, and other good scouts were hard to find, most of them now working for the Army on Indian campaigns, or working for surveyors in the north who risked Indian attacks while determining routes for even more railroads.

Lance simply took over again, to Jim Beck's relief. The men had exchanged looks, but neither had spoken about Jessica Françoise. When Lance first reported to Beck that he was on his way to Abilene for an emergency, he had simply told Beck with anger in his eyes that the original note was not from Françoise at all, but from Jessica. Beck had given him an "I told you so" look, and Lance knew the man understood how deceiving the woman could be.

"I'll not tell Françoise you ever went to Denver," he'd told Lance. "I'll simply tell him you have temporarily left duty to tend to a family emergency. I'll find someone to take over, but don't take too long, Raines. You're the best. I want you back."

Lance had agreed, and keeping his word, he had reported back for service with the KP, even though he knew that would take him right back to Denver eventually. It was a chance he had to take. It was a good-paying job, and there was Cassandra to think about. If anything should really come from the sweet feelings he had for her, he wanted to provide well for her. She'd suffered greatly the last year or so. She deserved something nice, a house, security. He had no doubt she'd make a fine wife some day, and he was surprised at his own thoughts in that direction. He couldn't even think of such things until the girl was at least sixteen. Later this summer she would only be fifteen. Maybe he'd been wrong to ask her to wait, wrong to put ideas in her head he couldn't even be sure he'd follow through with. He was telling her to wait for a "maybe," and that was cruel. But there were "maybes" on her side, too. Maybe she'd find a nice young man who would sweep her right off her feet. Maybe her feelings would change as she matured, and she would grow out of her childish crush on him.

Still, so many things seemed to point toward the inevitable. Had *Maheo* led him to her in the first place? He only knew that he'd missed her company and conversation these cold, lonely months. Her letters were warm and sweet, long, diarylike passages of her daily activities; concerned comments about Kate, whom she had grown to love; talk about school. He worried about the farm boys, who she told him never said anything verbally or bothered her any more, but who looked at her with what she called "evil eyes." He'd make a point to visit those young men when he returned later in the summer, and they'd not look cross-eyed at her again. He was grateful to Mattie for "putting the fear in them," as Cassandra had put it. But he couldn't be sure how long that would last, and he'd not stand for Cassandra being abused, even though she'd argued that he not do anything to the boys.

It angered him to think how some whites judged people and presumed things. Just because Cassandra had been a captive of the Cheyenne, people figured her to be "spoiled." Would they be any more satisfied if she'd been returned beaten and burned and scalped? Probably not. They'd still consider her "spoiled," even though none of it would have been her fault.

Rain ran off his hat, and he bent his head, wishing he could light a cigarette but knowing it was useless in the downpour. He realized he owed Cass a letter, but it seemed his letters were short and lifeless compared to hers, and his writing was poor. Maybe in a couple of years, with all that schooling and "civilizing," she'd change her mind about how she felt about one Lance Raines, a wild, roaming man who lived like an Indian half the time. Maybe the settled young farmers would seem more attractive to her, their offer of security more dependable.

He watched water run in little rivulets across the soil, and thunder boomed across the land, making the earth shake. The rivers and streams would be swollen now, snow melting in the mountains and running to lower regions. It was spring, a time when life awakened to greet the sun again, a time the Indians loved, for the spring sun brought warmth to their bones and tipis, and with it came the buffalo hunts. It made him sad to think of how their beautiful, free lives were changing. It seemed he was sad about a lot of things lately. The running waters made him think of Indian tears, and of White Eagle. The awakening spring made him think of Cassandra's awakening womanhood.

He had no doubt that when and if the time came that Cassandra became his woman, he'd find sweeter satisfaction than he'd ever found in any other woman, and he would be true to her forever. But the fact remained he was a man, and she could not be a woman for him yet. That left needs to be fulfilled, which Jessica was even better at than Mattie. But the thought of the woman brought an odd depression, a mysterious dread. That was the only word he could find for it—dread. But why?

A gust of wind whipped about him out of the west, and he was so certain he heard someone call his name in it that he looked up and stared at the horizon. There was nothing there. It was so real, and created such a strong feeling he must go to Denver, that he was tempted to kick Sotaju into a gallop and head in that very direction. He frowned, studying the horizon. Something called to him, but what? He wondered if he should tell Cassandra about his feelings. No. It would only worry her.

Jessica. He damned her witchcraft, her odd hold on him when there was really no obvious reason for it.

"Raines!" someone called, startling him from deep thought. Lance turned to see the surveyor pointing toward a rise on the right. He looked in that direction, and through the downpour he could see a long line of Indians. He sat quietly, studying them intently, seeing women standing among some of the men on horses. One horse came forward slightly, turning then and prancing back and forth in front of the others.

Lance squinted, noticing the distinct and unusual black and white spotted mount, its rump painted red. "Kicking Horse," he murmured, his heart pounding with a mixture of joy and apprehension. Where was White Eagle? And what did his Indian brother want? Lance did not care to get into a skirmish with them.

He raised his arm and made a sign of peace, then called out to Kicking Horse in Cheyenne that he was friend and brother—Rainmaker.

Kicking Horse stopped then, sitting still. Lance turned and rode back toward the surveyor, who was pulling his rifle from its boot.

"Don't use that thing!" he called out. "I think they're peaceful. They have women with them."

The surveyor looked from the Indians to Lance with a frown. No Indian came upon the railroad in peace. He cocked the rifle as Lance rode up to him, and Lance kicked out, knocking the weapon from the man's hand. "I said don't use it!" he barked. "I'll take care of this!"

The startled surveyor rubbed at his hand, looking angrily

249

at Lance. "If they ride down on us—"

"They won't, damn it! This is my job, Decker, so do what I say. I'm sorry, but I had to keep you from firing. Now pick up your rifle and load up your gear. Ride back to the next man and on from there until all of you are back at camp. Tell everybody to sit tight. I'll be there soon to report."

Decker blinked back some of his anger, a little surprised and awed that Lance Raines would stay behind alone. "You sure?"

Lance backed his horse. "I'm sure. Do like I say."

The man scowled. "All right—only because I've got strict instructions to do what you say. What if you don't come back soon?" The man bent down to pick up his rifle.

"Give me until sundown. I know one of them. They won't harm me."

Decker shook his head and mounted up. "Suit yourself. But if you don't show up by then, we're calling in troops."

Lance glanced back up at the Indians standing nearly motionless in the downpour, looking lost and forlorn. "Don't be calling any soldiers," he told the man. "They won't be needed."

He turned his horse and headed up the gradual incline. Like everything else in this land, it was steeper and the Indians more distant than at first perceived. Judging distance was always a trick in such vast emptiness. It seemed to take him longer than anticipated to reach the black and white mount that belonged to Kicking Horse. Lance did not ride hard, but at a slow gait, assuring the Indians who watched him that there was no urgency—that he was coming simply to talk.

He reached Kicking Horse first, and he saw the sad, hard look in the man's eyes. The two men held each other's gaze for several long seconds, both sitting proud and straight, reading each other's eyes.

"White Eagle is dead," Lance said, reading his brother's

thoughts.

Kicking Horse swallowed and nodded. "He did not live through last winter."

Lance felt a dull ache in his chest, and his throat hurt. "Too many things are dying," he finally spoke up. "Part of me died when the soldiers came and took me from the Cheyenne."

Kicking Horse studied his white brother, glancing far into the distance below where he could see the end of the tracks being laid. From his perch he could scan the land for many miles around.

"My brother still works for the iron horse," he said.

Lance looked at him with watery eyes. "Your brother sometimes wonders where he belongs. It isn't easy for me, Kicking Horse, to have known and loved two worlds. Now there is . . . a girl soon to be a woman . . . a girl I hope to keep for myself. She's white. I work for the iron horse to get enough of the white man's money so I can settle the white man's way and build her a house."

A faint grin passed over the face of Kicking Horse. "Could she be the same girl my brother rescued from Crooked Neck two winters ago?"

Lance sniffed and turned away, not wanting Kicking Horse to see his tears over White Eagle. "She is."

He felt Kicking Horse's hand on his arm. "This is a surprise, finding you this way. It is good. We come in peace, my brother, only to hunt the buffalo, which we have tracked this way. Are we safe to camp here so our women and children can get dry? Or will the people of the iron horse call the soldiers for help?"

Lance turned back, grateful for the rain on his face, which mixed with his own tears. "It's safe."

"Come then. We will have the women put up lodges. Three Stars Woman and her sister are with me." He grinned. "I am sure you remember my sister-in-law. She is now my second wife, but not the favored one. If you would

251

like her companionship, I would not object, nor would she."

Their eyes held. "My heart is too heavy," Lance replied.

Kicking Horse nodded. "Come. We will get dry—then talk." He turned his horse and headed back up the rise.

"You go on ahead," Lance told him. "I'll come in a few minutes."

Kicking Horse nodded. "I understand."

The man rode ahead, and Lance dismounted. In spite of the rain, he removed his blanket and his buckskin shirt, laying them both over Sotaju. The only father he truly remembered, and who had loved him as much as any son, was dead. White Eagle had taught him strength and skill, bravery and honesty. He had taught him everything he knew, for Lance had been determined never to be helpless again as he had been when his parents and sister died.

There must be a sacrifice. No true Cheyenne lost a loved on without letting blood in sorrow. The pain of the wound relieved the pain in the heart, and the sacrifice helped the loved one walk the milky road of stars to the place where warriors again rode free and hunted, where the buffalo were plenty and fat, and where he rejoined other loved ones gone before.

He removed his knife from its sheath and closed his eyes, praying for strength. He took the knife then, and quickly and deliberately gashed a long slice up his left arm. He stood there trembling in the rain, tears spilling on his cheeks and blood running from his arm to the ground, where it mixed with puddles and was washed into the earth, from where all men came, and to which they all returned.

Lance chewed on a bite of prairie turnip, a basic staple of the Cheyenne, gathered every spring by the women. He ate his raw, while Three Stars Woman cut some into a pot of water with fresh rabbit meat to make a stew. Lance and

Kicking Horse sat near a central fire, wearing only their loincloths, while their buckskin clothing hung on pegs nearby to dry out.

"What is happening in the north, Kicking Horse?" Lance asked between bites.

"For now things are good, but they will get worse again." Kicking Horse sat smoking one of Lance's cigarettes. "Red Cloud has won the war for the north country, forcing the soldiers out and burning all their forts. It is good. I rode in some of the battles. We claim much land now as our own, and the Great White Father has said he will provide food and supplies because we are surrounded by white settlement and the buffalo leaves us. But the White Father wants us to go all the way to the Missouri River to claim these things. This is many hundreds of miles. We are too few and sick and tired to go so far. Red Cloud refuses to go. He chooses to stay on the White River. He fears if we go all the way to the Missouri, the whites will come into our land while we are gone and claim it. Now Red Cloud has been invited to go all the way to that place where the sun rises to visit with the Great White Father and talk about it. I think he will go." He took a drag on the cigarette and glanced at Lance. "What do you think? What will happen there?"

Lance frowned. "He will see how great the white man's cities are. He'll see that there are more white men than sands in the desert, and that it is useless to fight them. He will hear promises from the white leaders that won't be kept. He can go, but it won't do any good."

"I fear the same," Kicking Horse replied. He sighed. "Why do white men always break their promises?"

Lance chewed for a moment. "They don't always break them," he finally answered. "But when it comes to land and money and possessions, they do whatever is convenient at the time. The white man has a great hunger for such things. I don't know why." He set the turnip aside. "I want money, too, but for a special reason. I'd never kill or cheat

253

to get it. Even I don't understand the extent of white man's lusts, and I'm white myself." He thought about Claude Françoise dealing in slave trade to get rich, selling human beings, breaking up families, tearing children from mothers' arms. He didn't care that he'd bedded the man's wife. He didn't care about Françoise or about Jessica.

"It is a sad thing," Kicking Horse said reflectively. "And very bad. Always the white man wants more land, more iron horses to get him to the hills and mountains where the golden metal lies. What good is golden metal? It means nothing to us. But already the whites send their little men with instruments into the north country to see about building yet another railroad to bring in more whites. Soon we will be at war again, to keep out the iron horse. It goes on and on, and I do not see how we can ever win, even under Red Cloud. I feel caged, my brother. Trapped and hunted. I know not where to turn. Sometimes it seems death is the only freedom for us now."

Lance rolled his own cigarette. He took a deep drag. "I'm sorry, Kicking Horse. I feel a part of you, and a part of that which you fight against." He lit the cigarette. "My heart is torn, and right now it bleeds for White Eagle. Perhaps it's best he died before worse things happen to the Cheyenne."

Kicking Horse nodded. "Perhaps." He glanced at the deep cut on Lance's arm. "You should let Three Stars Woman dress your wound."

Lance glanced down at it. He wanted it to hurt. It was necessary. "It will heal." He looked over at Three Stars Woman and her sister, thinking perhaps he'd have been better off living this life. Kicking Horse didn't have to make many decisions when it came to women, and with two beautiful wives he must be a very satisfied man. Lance already knew how pleasing the younger wife could be. She smiled at him now and he smiled back, but in his grief for White Eagle, he had no desire for her.

"Let her rub sweet oil on your cold, aching muscles," Kicking Horse told him. "You will change your mind about wanting her once she has helped you relax."

Lance turned his eyes to his Indian brother's and grinned more. "That's possible. But I told the railroad men I'd be back by sundown."

Kicking Horse shrugged. "So go back. Who says you cannot return here later?"

They exchanged teasing looks, and Lance laughed lightly, feeling better. "Some things will never change, no matter what else happens to us," he commented.

Kicking Horse nodded. "This is true. You will come back, then?"

Lance thought for a long time. He could relieve his frustration over Cassandra, at least temporarily. And in a way perhaps he could say good-bye to a people he loved, for it was becoming more and more obvious he could never return to the life of his youth. Somehow sleeping with Kicking Horse's young sister-in-law seemed a sweet and innocent good-bye. And he did not want to insult Kicking Horse or the woman, one or the other of whom might take offense if he kept refusing their generous offer.

He nodded then. "I'll come back after I report in."

Kicking Horse smoked quietly. "I thought you would." He sat up straighter. "See how I trust you, my brother? I know you will not betray me and bring soldiers."

Lance looked down at his arm again. "I would never do that, Kicking Horse. I may be white now on the outside, but in my heart I am the son of White Eagle."

The night was spent in sweet dreaming that he could stay with the People. But with the morning sun came the reality that he must go. There was little that could be said in words. It was all said in the eyes, and in the quick embrace Kicking Horse gave his white brother inside the tipi before

Lance exited. These were not the same old happy times. Lance glanced at Buffalo Woman, the young sister-in-law he had slept with. It was strange how Indian women could give themselves out of pure friendship without it being wrong. There was a beautiful freedom about these people, an unrestrained joy and an ability to get the most out of life and nature that the white man would never appreciate or understand. It seemed in the white man's world relationships were so strained, so full of responsibilities and rules. There were few rules among the Indians, and those they had were followed without question. Children were not disciplined; they were simply so loved that they obeyed out of that love. That was the way it would be with a child of his own. He knew already how he would feel about a son.

He walked up to Buffalo Woman, gently taking her face in his hands and kissing her forehead, thanking her in Cheyenne for her sweet friendship and hospitality. He turned then, unable to look back, walking out to his waiting horse and mounting up. The morning brought sun and warmth. The clouds were gone. With a heavy heart he headed down the hill toward the railroad camp, his mind swimming with memories of better times, and with confusion over Jessica and Cassandra, both women gnawing at him now more than ever, for different reasons. He decided it would be best not to see Jessica again. When this job was finished, he would go back to Abilene. Then his better sense told him he could not do that either, for Cassandra was barely fifteen. But he would go anyway. He had to at least see her again, see how she had grown over the winter.

After several minutes of riding, he approached the work crew and a pacing, impatient Jim Beck, who looked up at him with a scowl when he rode into camp.

"You didn't send for those soldiers, did you?" Lance asked, dismounting.

Beck sighed. "No, I didn't, against my better judgement. Those Indians are not where they belong, Raines. I should know better than to listen to you on something like this. I'll probably get axed for this one."

Lance walked around Sotaju to face him. "You won't. Why start something with peaceful Indians? They aren't out to harm anyone. Why start trouble where there is none in the first place?"

"And what would you do about it if I did send for soldiers?" the man challenged.

Lance gave him a hard, cool look. "I'd kill you, for starters."

Their eyes held, and Beck knew Lance meant what he said. The man swallowed and cleared his throat. "Well, at least you're honest," he said with a nervous smile.

"That's the only way to be with Indians, Beck."

The man sighed deeply. "All right. We'll let it go." He reached into a shirt pocket. "Besides, we're getting close. I'd say we'll be in Denver inside of three weeks. This message came by telegraph this morning out of Denver. It seems all of us in charge of things are invited to a grand celebration at the estate of one Mr. Claude Françoise when we reach Denver."

Lance frowned, taking the note.

"Send word soon as reach Denver. All crew leaders, scouts, surveyors, foremen, engineers, suppliers and cooks invited to celebrate with free whiskey and beef at my home. Time will be arranged upon arrival in Denver. You are also invited to help celebrate the birth of my son, Julien Pierre Françoise. Here's to the Kansas-Pacific, and my son!

"Claude Françoise."

Lance paled visibly. The birth of a son? How? Jessica had said she could not have children. And when was he born?

"It seems our lovely Mrs. Jessica Françoise is now a loving, doting mother," Beck was saying as Lance stared at the note. "I find it rather humorous, don't you?"

Lance kept staring at the note. A son. Julien Pierre Françoise. Why had Jessica lied about being able to have children? It made no sense.

"Lance? You in there?" Beck tugged at the note, and Lance blinked. He handed back the note without a word, mounting back up and riding away from camp.

A son. Jessica Françoise had given birth to a son, yet she had said she could have no children. Around and around the thought spun in his head as he tried to put it all together: Jessica, her promiscuity, the mystery about her reasons for running after men, her telling him she could have no children, and now she had a son. Again there was the odd pull at him, and he knew that though he did not want to go back to Denver, or to see Jessica Françoise again, he must do so anyway. There was something left unfinished, yet he wasn't sure what it was. There were questions to be answered, and before he gave his heart and life to Cassandra Elliott, he must finish whatever was left unfinished with Jessica Françoise.

Chapter Fifteen

The early evening mountain air was crisp, and the voices and fiddle music coming from the Françoise estate were easy for Lance to hear. He sat on Sotaju at the base of the hill on which the Françoise house sat. Most of the men who had decided to accept Claude Françoise's invitation were at the house now, drinking free whiskey and enjoying rich, roasted beef. Lance hesitated, still trying to decide if he should go at all.

Their arrival in Denver, a city which had grown to surprising proportions in the year Lance had been gone, had brought cheers and hails from Denver citizens, especially the businessmen; and the last days of construction had been spent under constant watch from curious bystanders and interested customers. Lance had quickly tired of people staring and asking questions, tired of remarks about his own Indianlike clothing, tired of the noise and movement of the city. But he needed his pay, and Françoise had insisted he wanted very much to see Lance Raines again and pay him in person. After all, it had been nearly two years since their first meeting, as Françoise's personal letter of invitation to Lance had pointed out. The man had mentioned having something to discuss with Lance, and he had left Lance little choice but to go.

Now Lance stared at the house. He didn't want to go. Not

only did he not want to see Jessica, but he especially did not want to see her while in the presence of her own husband. All he really wanted was to go home to Abilene. But he had not only been invited here; he had also been drawn here by his own intuition. He was still bothered by the fact that Jessica had given birth to a son. He had trouble admitting to his real suspicion. He didn't want to think it. And perhaps that was why he was afraid to go to the Françoise house. It wasn't Jessica he was afraid of seeing. It was the baby, and the look in Jessica's eyes. He would know by that look. He would know where Jessica Françoise's son had come from.

Surely it couldn't be. Yet so many things made sense when he thought about it now. She'd told him she was barren. Surely she'd done so to assure he'd bed her often and use no protection. Why? There was no answer but the obvious. She had deliberately planned to get pregnant. She had deliberately tried, and she had used Lance Raines in her scheme. Perhaps that was why there had been so many others—a strange attempt at getting pregnant. Was Claude Françoise impotent, or did he just have lifeless seed? Either way, why would Jessica go to such lengths to get pregnant?

Again he argued that none of it was true. It would be easy to argue that, if she hadn't told him she could have no children, as though to say he could bed her all he wanted. And if it was true . . . He counted the months again. Françoise's letter had announced his son had been born April 12th, 1870, nine months exactly from the five days he had spent with Jessica.

His heart tightened again. No! Surely it was not his own son! He didn't want to know. He didn't want to find out. He especially didn't want to see the child. If he saw him, he would know. He would feel the spark of knowledge that the Great Spirit would put into his heart. In a way, the spark had already taken place. He was almost certain that was what had made him feel so drawn to Denver.

If it was so, what could he do about it? He had to think

carefully. To try to say the child was his might endanger the boy's life, and Jessica's. She was his mother. He didn't want any harm to come to the child or the mother, much as he hated Jessica for what she had done. A baby needed its mother, and in spite of what she was, Lance sensed she would be a good mother. What would a man of Françoise's wealth and power do if he suspected? Would he have them discreetly disposed of? Who could tell with a man like that? Anyone who dealt in slave trade could not have much regard for human life, and in his anger, anything was possible.

He felt trapped. If by some cruel fate the boy was his, how could he leave Denver? How could he ever offer anything to Cassandra? A great share of his heart would lie right here in Denver, in one Julien Pierre Françoise. He had never bothered thinking until lately what it would be like to have a son, how he might feel about one. But every time he considered that Julien could belong to him, his heartbeat quickened, and a surge of love and possessiveness shot through him with fiery passion, more passion than he'd known for any woman. A son! He knew one day he'd want one, more than one. But not this way. If he had a son, he wanted him for himself, wanted to be near him, to love him, raise him, teach him, hold him. It was a need as old as time for a man to be with his son.

He dreaded going up the hill, yet he knew he must. Perhaps it would all be for naught. Perhaps he'd see in Jessica's eyes the boy belonged to someone else, maybe even to Françoise. Perhaps the boy was adopted. If Jessica could just come up with a logical explanation of why she'd told him she could have no children, he'd be happy. Somehow he had to find her alone, had to ask, had to look straight into her eyes.

He headed toward the mansion, where carriages lined the circular brick drive in front. He knew he would look and feel out of place, for he had chosen to dress as he always dressed. He didn't care about making impressions, hated stiff suits

261

and the way the rich had of talking. At least today most of the men here were not the wealthiest, and he knew them. They were all friends now. The heat of the summer and the cold of the winter on the plains were over. They had all been through snake bites, gunshot wounds, frostbite, Indian attacks and prairie fires. They had made it through the boredom without killing each other off. They had shared many things together, and Lance smiled bitterly at the realization that some of them had also shared Jessica Françoise.

Was it all her plan then to get pregnant? Jim Beck had said he suspected some ulterior motive, just as Lance had suspected. But pregnancy was the last thing he would suspect, and surely Jessica knew it. Yes. It did all make sense after all, and as he approached the mansion, his heart felt as heavy as lead. He dismounted and tied Sotaju. The music was louder now, and he could hear laughter from the back lawn. The smell of roasting beef filled his nostrils and teased his hunger, but an odd pain in his stomach accompanied the hunger. He wondered if once he saw Jessica he'd be able to eat at all.

He walked around the house to the backyard, where up to fifty men stood about, talking in small groups, some sitting on blankets playing poker. Many were the railroad men he knew. Others were Denver businessmen he did not know and didn't want to know. A huge side of beef was being turned over hot coals by two servants, and on a nearby table were several bottles of whiskey and glasses.

"Raines!" Beck called then from Lance's left. The man headed toward him, and heads turned. Françoise spotted him then also and started toward him.

Lance's chest tightened. Did the man know? Suspect? He glanced around the lawn but Jessica was nowhere to be seen.

"Here's the best man of the bunch!" Beck was saying about Lance. Françoise reached him at almost the same time, putting out his hand. Lance took it, searching the man's eyes, studying them, seeing no sign of animosity. It was obvious he didn't know or even suspect, and again Lance wondered how the man could live with a woman like Jessica and not know, especially when she'd been a prostitute before they married.

"Lance, I've heard a lot about your exploits out there on the plains!" Françoise was telling him, shaking his hand vigorously. "Especially the story of how you outran a pack of Indians with a surveyor sitting on your horse behind you."

Lance forced a smile and nodded. "Yes, sir. But I expect some of the stories got exaggerated."

The Frenchman looked him up and down. "I highly doubt it. You're a hell of a good man, Raines. I knew you would be. I know how to pick my men."

Lance nodded again. "Thank you." He looked around again. There simply was no Jessica, and no baby. He wanted to ask about them, but did not want to appear too interested.

"Well, I am glad to be able to give you men some refreshment and a big thank-you for a job well done," Françoise was telling him. "Today Denver, tomorrow all of Colorado!" He laughed, his eyes red from too much whiskey. He took Lance by the arm and pulled him around, introducing him to slick, suited businessmen who smelled of money, many of them overweight, men who laughed too easily, their eyes not matching the laughter.

Lance quelled an urge to tell them all what he really thought of them, for every time he looked into the face of one of these wealthy men, he could also see the face of a starving Cheyenne. The Indian bred into him made him long for the privilege of taking his knife to each man and watching each one sweat and beg for his life. How utterly enjoyable that would be. When it came down to it, no man was better than any other, and a man was proven by his strength and bravery, not his money. But men like this did not understand such things. These men had come to rape the land, shoving away or killing off anything and everything in their way. They were exploiting the West, exploiting the men who slaved away in their gold mines, exploiting the people from whom they bought land for the railroad, people who unwittingly sold their land cheaply, not realizing that one day it would be worth millions.

Again he wondered what he was even doing here. If there was still money to be made in trapping, he'd be doing that instead. But trapping had died out. There were not so many wagon trains a man could scout for now; the railroad had taken over most of the business of getting people west. He could not bring himself to scout for the Army, because that would mean hunting down Indians. So he had resorted to the railroad, good money for doing what he knew best. But as soon as he had enough, he'd quit this business and get on to what he loved most—horses, maybe a ranch—and maybe, some day, Cassandra. For once in his life he had begun to see what he really wanted.

But all of that might be ruined now. What of Jessica Françoise? What of her son? If only he had not fallen into her witch's spell, allowing himself to believe there could be no harm. His one last wild and reckless move might have cost him his happiness, and a son.

Voices and faces whirled about him. He answered questions about Indian life, prairie life, some of his own adventures. Yet he hardly heard himself speaking. He heard Françoise telling someone all the wives were inside where it was cooler and would be out later in the day. All the wives. Jessica, too? And the baby? Surely the man intended to show off his son.

He drank whiskey. He needed it. After an hour of answering trivial questions and accepting "thank-you's" from some of the crew, Françoise took him aside. Lance wanted to grab the man around the throat and tell him he suspected the man's son was his own, that he'd come to take the boy. But he knew it would be a foolish move. He had to see the child, see Jessica. He had to think about all of this.

"Lance, you're a hell of a good man," Françoise was telling him. "You're strong, smart, skilled and unattached. I'd like to keep you on."

Lance frowned, lighting a cigarette and studying the smooth Frenchman who bought and sold people like cattle. "Doing what?" He took a deep drag on the cigarette.

Françoise grinned. "It doesn't end here, Lance. Surely you know that. I believe I mentioned to you two years ago that plans were in the making to build a railroad north from Denver to meet the Union Pacific in Cheyenne. And we'll go south, too—all the way to Pueblo, and on to Santa Fe, if luck is with us. And there will be lines into the mountains, mining country. The railroad could make a fortune if it could reach those mines and haul the gold out. There is much more to come, Lance, and I'd like you to be a part of it."

"I don't understand. I'm a scout. A line going north or south from Denver wouldn't need too much in the way of what I do. You've chased just about every Indian out of Colorado, so what would you need me for?"

Françoise lit a pipe. "You're right about the Indians, Lance, although there are still a few renegades out there. But I'm not worried about that. I'm worried about losing any of my better men. You know the railroad business better now. And you have an air of authority about you. I'd give you more responsibility—crew leader—something like that. With your experience out here, your knowledge of the land and survival, you're a valuable employee. It would mean even more money." He winked. "That could help you buy a fine ranch some day to settle on with that little girl you were so worried about last summer when you ran off on Beck."

Their eyes held. Did he know Lance had gone to Denver first? From the man's eyes, Lance was sure he didn't.

"I'm sorry I had to leave; but the girl is special to me, and she'd been hurt bad—trampled by cattle. I had to go."

Françoise knitted his eyebrows and puffed the pipe. "No problem, Lance. I'd have come back from the other side of the world to be with Jessica when she had her baby."

Lance struggled to show no emotion. "Did everything go

well?"

The man beamed. "Perfectly. Jessica is such a healthy woman. That's part of the reason I married her, you know, to give me healthy heirs. But then no man can deny her beauty, right?"

He laughed and Lance smiled and nodded. "She is a beautiful woman," he agreed. Already he was beginning to see the picture. Had the man threatened to leave Jessica flat if she didn't present him with heirs?

"Well, the boy came a little early, considering he was probably conceived last summer after I came back from a trip to San Francisco. But he was born healthy and beautiful, every limb in place, alert and bright-eyed. At first his eyes were a light brown, but now they're changing to a beautiful green. Can you imagine that, as dark as my Jessica is? I'm trying to think who in my family might have had green eyes. I think I had an aunt with green eyes."

He looked straight at Lance, and Lance wondered if the man was just being clever, or if he was really that ignorant. His own eyes were an unusual green but Françoise didn't seem to even notice. Never had Lance had to struggle so hard to stay in control and hide his emotions. Green eyes! The boy had green eyes! It couldn't be. It hurt too much to think it. A son. A son he could never have for himself without a legal battle. And how could he ever win a legal battle against Claude Françoise? And even if he tried, what would Françoise do to the boy? Maybe he would even sell off both Jessica and the boy into some kind of slavery in another country. The man was capable of doing just that.

There was only one way now to be close to both Jessica and the boy until he could think straight and know what to do about the whole predicament.

"I'll stay on, Mr. Françoise," he told the man. "I do need the money, and I appreciate the opportunity."

Françoise smiled and grasped his shoulder. "I hoped you'd say yes," he told Lance. He frowned then. "Oh, say, do try to keep from punching out any more of my surveyors, though, will you?"

Lance grinned. "You heard about that?"

"Ah, yes. But then men do get a little edgy out there, don't they? By the way, how is that little girl in Abilene?"

Lance sobered. "She's better. But she almost died. The bones didn't heal right and had to be rebroken. That's why I stayed so long. She was healing fine when I left."

Françoise grinned. "Good! Good! But tell me what's this about her being so young?"

Lance took another drag on his cigarette. "The whole thing is nothing serious yet. I rescued her a couple of years ago from the Cheyenne. That's how I got to know her. Her entire family was killed, so I brought her to Abilene to live with the white woman who raised me. We became good friends. I can't say anything will ever come of it, but I have enough patience to wait until she's old enough to be looked at as a woman."

Françoise laughed from deep in his throat. "Take it from me, my man, there is nothing sweeter than taking a young one, in spite of how pleasurable a grown, appreciative woman can be. I dearly love my Jessica, but I've had my share of young Negro girls, and servant girls. Don't pass up a good thing if the girl is willing. Actually, I prefer it when they are unwilling."

Lance looked away, forcing himself not to punch the man in the face. He needed this job, needed it to stay close to Jessica and the boy. And he knew now more than ever that he did not want his son to be raised by such a man, raised into lust and evil, to put money above all other things and to have such little regard for human life.

"I prefer to wait until she's a little older. I care about her too much," he answered, throwing down and stepping out his cigarette. He wondered if the man had attacked any young Indian girls.

"Well, to each his own, my boy. I'm sure a man with your

physique and looks can have any woman he wants."

Lance looked him straight in the eye then. How tempting to tell him he'd had the man's own wife. "I've had my share," he answered.

Françoise laughed and slapped him on the back. "Take the rest of the summer off, Lance. Go home to Abilene and see to that little girl, if you want. Report back to Denver by November. It won't be long after that when the narrow gauge will begin construction."

"Narrow gauge?"

"Yes." He lowered his voice. "A lot of this is still confidential, Lance, but since you'll be a part of it, I'll fill you in a little. Under the direction of a Mr. William Palmer, a real railroad dreamer, we're building a narrow gauge railroad into the mountains. The tracks are only three feet wide rather than the over four and a half feet width of most railroads. This matches the narrow lines going into the mines, meaning no stopping to transfer loads. And a narrow gauge is lighter weight, the rails easier to work with, and its narrower bed easier to lay along the sides of mountains. The smaller engines and track bed mean smaller tunnels to blast. All around, it's the perfect railroad for a territory like Colorado; and, I might add, I forsee Colorado becoming a state in the not-too-distant future."

Lance shrugged. "I suppose that's good, for those who care."

Françoise chuckled. "You should care, son. You should care. You'll be a part of all of it. You're a part of this great land. You'll settle here some day."

Lance thought about White Eagle and the Cheyenne. "Maybe. Maybe not. I may settle in the Dakota's, closer to the northern Cheyenne, maybe Wyoming or Montana."

"Well, the same thing is happening everywhere, my boy. But you watch. Colorado will prosper more than any other territory, and Denver will be the hub of the entire West, thanks to the railroad."

Lance sighed, bored with the same old speech, and looked around again. Jessica. He had to see the boy. "I'll be back in November," he told the man. "I'm thinking of heading north and joining the Cheyenne for the Sun Dance after I leave Abilene. But I'll get back here in time."

"Good! Good! Go and cut yourself a slice of that beef over there, Lance. And there is homemade bread to go with it, and plenty of fruit and all the whiskey you want. I'll see you in November."

The man left him, and Jim Beck approached Lance, his eyebrows raised as he watched Françoise leave. "I have a game of poker going over here, Raines. Care to join us — while away the time until the women come out?"

Lance frowned. "Why not?"

"Hey, Raines, don't let that damned witch get to you."

"I didn't come here because of her!" Lance snapped. "Leave it alone, Beck."

The man shrugged. "I hope you don't feel guilty talking to Françoise like nothing ever happened. Neither one of those two is worth feeling guilty over."

"It isn't that. Where's your card game?"

Beck indicated with his arm and started walking. Lance was tired of these people, the babbling and laughter. It all rang in his ears. He supposed he would just have to wait it all out. He had to see the child, and Jessica.

The afternoon sun finally dropped behind the mountains. It had only been an hour, but seemed more like a whole day to Lance. Laughing, visiting women came out of the house then to join their husbands. Only the wives of the prominent businessmen were there, for the railroad men all came from other places and still had families to return to. Some of the women gave more than a second look to Lance Raines, who was not only fascinating by his size and dress, but the most handsome man there, standing taller than the others, holding back, quiet and observant. A few of the women insisted on being introduced, and they batted eyes and fluttered fans, the look in the eyes of some of them not much different from the way Jessica Françoise had first looked at him. He knew the only difference was that most of them would never follow through on their thoughts as Jessica had done.

A few of the men refused to even introduce their wives to the buckskin-clad scout, telling them he had once lived among Indians and could not be trusted. Lance could only grin at their remarks when he overheard some of them. He'd heard such remarks before. He was used to them. Besides, the only thing that was important was to see Jessica. But she was not about.

Finally Françoise came from the house, holding an infant. Lance's chest tightened, and he pushed through others to get closer, as Françoise shouted from a garden step, holding up a baby with dark hair and skin.

"Friends and fellow railroad men, I would like to introduce my first-born son, Julien Pierre Françoise, three months old today."

The crowd sighed and clapped and women jabbered. Lance stared as Françoise turned in a circle holding the boy on display like a statue. He couldn't take his eyes from the baby, fat and dark and beautiful. He could not quell the voice that told him this was his son, and he found it difficult to breathe.

"My wife and I are leaving on an extended tour of Europe," Françoise was announcing. "Jessica needs the rest. I will return in three months, but Jessica will stay in Spain for the winter, where there is eternal warm sunshine. So, this party is to let all of you see my son before he disappears for a while."

No! Lance wanted to run up and grab the boy from the man's hands. He couldn't take the child away! For months? Maybe a year? He stepped closer as Françoise lowered the boy and settled him into the crook of his arm.

"Ah, Raines, come and have a look!" Françoise called out. Several women surrounded the man, some of them using it as an excuse to get closer to the mysterious scout. Lance paid no heed to any of them. He had eyes only for the baby. The boy opened his eyes, his beautiful tiny mouth breaking into a toothless smile. The eyes were green, green as Lance Raines's eyes.

Lance swallowed, putting out a finger for the baby to grasp. And he knew. In his heart he knew. "He's beautiful," he told Françoise in a husky voice. He looked up from the child to see Jessica standing farther up on the garden steps. When their eyes met, Lance felt as though he'd been hit by lightning. She quickly turned and hurried away.

For the sake of his son, Lance forced himself to remain calm. He wanted to run after her, shake her until she admitted the truth, take her away if he had to and marry her just to keep his son. It was all there, in her eyes, so obvious, so undeniable! How he kept a straight face he would never know. He looked back at Françoise and smiled. "You should be very proud," he told the man.

"Oh, I am! I shall miss the boy greatly this winter, but I'd be gone so much due to our new railroad venture that it won't make much difference that Jessica stays in Spain. She gets lonely and bored here in Denver in the winters. The trip will be good for her."

"I'm sure it will." Lance glanced at the boy again, a beautiful child, perfect, strong, a fine son. He needed no proof it was his son, and his heart burst with love. "Excuse me, I'll let these ladies get their feminine pleasure over the child."

He turned away, talking through the crowd of guests and past Jim Beck, saying nothing. He casually made his way to a grove of aspen at the back corner of the gardens, where there was no one to see him grasp a tree and look up, his eyes filled with tears.

"Help me, *Maheo*," he groaned. "What can I do?"

He felt sick. Cassandra. How could he even think about Cassandra now? How could he think about anything but how to get his son? Maybe Jessica would consider leaving Françoise and going away with him.

But no. Jessica Françoise intended to keep her lifestyle. It all made sense now. She had presented her husband with a son, insurance that she would remain a part of the Françoise empire. She had told him once she never intended to give up the life she had found with the man.

He looked toward the house. He didn't dare make a scene, but if he could just talk to Jessica. He moved around the side of the house and to the front door. He knocked.

A maid answered, and he asked to see Jessica.

"I'm sorry, sir. Mrs. Françoise is indisposed. She doesn't feel well and has gone to bed."

He didn't believe it. "Give her a message," he said quietly. "Tell her—"

"It's all right, Marian," he heard Jessica's voice speak up. "I'll talk to him."

She exited from the parlor doors, and Marian nodded and hurried away. Lance remained in the doorway, his eyes watching her with a mixture of anger and pleading. She stepped close, standing just inside the open door.

Lance struggled to stay in control. How he wanted to beat her! If she were not Julien's mother . . . "You told me you couldn't have children!" he hissed between gritted teeth.

She shrugged. "I didn't think I could. What do you care?"

"He's mine!" he whispered savagely. "He's mine, isn't he?"

His eyebrows arched in surprise. "Whatever gave you that idea?"

"You know what gave me that idea! The timing from when we were together—"

"Together? You and I? And when was that?"

Her eyes flashed a warning. She would not admit it in a million years, and if she did not admit it, Françoise would never believe him. There was little hope, even with her cooperation. Without it, there was no hope at all.

"Why are you doing this?"

"I'm not doing anything. But I might ask what you think

272

you're doing, Mr. Raines. I believe you're supposed to be out back with the others."

He grasped her wrist. "Bitch! You haven't heard the last, Jess! You picked the wrong man to play your games with. That boy belongs to me! My blood runs in his veins, and I'll not have a man like Claude Françoise raise him!"

He gave her a push when he released her and walked down the steps and out to Sotaju, mounting up and riding off without another word. Jessica watched, blinking back tears of fear. Lance Raines could ruin it all. But what was worse, he must understand that Claude Françoise must never know, for fear of the boy's very life. It was just as she feared. Lance Raines would not be an easy man to control.

Lance spent the night in restless sleep on the open plains, thinking, praying, the face of the baby boy vivid in his mind. What could he do without endangering the welfare of the child? He had only to remember Jessica's face to know it was his. How she must have hoped she would not see him again, or that he would be the kind of man who would not care. But he did care! How could he go through life knowing the son of Claude Françoise was his, watching the child grow, reading about him in the news? Perhaps the child would grow to be as ruthless as Françoise. He could not bear that thought. Such a pretty child, so innocent, so perfect. His son!

By morning he fell into an exhausted sleep, waking when the sun was high. He was still at a loss as to what to do. He cleaned up camp and rode into town, paying for a bath and a shave. He had to see the boy again. He would use the excuse of visiting Françoise once more to find out more about his job. He rode to the mansion, which could be seen from town, nestled on the hill overlooking the city Françoise was helping support and build. Lance's chest hurt so badly he wondered if something was wrong with him. He urged Sotaju into a gentle run. If not for the predicament over his son, it would be a beautiful morning, for the sky was a vivid blue, the greens never greener, the reds never redder. But Lance saw no color. He saw only the face of a baby boy and for the first time was hit full force by the aching realization of what his wandering ways had cost him. He had gone from no responsibility to almost more than he could bear.

He headed up the hill again, to the outlandish mansion he was beginning to hate more and more. He dismounted and tied his horse and went up the familiar steps, knocking at the door. The maid did not look surprised when she saw him, for she knew him better now.

"Mr. Raines, is it?"

Lance nodded. "Is Mr. Françoise at home?"

"I'm sorry, sir. But both Mr. Françoise and his wife left early this morning in a buggy, with all their luggage and the boy. They boarded an early train east. They're on their way to Europe. Mr. Françoise will be back home in November, if you wish to call on him then."

Lance paled, his heart torn. "How . . . how long ago?"

"Oh, at least three or four hours, sir. Mr. Françoise ordered a very early train. For some reason his wife insisted on leaving early today. She's been quite irritable lately, you see. That's why Mr. Françoise agreed to let her to go to Europe in the first place. He—"

"Never mind," Lance interrupted. He turned and went back down the steps to Sotaju. He mounted up. If they had gone by train, there was no way he could catch up with them. Even if he could, what would he tell them? His son was being taken away, clear across the sea to another land. There was no chance of seeing the boy again until perhaps the next summer. There was nothing he could do now but wait and hope that when Jessica returned, some kind of miracle would make her admit the boy was Lance's, and she would come to him. Perhaps he should steal the boy, but then he would be a hunted man, always running with his child. He didn't want that, either.

He turned Sotaju and headed east. He'd go home now — home to Abilene and Kate — home to . . . Cassandra. What was he to do about her now? Perhaps he should be cruel to her and tell her to forget everything and find some nice young man to settle with, for he could not settle until he had his son.

But the picture of her pretty face and big, trusting, blue eyes haunted him. How could he tell her such a thing? Yet how could he want her but not touch her? How could he make promises he could not keep? How could he commit himself to her while some other woman was living halfway around the world with his blood son? Yet how could he bear the thought of some other man being Cassandra Elliott's first, invading that which Lance felt more and more belonged to him?

Maybe Kate could help. Yes, he'd talk to Kate. And even though he could make no commitments to Cassandra, he could at least see her again. He'd missed her bright smile and the way she had of making him feel better about things. Cassandra. She was nearly fifteen. How much had she grown?

Chapter Sixteen

Cassandra hung a sheet on the clothesline, noticing a rider in the distance. At first she thought nothing of it, but as he came closer, her heart pounded with joy and anticipation. Who else sat that tall on an Appaloosa horse. She could see the fringes of his buckskin clothing. Rainmaker!

She dashed into the kitchen. "He's coming!" she shouted to Kate, hurrying up the stairs. "I'm a mess!"

Kate turned from a pan full of dishes and wiped her hands on her apron, grinning and shaking her head at the girl's excitement. The words could only mean Lance was back.

She walked to the screen door and went outside, shading her eyes to see him coming closer then. He urged Sotaju into a gentle gallop and was soon riding up to the back door.

"It isn't exactly spring," Kate chided. "More like late summer."

Lance grinned and dismounted, and Sotaju put his head down and began nibbling at grass as Lance hugged the woman close. "It's good to be here, Kate."

She caught an odd sadness to the words, a ring of sincerity to his voice that told her this was not the usual devil-may-care Lance Raines. She leaned back, her hands at his waist, and looked up at him. "You look tired and thinner, Lance Raines. What's wrong?"

He smiled and put an arm around her, walking her up the steps and into the kitchen. "A lot of things. We'll talk later. Where's Cass? I want to see her."

He sank wearily into a chair while Kate took a pie from the shelf. "She came flying through here like a jackrabbit when she saw you coming. I think she intends to change her dress and comb her hair."

He met her eyes and she nodded. "Oh, yes, young man. Her feelings for you haven't changed one whit. So you just watch yourself while you're here. I've never seen her move so fast."

Lance grinned. "She okay? Those boys been leaving her alone?"

"Far as I know. But she might not say anything, just to keep from worrying me . . . and you. You'll have to ask her yourself." She set some pie in front of him, and he rubbed his stomach.

"Looks good, Kate. But I haven't had much appetite lately. I'm not sure I can eat the whole thing."

She frowned. "You not eat a whole piece of pie? You sick or something?" She came over and felt his forehead.

"No, I'm not sick. I am hot, though. You care if I take off this shirt?"

She stepped back, planting her hands on her hips and studying him. "There's for sure something eating at you bad. Is it something to do with that woman in Denver?"

His eyes cooled, and she worried at how his face hardened. "I said I didn't want to talk about it right now." He rose and pulled off his shirt.

"If you want to go around half naked, then do it outside. In here you can at least put on a vest. Go and get one before you sit down to that pie. I'll pour you some coffee."

Their eyes held, and she saw a pitiful sadness in his. He sighed and went out, still almost as obedient as a young boy around Kate McGee, but only out of respect for her.

277

He returned minutes later wearing a vest, and just as he was about to sit down, Cassandra came into the room.

Lance stood at his chair staring, at first speechless. He never dreamed a girl could change so much. She was even taller, perhaps five feet and three or four inches. Her golden hair hung in cascading waves about her shoulders, freshly brushed. She wore a bright blue dress that matched her blue eyes, and it fit her tiny waist tightly, but was gathered at the bodice to accent full, firm breasts. Part of their fullness could be seen just above white lace that decorated the slightly low neckline of the dress. It was obvious the dress was for a special occasion, but she'd put it on just for him.

She reddened under his appreciative gaze as his gentle green eyes moved over her inch by inch. His own surprise was obvious. Her face was beautiful, fair and smooth, her lips full and sensuous. Could she really be only fifteen? Even though the dress was full, he knew the legs and hips beneath it were slim and firm. Could the day ever come when those slender legs would be wrapped around him in the ecstasy of being one with him?

Cassandra felt hot and weak. Why was it every time she saw him he seemed more beautiful than ever? What had happened while he was gone? How did he feel about her now? How she loved him! Did he like the way she looked, the way her breasts had filled out, the way she brushed her hair?

"Hello, Rainmaker," she finally spoke up. Her throat felt dry.

He nodded, surprised at the mellow tone of her voice. He flashed a warm, provocative smile. "You get prettier every time I see you."

She reddened even more. He was so beautiful. His size and masculinity filled the small kitchen, overpowering everything: so broad, so dark, so muscular, the hair so thick, the eyes so green and beautiful. What must it be like to be Lance Raines's woman?

He walked up to her then, and she hoped she wouldn't faint when he took her arm. "Come sit down," he told her. Did he remember his parting words when last he came? He'd asked her to wait for him. Would she get to be alone with him again, get to find out if he still wanted her to wait?

She walked to the table, suddenly embarrassed and speechless.

There was so much she wanted to say, and she felt there was much he wanted to tell her also. But he was so much man. How could she begin to tell him anything? It seemed it was easier when she was younger than it was now. Was that because she was more aware now of man and woman, more informed about what a relationship involved, more overwhelmed at the thought of ever lying beneath this man of men?

Kate watched with some alarm. There was obvious magnetism between the two of them, and she knew how Cassandra worshipped Lance Raines. And not only was Lance Raines obviously impressed by Cassandra's beauty, he was also a man who no doubt knew how to handle women and had a healthy appetite for them. She shoved the pie closer in front of him.

"You going to eat this sometime this afternoon?" she asked.

He tore his eyes from Cassandra to meet Kate's warning look. He just grinned. "Yes, ma'am." He picked up his fork when Cassandra gasped.

"Rainmaker! Your arm! What happened to it?"

Kate followed the girl's eyes to a long, wide, white scar on his left forearm. Lance met Kate's eyes when he replied.

"White Eagle died," he told her, losing the smile he'd worn moments before.

The old woman nodded. "I'm sorry, Lance."

Cassandra frowned in confusion. "But your arm! What does that have to do with your arm?"

Lance sighed and cut a piece of pie while Kate answered for him.

"It's the Cheyenne way, Cassandra. When you lose a loved one, you make a blood sacrifice in mourning. The physical pain eases the pain in the heart."

The girl stared at the arm wide-eyed. He'd done that to himself? She remembered his fond parting from White Eagle when first he took her from the Cheyenne, remembered his sadness at the man's ill health. So, this was how deeply Lance Raines could love, that he would inflict such a wound in sacrifice for the loss of a loved one. Would he have done the same if she had died from her wounds? Her eyes teared.

"I'm sorry, too, Rainmaker, about White Eagle. How did you find out? Did you see him?"

He swallowed some pie. "No." He took a drink of coffee before continuing. "I saw Kicking Horse. He and his family and some others were moving south in search of buffalo and came across our railroad site. I had a hell of a time keeping the railroad men from calling in soldiers. They were there in peace. I stayed the night with Kicking Horse."

Cassandra's stomach wrenched with jealousy. Was Three Stars Woman's sister with them? Had he slept with her again? And she wondered about the woman in Denver. Had he been with her, too? And would he go see Mattie while he was in Abilene? The thought of his being with any of them made her hot with anger. But she could not show it. He was looking at Kate now, still talking.

"Things are worse than ever for them, Kate. It makes me sick. It isn't just White Eagle dying that bothers me. They're all dying, slowly but surely. And there isn't a damned thing I can do about it."

He sighed and leaned back, running a hand through his

dark hair.

"You go up and get some sleep," Kate told him. "You look terrible. Whatever it is that's troubling you besides the Cheyenne, you'd best tell me when you're rested. There's a sadness in those green eyes I've never seen before."

He rubbed at his eyes. "I do need to sleep. Where can I bed down?"

"Use Cassandra's room for now, your old room. We'll worry later about where you'll sleep for the night."

He glanced at Cassandra, who was flushed at even the thought of Lance Raines sleeping in her very bed! "You mind? I need a bath, but I'm tok tired even for that."

"Of course I don't mind," she answered.

His eyes moved over her again. How nice it would be to hold her in his arms as he slept. He had so many things to tell her. Yet how could he tell her he had a son? How would she react to such news? He got up from the table then and put one hand on the table and the other on the back of Cassandra's chair, leaning over her.

She looked up and met his eyes, trembling at the thought of his strong arms around her. Would he ever truly embrace her, truly kiss her the way a man kissed the woman he wanted? She would never forget that first kiss, but it had been a light kiss of "maybe." Would there ever be a lingering kiss of "promise"?

"Do me a big favor and unload and brush down Sotaju, would you, Cass?" She smiled, and he wanted desperately to taste her mouth.

"Yes. I'll take good care of him."

"I know you will." He breathed deeply before straightening, as though to fill his nostrils with the scent of her. He looked at Kate then. "Don't wake me till I wake up by myself, which might not be till tomorrow morning," he told the woman. "I haven't really slept well in weeks."

"Then you go get that rest right now. We'll not bother you."

281

She rose and walked around to him, patting his arm. "Whatever is troubling you, you just forget it for now and sleep," she told him. "We'll work it out, like we've worked other things out, Lance. You hear?"

He smiled sadly. "I hear." He bent down and kissed her forehead, then walked on weary legs up the back stairs to Cassandra's room. He felt pleasant urges at its bright cheeriness, its feminine touch, the light scent to the air. Yes, he was more and more sure what he wanted. If not for having a son . . .

His heart tightened again at the thought of it. His son. His little boy, thousands of miles away from him, overseas in a strange land. What if Jessica chose never to come back? What would he do then? His throat ached again with the lump that seemed constantly there of late. He pulled off his leggings and moccasins after removing his weapons belt. He threw everything, including his vest, on the floor and pulled back the covers to the bed. He crawled into it and was soothed by the softness of the sheets, the light scent of Cassandra Elliott. If only he could hold her, sleep with her, make love to her. Fifteen wasn't such a terribly young age to him now, but it would be to Kate; and he knew that to take her in such youth when he couldn't pledge his life to her would be cruel. How could he pledge himself to anyone until he had his son? And how was he ever to get the boy?

"Julien," he whispered, hugging a pillow. He was glad there was no one to see his tears.

The room was dark when Lance stirred to the sound of a squeaking dresser drawer. He shifted in the bed, opening his eyes for a moment and sensing someone else was in the room.

"Cass?"

He heard a sigh. "I'm sorry," she replied softly. "I came

in to get my gown. I know right where it is. I thought I could get it without disturbing you. Darn this old dresser."

He stretched. "Where are you? Come sit on the edge of the bed a minute."

The room was silent, and he sensed her hesitancy.

"It's all right, Cass."

He heard her soft footsteps as she came to the bed and sat down on the edge, her back to him. He felt for her arm and grasped it, and she shivered with the thought of being in a dark room with Lance Raines, sitting on the same bed with him. He in turn fought a strong urge to pull her down close and let what happened happen.

"I . . . I shouldn't be here," she whispered.

"Don't worry about it. I just wanted to tell you—" he squeezed her arm—"you're beautiful, Cass. More beautiful than I imagined you'd be."

There was another moment of silence, then a sniffle. "Am I truly?"

"Yes, you are." He gently squeezed the arm again. "I told you to wait for me, Cass. And if I seem . . . distant . . . it has nothing to do with you. All I can tell you for now is the wait might be longer than I thought. It isn't your fault, or even because you're so young. It's . . . something else."

He heard another sniffle. "It's that woman in Denver, isn't it?"

"Not exactly. You just have to trust me, Cass. We'll talk about it, but first I have to talk to Kate. Is she still up? What time is it, anyway?"

"About ten. Kate's down in the kitchen."

She heard him sigh. "I think I'll go and talk to her. How has she been?"

"Better, I think. She hasn't acted sick or complained much."

"Good. Go ahead and get your gown on. I'm going downstairs. Can you sleep with Kate tonight?"

"Yes."

There was another moment of silence, both of them thinking the same thing.

"You'd better get out of here before I do something that's against my better judgment," he told her quietly.

He heard her swallow. "I wouldn't care."

He leaned up and grasped a handful of cascading, golden hair.

"Go on, Cass."

She sighed. "Rainmaker?"

"What?"

"Would you . . . would you go to a dance with me?"

"What dance?"

"Friday night. It's for all the young people around Abilene. It's being held at my girlfriend's farm, in a big barn — fiddle music and dunking for apples, and popcorn and all sorts of other things to eat. People can go alone, or they can bring anybody they want. I've told all my friends at school about you. I would so love for you to be the one to take me."

He thought for a moment. "I don't think so. Maybe I could just sort of show up later on, to keep an eye on you. But it wouldn't look good, a man my age and all taking someone so young."

"Please, Rainmaker. I don't want to dance with anyone else."

"You're the prettiest girl in Abilene. A lot of young men will want to dance with you."

"But I don't care. I just want to go with you, be just with you."

He sighed. "I don't think so, Cass. Are those farm boys still giving you trouble?"

"Sometimes. But they don't push me around or anything. They just talk and look at me."

"Bastards!" he whispered. "You go to that dance," he spoke up louder. "I'll be watching for that bunch from the shadows."

"Oh, please go with me, Rainmaker."

"No more arguments. And get your gown and get out of here. You're being cruel to me sitting here on my bed in the dark."

She got up. "How am I being cruel?"

He moved to the edge of the bed and put his feet on the floor. "If you don't understand that, you still don't understand everything about men, which is all the more reason for me to stay away from you. Now get going."

She walked toward the door. "I said I'd wait forever for you, Rainmaker. I meant it."

"I know you meant it," his voice replied through the darkness. "And I'm sorry I'm so unsure about it all. You're a fine girl, Cass. It's like I said. If some young man comes along offering you all a woman could ask for, you think real hard on it."

The door opened, and he saw her silhouette in the hall light. "You're all a woman could ask for," she answered. She quickly left and he grinned at her boldness. He rose and pulled on his leggings by the light of the hall, then fished around on top of the dresser for his tobacco pouch, picking it up and heading out of the room and down the back stairs.

Kate was untying her apron and hanging it over a chair when he came into the kitchen. She looked surprised when she saw him standing there, his eyes sleepy and his hair disheveled.

"What are you doing up? You're supposed to stay in bed the rest of the night," she chided.

"Cass came in to get a gown and it woke me. I don't sleep too well lately." He sank into a chair and put his elbows on the table, holding his head in his hands. "I'm in trouble, Kate."

The woman quickly sat down. "Trouble? What kind of trouble? Did you go and kill some man without thinking,

285

like that one up in Nebraska? If I hadn't argued your way out of the noose for that one—"

"No, nothing like that," he interrupted. "It's worse than that. At least to me it is."

The old woman frowned, putting a hand on top of his head and smoothing his hair. "What is it, Lance? You know you can tell Kate."

He sat there silently for a moment. "My God, Kate," he finally spoke up brokenly. "I have a son."

She moved her hand to grasp his arm. "A son! Where? How? Are you sure he's your own?"

"I'm sure. I don't need any particular proof but my own gut feelings, his green eyes, and the look on his mother's face when I saw her."

"The woman in Denver?"

He nodded and sighed, dropping his hands. His eyes were red and watery. "She's a witch, Kate. That wealthy Frenchman she's married to thinks the boy is his. But his wife is no better than a whore. Mattie Brewster is a better woman than that one. She flaunts herself, literally begs a man to take her to his bed. Any man would have done what I did. But it was all a strange game with her. She deliberately tricked me."

Kate leaned back, folding her arms. "Tricked you? Lance Raines tricked by a woman? I find that hard to believe."

He clenched his fists out in front of him on the table and stared at them. "It's true, Kate. She told me she couldn't have children, and while her husband was away I spent five days with her."

Kate sighed and shook her head. "You pay a price when you don't settle, Lance. I've told you that before. And I warned you that woman was trouble. You had no business messing with a man's wife, no matter how bad a woman she was. I know Indian wives sometimes leave their husbands and go to another man; but that culture isn't like ours, and you've got to learn to live by white man's rules." She leaned forward, resting her arms on the table. "So what is this about a son."

He met her eyes. "I went back to Denver to see her husband about getting my pay. He gave a big cookout for all the railroad men when we reached Denver. He's offered me a job on a new railroad venture. At any rate, he announced his new son, born April twelve of this year. Yet his wife had told me she could have no children. I counted back. April twelve was exactly nine months from the week I spent with Jessica. I got suspicious. Why did she tell me she couldn't have children? And why did she literally beg me to make love to her? I'd wondered before, but couldn't put it together and didn't care. But when she had the baby, I realized what she'd been up to."

"She used you to get pregnant?" The woman rubbed at her neck. "That doesn't make sense."

"I'm afraid it does, Kate. Jessica told me once she'd never give up the rich lifestyle her husband affords her. For some reason she'd never gotten pregnant by him. She was testing—finding out through other men. She wanted to give that man a son, to ensure he'd keep her and she'd never lose her life of luxury. A baby was her insurance, Kate. Don't you see? Now that she's given her husband an heir, she'll be more special to him."

Kate shook her head in dismay.

Lance opened the tobacco pouch and took out a paper, then began rolling a cigarette. "I know I'm right. I was only half sure when I went to that party. I knew if I could see Jessica and the baby, I'd know if the boy was mine. Now that I've seen them—" His voice choked again, and he lit the cigarette, taking a deep drag and rubbing at his eyes. "He's mine, Kate. Take my word for it. That boy is mine, and I want him!"

She leaned back again "You want him? You have no rights to him, Lance Raines. And if you go claiming him, there's no telling what a powerful man like this one you've described would do to you. You leave it be, you hear me? You leave it be."

His teeth clenched, his eyes so watery that one tear spilled onto his cheek. He quickly wiped it away. "I can't," he replied in a low and heated voice. "He's my son, Kate!" He got up from his chair and took another drag on his cigarette. "If I had gone into that knowing she could get pregnant, I'd agree I have no right to the child. But she deliberately lied to me in order to conceive. It was a cruel trick, and her deceit gives me a right to that child. I never would have risked a child if I thought for one moment I could never have him. If I got a woman pregnant, I'd marry her, just so I could be with my son. But there's no marrying this woman. She'd never leave her husband for what I have to offer her. Now she's gone off to Spain. Spain! With my son! Good God, they might not even be there yet. I don't know how long it takes a ship to get overseas. What if the ship sinks? What if she chooses to live in Spain? I might never see the boy again!"

Kate hung her head. "Lance. Lance. What am I to do with you? I don't know how to help you with this, son. And you must remember that to fight this woman's powerful husband could mean harm to the boy and his mother. God only knows what he might do to them."

He turned and sank back into a chair, laying his cigarette in an ashtray. "I wish you could see him, Kate. He's beautiful. He's so perfect: healthy, dark, a wonderful smile, thick, dark hair, and eyes green as the sea."

She smiled, her own eyes tearing. "Like yours."

He put his head down on the table, and she stroked his hair. "What am I going to do, Kate? I might never even see him again."

"All you can do is pray, Lance. Pray that something will happen that will mean you can have him for yourself. But if God chooses that that child should stay with his mother and her husband, you have to accept that. You risk such things when you live a wild and reckless life. Why do you think I've always been after you to settle?"

He sighed, feeling like a little boy. "I want my son."

"Then I shall pray for you, too. Oh, how I'd love to see any child of yours." She kept stroking his hair. "Have faith, Lance. I'll have faith in my God, and you have faith in yours. Things have ways of working out the way they're supposed to be." She sighed deeply, a pain gnawing at her chest again. But she said nothing about it. "What about Cass?" she asked "You should tell her, you know."

"I know. I'm all mixed up now. I can't make her any promises, Kate, and she's still so young."

"You'll just have to explain. And you'd best not touch that girl until you know what you're going to do about your son and that woman in Denver. You understand that, don't you?"

"I know." He ran a hand through his hair and raised his head, picking up his cigarette and taking two last drags before there was not enough left to smoke. He put it back in the ashtray to burn out. "She said something about a dance Friday . . . wanted me to take her. Maybe I should do that much. It seemed so important to her. Do you think it would look bad?"

Kate stood up herself, patting his arm. "I don't think you should worry much about that. She'd be so thrilled if you took her. Just remember her age and her soft heart. Don't break that heart, Lance. Don't go laying claim to something you can't really have yet. You might even have to be marrying that Denver woman. Right now it's that boy that has control of your heart, and that's something you've got to deal with first. I don't know what to tell you to do about that, or about Cassandra. You talk to her. Take her to the dance if you want. But you remember your place."

He stood up and put an arm around her tiny shoulders.

"I always feel better when I talk to you, Kate. I know I've not been around much, seem damned ungrateful sometimes, but I don't mean to be. I love you, Kate."

She patted his stomach. "I know that. And I love you."

"How are you feeling? You doing okay?"

She smiled. "I'm just fine. I just get tired, but all old people get tired. And I think we'd both best get some sleep now." She stopped and looked up at him, tears in her eyes. "I hope you find a way to get your son, Lance. But whatever happens, always keep him above all else. Don't let your own pride and passion for the boy endanger his life."

Their eyes held, and he embraced her, unable to answer because of the tightness in his throat.

Chapter Seventeen

Lance finished dressing. It was the first time in years he'd worn white man's clothing. But it was for Cassandra. He couldn't take her to the dance dressed like an Indian. People made enough remarks already about her captivity. He looked in the mirror, adjusting the uncomfortable jacket of the black suit over a white shirt that was pleated in front. He studied the black silk tie and decided he didn't like the way it looked. He quickly untied it and retied it into a flat bow at the throat. That was supposed to be the style, but he didn't like it at all.

He frowned at himself, turning his head and smoothing back his hair. Yes, he was truly a white man when he dressed this way. He sometimes wished he could change that, but there was no denying the green eyes, or the fact that he would some day settle and live like a white man. But until he knew what to do about Julien, there would be no settling.

He turned and looked at his weapons belt on the bed. He was not accustomed to going anyplace without weapons, and he decided to at least take his knife. He removed his belt and took the knife and sheath from his weapons belt, hooking his dress belt to the loop on the back of the sheath. He turned it backward so that he could shove the knife inside his pants at the side, where it wouldn't show. It would be uncomfortable, for it was a large hunting knife. But he felt better carrying something. Perhaps it was left over from his days with the Cheyenne, but he couldn't bring himself to go anyplace completely unarmed.

He turned again and adjusted everything, making sure the knife didn't show. He used one of Kate's guest rooms, insisting on paying her like any other guests would do. He had also deposited more money into a special bank account to be used for Cassandra and had paid off some of Kate's debts. Even after all of that, he had plenty of money saved. He had that much for which to thank Claude Françoise. He was making more money than he'd ever made before in his life. The more and sooner he saved, the sooner he could think more seriously about Cassandra.

Envisioning her as his wife, sleeping with him every night, cooking for him, carrying his babies, all was sweet to dream about. But also in the dream he had Julien with him, too. If not for his unfortunate decision to sleep with Jessica, he would be the happiest man alive at this moment. But the thought of a son existing somewhere left a dark spot in his heart and brought an ache to his chest that would not go away.

He supposed he was as ready as he'd ever be. He still didn't feel completely right about taking Cass to the dance; but he owed her some little bit of pleasure, and she wanted this very much. He left the room and went down the back stairs to find her already finished dressing and ready to go. She stood in the kitchen talking nervously to Kate, asking if she looked all right, turning around in a white dress with blue and yellow flowers printed on the material. The short sleeves were puffed, and the scooped neckline revealed just enough virgin bosom to send a man's thoughts wandering. Her skin looked so soft he wanted to run his fingers over it just to see. Her long, golden hair hung down her back in curls, drawn up at the sides and held there by pins. Fresh flowers decorated her hair on each side. She was the image of innocence and beauty, and when she turned and saw him watching her, she blushed.

He flashed a handsome smile. "You look beautiful, Cass."

She put a hand to a hot cheek self-consciously. "Do I, truly?"

"Why do you always ask that? I only speak the truth, Cassandra Elliott." Would his life always be this torture, longing for a son he could not have, and for a beautiful young girl he could not touch? Her gaze was running over him now, and Kate stood back staring also, smiling and nodding.

"I've never seen you in regular clothing before," Cassandra spoke up. "You look . . . wonderful." She smiled. "I'll be with the most handsome man in Abilene. My girlfriends will envy me."

He grinned bashfully then. "I don't know about that. If they knew all my wild ways, they wouldn't be so envious."

She stepped closer. "That doesn't matter. I know what a good man you are." She swallowed. "Thank you for taking me, Rainmaker."

He took her hand and bowed ceremoniously, kissing the back of her hand. "My pleasure, sweet lady," he told her with a wink. He looked over at Kate, putting an arm around Cassandra and leading her toward the door. "Don't wait up, Kate. I may keep her all night."

The woman's eyes widened. "Lance Raines, you mind your business!" she warned.

Lance just laughed. "When are you going to learn not to take me so seriously, old woman? I'll have her back by ten o'clock."

She grinned then. "See that you do."

Lance led the girl through the door to a horse and buggy he'd rented from the livery. He lifted her by the waist into the buggy as though she were a feather, and the touch of his strong hands about her waist sent pleasant feelings through her body. He walked around and climbed up himself, picking up the reins and pushing off the brake, shouting to the horse to get moving.

Cassandra sat staring ahead, suddenly self-conscious and nervous. They were alone for the first time since he'd arrived three days earlier. He'd spent most of his time sleeping and taking care of banking business. She suspected with a hot jealousy he'd been to see Mattie Brewster, but wasn't sure and was afraid to ask. He still had not told her whatever it was that bothered him, the reason he'd said she might have to wait longer than expected for him to make any decisions.

"Will there be a lot of people at this thing?" he was asking her.

"Probably. You just go straight through town and east of it. The barn is so big you can see it from the end of town. Susan Greene lives there. Her father agreed to have a dance for all the young people before school starts again. Susan is a good friend. She was nice to me, even when I first came here."

"Well, then, she must be a very nice person."

"She is. I've told her a lot about you. She's anxious to meet you." She looked at him then. "You won't dance with any of the other girls, will you? You'll just dance with me?"

He grinned. "Just with you. But I'm not much good at this dancing business. About the most dancing I've done is swinging around to piano music with a glass of whiskey in one hand and a pros—some wild woman in my other arm. But I suppose I know enough that I won't embarrass you."

She quelled the burning jealousy his mention of other women always brought to her heart. "You could never embarrass me, Rainmaker."

They rode on silently for a moment. "Will those boys be there," he asked then, "the ones who gave you trouble?"

She adjusted her dress so it wouldn't wrinkle. "I don't know. I suppose they will."

"Good," he said coldly. "You'll have to introduce me."

She looked at him again in surprise. "Introduce you? I wouldn't introduce a pig to those smelly boys!"

"Well, you'll introduce me. Promise me you'll point them out and introduce me if they're there."

She frowned. "You won't get yourself in trouble, will you?"

"I won't get in trouble. Don't worry about it."

She studied the strong, dark hands that held the reins. How long would it be before she could enjoy him in every way, give him pleasure in return? When would he start looking at her like a woman? What was troubling him now, the reason for the odd sadness in his eyes all the time? He was a changed man since he returned, calmer, less good-humored, sad.

It took twenty minutes to get to the Greene farm. Lance climbed down and tied the horse, then came around and helped Cassandra down. For a moment he just stood there, his hands at her waist, as though he didn't want to let go of her.

"Cass." She looked up at him. "Promise me that . . . you won't hate me for anything I might have to tell you."

She shivered. "I could never hate you. What is it, Rain-maker?"

To her surprise he bent down and kissed her cheek. "We'll talk later." He took her arm and walked her to the barn from which fiddle and banjo music could be heard, as well as someone calling square dances, voices and laughter echoing through the soft night air.

When Lance and Cassandra walked in, several people turned to stare. A few knew Lance Raines, knew the untamed man that he was, knew of his strength and skills and that he was seldom crossed by another man. But quickly some of them began whispering. Was he actually the escort of young Cassandra Elliott? What had really happened when he rescued her two years ago? Had the Indians raped her or not? Had Lance Raines laid his claim on the poor girl?

Many others didn't know who Lance was; for he'd not been around Abilene much these past two or three years, and a lot of new people had come in since then. Those who knew him whispered to those who did not. "That's the man who lives with Kate McGee sometimes. She took him in after soldiers took him away from the Indians. He's white, but he lived like an Indian and sometimes he still does." . . . "I've heard he's killed a lot of men and can be very vicious." . . . "That's the girl he rescued from the Cheyenne. But she's so much younger. She shouldn't be with a man like Raines."

All the while they clucked and whispered, the men were simply covering their jealousy of Lance Raines's looks and reputation, while the women were covering their inner curiosity of what such a man would be like in bed. Several young girls walked up to Cassandra, some giggling, all staring, some blushing at the sight of her handsome escort. What was it like to be with such a virile, wild man. And such beautiful green eyes!

Cassandra introduced them, using Lance's real name. "But I call him Rainmaker," she added. "That's his Indian name."

"Did you really live with Indians, and ride in war parties and all those things?" Susan asked, wide-eyed.

Lance grinned, feeling like a statue on display. It irritated him, but he went along with it for Cassandra's sake. "I really did," he replied with a slight bow.

The young girls all gasped and giggled, and Lance urged Cassandra away from them toward a table where punch and food were set up. "You want something?"

"I guess a little punch."

A square dance was called, and several people danced in the middle of the dirt barn floor, whirling and stepping to the calls.

"I'm sorry if my friends embarrassed you, Rainmaker," Cassandra was saying.

"Never mind about that." He thanked a gawking farm wife for two glasses of punch and handed one to Cassandra. They both watched the square dancing.

"Don't ask me to square dance," Cassandra said with pleading eyes. "I get all mixed up at the calls."

He winked. "I'm not much at such dancing myself." He looked around the room. "Those boys here?"

Cassandra searched the large barn carefully, spotting the three troublemakers sitting in a loft and staring down at her, pointing and laughing. "They're in the loft," she answered. "The biggest one in the red-checkered shirt is Huey Brown. The skinny one with blond hair is Johnny Sorrell, and the other one is Richard Gobles."

Lance glanced up and watched them. When they caught him looking at them, their smiles faded, and they pretended to be looking at others. The square dance ended, and the fiddles whined away a waltz. Lance took Cassandra's arm. "Shall we?"

She reddened. "Oh, I don't know if I can do it very good."

"Nonsense! What better excuse to put my arms around you?" He led her out to where several farmers and their wives, as well as a few young couples, whirled around, some in fine dresses, some in simple cotton frocks. In this land such events were exciting and appreciated, for there was little to do in the way of recreation; and when a fair or a dance was held, nearly everyone in town showed up. It seemed that way tonight; and Cassandra was grateful there were so many, for they hid her own attempt at dancing smoothly.

"You're doing fine," Lance told her, his right hand at her waist and his left hand holding her right arm.

She looked up at him. "Am I truly?"

He laughed lightly. "There you go again. Yes, truly."

She smiled, feeling warm and happy. Their eyes held as they turned and swayed, and it was all said in that moment. Somehow, some day, they would be together; Lance Raines would lie naked with her, invade her, claim her, and she would know man. A vibrant, radiant feeling swept through them both, and he wanted to pull her tight against him but didn't dare. She couldn't remove her eyes from his handsome face and hypnotic eyes until the spell was broken by words that came from somewhere in the crowd.

"Squaw girl's with her big buck" came the voice of a young man.

Cassandra reddened and stiffened, and their dancing slowed. "Just keep dancing," Lance told her, squeezing her hand. Others kept dancing, pretending they hadn't heard the remark, embarrassed for poor Cassandra. Lance saw her eyes tearing, and he was consumed with rage. They finished the waltz, and Lance glanced up at the loft to see the three boys were not there. He quickly scanned the crowd to see them all laughing and heading out of the barn. "Stay right here," he told Cassandra.

"Wait! Rainmaker!" she called out. But he was instantly gone. She put a hand to her stomach. What would he do? Would he get in trouble? It would be her fault if he did. He was so much older than the farm boys, and wild enough that the townspeople might demand some kind of punishment if he hurt them, maybe even a hanging.

Lance quickly followed the three boys out of the barn. His keen well-trained eyes could see them even in the darkness, and he recognized them by the red-checkered shirt Huey Brown had worn in the loft. Like a stealthy Indian, he sneaked up on them as they stood outside the barn lighting pipes and cigarettes, pretending they were grown men. He waited and listened as they laughed about the remark that had been made by the biggest one, hearing them make dirty remarks about Cassandra, asking each other if they thought the man she was with tonight was the one called Rainmaker, and if maybe she slept with him.

He stepped into their circle then. "Why don't you three ask me personally about Cassandra Elliott?" he asked.

The three boys fell silent and stared at the tall, broad man who faced them in the moonlight.

"I'm called Rainmaker by some," he told them. "Lance Raines by others. I rescued an innocent little girl once from the Cheyenne, a sweet child who'd seen her parents slaughtered, as well as her little brother. That little girl was braver than all three of you filthy bastards put together! And to answer your dirty questions, the Cheyenne didn't touch that girl, nor have I. Is there anything else you'd like to know?"

The biggest one dropped his pipe. "N-no."

Lance whipped out his blade, and it flashed in the moonlight. As he drew it, he grasped Huey by the front of his overalls and jerked him forward. The other two wanted to run, but were torn between that and protecting their friend. Lance laid his knife against the boy's cheek.

"I've come out here to give you boys fair warning," he hissed, his face close to Huey Brown's. "Stay away from Cassandra Elliott! I'll be leaving Abilene again, and if I find out when I come back that you've been bothering her, I'll run this blade right around your head — slowly — and watch the blood drip down your ugly face while I lift the hair right off your scalp! You understand me?"

At that moment there seemed to be nothing civilized about Lance Raines. Huey Brown shivered and swallowed, his eyes bulging. The other two just stared. Even though there were three of them, none of them doubted Lance Raines could lay them all to rest even if they jumped on him all at once.

"Yes, sir," Brown squeaked. "I understand."

Lance yanked on the bib of the boy's overalls, and in a flash the big blade cut into them, slicing through the bib so that there was nothing to hold them up. He let go, and the overalls fell as Huey Brown stood frozen in place. Lance gave him a shove then, and he tripped on the overalls and fell backward. Lance shoved his knife back into its sheath.

"A warning to all three of you. You make up some lie

about what I did here tonight, and by God I'll come after you. I want no trouble over this, and none for Cassandra. You make trouble, and you'd better know you'll be looking over your shoulders night and day to see if I'm behind you! If you think you're all men, then you'd best be prepared to die like men!"

He left them then, and Huey Brown stood up, jerking up his overalls and holding on to them as all three of them started running.

When Lance reentered the barn, he saw Cassandra standing against a wall, avoiding others and watching the entrance for him. She walked quickly to meet him, looking him over as though she thought he might be hurt, yet knowing there was no way boys like Huey Brown could bring any harm to Lance Raines. But what had he done to them?

He just grinned and gave her a wink. "Everything is just fine. I don't think they'll bother you anymore, and if they do, you tell me, understand?"

She glanced over at the entrance. "Where are they?"

"I don't think they'll be back."

She put a hand to her chest. "What did you do to them?"

He led her back toward the dance floor. "It isn't what I did to them. It's what I threatened to do to them if they ever bothered you again. I think they got the message."

They were stopped then by a middle-aged, heavy-set man who smiled and put out his hand to Lance. "Lance Raines, I'm told," he greeted. "You're the brave young scout who rescued little Cassandra here from the Cheyenne a couple of years back."

Lance shook the man's hand. "Well, I got her back. I don't know about the bravery part of it."

"Why, of course it was brave!" the man answered, releasing the handshake. "I'm Bradley Greene, Susan's father. Why, Cassandra here has told us many times how you had to fight an Indian warrior to get her back, how you were

300

wounded and all."

Cassandra blushed and could not meet Lance's teasing eyes. She was sure he suspected she'd exaggerated the story, but she hadn't at all. It truly was a brave sacrifice he'd made.

"I lived among the Cheyenne for many years, Mr. Greene," Lance was telling the man. "It was my knowledge of their ways that helped get her back. And I suppose any man would have tried."

"Oh, don't be so humble, Raines. It isn't true that just any man would have tried. A lot of people in Abilene must have known the girl was out there, but you're the one who went after her. I thank you, for I know that if it had been my daughter Susan, you'd have done the same thing. Susan and Cassandra are good friends, you know."

Lance nodded. "Yes, sir."

"Well, it's nice to meet you finally. Any friend of Cassandra's is a friend of ours. I hope you enjoy our little get-together here."

"It's very nice of you to have it."

A moment later Greene was introducing his wife and some other friends. Susan moved close to Cassandra. "He's the most handsome man here!" she whispered excitedly. "You see, Cass? Most of the people are nice."

Cassandra's heart swelled with pride at the way people looked at Lance and were suddenly asking questions about scouting and the railroad and Indians. Lance seemed to know all there was to know, and she realized how worldly he was and how boring she must seem to him. There was a whole world out there for him, and all the women he wanted. Why would he think of settling with the likes of Cassandra Elliott? Perhaps she had exaggerated everything in her mind. Still, he had asked her to wait. And he had brought her to the dance, allowing her to show him off, meeting her friends. And the way he looked at her sometimes . . .

After an hour or so, Lance led her toward the door. "Let's

go for a buggy ride," he suggested. "All these people make me nervous. I want to be alone."

Her heart surely skipped a beat. He led her outside into the warm night air and helped her up into the buggy. He untied the horse and drove off, around the outskirts of Abilene. He halted on a low rise from which they could see most of the town, then put on the brake and wrapped the reins around a post on the buggy to hold the horse. He turned to her then, looking even bigger in the moonlight, his sweet masculinity overpowering her. Their eyes held, and then their lips met.

This was a kiss she'd been waiting for, the kiss that said she was a woman, not a child. His lips were gentle but demanding, parting her own with expertise, lightly moving his tongue to taste her mouth as he pulled her against himself, pressing the firm, young breasts against his hard chest. She could not tremble because he held her too tightly in sure, strong arms. Yet she was sure that if he let go of her she'd fall to pieces.

This was Rainmaker! This was the beautiful man she'd loved since he'd taken her from the Cheyenne. He was touching her, pushing her against himself, tasting her mouth hungrily. How she wished she knew what to do, wished she knew what followed a kiss, wished she was not so afraid of it in spite of this being her beloved Rainmaker.

His lips left her mouth and traveled over her throat, while one hand moved up to cup a breast and his lips traveled over her chest, gently kissing the whites of her breasts and forcing a whimper out from her throat. Never had she experienced such an utterly exciting, joyful, passionate feeling. He wanted her! He wanted her!

But then he seemed to go limp, letting out a long sigh and pulling her into his arms, resting her head on his shoulder.

"I shouldn't have done that," he said in a husky voice. "I'm sorry, Cass. I had no right."

"Yes, you did. I love you. You know I love you, Rainmaker. Kiss me a hundred times, a thousand times. Do whatever you will—"

"Cass, don't." He held her close, kissing her hair and placing a hand gently against the side of her face. "Cass, I have to tell you. There's something . . . something that keeps me from being able to just sit here and say for sure I'll come back when you're sixteen and want to marry you. I shouldn't say it that way. It isn't that I wouldn't want to, but I . . . might not be able to."

She frowned, turning her face to kiss his hand. "I don't understand."

He took a deep breath. "Cass, I . . . I have a son."

He felt her stiffen, and he held her tightly. "I know we've never really talked about us, Cass. It seems I've been waiting forever for you to get older. Now that you are . . ." He sighed deeply. "I've thought a lot about you, Cass. I thought when you were sixteen, maybe that wasn't so terribly young for marrying . . . having babies . . . if you wanted me for a husband. But now I've discovered I have a son . . . in Denver—"

"It's that woman!" she wailed, pulling away from him. "It's that horrible woman in Denver! And now you love her more, and you're going to marry her and be with your son—"

"No!" he interrupted, grasping her shoulders. "It isn't like that at all." He searched her disappointed eyes. "How can I explain it? She's already married, Cass, to a wealthy man she's not about to leave. We . . . we had an affair. She's no good, Cass. She's not the kind of woman you'll be—sweet and beautiful and loyal. She's worthless. It was just one of those things . . . just another woman. But then I found out she had a baby."

"It's probably her husband's," the girl wept, turning away from him.

"No, Cass. It's mine. I know it by the timing, and I was more positive when I saw the look on her face when I was in

Denver and her husband showed his new son to all of us. And as soon as she found out I was around, she left for Europe. She's on her way to Spain with my son, and God knows when or if she'll come back. He's mine, Cass! He's mine and I want him, and until I decide what to do about it, I can't make any promises to anyone."

"Oh, why!" she wept. "Why do things always turn out this way for me!"

Her tears tore at his heart. "Damn, I'm sorry, Cass."

"I can't bear it!" she wept. "I can't bear the thought of you being with other women, doing to them what I want you to do to me! And now . . . some other woman has given you a son . . . given you a son before I could! Maybe it will be years . . . before you find a way to keep him for yourself, if that's what you want. Maybe you'll even marry that awful woman to be with him!" She covered her face and wept. "Take me home," she wailed.

He sighed deeply and picked up the reins, kicking off the brake. None of this had turned out as he'd hoped—sweet promises from both sides, a gentle understanding on her part. But how could he expect her to understand, a fifteen-year-old girl sick with love for him. Girls her age didn't know how to handle such things, didn't know how to handle jealousy. Now he'd ruined her night, and he'd never felt more like a criminal.

He drove near the house saying nothing, then drew the carriage to a halt again. "Cass, please try to understand. I . . . I love you."

She looked at him then, her face covered with tears, her chest jerking in sobs. She took his hand and pressed it against her breasts. "If you love me . . . then show me!" she wept. "I don't care . . . about that woman . . . or the baby . . . or any of it! You're the only man I want, Rainmaker! And I want you to make me your woman . . . even if we can't always be together. I want you to be first. Prove that . . . you love me. Come to my room tonight, Rainmaker. I won't . . . be afraid. I just . . . want you to be mine . . . and nobody else's. You don't have to marry me. We can . . . still be together . . . and some day maybe you'll get to be . . . with your son."

She cried harder and climbed down, running toward the house in tears. He watched after her, kicking the running board of the buggy angrily, hating himself, hating Jessica Françoise, hating life itself. He turned the buggy and headed for Mattie's.

It was deep in the night when Lance returned, his heart reeling with love for poor Cassandra, a love made more passionate by too much whiskey. Cass. She'd asked him to make her a woman. Why not? He'd been putting it off too long as it was. Mattie had tried to console him, reason with him, stop him from leaving. He grinned at the realization he'd not even been able to make love to Mattie. That had never happened before. But it wasn't Mattie he wanted. It was Cass—sweet, young, innocent, beautiful, loving Cass. She was perfection—untouched perfection.

He groped his way to the back stairs and climbed them, but at the first landing, before another curving set of steps to the top floor, he was met by Kate.

"You smell of whiskey, Lance Raines," she said quietly. "You get yourself right back outside and sleep under the stars, or go back to that Mattie."

He took a deep breath. "Get out of my way, Kate. I'm going to sleep with Cass."

"Oh, no you're not," she said calmly.

He shook with anger. "I have to!" he hissed. "If I don't, I'll go crazy!"

"You've got women like Mattie for that."

"That isn't what I mean!" he shot back, trying to keep his voice down. "I'm not some kind of animal! I only mean . . . it's not the same, Kate. It just has to be Cass, that's all. I love her."

"Is that why she came running in here crying earlier? Her heart's broken enough knowing you have a son and can't make her any promises now. She's been crazy about you since you first brought her here. But she's still a child, Lance Raines, and you have a little matter to settle regarding a son in Denver, remember? You can't go into that room without marrying that nice girl, and you can't marry her until you get matters straight over that boy, because he'll haunt you and pull at you and it won't be good for your marriage. You get your mind straight about your son before you go making a woman out of that child in there."

He trembled, hanging on to the railing. "I love her, Kate."

"I know that. And if you truly love her, you'll turn around and walk right back down those stairs. That's the kind of man I know you to be, Lance. Don't disappoint me."

Their eyes held in the dim light of an oil lamp on the wall of the landing. Never had Kate McGee felt so sorry for anyone, but she would not let him do something she knew he'd regret later.

"Go on with you, Lance. You'll know come morning I was right."

He stood there several more long seconds before turning around without a word. He half stumbled back down the stairs. Kate was right. Kate was always right. Why was it he could handle himself so well when it came to grown women, but did crazy, stupid things when he was around a half-grown girl? For not knowing much about men, Cassandra Elliott was certainly turning him in circles.

"Kate?" he called up to her.

"I'm here."

"Would you pack my things in my room? And wake me up early. I'll leave in the morning. I'm going to the mountains for a while, then I'll report for duty in Denver. I have to stay around there until Jess comes back with my son. Can you understand that?"

"Of course I understand. You go to Denver, son. And you be sure to let us know what's happening."

He swallowed. "You and Mattie are more alike in your thinking than you'd suspect," he told her with a light, bitter laugh. "She told me not to come here." There was a pause. "I'll . . . uh . . . I'll go back to Mattie's. Tell Cass I'm damned sorry I spoiled her night. I'll talk to her myself in the morning, before I leave."

"You do that, honey. You're a better man for leaving her alone tonight. You know that, don't you, son?"

There was a moment of silence. "Sure," he finally answered.

She heard him leave then. The door closed, and the buggy soon clattered away. Kate sat down on the landing and wept. Was there anything stronger inside a man than the need to be with his son, especially a man raised by a nation of people who treasured children above all else? If Lance Raines could not be with his own son, he would be a tortured man all of his life, and poor Cass would never be able to have him for herself.

Chapter Eighteen

Lance saddled Sotaju, every bone weary from a poor night's sleep. When he straightened to slide the bit into the horse's mouth, he saw Cassandra coming out the door. Their eyes caught, and she looked at the ground and started walking toward him. Lance placed the bit and drew the bridle over the Appaloosa's head, checking it for fit as Cassandra came closer. He stopped then, hanging one arm over Sotaju's neck, aching at the sight of her golden hair in the morning sun, the full breasts covered now by a dress that came up to her neck.

"I'm sorry, Rainmaker," she said in a subdued voice.

"You're sorry?" He tightened a strap on the bridle. "I think I'm the one who should be sorry. I could have picked a better time to tell you about Julien."

She looked up at him then. "Is that his name? Your son?"

He met the blue eyes and nodded. "Julien Pierre Françoise—only some day it's going to be Julien Raines."

She folded her arms nervously in front of her. "That's what I'm sorry about, Rainmaker. I'm sorry I didn't stop to understand about your son—your feelings. I acted like a stupid child, and I've been trying so hard not to be a child around you. I truly am sorry. And I truly do care."

He sighed and reached out to touch a strand of hair.

"You 'truly' are a lot of things, aren't you? I like the way you use the word."

She blinked back tears. "But I do mean it. Please tell me about it—about him. Are you sure he's yours?"

He turned away. "I'm sure." He ran a hand through his hair. "I tried to explain last night, Cass. The woman means nothing to me. It was just . . . just something she'd done with who knows how many other men. But this time it was me. I was with her for five days, and nine months later she gave birth to a son, with green eyes."

Cassandra struggled to stifle the horrible jealousy she felt over the words. Five days! And only last summer. It must have been while he was in Denver, before he came to her when she was hurt.

"It isn't just the eyes," he was saying. "It's . . . a gut feeling. I've felt drawn to Denver for months. The woman told me she couldn't have children, and then she did have one. None of it made sense. I suspected but didn't want to believe it. It must have been her husband who couldn't give her good seed—whatever." Cassandra blushed at the words. She had no doubt Lance Raines's seed was strong. How she wanted it to grow in her own belly! "At any rate, this last time I was in Denver I saw the boy. He's about four months old now. When I saw him, it was as though God Himself came down and gave me a message that he was my son. I . . . touched his little hand . . . saw his smile." His voice choked, and he took a deep breath, his back to her. "And then I saw his mother—Jessica—and I knew by the way she looked at me that the child was mine. A woman knows those things. And then it all fit. Françoise wanted a child very badly. So she found a man who could give her one. By presenting the man with a son, she ensured her continued role as the wife of Claude Françoise. And I don't think she'll ever give that up for anything." He rubbed the back of his neck. "So I guess I'm in a fix, because I don't want my son raised by Claude

309

Françoise. He's a ruthless, money-hungry man, with no regard for human life—a man who once dealt in slave trade."

She cautiously put a hand on his arm. "I want to understand, Rainmaker. I . . . I want you to know that if you ever get your son, I could love him as much as any mother. And I'll wait for you forever if I have to. Just don't . . . don't marry that woman. Please!"

He turned to face her with watery eyes. "I can't promise that I won't, if that's what it takes, Cass. But I don't want to. I want to marry you. I love you. And it's because I love you that I didn't come to your room last night. I wanted to. I wanted to more than I've ever wanted anything in my life."

She looked down. "I threw myself at you like a . . . like a bad woman. I didn't mean it . . . like it seemed. I just . . . love you so much."

He pulled her close, petting her hair. "Don't ever be ashamed of your feelings, Cass. I understand. When I think of other men touching you . . ." He squeezed her closer, kissing her hair. "But the way things are . . . I'd be cheating you by coming to you now. And last night, when I did come home . . . I was drunk. Thank God Kate stopped me. If I had come to you that way, I'd have hurt you. I don't want it to be that way for you, Cass, quick and frightening."

"Tell me again, Rainmaker. You do love me, don't you?" she asked, her face buried against his broad chest. She breathed deeply of his tempting, masculine scent.

"God help me, I do," he answered. "I do love you, Cass. But you're still so young, and my life is so messed up now. Maybe somehow—some day—it will all work out."

"Don't go away, Rainmaker!" she wept. "It's too soon."

"It's none too soon. I can't stay so near you right now, and I have a lot of thinking to do. I'm going to the mountains, and you have to be patient and pray for me,

Cass. Then I'm going on to Denver." He pulled away, gently grasping her arms. "I'll be working for Françoise again, on the Denver and Rio Grande Railroad, a new venture. It's the only way I can be close to my son. I'll just have to think of something once I'm there. But first I have to pray that he'll even come back to Denver."

She frowned. "What do you mean?"

"I told you last night that his mother took him to Spain. For all I know he'll be a year old or better before I see him again. I think she went partly because she saw the look on my face and knew I wanted him. She's afraid her husband will find out, but I'd never tell him because I don't trust him not to harm the child if he knows. And he might harm Jessica."

He saw the flash of angry jealousy in her blue eyes again, and he squeezed her arms tighter.

"Cass, I only care because she's the boy's mother, and in spite of what she is, she loves him. I can tell. I can't bring myself to harm her or to let anyone else harm her. Can you understand that?"

She closed her eyes and sniffed. "I . . . want to. I'm trying hard to understand. Just tell me again. Tell me again you love me."

She was answered with the feel of gentle lips on her mouth. She flung her arms around his neck, and he pressed her close, one arm around her slender back, the other grasping her around the hips and lifting her so that her feet could not touch the ground. The kiss was sweet and hungry, and her jealousy faded again. He moved his lips to her cheek.

"I do love you, Cass. That's why I'm leaving and giving you another year to grow, and think. Maybe by then I'll know what to do."

"I love you, too, Rainmaker, more than anything on this earth! I love you! I love you!"

He clung to her a moment longer, then lowered her as

Kate came out the door with a sack full of fresh biscuits and cookies. The woman's heart ached at the sight of the two of them embraced. If only they could be happy together.

"Food for your journey, my wandering adopted son," she spoke up, coming closer. Lance gently lowered Cass to her own feet, then reached out and took the sack, shoving it into a saddlebag. He turned then to hug Kate, afraid to squeeze too tightly for fear her tiny bones would break.

"Thank you, Kate," he said emotionally. "Thank you for all of it. I'll be back. That I promise."

"Well, you don't need to take too long in doing it," she answered, patting his shoulder. She pulled back and looked up at him. "You take care of yourself, Lance, and be careful how you handle the mess over that boy. Don't get yourself or him in trouble." She squeezed his hands. "I'll be praying for you, son. I'll be with you everyplace you go. You remember that. I'll be leaving you now to Cass. You write, hear?"

"I'll write."

Their eyes held, and then she turned and walked briskly back to the back door. She stopped there a moment, turning and looking at him once more, then went inside. Kate wasn't one for mushy good-byes, but Lance was sure he saw something more in that look, as though she might never see him again. His heart tightened. He loved her. He looked down at Cass.

"Take good care of her, Cass. Don't let her work too hard."

"I'll watch out for her," she replied.

Lance grasped her shoulders. "Some day we'll be together, Cass. And we'll let Kate live with us, and we'll all be happy. Somehow I know it will happen."

She flung her arms around his waist and hugged him tightly. "It has to! It has to!" she whimpered.

He pulled away again, bending down and kissing her

cheek. "I'll write. But I can't make any promises about anything that might happen."

"I know." She sniffed and wiped at tears. "Just so you love me. Say it again, Rainmaker."

He smiled sadly. "I love you. I guess I've loved you ever since we met. But you were so young, so small. Even now it doesn't seem right telling you. But I feel better saying it."

They looked into each other's eyes. What more was there to say? He kissed her forehead. "May the wind always be at your back, *Kseé. Nemehotatse.*"

"Nemehotatse," she answered, bursting with love for him.

He turned away and mounted up, the horse prancing in an eagerness to leave. "Good-bye," he spoke brokenly.

She could not answer. She shook with tears, her blue eyes forgiving and loving. He turned Sotaju and rode off, heading for the mountains . . . and Denver.

Cassandra listened to winter winds whip against the kitchen door, their wail as lonely and desolate as she felt in her heart. She looked at Kate. "Do you think he'll ever come back, Kate?"

"Sure. He'll come back. And if I know Lance, some day he'll come back with that boy. I just hope he doesn't try some Indian trick and steal the child as though he were on an Indian raid. He'd be hunted down and hanged for sure. I hope I've taught him enough sense that he can't do that."

"That's what's always made it hard for him to settle, isn't it? Being raised by Indians and all. It seems like he's an Indian one minute and a white man the next."

"That's a fact. That young man has had a struggle going on inside himself ever since the soldiers took him from the Cheyenne. I don't doubt he'd have been a lot happier if they had left him there, Cass. His blood is white, but his heart is much more Cheyenne. And that whole culture is so different from ours. They don't play by the same rules.

313

I feel sorry for Lance. I guess that's why I've been able to put up with some of his reckless ways."

Cassandra walked to look out a window. Snow danced around its panes. She tried to keep track of one particular snowflake, but with the wind so wild, it was impossible. "Kate, do you think if he ever does settle, with one woman, he'll be true to her?"

Kate glanced at her and grinned. "I have no doubts whatsoever. All those other women are just a way of taking care of many needs. But if he has a wife he loves, and who loves him and makes him happy, he won't have need of those other women. Lance has a good heart, Cassandra. He'd not be untrue to the woman he loves."

"He told me that once, when we talked after I'd been hurt. He said if he had a wife, he'd not need any other women." She sighed and turned to look at the old woman. "Do you think I'll ever be his wife, Kate?"

Kate threw some dough into a bread pan. "I only know that's what he'd like, honey. But with this thing over his son, I'm not sure what he'll do. You've go to face the fact that he might try to get that Jessica woman to marry him, because no matter how much he loves you, that boy will win out in all decisions. He's got a craving to have his son, and he'll do what it takes to get him."

Cassandra's throat tightened, and she looked out the window again. "I don't know what I'd do if he married her. I'd . . . I'd probably be a bad woman . . . because I'd go to him, Kate, if he still wanted me, even if he was married." Her voice broke. "She'd . . . never love him, Kate . . . not like me. He'd never . . . really be happy. He can't marry her. He can't! I'll kill myself if he marries her!"

Kate left the table and walked over to embrace the girl. She wondered if she was shriveling, or if Cassandra was just growing more, for the girl had to bend her head to weep on the woman's shoulder. She patted the girl's back. "You listen here, Cass. If that man loves you, he'll do anything he can to make it all right. You just believe that and don't be fretting over something that hasn't happened yet. You just love him and pray for him. That's all you can do, child."

"It isn't fair!" she wept. "I've loved him . . . for so long."

"I know, honey. I know." Kate closed her eyes and said a quick, quiet prayer, not just for Lance and Cassandra, but that she would live long enough herself to see her Lance again and see them together.

Lance grabbed one of the two fighting men who had disrupted a smoothly running work crew when an argument broke out over a gambling debt from the night before. Jim Beck, another employee kept on by Claude Françoise from the Kansas-Pacific work crews, grabbed the other man. Lance's man continued to scuffle, and Lance turned him around and landed a big fist into the man's face. The crewman sprawled flat out on the ground.

"Everybody get back to work!" Lance ordered the rest of them. "Settle your arguments on your own time!"

None of them cared to argue with him. The second man picked up his shovel and walked away. Lance bent down to check the man he had punched. He pulled him out of the mud and set him on a grassy bank to come to on his own.

He stood up then, rolling and lighting a cigarette. He held it in the corner of his mouth while he flexed his right hand, sore from the punch. It felt good to punch someone. He'd like to punch everyone in sight. He'd like to hit and hit until his hand was broken, then do the same with the other hand. Never had he known such frustration as he'd known over the past long, cold, lonely winter.

Progress was slow on the Denver & Rio Grande, and now with March melting snows in the mountains, things were only worse. Streams were swollen and the earth was soft. And at the base of the Rockies, one could only expect sudden spring snowstorms that could bury them again, forcing them back into their boring card games. It was no wonder the men were at each other's throats. He could bear it better himself if it weren't for the quiet mountain nights, when he thought about Cass and what it would be like to bed her. He knew instinctively that if and when he went back to Abilene, he'd never be able to keep from claiming her, no matter what. She'd be sixteen. Sixteen and in every way a woman. It was amazing how three short years could produce such a change in a girl that age.

He looked up at the Rockies. He ached for her. Yet this place held him. He could not go back to Cass until he saw his son again, talked to Jessica again. Maybe he could never have Cass.

Beck walked up to him. "You all right, Raines?"

Lance turned tired eyes to the man. "Sure. I kind of wish the guy had punched back. I feel like getting into a good brawl."

Beck grinned. "Yeah, I guess we all do. You shouldn't have hit him so hard. You ruined your chances for a good fight."

Lance flexed his fist again. "I guess I did."

"Listen, is something eating at you, you need to talk about? You've been wound up like a spring all winter, distant, quiet, half angry all the time. Maybe you should go to that little girl in Abilene and get it over with. She's getting to be old enough, isn't she?"

Lance took a drag on the cigarette. How could he tell the man about Julien? No one must know. "I expect she is," he replied. "I'll wait till later this summer. She'll be sixteen."

"Well, I'd say that's old enough. You let me know when you want some time off, and you go get that pretty little thing out of your system. The way you describe her, I envy you, Raines. I haven't found any special woman since my Ann died a few years back." They exchanged a look of understanding then. Jessica. Beck sighed. "That one doesn't count. She can't be special like Ann, or your Cassandra."

"That's for damned sure," Lance replied. "You hear anything from Françoise lately?" he asked cautiously.

"Yeah. He visited the base camp just a couple of days ago, while you were working ahead of the line. I guess the illustrious Jessica will be back home in May."

Lance's heart tightened. Julien!

Beck was shaking his head. "I don't know how a man can stand to go that long without seeing his son, especially considering how they grow that first year. He's probably walking and saying a few words by now. He must be about a year old."

"April," Lance spoke up, staring at the mountains again.

"What?"

"April. He'll be a year old in April."

Beck studied him, suspecting things he didn't want to suspect. He liked Lance Raines. He'd not tell a soul of his suspicions, and he was sure that if he did, Raines just might kill him. Lance turned to look at him then.

"Listen, I might go back to Abilene in May instead of later," he lied. "Would that be all right with you?"

Their eyes held. "Sure," Beck answered. "You do what you think best."

Lance stepped out his cigarette and walked back to the crew. May! Julien would be home in May, and he could see him again!

Jessica put away the last garment from her many bags. She felt refreshed, a new woman. Her year in Spain had been exciting indeed, with a long line of handsome Spanish gentlemen ready to show her the sights, and to share her bed. She had lain on sunny beaches, had enjoyed total freedom. She had considered never coming back, but knew if she did that, Claude would suspect, and would soon divorce her. A wife's place was beside her husband, boring and irritating as that might be. But if she did not keep up this game, she would lose it all. She could always go back. At least she had returned when warm spring winds brightened Colorado and most of the snow was gone. And she could walk the streets of Denver, showing off her fine son.

She had learned to ignore the catch in her heart that seeing her son brought, for to look at him was to look at Lance Raines. She wondered why her husband did not notice. Perhaps he simply didn't want to notice. It had been close to two years since she shared those five glorious days in Lance Raines's bed. Too much time had gone by for Claude Françoise to start putting together any dates. It was just as well. If only the boy didn't have those green eyes, yet that was what made him such a beautiful baby. And how she loved him! She did truly love him. Her only worry was that Lance Raines would spoil it all. Maybe he had given it up by now. Maybe after going so long without ever seeing the child, he had decided it wasn't all that important. After all, the boy would be raised in wealth and comfort. That was something to consider. And there was that stupid child in Abilene he'd run off to help. Maybe he had married the silly girl by now and was settled in Abilene. She didn't want to ask Claude, for she didn't want to bring any attention to Lance Raines in any way.

She walked into the adjoining nursery. The room was dark, except for the light that filtered in from her own room. She bent over the baby bed to check on Julien and smiled at the sight of him sleeping peacefully. Such a strong, chunky, handsome boy he was! Everything was perfect. She had wealth, and she had this son for insurance. But he was more than that to her now. She loved him as any mother would love a son. She never dreamed at one time she'd have a child and live like other women.

Who cared that she had used another man to get this?

Suddenly she shivered and straightened, sensing a presence in the room. At first she was afraid to even move. Was the room haunted? Was there a thief lurking somewhere? After all, Denver was full of all sorts of no-goods, and there were many valuable items in the house. She reached for Julien, then gasped when a hand went over her mouth and a powerful arm wrapped around her, pinning her own arms.

"Don't scream" came the husky voice. "It's me—Lance. Promise you won't scream."

Her heart beat wildly, and her breathing was quick and shallow. She nodded her head, and he took his hand from her mouth.

"How did you get in here!" she whispered.

He jerked her around. "I was raised by Indians. Remember?"

"Get out of here!" she hissed. "If Claude finds you here—"

"I'm not leaving without my son," he growled.

"He's not your son!"

He jerked her close, bending her arms behind her. "He is! You just don't want me to believe it, because you know I'd want him! And I do! My God, Jessica, why? Why did you do this?"

"You get out of here!"

"Come with me, Jess. Bring Julien and come with me. I have a lot of money saved. I want my son. You'd still be a respectable married woman, only married to me."

"I told you once I would never leave Claude Françoise's wealth!" she sneered. "That boy ensures that I can stay here forever! Nothing and no one will ever take either of them from me!"

His face was close to hers, his body pressed against her own. "And you have no feelings at all for me? I'm your son's father, Jess! And you can't deny we're good in bed together. That isn't much, but it's a beginning. Tell me you don't have any feelings for me, Jess. Tell me there isn't a soft place in your heart for Julien's real father."

Her breath caught in her throat, and she did not fight him when his lips met her hungrily, bringing back all the flaming passion he'd always been able to stir in her loins. But he was not rich like Claude Françoise. She turned her head away.

"It isn't enough, Lance," she told him. "I will not leave Claude. I will not leave this life."

He pushed her away then. "Bitch!" He reached into the baby bed, picking up Julien.

"What are you doing!"

"When I rode with the Cheyenne, we sometimes raided other Indian camps—enemy Indians. Children were taken and adopted into the tribe, loved as their own. I'm conducting my own little raid, Jess. I'm taking him with me."

She grasped his arm. "No! You can't take your son away from his mother!"

He held the boy tight in his arms. "So, you do admit it. He is mine!"

She broke into tears. "Yes. But, Lance, you can't take him! You must listen to me! If you take him, Claude will send men after you. And when they find you, which they will, they'll kill Julien! Claude will know why you took him, and he'll have the boy killed! I know him, Lance. Please! Think of our son! Don't do this!"

He trembled, holding the boy close and kissing his soft hair. Finally! Finally he had his son in his arms. He was a hefty armful. He walked him closer to the light from the other room to study the boy's angelic face. "Is he walking?" he asked brokenly.

"Yes. And he talks. He says many words already, and even some in Spanish. He's so good, Lance."

He met her eyes. "You test my love for him. What about your own? If you would just divorce Claude, you

320

could come and live with me."

"Claude would make sure I could not take the boy with me. He treasures his son. He is determined the boy will be raised a Françoise, inherit the Françoise fortune. It would never work, Lance, don't you see? Even if I left him, it would never work. He would want the boy. The only way he would not want him would be if he knew the child was not his. And if he knows that, he will kill him out of vengeance."

"Then it's dangerous for my son to even be in this house! He stands a better chance if I take him away. I know a million places to hide. Come with me, Jess. We can do it."

She stepped back. "Please, Lance. Leave him for now. Give me some time to think. Please!" She inched her way toward the doorway to her bedroom.

"You'll consider coming with me? I don't want to take the boy from his mother, but I will if I have to. I'll find a way to get him, Jess. If you want to come with me, I can arrange it. I know we can do it."

"I . . . I'll think about it. Please. Just give me a few days. I . . . I can't think that quickly. And you must go before—" She cocked her head as though hearing something. "Wait there in the shadows!" she whispered. She darted into the bedroom while he stood waiting in a dark corner of the nursery, relishing the privilege of holding Julien. He kissed the boy's cheek and nuzzled him, breathing in the sweet baby smell, loving him—loving him so automatically. He needed no one to give him any proof who the beautiful boy belonged to. And now he had hope, a dim hope of getting the boy for himself. It would be risky, but worth it.

In seconds Jessica was back inside the nursery. "It's all right. I thought I heard someone coming. But you must leave now, Lance. We cannot do anything without making plans."

He sighed, laying the boy back in his bed, reluctant to let go of him. "Three days," he told her. "Meet me in room five at the Denver Inn on Monday morning. Tell me then. You could even bring the boy with you, and we'd have a head start before anyone knew what was happening."

"Three days. Yes." She came closer then. "Hold me, Lance."

He reached out and embraced her. If only he could bring himself to love her. But he had no respect for her, other than the fact that she was his son's mother. If she chose to go with him, how was he to forget Cass? Sweet, beautiful Cass. His heart ached for her even now as he held his son's mother in his arms. He could never love her, but he would sacrifice Cassandra's true love to be with his son. He must do it.

He moved his mouth to meet Jessica's lips, lips he once shared in animal passion, but lips which now seemed cold and brought no passion at all, in spite of her beauty. He moved his lips to her neck.

"Think hard on it, Jess. And don't run off on me this time. I'll find you, I swear it, even if you go across the ocean!"

"I'll not run off," she answered.

It was then he heard the muffled shot and felt the searing pain in his middle. He stood rigid for a moment, half hanging on to her; but then she backed away, and he stumbled backward.

"I'll not run off because I'll never leave Claude Françoise or this life!" she hissed. "And now you will not bother me again!" Lance stumbled toward the window as her sneering words came at him like a twisting knife. "I have killed you, Lance Raines! This gun is small, but it makes big holes. Soon I will tell my husband I heard an intruder, and when you are found, they will know it was you. After all, you are a wild man, half savage. Any white man would believe you are capable of turning wild and doing something foolish, like sneaking into your boss's home, perhaps to steal from him, perhaps to rape his wife! I have shot at an intruder."

He turned and managed to climb through the window, grasping his stomach and unable to talk at all. Another shot was fired, a tiny "bang" that sent another very big pain, this time in his back, in his upper right shoulder. He heard his son's frightened cries rising in the night air. His only thought was of Julien. He would not die! He would somehow live through this for Julien, and just to spite Jessica Françoise. He heard her screaming for help then. He scrambled down the trellis he had used to climb up. How he managed any of it, he could not tell. He was moving on some inner strength that kept shock from taking over. Or perhaps it was shock that kept him going, kept the pain from being worse than it was. His belly was on fire, and he felt the movement of his right arm beginning to leave him.

He ran to Sotaju, tied in the shadows, and grunted as he mounted up. He knew he could count on the animal to outride anything Claude Françoise might send after him. And it was night. By the time a search party could be gathered and it was light enough to see his tracks, he would be far away. He headed the animal east.

In Jessica's bedroom, the woman stood shaking and grasping the little gun she kept near her bed for protection. Claude Françoise was holding her, gently urging her to give him the gun.

"Someone . . . tried to break in . . . through the nursery!" she told her husband, putting on a fine display of fright. "I didn't know . . . what to do! If I called for you, he might have hurt Julien. I had to think of Julien!"

"Of course you did, dear," Françoise replied, patting her shoulder. "Do you think you hit him?"

She put a hand to her head. "I think so. Oh, Claude, it was so terrible."

"Now, now, dear. Thank God I made you keep that gun handy. Out here a woman needs protection. And you just remember our Julien. You were protecting him, too, so don't be too upset that you might have shot someone. I'll have the grounds searched in the morning, and inquire in town if anyone showed up at a doctor's office wounded. That's the most we can do."

She nodded, praying that Lance Raines would die somewhere away from town and lie in the sun and rot. She clung to her husband, weeping. It was so easy now to win his affection and concern, for she had given him a son.

Chapter Nineteen

There is a secret strength in some men, a determined stubbornness that only desperate love can draw forth. Now it was Lance Raines's turn to pull on that source, made easier by his Indian upbringing, the Sun Dance ritual during which he learned to bear pain. This, then, would be his sacrifice, to suffer as he was suffering now, in payment for having a son by such a woman as Jessica Françoise. Perhaps if he endured this suffering, the Great Spirit would bless him and some day make it possible for him to have his son.

He rode east slowly, not even sure where he was going, struggling to keep from dying. How many miles Sotaju had gone, he could not be certain. He only knew that if he got off the horse, he would never get back on. He must stay on, must find help. There was no way he could reach Abilene and Cass and Kate. And what would happen to him if he went to some farmer for help? He could not take the chance of the law being brought in while he was helpless. It was hard telling what Jessica would tell her husband, what Françoise would do. And he had to think of Julien. He must protect Julien. That was the only thing he could be sure of about Jessica. She was a scheming, lusting, murdering woman, but she would not let harm come to her son.

Jessica! How he hated her! How could he have been such

a fool? She was worse than he had thought, more hungry for wealth than he had anticipated. He had hoped she would put her son first, realizing he should be with his real father, that no child should be raised patterned after Claude Françoise. She was truly a witch, a deceiving devil, and if he could ever find a way to get revenge, he would do it. It would be his all-consuming goal now. Revenge against Jessica, and his son in his arms. In all his years with the Indians, and in scouting and living in this untamed land, no man had gotten the better of him. Now a woman had done it, asking for his embrace while exploding a gun in his middle. It was the ultimate deceit, and his disgrace. He was glad he was suffering. He deserved to suffer.

But he must not die! He must not die! Visions of Cassandra and Julien floated through his confused mind: the sweet smell of both of them, his son's chubby, soft face, Cassandra's beautiful blue eyes. What a sweet mother she would be. Surely if he could get his Julien, Cass would love the boy, just because he was Rainmaker's son. Yes, she would love him. He would go to Cass. He would talk about it with her. Somehow he would find a way to get Julien, and they would all be together.

Cass. He groaned her name. All night and most of the day he had ridden in a general northeast direction. Sotaju sensed his master's predicament, and ambled slowly. He was given no direction, and so headed on his own toward water. Soon they were at the South Platte, many miles from Denver, no settlements in sight. The stallion halted at the river, bending his head to drink.

Lance tried to hang on, but when Sotaju's neck sloped down, Lance lost his grip. He felt himself sliding and could not stop himself. Seconds later he grunted when his body hit the soft earth beside the river, the wound in his back dried and crusted now, his right arm almost lifeless and his legs feeling numb. His stomach still bled badly, and he knew that with every drop of blood, more life oozed out of him. How much longer could he survive without help? And what would happen to Julien if he died? And what about Cassandra? Poor little Cassandra. He was supposed to take care of her. He couldn't let some other man do that. No! Cassandra belonged to him. And so did Julien.

Sotaju casually drank from the river, whinnying softly when he sensed the approach of humans. By then, Lance was too far into near unconsciousness to know or care what went on around him. Flies settled on his wound, biting at him. Julien. His son's charming, chubby face was before him, the sweet little mouth smiling, the green eyes looking to him for help. He heard voices, but could not place them. How long had he lain here? One hour? Three?

Someone touched him. He wanted to resist. He should go for his weapon. But nothing would move. He was being lifted, and there was nothing he could do about it. A subconscious panic built in him, and outwardly he was screaming and didn't even know it, for deep in his mind he knew he could not move anything. Paralyzed! Yes. One of the bullets, perhaps both of them, had done something to him so that he could not move. It would be better to be dead. And maybe he was dead. Maybe the spirits were lifting him, helping him to walk *Ekutsihimmiyo,* the great Hanging Road that leads all Cheyenne to the great hunting grounds in the heavens. Yes. That must be it, for those who helped him were speaking Cheyenne.

More hours passed as his mind swam in blackness while he bounced along on a travois, unaware of where he was or where he was going. It was not long after that when he could smell a comforting, familiar smell — the rich aroma of a tipi that had known many smoky fires. Then came a chanting in Cheyenne, beautiful singing, the smell of herbs placed on a smoky fire, the smoke waved over his body by a Cheyenne shaman.

It was then the horrible pain gripped him in all its ferocity. What was happening? Something dug into his belly with unrelenting deliberateness. Pain enveloped him, not just his belly, but his entire body, every nerve ending, every muscle. Someone sponged his perspiring face with cool water, and more water was dribbled into his hot, dry mouth. It seemed hours before the pain subsided; but then it came again when someone rolled his helpless body onto his stomach, and again horrible fingers of pain dug into him at his back. In the deep recesses of his mind he knew someone was removing bullets; but he didn't know who, and only the recurring vision of a baby's face made him want to hang on through the pain and live.

He moved back and forth from subconsciousness to total unconsciousness, never sure if he was alive or traveling to the heavens. He must be alive. Surely this pain meant he still had life. Someone gently rolled him onto his back again, talking soothingly. Again his face was bathed in cool water and more water was put in his mouth. He could smell the pungent magic smoke of the shaman. He wanted to speak, but could not — wanted to move, but could not. When he managed to open his eyes at times, he saw nothing but blurs, and in moments they would close again. In his mind he called for Cassandra, then spoke Julien's name. Yes, if this pain meant life, then he would bear it. He would live. Somehow he would see both Julien and Cass again.

Eight days went by before Lance was conscious enough to think with reasonable clarity. When he opened his eyes, he said nothing at first. He looked cautiously around him. He was tied tightly to a travois so that his body would not bounce or sway too severely. Several Cheyenne men rode beside and behind him, and several women walked behind, a few riding, many carrying cradleboards on their backs. He moved his head and eyes to the left, but felt pain in his neck when he did so. In the distance he could see the usual herd of fine horses that usually accompanied a traveling band of Cheyenne. Horses were their treasure, and most men had several, each horse trained for different tasks, some for riding in battle, others for the buffalo hunt, others used strictly as pack animals.

He breathed deeply of the fresh air, enjoying the feel of the warm sun on his face. He was alive! Somehow he had managed to live through Jessica Françoise's attempt at murdering him. The thought of it made him want to clench his fists, but he couldn't seem to close them. In his joy at being alive, he wanted to stretch and sit up and shout. But nothing would work. Was it only because he was tied so securely? It couldn't be. He would surely still have feeling, sensations in his limbs. But he felt nothing.

He tried to close his fists again, to move his feet, stretch a little. Nothing. His heart pounded, and sweat broke out on his face. His breathing became labored.

Someone near him shouted in the Cheyenne tongue that the "white brother" was awake and moaning. The entire band halted, and a man came around to Lance's travois, kneeling near him while Lance struggled just to breathe.

"Do not move, my friend" came a voice. "With many prayers and a long rest, surely some day you will rise and walk again. You must give yourself time to heal. We will help you."

Lance swallowed, his throat dry. "What's . . . wrong with me?"

"We are not sure. We found you badly wounded. We removed the evil bullets that were bringing death to you. Many times you groaned that you could not move, although perhaps you do not remember. We did what we could, my friend. You will stay with us until you are well. We owe you this."

Lance blinked and focused on the face of the man who spoke to him. He looked familiar.

"I am One Cloud," the man reminded. "You helped us

once when we were starving. You took us into the wooden house of the iron horse and warmed our bones, fed our horses. You buried an old Indian woman for us, in spite of the frozen ground. She was my wife's mother. We have not forgotten. When we found you, we remembered the white man who dresses and speaks like a Cheyenne, and who calls Kicking Horse his brother. You helped us, so now we help you."

"You must lie still" came a woman's voice. Lanced turned to see another familar face — the woman who had held the old Indian woman in her arms in the boxcar and wailed when the old woman died. She laid a buffalo-skin water bag to his lips and tipped it, and he took a swallow.

"This is Deer Woman, my wife," One Cloud told him. "She has been caring for you."

Lance tried to quell his panic. He could not move! "I am . . . grateful," he said in a weak voice.

"Who did this to you? " One Cloud asked.

His breathing quickened again as he remembered the horrible explosion in his side while he embraced the very woman who pulled the trigger, the woman for whom he was ready to sacrifice his true love, sweet Cassandra, just so he could be close to his son. "I . . . can't tell you that," he moaned. He gritted his teeth, trying to move something, anything. "My God . . . move anything!" he growled.

"Ho-shuh," Deer Woman told him gently. "You must give yourself time. Do not be afraid. The spirits will bring all life back to you. What are you called? We have forgotten."

"Raines. Lance Raines. The Cheyenne . . . called me . . . Rainmaker."

She rubbed a cool rag over his face. "Then we shall call you Rainmaker, also. And one day when you are stronger, you can tell us about your days with the Cheyenne, and how you have come to know about us so well, speak our language, call Kicking Horse a brother. We know you once lived among us, for you bear the scars of the Sun Dance."

330

"We hunt along the Republican," One Cloud added. "We must be very careful, for if we are spotted out of treaty territory, we will be hunted. But we are forced to come this far in order to find buffalo. Soon we will head north to join again the Sioux, our friends. Perhaps we can help you find Kicking Horse."

Lance closed his eyes. "I would like that. I am . . . grateful, One Cloud. You have saved . . . my life."

"As you once saved all of ours." The Indian put a hand on Lance's shoulder. "Tell me. Who is Julien? Many times you spoke his name."

Lance did not reply right away, and in his agony and panic and depression, he could not stop tears from finding their way from beneath his closed eyelids and running down the sides of his face into his ears.

"My son," he finally whispered, ashamed of the tears he could not stop. He felt a gentle squeeze on his shoulder.

"The sun is bright today," One Cloud reasoned quietly. "It makes a man's eyes water."

The Indian left him then, and the woman wiped at his tears with the cool cloth. "Day always follows night, Rainmaker," she said softly. She also left him then, and soon he grunted with the jerk of the travois as they were off again.

Kate read the telegraphed message over and over. *"Tell Lance Raines he must return soon. We need him badly."* It was signed *"Jim Beck, Denver & Rio Grande. Reply via D&RG R.R. office, Denver, Colorado."*

The woman tried to calm the panic in her chest. Had Lance planned on coming to Abilene for some reason? If so, where was he? She decided not to say anything yet to Cassandra. She sent a message back to Jim Beck.

"Lance Raines has not been here since left to work on D&RG summer of 1870. No letters in five months. When did he leave for Abilene?"

There was nothing to do but wait after sending the telegram. It was now August 1871, a full year since Lance had been home. She would not be so worried if it were not for the determination she saw in Lance Raines's eyes when he left — a determination to find a way to be with his son. Had he stolen the boy and run away with him, to Canada perhaps? Or had he been caught and killed? How could she tell Cassandra no one knew where he was?

It was two days before the reply came. *"Lance Raines left for Abilene this past May. Said he would return within a month. Can no longer keep him in employment if does not show up soon. If he does not show up by September 1, employment is terminated. Apologies. It if is discovered his failure to return was due to uncontrollable circumstances, please inform."*

"Uncontrollable circumstances." Kate did not like the words. With the kind of life Lance lead, all sorts of things could have happened to him. Why had he told the railroad he was coming to Abilene? For Cass? And what could possibly have stopped his arrival other than foul play? It was the only explanation for not even having heard from Lance himself by letter or wire.

How was she to tell Cassandra? Where did she begin looking for Lance? Perhaps he wasn't even alive. There was nothing she could do but wait. She would put off telling Cassandra as long as possible that Lance Raines was missing.

In Colorado, Jim Beck studied Kate's reply again. So, Lance Raines had never even gone to Abilene. Perhaps he had started there and had met with foul play. Or perhaps he had gone someplace else, like Denver. He frowned. Was it possible his suspicions about Julien Françoise were true? There had been rumors that there was an intruder into the Françoise home not long after Lance had left for Abilene. Word was Françoise himself had shot at the man, but the man had not been caught. Lance had never shown up again, either at the railroad or in Abilene.

Beck wadded up the note and threw it down. He liked Lance and hated Jessica Françoise even more for what he suspected happened, but would not betray Lance by voicing his suspicions. Perhaps Lance was still alive and had some kind of plan. And if the boy belonged to Lance Raines, Beck didn't want any harm to come to the child, although he wouldn't mind harm coming to Jessica Françoise, whom he had once loved himself. But that was a long time ago, and he'd been a fool. For the moment he was helpless to do anything more than the old woman called Kate could do, and that was wait — wait and see if Lance Raines ever showed up again. But after this long, he could only come to the conclusion that it was Lance Raines Françoise had shot, and that Lance had died alone somewhere on the prairie, his body probably rotted to an unidentifiable nothingness by now. Jessica Françoise had ruined another good man.

Winter winds howled about the tipi, which sat half buried in drifts. Buffalo Woman put another robe over Lance. He was grateful to have been brought to the camp of Kicking Horse in the Dakotas, to again be with Three Stars Woman's sister and Kicking Horse's second wife, Buffalo Woman. But this was not the Lance Raines who had so gladly shared Buffalo Woman's bed on his visits to Kicking Horse. This Lance Raines could barely move, and wondered if the day would come when he could make love to any woman again. He was thin and pale, withdrawing from life, ashamed of his helplessness. He wanted to die, for to live as he lived now was worse than death. He could not care for his son this way, nor could he take a wife. He would not want Cassandra to see him now, or poor Kate. Surely they both thought him dead anyway, and he might as well be.

Buffalo Woman cared for him with undying patience. She was a good woman. She had given Kicking Horse a son and had become an accepted second wife. Lance had no more desire to bed her himself, even if he could. But they remained friends, and her patience and concern were touching.

Some movement had returned to Lance's extremities, hands and feet. But still he could not fully move his arms or legs or even sit up, and his determination to survive was dwindling. Buffalo Woman talked to him constantly, assuring him that today he moved his feet, tomorrow it would be his legs.

"As soon as the warmth of the spring sun moves into your bones, you will walk again, Rainmaker," she kept promising him. "Do not give up. Remember your son, and the pretty girl in Abilene."

By now there had been plenty of time for conversation. He had told Kicking Horse and his family about his feelings for the girl he had rescued from these very people over three and a half years ago now. And he had told them about Julien. Many nights had been spent pondering what could be done about his son. But the fact remained that he could do nothing at all until he could walk again. If that did not happen, he had already decided that if he was still this way by the next winter, he wanted to be left on the plains to freeze and die. He was useless and ashamed. No man could live this way, nor would he go back and face his loved ones in such a condition. He had no doubt Kate and Cass both would care for him forever, and he remembered Cass's sweet, loving words when he rescued her, telling him she would take care of him forever if the Indians should "cut off his legs." The memory hurt. His legs might as well be cut off for all the good they were to him now.

Yes, Cass would take care of him. But he'd not go to her and deprive her of a normal life with a normal man, much as the thought of it hurt. And day by day his hatred of Jessica Françoise grew. This was all her doing, from beginning to end. From that first moment their eyes met and she cast him that animal hunger, all the while scheming to mate simply to bear a child for Claude Françoise, who apparently could produce no good seed; all of it had been carefully planned by the witch Jessica. And she had won. It wasn't right that a woman like that should win at anything, and he vowed that if he ever walked again, she would pay, even though she was Julien's mother. He could not bear the thought of his son being raised by a whoring, money-hungry, murderous woman, and a man who would stoop so low as to buy and sell humans in order to get rich.

But the fact remained that he lay helpless in a tipi, far from Abilene, far from Denver, half buried in snow drifts, no one but a small camp of Cheyenne even knowing he was still alive. There was nothing to do but allow his hatred of Jessica, and his love for Cassandra and Julien, to keep his blood flowing, keep up his failing determination to walk again. Perhaps Buffalo Woman was right. Perhaps the spring warmth would bring warmth to his seemingly dead bones.

Cassandra stood at the doorway gazing at wildflowers struggling to come up and bloom though the now-melting snow. It was March 1872, and over a year and a half since Lance Raines had left Abilene—eight months since he'd been reported missing by the railroad. Summer was coming. It would be two years then since she had seen Rainmaker, but her love for him had not dwindled. She would be seventeen late this summer, and her body and stature made her seem even older, a woman in every way. Lance was to have come home for her sixteenth birthday the summer before, but had never arrived.

No. She would not believe he was dead. Just as the flowers struggled to life after a hard winter, so did Lance Raines still live. What could kill a man like her Rainmaker? He was invincible. Whatever had happened, he was not dead. He would come to her. He had promised. She would wait forever.

"That nice young banker is here to see you, Cass" came Kate's voice behind her. Cass did not turn around.

"I don't want to see him. Send him away. I'm tired of him bothering me."

"I think you should at least go and talk to him, child."

"I said send him away!" the girl snapped. "There is only one man I want to see and talk to. I wish you wouldn't keep telling me to see other men, Kate."

She turned with angry eyes to meet Kate's sad ones and was immediately ashamed. "I'm sorry," she said quietly. "Please send him away, Kate. Tell him I'm sick or something."

The woman sighed and left. Cassandra heard voices, then a door closing. Kate returned to the kitchen then and their eyes held.

"He's alive, Kate," the girl told the woman. "I know it in my heart. He's alive, and something is keeping him from coming to us. That's all it is. He'll be here."

The woman turned to a pot of stew and began stirring it. "I like to hope you're right," she replied. "I put a lot of years of hard work into that young man. He's thirty now — if he's alive. He was only fifteen when he came to me."

For what seemed the hundredth time, Kate went over the story of how Lance had been brought to her, as wild as any Indian boy. Over and over the woman told the story, as though telling it would somehow keep Lance Raines alive and bring him home. And as always, her voice broke before she could finish. She stirred the stew quietly then, her thin shoulders shaking.

"It's that woman in Denver," she sobbed, a theory she had suggested as many times as she had told the story about Lance. "She's behind this. I just know it! It's got something to do with that damned woman. He tried to get his son. I just know it, Cass. He tried to get his son, and something terrible happened to him! That woman knows! I'll bet she knows!"

Cassandra stared out at the wildflowers again, feeling sick at the thought of Lance's being with the mysterious Jessica, planting a baby inside the wicked woman. She wanted to be the one to give him babies. She was the only woman who really loved him as a woman ought to love a man, yet she was the only one he had not touched. It wasn't fair. Was he dead now? Would she never have the opportunity of being held in his strong arms again, taste his lips again? Would she never experience the glory only Lance Raines could bring her by being her first man?

The agony of it was almost unbearable. It would be better to know for certain he was dead than to bear this dreadful waiting and wondering. How much longer should she wait without giving him up for dead? Somehow she simply could not do it. Men like her Rainmaker did not die. He would come. Rainmaker would come.

Lance lay listening to a nearby waterfall. Buffalo Woman had been right. The spring sun brought new life to his blood. It had taken many months for his wounds, especially his belly wound, to heal, although they left their scars. Several infections and a lot of sickness were behind him now. And a month ago he had begun to feel life in his limbs. He immediately took hope in that life, drawing on strength his love for Cass and Julien had sustained, praying to *Maheo* to accept his pain and helplessness as a sacrifice toward righting his wayward life. He was thirty years old now. He wanted a wife, and he wanted his son.

It all became more clear to him now. Somehow he must have both, but first he must get well. He forced back a temptation to give in to the awful pain as he began forcing movement, sweating and gritting his teeth as he began bending his arms up and down, holding light rocks Buffalo

337

Woman put in his hands. By April he was walking with the use of crutchlike devices made of tree limbs; but his legs were half dragged, and he could only stay up for a few minutes. It was then he asked Kicking Horse to make a camp for him near a stream and waterfall, leaving him there alone with supplies and Sotaju. Kicking Horse objected, but Lance was determined to pray and to concentrate on his inner faith and strength, that which had been instilled in him by suffering the Sun Dance ritual. He was, after all, Cheyenne on the inside. He would be strong. He must be strong—for Cassandra and Julien. He must be left alone to survive, to learn not to rely on anyone's help. It was the only way he would force himself to get stronger faster, for there was much to be done.

Now it was early May. He lay on the bank of the stream, lifting his legs up and down, then sitting up and bending his arms in and out while he held rocks. He was eating well now, his stomach finally working right. He knew he was gaining weight, and he let the welcome sun burn into his skin, darkening it again to a color almost as dark as his Cheyenne friends.

May turned into June. Little Julien was over two years old now. Lance could not help but wonder how he looked, how big he was. And what of Cass? She would be seventeen soon. Surely she was more beautiful than ever. Was she still a virgin? Had she given up on him and perhaps become interested in someone else? He must work hard at building his strength. His faith and determination and undying love for both Cass and Julien had brought life back to his bones and muscles. The Spirits had been good to him. He felt like a new man, ever stronger, forgiven, more sure of what he wanted in life. Perhaps it was good he'd been forced to lie still all winter, forced to think about his life, forced to slow down and remember his Cheyenne teachings. Every day his strength grew, as well as his renewed faith and determination. He spent the days in almost constant exercise, until he

338

could actually run. He ran and ran, Sotaju trotting beside him, as though to ask why he didn't ride his horse instead. He breathed deeply, glorying in life and sun and warmth. Surely if the Spirits had let him live and walk again, they meant for him to be with Cass and Julien.

Life! It was good. The stronger he became, the more he desired Cassandra, wanted to see her, touch her, use her to prove to himself he could again be a man in every way. Soon. Soon he would leave. He would go to Abilene first this time. He would go to Cassandra, and nothing and no one would keep him from branding her as his own. Then he would find a way to be with Julien.

Cass sat by Kate's bed. She was relieved that the good doctor who had kept her from being crippled was still in town, and now could help Kate. Abilene had grown and changed, most of the cattlemen herding their beef to Dodge City now, farther south. The Atchison, Topeka and Santa Fe line now ran south of the Kansas-Pacific, and had stolen most of the cattle business, to the relief of most Abilene citizens.

But none of it mattered at the moment to Cassandra. Kate was ill, very ill. The doctor had set up a small clinic, where Kate had been brought, for Cass wanted the beloved woman to be near help at all times. The girl's heart was heavy with grief. Kate seemed to be dying, and Lance had still never returned. It was close to two years now since his last visit, when he had kissed her so passionately in the buggy, professing his love for her but an equal determination to have his son. How could she continue to believe he was alive? That was what was killing Kate now. The woman was sure Lance Raines was dead and she would never see him again. After losing a husband and son years earlier, this was the final blow in her old age, for Lance had become like a second son to her.

Cass didn't know what to do, for she herself had no hope. She had nothing to draw on to give Kate reason to want to live, other than to tell the woman how much she loved her and needed her to get better. The woman lay breathing in shallow gasps, her face pale, her hands limp when Cass held them. Cass could do nothing but pray, both for Kate and for Rainmaker. But her faith was dwindling to nothing. What would she do if Kate died? Where would she go? The thought frightened her. She had no one but Kate — and Rainmaker. He was going to marry her, take care of her. But he might never come back now, and if Kate died, she wouldn't want to live at all.

Dusk turned to darkness, and the doctor urged Cassandra to go home and get some rest. She bent over and kissed Kate's cheek.

"I love you," she told the woman, squeezing her hand. "He'll come, Kate."

She moved away from the bed then, to go home again to an empty house. Without Kate, she could not handle boarders, and in her youth was afraid to allow men to take rooms. She had taken in a few women. She tried to keep the house in shape, cleaned and ready for when Kate would be better and come home. She had to hope that would happen. She left the clinic and headed toward the house at the end of town, lost in thought. Rainmaker. What was she to do? If only she could talk to him, could be held by him and comforted by the strong arms. Fear gripped her. She was alone again, just like when she'd been taken by the Cheyenne. She felt almost as lonely and helpless. Rainmaker had come then. Would he come now?

She hurried on, realizing she had let it get darker than she usually did before leaving the clinic. Abilene had a sheriff, but was still suffering the remnants of the lawless town it had become when the cattlemen half ran the town. It was still not the safest place to walk at night. She walked faster, but as she passed a dark alley not far from her house, someone grabbed her, someone strong and smelly.

She gasped and struggled, but others held her, pulling her arms back and tying them while something was stuffed into her mouth and someone else tied her ankles together.

"I want to look under her dress," she hear Johnny Sorrell whisper.

"Never mind" came the voice of the dreadful Huey Brown.

Her heart pounded furiously. They had not bothered her in months, and she hadn't even gone to school that year. She had received all the schooling she needed.

"Those men said they'd pay fifty whole dollars for her," Huey was saying as he gripped her tightly against him, his arms wrapped over her breasts. "But we can't touch her."

"Why not? The Indians did," Richard Gobles protested.

"That's different. That's what the men said fascinates Mr. Farr. He wants him a young wife, but one who's broke in some. Wait till he sees this pretty package!"

They all laughed, and Huey dragged a helpless Cassandra to a horse. The other two boys held her as Huey mounted up, then handed her up to him.

"They're waiting in that grove of cottonwoods north of here," he told the other two. "I can take care of it from here."

"You'd better split the money with us, Huey Brown," Johnny warned. "And you'd better not get under her skirts without letting us do it."

"Don't worry. I don't want all those men mad at me. Quentin Farr is a big rancher. I don't want to cross him. Now wait here for me. Maybe we can use some of the money to go to that Mattie woman's whorehouse and have a good time with some real women."

They all laughed again, and Huey Brown turned his horse and rode off, to a fate unknown to a terrified Cassandra.

Chapter Twenty

Lance noticed there were no boarders' horses in the stalls when he arrived at Kate's house. This time of evening, there should be a few there. He rode up to the back gate and dismounted, squinting with an aching tiredness. In spite of all his rest and exercise, the nearly month-long ride south to Abilene from the Dakotas had left him spent. It would be a long time before he was back to full strength, but he was well enough to get to Cass and Kate and let them know what had happened.

He went to the back door and discovered it locked. He walked around to the front door then, noticing that the roses Kate always took good care of were becoming overgrown with weeds.

His chest tightened. He'd been gone nearly two years. Kate! Had she died? What had happened to Cass? He went to the front door to find it also locked. He walked to a side window where a key was kept hidden beneath the sill, then retrieved the key and let himself inside. The house was well kept. He called out Kate's name, but the place was quiet as a tomb. His heart beat faster, and he ran up the stairs to Kate's room to find it tidy, her bed made. He charged through the adjoining room to Cassandra's room, and to his relief, some of her personal items were still there. Perhaps they had both merely gone some-

342

where, but where would they go? He hurriedly searched the other rooms. All were tidy, beds made. There had apparently been no boarders for quite some time.

He tried to remain calm. Kate! Was he too late? He ran down the back stairway several steps at a time into the kitchen. It had been little used. There was no bread baking, no pies ready. Kate's apron hung over the back of a chair. He ran his hand over it lovingly, an ache in his throat. After all he'd been through, there was nothing he looked forward to more than seeing Kate and Cass again. But all signs indicated there was definitely something wrong.

He walked through the dining room and into the hall-way to the front door, going out and relocking it and putting back the key. He hurried around the fence to Sotaju and mounted up, ignoring his own aching weariness. There was no time now for rest. He rode into town to the saloon where Mattie lived upstairs, dismounting and retying Sotaju.

"Hold on, boy," he told the animal, patting his neck. "I'll unload you eventually."

He strode inside, seeing several familiar faces and nodding to them, but also seeing a lot of new faces. It struck him then that in his concern he'd not noticed how Abilene had changed—bigger but quieter, cleaner.

"Lance, you been to see poor Kate yet?" the local livery owner called out to him.

Lance walked over to the man's table while a piano player began plunking out a tune, and Mattie Brewster came hurriedly down the stairs when she spotted Lance.

"What do you mean?" Lance was asking the livery owner. "I just got here to find Kate's house empty."

The man frowned. "She's over at the new doc's office, Lance. Not doing too well, the way I hear it."

"Is Cassandra there with her?"

The man looked at the other men, who all shrugged. "Nobody has seen her for two or three days now," the man replied.

Lance paled visibly. "What the hell are you talking about?"

"Just that, Lance. She stayed faithfully by Kate's side every day, went home at night and came back the next morning. Then she just didn't come back. Only reason we know about it is the doc was asking about her. Her not being there has Kate worried."

"What's wrong with—"

"Lance!" Mattie came up to him then, and he turned and hugged her gratefully, actually relieved to find someone he cared about still around.

"I was beginning to think I'd come back to the wrong place," he told her. "What the hell is going on? What's wrong with Kate, and where's Cass?"

She led him to a separate table and yelled to the bartender to bring some whiskey. They both sat down and she took his hand. "You don't look so good. Where have you been, Lance? It's been almost two years!"

"It's a long story. A few months ago I couldn't even walk. I suffered a bad gunshot wound." He rubbed at his eyes. "I don't have time for that now, Mattie. What the hell is this about Kate, and where's Cass?"

The woman sighed and squeezed his hand. "Kate took sick, Lance. The doctor thinks it's her heart. She was getting better. I checked on her myself, for your sake. But then . . ."

The bartender brought a bottle of whiskey and two glasses, pouring two drinks and then leaving them.

"Then Cassandra didn't show up. That was about three days ago. By the end of the first day, the doctor went to

Kate's house to inquire, because Kate got so upset that the girl didn't come. Cassandra wasn't there. We've looked all over town for her, and we told the sheriff. But nobody knows what could have happened to her. We've got to find her or poor Kate will never get better. But seeing you will help. All she does is ask about you, hoping she'll see you again before she dies."

"My God!" he groaned, slugging down the drink. "Jessica Françoise has ruined my life in more ways than one! How long does a man have to pay for his mistakes!"

"That woman in Denver the reason you got injured? What did you do, Lance, try to steal the kid?"

"There's no time now. How was Cass? Was she still . . . waiting for me?"

The woman smiled slyly. "If you are asking if she was still single and pining away for you, the answer is yes. She never gave up hope that you were alive and would come. And she was so faithful to Kate. I can't believe that anything but foul play is involved, Lance. You've got to find her. If I were you, I'd go talk to those farm boys who were always giving her trouble. The sheriff already talked to them, but they said they didn't know anything about it. I'm sure you have ways of making them talk that the sheriff couldn't use."

His eyes smouldered. "I have ways," he growled.

"It's just a suspicion, mind you. But it's worth looking into."

"Do you know where they live?"

"Sure." She swallowed some whiskey. "I hope you find her, Lance. She's sweet and beautiful, and she's waited for you faithfully. I hope . . . I hope she's still untouched when you find her."

He picked up the whiskey bottle with a shaking hand. "If she's been touched, I'll kill every man who had anything to do with it," he said with a quiet, determined coldness. He slugged down more whiskey. "I came back here to marry her, Mattie. I can't stay away from her any longer. What I'll do about my son, I still don't know. I can only take one thing at a time. Where's Kate being kept? I'd better go see her right away."

"Just up the street. Used to be the hardware store. The doctor took over the whole building, made it into a little hospital."

He closed his eyes, wondering when he would explode. Cass! What had happened to Cass! He must waste no time. "Give me those directions, Mattie. I've got to get going. And don't tell the sheriff. I'll handle this myself."

Kate lay still as death, forcing herself to keep breathing. What was there left to live for? What had happened to poor Cass? All alone. The girl had been all alone. God only knew what had happened. Someone surely had abducted her. Nothing else would have kept her from coming. The doctor had carefully told her they couldn't find the girl but were searching diligently. But Kate knew that mattered little. Where was there left to search? If only Lance were here. Lance would know what to do. Those farm boys were lying; she was sure of it. Lance would know how to make them talk.

She struggled to keep from crying. Crying only made her worse, made the breathing even harder. She closed her eyes and sniffed, and unwanted tears spilled down into her ears. Someone came inside then, but in this big room full of several patients, many people came in and out to visit. She was certain there would be no visitors for her, and she didn't bother opening her eyes. She didn't want to be disappointed again.

346

Then she felt gentle hands on her face, fingers wiping away the tears. Someone bent close and kissed her forehead, and she recognized the familiar manly, outdoor scent of him. She opened her eyes, but couldn't see well because of the tears. "Lance?"

"It's me" came the reply. "What are you doing lying around like a lazy old woman, Kate McGee? Who's going to bake my pies?"

"Oh, Lance," she squeaked, putting a frail hand to her mouth.

"Don't get all excited," he warned. "It isn't good for you." He pulled her up in strong arms and cradled her against him, his heart aching at how thin she was. "Everything will be all right, Kate," he assured her. "You're going to get well because I won't let it be otherwise, and I'll find Cass. Don't you worry about that."

She clung to his buckskin shirt. He was all she had left in the world. "I was so afraid . . . of dying . . . all alone," she wept.

"Hush, Kate. You aren't going to die, and you aren't all alone. What have I told you about sharing spirits? Did all that Indian teaching go in one ear and out the other? You used to scold me for not remembering my lessons. Now you've forgotten yours. Even when I'm gone, my spirit is here with you, because you're in my heart and mind all the time. Remember when I told you that?"

"I remember."

He rocked her gently. "The doctor says if you'd get your spirits up, you'd get better. You'll never be able to work as hard as you have till now, but you could live a lot of years yet, Kate. So you just quit thinking you're all alone. I've come to marry Cass, and then I'm going to do something about getting my son and we'll all be together. You'll see. I'm taking care of you from here on, Kate. We'll make it.

I may leave once more; but I'll be back, and I'll never leave again. That's a promise."

"But . . . Cass . . . she's disappeared. My poor Cass!"

He gave her a hug. "Don't you worry about Cass. I'll find her, Kate."

"I kept praying . . . you'd come. I knew you'd know . . . what to do, Lance."

He helped her lie back down, and she looked at him lovingly, hoping she wasn't just dreaming. "What happened to you? You're thinner, son. Why were you gone so long?"

He held her hands. "It's a long story. I took a bad bullet wound. I spent half the winter paralyzed and all spring learning to move and walk again. I was with Indians. There was no way I could get word to you. I'm sorry, Kate."

"But . . . how? Did you try . . . to steal that boy? I told you—"

"Not exactly. I'll explain when you're better and when I have more time. Right now I've got to find out what happened to Cass. I'll have to be gone for a few days, Kate; but I'll be back, and I promise I'll have Cass with me when I come. But you have to promise you'll be better by then."

She forced a smile. "Now that I know you're all right—" She broke into tears again. "I thought . . . you were dead . . . but little Cass never gave up hope . . . you were still alive. You have to find her, Lance."

He bent down and kissed her cheek. "I'll find her, old woman. And you'd better be well when we get back. This is the first time I've come home to no pies. I'm very disappointed in you."

She smiled through her tears. "You be careful, Lance. I'll get better now that I know you're all right. I thought

348

. . . everything I loved was gone. What is there for an old woman . . . after that?"

He squeezed her hands. "You do everything the doctor tells you. I'll be back as soon as I can get here. Just don't panic if it takes me a week or two, all right?"

She nodded. "I promise. God bless you, Lance."

He smoothed back some of the gray hairs. "The blessings of *Maheo* on you," he replied. He stood up and patted her cheek lightly. "Get well, Kate. It's the same for me, you know, especially if something has happened to Cass. You're all I have."

She blinked back tears. "You have a son. Always remember that, even if you can't be with him. You have . . . a son. And I just know . . . somehow . . . you'll have him for yourself some day."

A sadness filled his eyes. "Good-bye, Kate. I'll see you in a few days." He turned quickly away, not wanting her to see the tears in his eyes. She was upset enough. He quickly left, wondering if she really would live until he returned. He had never considered so seriously that she really could die, and he wanted to cry. Not Kate! He hurried outside and mounted up, riding east, to the farm where Huey Brown lived. His sorrow over Kate and thirst for vengeance for what might have happened to Cass filled him with the strength he needed to keep going. He was weary and not really ready for this, but he could not worry about that now. He'd find Cass if he died doing it. And if Huey Brown knew anything, he'd talk when Lance Raines got through with him!

Huey Brown set down the bucket. He hated early morning chores, and cussed his father out under his breath as he picked up a stool and set it down beside the first cow that had to be milked. He pushed the bucket under the cow and sat down to begin milking, wondering if the money he'd made selling Cassandra Elliott to the rancher was enough for a boy to run away on. He'd kept half the fifty dollars for himself, telling Johnny and Richard he deserved more than they because he was the one who had actually ridden out to the ranch hands to deliver the girl. Neither of his friends had argued much, for Huey was much bigger, and they didn't care to feel his fist in their faces.

He had considered spending some of his money on the local whores but was afraid his parents would find out. Besides, what he wanted more than anything was to get out of Abilene. Maybe he'd go to Denver, or even San Francisco. He had to get off this farm, that was sure, and the squaw girl Cassandra had helped him realize part of that dream. Who cared what happened to her now? She was already used by the Indians anyway. No one could convince him otherwise. And that man called Rainmaker hadn't been back in two years and would probably never come back. Even if he did, he'd just wonder like everyone else what could have happened to Cassandra Elliott.

The boy grinned to himself. He couldn't help but at least have a look under the pretty girl's clothes. There hadn't been time for anything else, for the men had been waiting. But he'd stopped and pulled up her dress, reaching inside her underthings for a feel of a real girl. He'd felt her breasts, feeling hot and excited at her struggles all the while, and contemplating just riding off with her and having fun with her. But the ranch hands might have come after him. He'd already made a deal, and he had to go through with it; so he delivered her and had twenty-five whole dollars hidden under his mattress for it.

He stood up, preparing to move on to the next cow,

when a hand suddenly grabbed his left arm and jerked it behind him painfully, and a huge knife flashed before his eyes.

"Where is she?" someone growled.

The boy wondered if he would faint. How on earth had someone managed to sneak up behind him without a sound? And what was he talking about?

The boy shook. In spite of his size and strength, whoever held him was much stronger, and from the looks of the knife and the buckskin shirtsleeve in front of him, he realized who it must be. But how could he know?

"R-Rainmaker?"

"Where's Cassandra Elliott?"

"I . . . I don't know what you're talking about!"

The knife came against his cheek. "The hell you don't!"

"You . . . you don't dare harm me! They'd hang you for murdering a boy!"

He felt a jolt and he was on his face, a knee in his back. "How old are you, Huey Brown?"

"I . . . I'm seventeen."

"Maybe that's a boy by white man's rules, but it's long a man by Indian rules. An Indian boy becomes a man when he endures the Sun Dance ritual, or kills an enemy or a buffalo. Have you ever done those things, boy?"

"N-no. What's a . . . Sun Dance ritual?"

A powerful arm jerked him around, and he was on his back. Now the knee was in his chest, pressing so hard he could barely get his breath, leaving him helpless. Lance held the knife against the boy's nose.

"It's a test of manhood," Lance sneered. "Wooden splints are pierced through a man's breasts and arms and back. Rawhide strips are tied to them, and the man is lifted so that he hangs by his skin. Maybe you'd like to test your manhood that way, Huey Brown! I can arrange it!"

351

The boy's eyes widened. "No!"

Lance rose and jerked him up. "Where is Cassandra Elliott?"

"I . . . I don't know what you're talking about! Honest!"

Lance just grinned wickedly, his eyes glittering. "We'll see about that!" He shoved the knife into its sheath, and before Huey could react, he slammed a fist into the boy's face. Brown slumped to the floor of the barn, and Lance quickly tied his wrists tightly behind him. He stooped down and lifted the boy's heavy body, perspiring as he hoisted the body over his shoulder and walked out the back of the barn. It was so early in the morning it was still almost dark. He slung the body over Sotaju, then mounted up himself and rode off.

When Huey Brown came to later, he found himself hanging by the wrists from a tree limb, a crying Richard Gobles hanging beside him. Huey looked around in bewilderment, realizing they were in some kind of ravine shrouded by thick overgrowth, where no one would ever see them. He shook his head as mosquitoes bit at him.

"Richard?"

The other boy sniffed. "Huey! I thought you were dead."

Huey licked at a swollen, sore lip. "Where are we?"

"I think we're at Thorn Creek. That Rainmaker brought me here. He snuck up behind me while I was plowing and put some kind of gunnysack over my head and told me if I yelled he'd knife me. I believed him, Huey. Then he brought me here and tied me to this tree. I'm scared, Huey. He knows!"

"No he doesn't. He's just guessing. He thinks that if he scares us we'll talk. Just act innocent no matter what he does. He doesn't dare really harm us. The law would be after him!"

"I don't think he cares, Huey!"

Huey swallowed. "Where is he now?"

"I don't know. I bet he went after Johnny." The boy started whimpering again. "God, Huey, I can't stand it. My arms!"

"He won't do anything."

"Yes he will! You better talk, Huey. I'm only sixteen. I don't want to die!"

"If you say anything, I'll beat the hell out of you when we get through this, Richard Gobles! You keep your mouth shut!"

The boy whimpered softly, and Huey fought his own fear. He was determined the man called Rainmaker would get nothing out of him. It seemed hours before Lance finally came riding into the ravine, a wide-eyed Johnny Sorrell riding in front of him, his wrists tied together. The boy stared at Huey and Richard, then turned to look at Lance.

"What are you doing?" his voice squeaked.

Lance shoved him off of Sotaju. "All three of you know what I'm doing." He jerked the boy up, taking another piece of rawhide from his saddlebags and dragging Johnny to the tree. He yanked up the boy's arms and tied him to the limb with the other two, pulling him just high enough that his toes barely touched the ground. Lance stepped back then and lit a cigarette, studying all three of them. He'd done no real harm to any of them yet and reminded himself of white man's laws. But it was difficult not to be Indian at this moment. If he had to be, he'd do it, if that was what it took to get Cassandra. These boy's knew where she was, and they'd tell.

"Which one of you is going to tell me where Cassandra Elliott is?" he asked. "Did you rape her? Kill her?"

"No! No!" Johnny squealed.

"Shut up!" Huey demanded. He looked at Lance. "What would we know about her? Johnny said no because he doesn't even know what you're talking about. And you'd better take us back home or you'll be in a lot of trouble, Rainmaker! People already think you're half savage anyway."

Lance took out his knife, walking up to the boy and ripping open his shirt. He pushed the point of the knife against the boys chest just enough to make a pinpoint cut that drew blood. Huey shook and gritted his teeth, and the other boys stared wide-eyed, one of them whimpering.

"They're right, Huey boy. I am half savage," Lance sneered. "Tell me where that girl is."

Perspiration poured from Huey's face. "I said we don't know what you're talking about."

Lance stepped back, shoving the knife back in its sheath. He took some wooden skewers from his saddlebags, in which rawhide strips had already been tied through a hole pierced in each end. He untied one strip from the end of one of the skewers and walked up to each boy, holding it in front of him.

"These are what are used for the Cheyenne Sun Dance ritual. They're placed under the skin of each breast." He opened Johnny's shirt and just poked him with the skewer to show him. The boy gasped. "One is also placed in each upper arm, sometimes also in the back muscles. The rawhide strips are tied to something higher, and the man hangs by his skin until he faints and stays there until the skin rips away and he falls to the ground. It's a test of manhood. You boys seem to think you're men. I'm going to see just how manly you are today."

He set the skewers down and walked up to Richard, taking out his knife and slicing through the boy's overalls so that they fell down. He jerked off the boy's shoes,

354

ripped off his shirt and yanked off his underwear. The boy began crying as Lance moved to Johnny, doing the same, then to Huey, so that all three of them hung there stark naked. He kept the knife in his hand then and walked up to Huey, grasping the boy's privates.

"Now, one of you is going to have this thing sliced off, and the other two can enjoy the Sun Dance ritual and see what men you are. You three decide which punishment you want to take. You have about three minutes to decide."

He shoved his knife back in its sheath, and mosquitoes bit at the boys' bodies as they all hung there looking at each other and crying. Lance rolled and lit a cigarette, their weeping music to his ears. He'd do exactly what he said if he had to, if it meant finding and rescuing poor Cassandra. Cass! Poor Cass! What had happened to her? And what if these boys really didn't know?

"What if we tell you where the girl is?" Richard spoke up.

"Shut up, you idiot!" Huey growled.

"You shut up, you big, fat slob! I'm not going to let him do that to me, not for any girl or any money."

Lance's heart leaped with excitement. He threw down his cigarette and stepped up to Richard. "Where is she?"

"We . . . we sold her."

Lance's face darkened in hideous hatred. "Where? When?"

"Three or four nights ago!" the boy answered quickly. "To some men who worked for some big rancher. They . . . they were in town. We saw them watching her walking by and talking to each other, wondering who she was and all. We . . . we told them . . . and they asked all about her . . . if she had folks and all. We told them about . . . about her being alone . . . and once being

355

taken by Indians. They said if we could figure a way to get her out to them without the law finding out . . . they'd pay us for her. They said their boss . . . the man who owns the ranch . . . is kind of a hermit and wanted a wife but never left the place to find one. He said the man or men . . . who brought him someone to be his wife would be well paid. So they came to Abilene looking. They saw Cassandra . . . and we all figured since she'd already been took by Indians . . . and had no folks and all . . ."

Lance clamped a strong hand around the boy's neck. "You figured? You figured wrong, boy! Where is this ranch? What's the man's name!" Never had he struggled so hard not to kill someone. Cassandra! Had the man already made her his wife? What kind of man sent others out to kidnap women for him? What horrors had she suffered? How often had he dreamed of being her first man? It must be beautiful for her. It must be just right. It couldn't be at the hands of some cruel hermit who wanted a woman strictly for labor and sexual pleasure.

"I . . . I don't know his name!" Richard gagged. "Honest! Please . . . don't kill me! Only Huey knows his name!"

Lance reluctantly let go of the boy and turned to Huey. He whipped out his knife. "There's no sense holding back any longer, Huey Brown," he snarled. "What's the man's name?"

Huey swallowed, looking down at the knife. The tiny cut on his breast stung. "They know the name. They're just saying they don't. They want me to be the one to tell!" the boy argued.

Lance laid the knife against the boy's groin. "Then tell," he hissed. This time Huey Brown lost his courage. The look in Lance Raines's eyes told him the man would do anything now to make him talk.

"Farr. Quentin Farr," the boy finally told him. "I'm not sure where his ranch is, except that it's north of here, almost to the Republican River."

Lance reached over the boy's head then, slicing through the rawhide that held him to the tree limb. Huey slumped to the ground, groaning from the pain in his arms and shoulders.

"Did they ride straight there?" Lance asked, slicing through Richard's ties then.

"I don't know," Huey answered dejectedly.

Lance cut down Johnny then. "Will the men who took her leave her untouched?"

Huey swallowed, not about to tell the man he'd toyed with the girl himself. "I think so," he answered. "They were supposed to take her to their boss and told us we'd better not mess with her. So I don't think they'd do anything to her, either." He watched as Lance shoved his knife into its sheath. "You going to let us get dressed and go home now?"

Lance mounted up on Sotaju. "No. You're going to admit to what you've done. We're about two miles from town. Get up and start walking." He pulled out his rifle.

"But . . . our clothes!" Johnny protested.

"I said start walking!" Lance growled. He fired the rifle, hitting a stone no more than an inch from Huey's arm. All three boys jumped up and climbed out of the ravine.

Mattie rushed out of the saloon at the sound of the general commotion outside.

"My God, they're naked!" someone shouted.

She heard gasps and laughter and pushed through a

357

crowd that had formed to see three naked, red-faced boys walking right down the middle of the street, Lance Raines riding behind them, rifle in hand.

"What's that man doing! Why are they naked?" someone commented. General laughter and talking rippled through the street, and Mattie grinned. She would miss the Rainmaker. If he found Cassandra, she'd not see him again, she was sure. In spite of her smile over what was happening now, her heart was heavy at the thought of it.

The sheriff moved through the crowd then. "What's going on here!" he demanded. "What do you think you're doing with these poor boys!" he shouted to Lance.

Lance stayed on his mount. "They kidnapped and sold Cassandra Elliott," Lance replied. "She's at a ranch owned by a Quentin Farr, near the Republican. I'm going after her. You going to help me?"

The sheriff studied the three boys. "That true?"

Richard hung his head. "Yes, sir."

The sheriff scowled. "You boys are in a lot of trouble." He looked up at Lance. "That's out of my jurisdiction, mister. I looked for the girl myself and came up with nothing. That far north, I don't think there's any particular law except the territorial marshal. But he might be hard to find right away."

"Then I'll go alone. I'll not wait around for anyone."

"Suit yourself. Let me know what's happened to the girl. I'll see that these boys get their just punishment." He turned to one of the men.

"Bill, you ride out and get their folks and bring them into town."

The boys paled at the words, and the sheriff herded them toward the jail. People stared at Lance, while others walked away visiting and laughing. The sight of the three naked boys walking down the middle of the street would be a topic of conversation for a long time to come.

Lance turned his horse and rode over to Mattie. "Tell Kate I found out where Cass is and went after her and not to worry. Would you do that? I don't have time to go see her first."

"You look tired, Lance." She patted his thigh. "You be careful."

"That's not always easy."

Their eyes held. "I hope you find her. If things go wrong, you come to me. I'm always your friend, Lance Raines. But I won't be here in Abilene. All the business is in Dodge City now. I'm heading that way myself day after tomorrow."

He nodded, smiling sadly. "A woman like yourself has to go where the business it. You told me that once."

She smiled, her eyes tearing. "Sure." She rubbed his thigh. "I'll always remember you, Lance."

He took her hand. "It's been good, Mattie."

"I hope you find her. And I don't know what all happened over your son, but I hope that works out, too."

He nodded. "Good luck in Dodge City."

Her lower lip quivered and she nodded, turning away then. "Good-bye, Lance." She hurried inside, and Lance turned his horse and headed north. If Cassandra Elliott had been raped and made the wife of Quentin Farr, a lot of men would die!

Chapter Twenty-one

Cassandra sat on the bed in the room in which she had been held prisoner for the past seven days. Her only saving grace had been that the man called Quentin Farr had been gone on a cattle-buying trip when she arrived. From what she could determine, it was the only time each year he ever left the ranch, and for that matter, he seldom even left the house. This she surmised from the talk among the other men on the ranch, those who had brought her to this hated place, and those who brought her food, untying one hand so she could eat it.

The way they looked at her made her feel ill. And now the one called Quentin Farr was back. He had arrived only this morning but had already been to see her. The thought of his next visit made her want to vomit again, as she had done after his first visit. He had looked her over, felt her body, and approved of her as though she were a prime calf.

"Clean her up" was all he'd said to a Mexican woman who was with him. He'd grabbed Cassandra's face then in a strong hand. "You'll be my commonlaw wife, fair one. I don't doubt you'll make a good one. I'm told you've already been broke in by Indians, so I won't be taking the time to be slow with you, understand? I'm needing a woman in my bed, and I'm told you've got nobody to be coming for you. So there's no sense in fighting it. This is a fine ranch. You'll be a well-kept wife."

She could only stare in horror. He was a big man, perhaps two hundred and fifty pounds, most around his middle. He was bald and aging, but strong as an ox, it seemed to her. He looked her over again then, pushing up her dress and feeling her legs.

"A little more weight and you'll be just right." He turned to the Mexican woman. "I'm going to take a bath myself. Clean her up and put that pretty gown on her I've been saving. Then bring her to my bedroom after supper tonight." He looked back at Cassandra. "I'm called Quentin Farr. You can call me Quin. How many ways did the Indian bucks do it to you? How experienced are you?

She only blinked at the horrid question. He grinned. "No matter. I'll find out, soon as you lose that fear in your eyes. I'll warm you up quick enough. Then you'll stay in bed and do my bidding for a few days, besides eat. You're too skinny." He rubbed at himself between his legs then. "I'll say one thing. The men did a right fine job picking you out. I've got me the prettiest wife in the territory."

He'd left then. His words still rang in her ears, words of horror and filth. For seven days she had wept and prayed, wondering how she could kill herself when she got the courage. What was there left for her? Kate was probably dead by now. And Rainmaker! What had happened to Rainmaker! Without him, all was lost. There was no purpose in living. This, then, must be her fate—to be eternally miserable—abused, unloved, used by men she did not love, never touched by the only man she cared about. Her misery knew no bounds. She could not eat, and could not stop the daily vomiting. She was sick, but not truly from anything physical. She was sick emotionally, sick with fear and horror. How many times had she

361

dreamed about Rainmaker breaking her into womanhood? Now this fat, brutal man would be the one, and she could do nothing about it. Would he bring in other men to hold her and watch? What did he mean by the "ways" the Indian bucks did it to her? How many "ways" were there?

She had trembled all through the rude bath the Mexican woman had given her, vomiting again, only to be hit and scolded by the woman. She was given water to rinse her mouth, then powdered and oiled and perfumed. She stood limp and exhausted as the woman put a flimsy silk gown over her naked body and led her back to her bed.

"You will wait here until after supper," the woman told her, tying her wrists again, then tying one ankle to a post at the foot of the bed. "Then you will go to your master's room." The woman giggled. "You will have a fine time tonight, fair one. A naughty night, no?" She laughed wickedly as she left, closing the door behind her.

Again Cassandra struggled with the rawhide bindings. Her skin was raw. There was no getting out of the expert knots. She lay back and wept, praying that somehow she would die before supper, die before the huge Quentin Farr did hideous, painful things to her. Rainmaker! If only he would come again like he'd come when she was with the Cheyenne. Rainmaker! How could she bear the thought that he might be dead, that she was doomed to live a life as a used, commonlaw wife of a half-crazy rancher. She wasn't even sure where she was. And how would she ever know what had happened to Kate? Poor Kate! Dying all alone. Who was there to know where she was? Those awful boys who had sold her would never tell. Those who might care had probably already stopped searching for her. There was no hope left but to hope she would die. Maybe if she just stopped eating all together, she could hasten her death. She had already started trying, eating nothing for the last two days. And she was too sick to care.

She could hear voices and men's laughter downstairs. They must be gathering around the table for supper! Soon! He would come soon!

"Oh, God!" she whimpered, tugging at her bindings again. Her stomach ached terribly; every muscle was tense. How could she stop the inevitable? The door opened a crack then and she gasped. Surely he wasn't through with supper already. She watched wide-eyed as the door opened further, as though someone was being cautious, and she saw a dark hand, an arm covered by a buckskin sleeve, its fringes dancing from a soft breeze through a nearby window. Her heart stopped beating. It couldn't be.

Lance Raines darted inside, putting a finger to his lips as she gawked at him as though he were a ghost. He quietly closed the door and moved to her bed on soundless feet. She wanted to scream her joy, to shout his name, but dared not. Rainmaker! Surely God was good after all! Rainmaker! Rainmaker!

He removed his knife and deftly slashed it through the rawhide bindings at her feet and ankles, then shoved the knife back into its sheath. He bent to pick her up, and she grabbed him around the neck, breaking into almost hysterical sobbing but stifling her tears. He grabbed her close, so close she could barely breathe. How beautiful she was! But was she still just his?

Her throat was too full of sobbing to speak. And what was there to say just now? He was not only alive, but he had come for her before the horrible Quentin Farr could touch her. She clung to him desperately, with an amazing strength for her size, little pitiful squeals coming through her lips, her breathing in quick gasps of frenzied joy and relieved terror. Rainmaker!

"There's no time for talking," he whispered, "or even for reunions, Cass. We've got to get out of here."

She could only make little squeaking sounds, holding on to him for dear life, unable to let go.

"Cass, if you want both of us to live through this, you've got to let go of me, baby."

What a sweet sound. Baby. What a wonderful smell — Rainmaker — leather, fresh air, man, sweet and gentle man, not the ruthless kind. He pried her arms away and searched her eyes, his eyes quickly dropping over her, drinking in the sweet breasts that could be seen through the thin gown, the slender legs and bare hips. Cass! She was all woman. But he couldn't know if she was still his woman, and there was not time to talk about it. There was a step at the door and it opened.

Lance whirled to see the Mexican woman. She opened her mouth to scream, but Lance grabbed her tightly around the throat and jerked her inside. He squeezed tightly until her face reddened and her eyes bulged.

"Don't you scream, lady, or I'll sink a blade into you!" he hissed. "I swear it!"

He ripped off her apron and pushed her to the floor, stuffing the apron into her mouth and tying it behind her head. He used Cassandra's own rawhide ties to tie the woman's wrists, then picked her up and laid her on the bed, tying her wrists and ankles to the posts so she couldn't pound against the floor or walls. Cassandra watched in surprise at his speed. She never dreamed he could hurt a woman, but she knew instinctively he'd have killed this one if she had screamed. Yet it didn't seem to matter. The woman had been cruel, as cruel as the men. He came around to Cass, who stood now near the bed, watching him in total rapture, total astonishment that he

364

was there at all. Truly he was a spirit. She was full of questions. Where had he been? Why had he been gone two years? How was Kate? What about his son? Why was he thinner? Was he sick? What about the woman in Denver? Did he still love her? He took her arm.

"We have to move quickly. Do everything I tell you. I worked my way up here through the tall grass. Luckily they haven't cut their feed grass yet, and they don't trim anything around the house. I climbed into a back room and made my way upstairs as I could. We'll have to go out a window at the end of the hall and sneak back through the grass. Sotaju is tied several yards from here in some cottonwoods."

How she wished there was time to talk! Time to hold him! Time to tell him she loved him! What if he was killed trying to save her? He took a rope from his belt and opened the door carefully, then hurried down the hall with her to a window. He tied one end of the rope to the leg of a heavy dresser sitting in the hall, then threw the rope out the window.

"Climb down, Cass," he said quietly. "You might get a little rope burn, but it's better than staying here. Hurry, honey. Don't be afraid."

She wasn't about to hesitate and foil his plans. She crawled over the sill and took hold of the rope. Just as she started down, Quentin Farr came out of another room, half dressed. When he had come upstairs, they couldn't guess. But he apparently had already gone into his own room and now wondered why the Mexican woman had not returned with Cassandra. His eyes bulged when he saw Lance.

"Hey!" he shouted.

Lance pulled his knife and did not hesitate in lunging in into the man's heavy chest. The man grabbed Lance

365

around the throat with massive, strong arms, and in Lance's tired and still-unhealed condition, he had trouble pulling the man's hands away as Farr squeezed with amazing strength in spite of the deep wound in his chest. Lance finally managed to push him away, and he stabbed again as Cassandra watched in wide-eyed horror. Farr fell backward, and men began coming up the stairs then in answer to Farr's shout. Lance quickly shoved his knife in its sheath and pulled a handgun, firing twice.

"Get down the rope!" he shouted to Cassandra.

"Oh, God!" she squeaked as more shots were exchanged. She slid down, the gown protecting her legs most of the way, but her hands taking a skinning. She looked up and Lance was right above her, almost landing on her. He grabbed her in one arm and started running with her. More shots were fired, and she screamed. Lance stopped and turned, firing back. She heard someone cry out. He ran again, holding her in his arm like a rag doll. He ducked into the grass once, lying on top of her as bullets whizzed by. He quickly reloaded. Then he rose and fired again.

"That's most of them who were in the house," he told her. "Let's get going before the ones out in the bunkhouses realize what's going on and get to their horses."

He got up and ran with her again. The clump of cottonwoods seemed miles away, but finally they reached them. He mounted up, grabbing her arm and pulling her up behind him. She grasped him about the waist, and they were quickly off, Lance kicking Sotaju's sides.

"Hopo! Hopo!" he shouted. The stallion took off at a furious gallop. Lance bent forward, Cassandra hanging on for dear life. Men were coming from bunkhouses then, running around in confusion, unsure what was happening. Sotaju ran with all the speed his heart could muster, for

he sensed that of all their dangerous moments, this was the most important time for him to be as fast as he could be. He sensed his master's urgency. This was more important than running from the Indians, or running down a buffalo.

"Get to the river, boy!" Lance was shouting. "We'll lose them at the river!"

They splashed along the edge of the river, night falling. "We'll keep going until after dark," Lance spoke up finally. "They can't follow us in water and can only guess which way we'd go. We'll head north, then west, then come south and back to Abilene. They won't spend a lot of time searching for us, especially with Farr dead. What they did was against the law anyway."

His only reply was tears and trembling arms. He halted Sotaju and turned, pulling her around in front of him. She shivered as he embraced her. "My God, you must be cold," he muttered, realizing she still wore the flimsy gown. "You should have said something, Cass."

"It didn't matter," she whispered. "We had to get away." She hugged him tightly. "Oh, Rainmaker . . . you're alive! Thank God! Thank God! I can't . . . believe you're here. It was all . . . so horrible. And I thought you were dead . . . and I'd have to live at that horrible place forever."

"Hush, *Kseé*. It's all over now. Kate's still alive, and we're going home." He reached around behind him and untied a blanket, then put it around her shoulders. "I know you're tired. So am I. But we've got to keep going for a while. You ride in front of me so I can hang on to you."

"Like . . . the first time you came for me," she sniffed, her head against his chest.

He kissed her hair. "Like the first time."

She leaned back and looked up at him then, studying him in the moonlight. He kissed her eyes. "Tell me those men didn't touch you," he groaned.

She gasped in a sob. "They didn't, Rainmaker. That . . . big man you killed . . . he was going to make me his . . . commonlaw wife. He was going to come for me after supper . . . and I just wanted to die. He said terrible things to me . . . and he looked at me . . . and that woman . . ."

He kept kissing her cheeks, her hair. "But none of them . . . none of the men . . . Quentin Farr . . . they didn't force themselves on you? Rape you?"

"No," she whispered. His lips met hers then, hungrily, gratefully possessively. He moved to her neck, trembling.

"You belong to me," he whispered. "I was so afraid they'd already touched you. You're going to be my woman and no one else's, Cass. I never knew how much I wanted that until I learned those men had you. I'd kill every one of them if I had to."

He drew back, smoothing back some of her long hair. "Can you keep riding?"

She sniffed and nodded, pulling the blanket closer around her. "My legs . . . are chafed, though." She drew the blanket over her knees in embarrassment. "I . . . don't have anything on under this gown."

He frowned. "You can't ride that way." He moved his mount up onto the bank. "We've got to move quickly." He helped her down, then removed his shirt. "This buckskin is soft. You can sit on it. I have a salve we can put on your legs. If we don't do it now, you'll be sore as hell in a few more hours." He searched through his saddlebags and retrieved a small jar. He unscrewed the lid. "Here. Put some of this on."

She took the jar hesitantly. "Don't watch," she said in a tiny voice.

He had to grin as he turned away. Before long he would see everything she bashfully kept from him now, touch it, taste it, invade it.

She quickly smeared on the salve, then put the lid on the jar and touched his arm. "Here."

He took the jar and put it back, then turned, pulling her close. "God, Cass, I can't believe we're here together any more than you can. Last winter I didn't even think I'd live to see spring."

She relished the warm comfort of his arms, the security, the wonderful, wonderful security of it. "What happened to you, Rainmaker? Why didn't you come back?"

"We can't talk about it now. I know a place we can go. It will take a few more hours, but we'll be safer there. We've got to get going." He threw his shirt over the front of the saddle, then lifted her up, positioning her over the soft shirt. "That feel better?"

"Yes" came the tiny reply.

He mounted up behind her then, guiding the stallion back into the water. For another hour they felt their way along in the moonlight, sometimes having to go up on the bank because the water became too deep. Cass wanted to shout with relief and happiness. He was here! Rainmaker was right behind her, holding her, rescuing her, claiming her. He wanted her for himself. He'd said so. And the only reason he'd been gone so long was because he'd been hurt. He hadn't married that awful woman, and he wasn't dead. The horrible Quentin Farr would never touch her, and soon, surely before they reached Abilene, she might become Rainmaker's woman in every way. The thought sent shivers of trembling anticipation through her body, fear of the unknown mixed with the utter ecstasy of the thought of pleasing Rainmaker in that way. He would never leave this time without branding her for himself, and she didn't care how much it might hurt. She would bear it for Rainmaker, and eventually it would be beautiful, once the pain went away. That's the way Kate said it happened.

They headed out of the water then and rode west, grateful for a bright moon.

"If I remember this country correctly, there's a huge hill about two hours ahead, with a rocky side to it and a few small caves. It will be good shelter. I may have to chase a few wolves or something out of a cave, but I'll find us a good place to rest. If anyone is still chasing us, which I doubt, they'll have a hell of a time finding us now."

He urged Sotaju forward, grinning as Cass's head lolled against him in a much-needed sleep, the darkness and the rhythm of the horse, along with his comforting arms, bringing the sweet peace she needed to be able to rest. He kissed her hair, tears in his eyes. Thank God she was still his. Maybe life would be good to him after all — good to both of them.

"I love you, *Kseé*," he said softly.

They slept. For hours and hours they slept. First there had been a quick scouring of the cave with a torch made out of a cottonwood branch and a rag. There were no dangerous animals in sight. Lance had quickly made a fire, building it up to frighten away any wildlife that might be about, and to dry the dampness of the cave, which was not a deep cavern, but more like a hole in the side of a hill, perhaps ten feet deep. The floor was earth, and blankets over that made a soft enough bed for two weary people. A buffalo robe provided enough warmth, for they had each other for keeping warm. They had eaten a meal of beans and potatoes that Lance had in his supplies, and it was the first time Cassandra had had an appetite in a long time.

By then they were too weary to talk about what had happened to either of them. They settled in together under the buffalo robe, Lance stripping to his loincloth first. It was all taken for granted, and Cassandra was not afraid. She would sleep in the blessed, strong arms and never be afraid again. And if he wanted to make love to her, she would let him. But first must come rest and quiet and just enjoying being together.

It was Lance who awoke first, his face buried in her thick golden hair, his arm around her, her back pressed against him. He breathed deeply of her sweet scent, and he could no more control his love and his needs than he could control the sun. He pressed her closer, kissing the back of her neck, gently moving his hand to cup a breast through the thin gown.

She stirred, jumping awake at first and turning, forgetting where she was, who she was with. Their eyes met. "It's just me, *Kseé*," he said softly, nuzzling her neck. He pulled her close, moving a hand down to catch the hem of her gown, then up beneath it, caressing firm, bare hips. "I want you, Cass," he whispered.

She closed her eyes, trembling, exploding with joy and fear. "I . . . don't know what to do," she said softly.

"You don't need to know." He met her lips then in savage passion, moving his hand over her hips, then around over her belly and between her legs, his powerful arm pulling one leg gently up, forcing her legs to open while the whimpers from her lips told him it was all right. He knew that at first it would seem he couldn't get enough of her. He warned himself to be careful and slow. This was

371

not Mattie or Jessica. This was Cassandra, and he must not frighten her. He moved his lips to her neck, kissing, tasting.

"Don't be afraid, Cass. I'd never hurt you," he told her, his voice husky with desire. He breathed deeply of her scent, nuzzling her breasts as he pushed up the gown, then raised up slightly to pull it over her head so that she lay there completely naked. She reddened and curled up as he drank in her nakedness, and he untied his loincloth and discarded it.

She shuddered at his masculinity, the fact that this beautiful man of hard muscle and bravery and skill had chosen her. His green eyes were glazed with desire, his jaw rigid, his breathing deep, while her own heart pounded wildly. He took her hand and placed it against that which she had never touched before. She couldn't bring herself to look. Maybe some day she could. But for now she would touch, because he wanted her to touch. It was velvet soft, to her surprise. He took her hand then and brought it up to his mouth, closing his eyes and kissing her palm.

"To mate is as natural as to breathe, Cass," he told her, kissing her eyes then, "when two people feel as we do. When it's natural and necessary, the pain is not so bad, and then that goes away, too, until there is nothing but joy and a desire to please and take pleasure in return. *Nemehotatse.*"

His mouth covered hers then, while one arm pulled her close and he moved his other hand over her breasts, down over her belly, reaching into the velvety moistness that told him that most womanly part of her was preparing to take a man for the first time.

She began whimpering and returning his kiss wildly at the touch of his fingers in magic, secret places never

372

touched before. Rainmaker! How beautiful he made her feel! What was he doing to her to make her so wildly passionate, so eager to let him touch her more, let him do whatever he wanted? How was it he could make her lose her shyness this way and want to be touched and tasted? It was more beautiful than she had even imagined.

His big hand explored and manipulated, while his lips moved over her throat, then down to the virgin breasts, their pink nipples erect from excited desire, and for the first time Rainmaker tasted them, ever so softly, lightly sucking, seemingly pulling forth from her all the buried, unknown, awakened passions she never knew existed within her soul. She could not help crying out, whimpering his name, grasping his thick hair as his lips traveled over her, kissing her belly, kissing the soft hairs between her legs, kissing her thighs, looking, exploring, his hands gently massaging, breaking down every last bit of resistance she might have until she felt a pleasant explosion deep in her belly, a marvelous throbbing that made her cry out his name.

He moved his lips back up over her breasts to her throat, her lips again, kissing with heated passion that nearly took her breath away, his tongue forcing her lips apart, his arm moving between her legs again, bending one leg up and out. He moved on top of her, his manliness pressing hard against her belly, while his lips never left her own.

Finally! Finally she was lying naked beneath Rainmaker, pleasing him like all the others had done, only she was the most special. He loved her! Finally she lay in the glorious ecstasy of Rainmaker's naked skin touching hers, Rainmaker tasting, loving, devouring. But the moment had come, the real moment of becoming a woman, and her heart beat wildly with a mixture of fear and excite-

373

ment.

"Hang on, *Kseé,*" he whispered.

In the next moment she knew only pain and could not help crying out with it. But there was no way he could stop now, and there was only one way to get it done. His heart ached at her screams, but he pushed deep, shuddering with the glory of it, with the knowledge this truly was her first time and finally he was making a woman of Cassandra Elliott, little Cass. But she was not the little girl he had rescued. She was a woman. He moved rhythmically, every plunge bringing a whimper from her now. He poured his life into her, afraid to take too long the first time.

He sighed deeply then, pulling her close as she whimpered in pain. "Please don't cry, Cass. I'm sorry I hurt you. How else could it be?"

She hugged him tightly. "I'm not . . . crying from that," she whimpered. "I'm just . . . so happy . . . you're finally mine."

They kissed, over and over, and he rubbed her belly gently after moving off of her. He looked down to see blood on himself. "Damn!" he whispered. He bent down and kissed her breasts, her belly. "You lay right there. I'll heat some water, and we'll hold some warm rags against you. I won't touch you any more today."

She reached out to him. "It's all right, Rainmaker. You can do it again if you want."

He grinned and leaned back down, pulling her into his arms and kissing her hair. "I probably could, but I'm not an animal, Cass. This is enough for today. We'll try again tomorrow, and every time we make love, it will get better and better. I promise."

"I believe you. I'm not afraid of the pain."

He studied the wide blue eyes. "I love you, Cass. Right

374

now that's all I'm going to think about. We'll stay here, maybe three or four days, and just be alone, enjoy each other, talk. We have many things to talk about."

She ran her hands over the muscular shoulders and the dark hairs of his chest. "I've never been happier than I am right now," she answered, her eyes tearing. "I love you, too, Rainmaker. I've loved you for such a long, long time. I never thought this moment would come. When I began to believe you were dead, I wanted to die, too. And then Kate got sick, and those awful boys—"

He put a hand to her mouth. "None of that. Not yet. I'll wash you and put something warm on your belly, and we'll sleep some more. Then we'll talk. And after that we'll do nothing but sleep and eat—" he cupped a breast and bent down to kiss the nipple—"and make love. We'll make love until I've shown you all the ways there are to be man and woman together, until you have no more pain. I've had a hunger building for you that will take a long time to fill."

Her body tingled at the words. Rainmaker would teach her all the ways of being a woman. He was here and alive, and she had been one with him. She couldn't think beyond that for now. They would lie alone in this cave somewhere in the middle of Kansas, and when he finished with her, there would be nothing left of the little girl in her. She would be woman, Rainmaker's woman.

Chapter Twenty-two

When Cassandra awoke later in the morning, it was to the smell of coffee. She turned, pulling the buffalo robe around her shoulders, to see Lance knelt by a rekindled fire, wearing only the loincloth. A wave of passion swept through her at the realization that the beautiful man she looked at had made a woman of her just hours earlier. Rainmaker! She had not dreamed it after all. He really was alive. He really had come for her. And he really had claimed her. There was even less doubt about it when she moved to sit up; for her loins ached, and she felt a cramp deep inside her belly. She winced and curled up, and Lance was at her side in the next moment.

He sat down beside her, stroking her hair. "You hurting bad?"

She reddened. "Not that bad. I'm sure I'll make it just like most other women." She closed her eyes, enjoying the gentle strokes of his big hand. "I want to do it again. I don't care how much it hurts."

"Well I do. We'll do it again, but not today."

Her eyes teared. "You don't think I'm bad, do you, Rainmaker?"

He frowned. "Now, why would I think that?"

A tear slipped down her cheek. "I'm not your wife. Only bad girls do what I did."

He sighed, lying down and resting on his elbows, hovered over her. "Don't you ever say that again, Cassandra Elliott. You're the sweetest, nicest girl I've ever known, and if I didn't intend to marry you, I never would have touched you."

He kissed her tears, and her heart swelled with love. "Do you mean it truly? We'll be married?"

"I mean it truly." He flashed the smile that made her ache with love for him. He wiped at her tears with gentle fingers, sobering. "That is, if you will have this worthless, wild man."

She reached up and touched his face. "You know I will. I've loved you ever so long."

He kissed and nibbled at her fingers. "I'll be true to you, Cass. I'm ready to settle. I want a wife and I want . . . " Pain filled his eyes and he sat up, turning away. "I want sons."

She quelled the jealousy the thought of his being with Jessica Françoise brought to her young heart. She knew he was thinking of Julien. She sat up and kissed the scar on his back, ignoring her own pain, then hugged him from behind, running her fingers over the scar on his stomach.

"You said you were shot and almost died last winter—that Indians helped you. That's all you told me, Rainmaker. What happened? Was it something to do with your son in Denver?"

He watched the coffee begin to boil. "His mother

shot me," he answered quietly.

She sat up straighter, pulling the buffalo robe around her naked body. "His mother! She shot her son's own father? How? Why?"

He ran a hand through his hair. "I'd gone there to see if I could talk her into leaving her husband and marrying me so I could be with my son." He sensed her disappointment and jealousy without looking. "It was something I had to try, Cass. God knows how long I could have stayed with her without going crazy with the want of you. I'm sorry if it hurts you, but I didn't know what else to do." His fists clenched. "She said she'd consider it, asked me to hold her." He snickered bitterly. "I've been with a lot of women, Cass, but none have ever used me or fooled me like she did. She truly is a witch." He spit the words out. "I guess I wanted to believe her because I wanted Julien so bad. That made me stupid—stupid with love for my son, I guess. The next thing I knew there was an explosion in my gut, and she just smiled. I don't know what she intended to tell her husband if I had died right there in the nursery, but as clever as she is, she'd have thought of something, I'm sure. But I didn't want to risk any explanations leading to Julien. I didn't want her husband to know the boy might not be his, especially when I'd be helpless to keep my son from harm. So I ran. She shot me again as I climbed through the window. I managed to get to Sotaju and get away in the darkness, but I felt everything slowly going numb. I thought I was a dead man. When the Indians found me, I didn't even know what was going on. I spent most of the winter paralyzed, wishing I'd die. If not for the support of Kicking Horse and Buffalo Woman, and if not for the memory of your love and little Julien's face, I would have just let myself die. Then movement finally came back to me, and I asked Kicking Horse to take me off alone so I'd have to fend for myself. I knew it was the only way I could find out whether I could make it, be a man again."

She hugged him again, resting her face against his muscular back. "I knew it was something terrible, but I also never stopped believing you were alive, Rainmaker. I prayed for you every day." She kissed his back. "That awful, awful woman! How could she do that?"

His jaw flexed with anger. "Jessica Françoise is capable of doing anything. That's why I can't stand the thought of my son being raised by her, and by a man as ruthless and unfeeling as Claude Françoise, no matter how much they might think they love that boy. That's not the kind of love a boy needs. I want him to be free, to know real love, to feel the wind in his face and ride bareback and learn to hunt, to love the land and nature, to have compassion. That's one thing he'd never learn with those people—compassion. I don't give a damn how much money they have. I don't want him growing up there. He's mine, Cass! He's mine and he's beautiful and smart and perfect. And he's over two years old now." He ran a hand through his hair again. "I don't know what to do, Cass. If I go to Françoise and just tell the man the boy is mine, God only knows what the man would do to him. I obviously can't look to Jess. If I kill one or both of them and get caught, I'll hang and never get to see you or my son again. And no matter what she's done to me, I can't bring myself to kill the boy's mother. If I just kill Françoise, Jess would know who did it. She'd have the law on me, and that would be that. No matter how I look at it, it seems that evil witch wins at every turn, and I feel sick with hatred for her and with love for my son."

Cass swallowed back the ache in her throat and hung her head. "It will always be this way, won't it?"

He turned to look at her with watery eyes. "What do you mean?"

She met his eyes with sad blue ones. "You love me. But there is someone you love more. You can't marry me yet, Rainmaker. Half of you is someplace else, and you'll never be able to truly settle until you decide what you're going to do about Julien. I don't want just half of you. I want all of you. And I can't have all of you until you either get Julien for yourself, or make up your mind to leave the boy where he is and get on with your life."

The look on his face told her she was right, and the utter happiness she'd known the moment before was tarnished. It wasn't over yet. In spite of the fact that Lance Raines had claimed her, she still could not yet truly belong to him. Her lips trembled.

"Just remember it's my life, too, that has to have a future," she told him. "I don't want any future but with you, Rainmaker. But we can't get married yet. Not until you decide what to do about Julien. To leave things this way will only eat at you and make you an unhappy man. You have to get things right . . . in your heart, Rainmaker." Her voice began to shake. "You have to make peace with yourself, resign yourself to whatever must be." She wiped at a tear. "I could give you babies, Rainmaker, as many as you want. They'd be your children, too, to love and nurture."

He reached out and petted her hair. "Don't cry, *Kseé*.

I hate it when you cry."

"I can't . . . help it. We still . . . can't really be together."

He pulled her close. "Yes we can. I'll find a way. I promise, Cass. I swear to *Maheo* and your Jesus that I'll find a way." He hugged her tightly. "Don't cry. No matter what else happens, the next couple of days are just ours, right here alone. I'll not let anything change that. Then I'll take you back to Kate, and I'll think of something. Maybe I'll just . . . just let it go. To do anything else would only mean harm to Julien. Maybe I have no choice but to let it go. I can't even tell the law what Jessica did because then I'd have to explain everything else. She's used everyone, Cass. She's even using Françoise."

"God will make it right somehow, Rainmaker. I just know He will. He has to! He just has to! Just look what He's already done. You're alive and walking, and you found me." She pulled back then. "How did you find me, Rainmaker?"

He kissed her forehead and moved away, pouring coffee into two tin cups. "I had a talk with those farm boys. I figured they'd be the best ones to start with." He handed her a cup. "If you will remember, I make terrible coffee."

She watched him wide-eyed, taking the coffee. "What did you do to them?"

He knelt by the fire. "Nothing, actually. It's what they thought I was going to do that made them talk. They're in the hands of their parents and the sheriff now. I don't think you'll have any more trouble with them."

He took some jerky out of his saddlebags and handed

her a piece. "I'll go out later and try to find us some fresh meat. I don't have much food left—a few cans of beans and a few potatoes."

She watched the muscle of his arm as he handed her the jerky, curious at what he'd done to the boys, remembering again his valiant rescue from the Cheyenne and again from Quentin Farr. She remembered his ruthless stabbing of Farr, realizing he could break her in half easily. Yet he'd been so gentle with her. When she was with Rainmaker, she felt so safe and loved and protected. Surely that woman in Denver was a witch. How could she not love a man like Rainmaker? How could she let him hold her while she exploded a gun into him? Surely she was a hideous, wicked woman.

She bit off a piece of jerky, drinking in the sight of him as he sat down Indian style across the fire from her. With only the loincloth, he might as well be naked. She could hardly believe the magnificent man she looked at had actually been one with her hours before, but her aching insides told her so. The pain of that first intercourse had been worse than she had imagined, yet it didn't matter. It had been Rainmaker. She believed him when he said it would hurt less each time. Even if it always hurt the same, she knew she'd let him take his pleasure in her anyway, because men like Rainmaker deserved their pleasure. She would take him and take him, and bear his children. She could only pray that somehow something would get settled over Julien, so that he truly could belong to her.

"If we ever get to all be together, Rainmaker, I'll love your little boy and be a good mother to him. I promise."

He glanced at her with sad eyes. "I know you will,

Kseé. That's why I hope some way I can have him. Better to be raised by you than someone like Jessica Françoise." His eyes turned cold then, so cold it made her shiver.

The hot Kansas sun shone down in all its August heat. From first glance, no one would guess there was anything alive in the vast, hot, empty prairie, for it was wide-open nothingness, with not even a farmer's house in sight. But there were two people who did not mind the loneliness, who wanted it, who lay together in a cool cave in the side of a hill.

Lance had spent the first day watching, but there was no sign that anyone had followed them there. They were as alone as if they were on a deserted island. He felt lucky that there were even prairie dogs about, and ended up shooting those for food, but not until the second day, when he was more sure no one was coming after them, for he didn't want anyone unwanted to hear the shots.

They all needed the rest, even Sotaju. Neither Lance nor Cassandra wanted to think about going back, about making decisions, about having to part again. There was only now, this moment, and the awakening of long-buried passions.

Never did Cassandra imagine being a woman could bring so much joy and pleasure. In that short time, the pain could not subside completely, but the things Rainmaker did to her before invading her brought her to such ecstasy that it made it easier to bear the actual intercourse. His patience was sweet, his skill at bringing her to peaks of glory amazing, his soft Cheyenne words beautiful music. It was not difficult to understand why women came easy to him, but neither did she doubt his ability to be true to the one woman he really loved. To her utter joy, that was herself. Finally, after her years of waiting, she was Rainmaker's woman. She struggled not to let the reality of his son's existence spoil the moment. Something would happen to allow them all to be happy. She had to believe it. She had to be his wife some day, like he wanted, bear his children, sleep in his arms every night, help him raise Julien.

The first day moved into the second, and then the third, ever closer to the time when they must go.

"We have to think about Kate," Lance said quietly the fourth night. He sat across the fire from her, smoking, studying how lovely she looked sitting on the buffalo robe, wearing one of his buckskin shirts like a dress. It came nearly to her knees, and the sleeves were rolled up several times; but at least it was covering. She had left the Farr ranch with nothing but the flimsy gown.

"I know. I'm worried about her, too. If she knows we're all right, I just know she'll get better."

"You up to riding to Abilene in the morning? It could take two or three days. I want to swing farther west yet, then come down from the north and follow the Kansas-Pacific back."

"I can do it. I feel better every day. I was only sick at that horrible ranch because I was so afraid and so sure I'd never see you again."

Their eyes held, and he wondered if he would ever get enough of looking at her, ever stop wanting her with such fierce passion. Every time he took her it was like the first time all over again. Everything was new to her, and because she was his first virgin, it was new to him, too.

"You're still too thin," he told her.

"I'll get fat soon enough." She reddened as soon as she made the remark, for it sounded like she meant pregnancy.

"I've thought of that, Cass."

"I didn't mean—"

"I know. But we have to face the possibility. When we get to Abilene, I'll leave you with Kate, and I'll go to Denver once more. I've already decided there's nothing much I can do but see my son once more and try to get on with my life. I'll come back, Cass, and I won't take too long doing it. We'll be married, once I get this last thing out of my system. I just have to see him once more."

She dropped her gaze. "You might stay forever. You might not come back once you see him."

"No. I'll come back."

"He'll be talking, walking. He'll win your heart, and you won't be able to leave him, no matter how much you love him. You'll stay in Denver just to be near him." She met his eyes then. "I can't live there, Rainmaker. I can't live near that horrible woman, see her and . . . and know. . . ."

"I never asked you to live there. I'll come back and we'll settle around here, and once in a while I'll go and get a look at him. That's the most I can hope for."

"You might get in trouble if you go back. You don't know what she might have told her husband that night she shot you."

He shook his head. "She doesn't dare name me if she can help it. My guess is that boy is growing to look more and more like me, and she doesn't want her

385

husband to notice that and make a connection. As far as I can determine, my name has never been linked with anything but being an employee of Claude Françoise. When I go back, I'll just tell Françoise I couldn't stand the daily boredom of the job and I left. He'd believe that of a wild, unsettled type like me. I'll collect my money, see Julien again, and come back."

He took a deep drag on his cigarette, and she watched the finely etched lips, shuddering with renewed desire at the thought that those lips had tasted and savored every part of her, those green eyes had seen all there was to see, and she had pleased him. Her heart tightened with aching love.

"I don't want to leave here, Rainmaker," she said, her voice choking. "It's been so wonderful, so peaceful, just you and me."

He threw down his cigarette and came to her side, kneeling beside her and kissing her lightly. "I don't want to go, either, but the cold, hard reality of life outside of this place awaits us. We'd best head out in the morning and get back to Kate."

Their eyes held, and in the next moment they kissed again, each as hungry for the other as the first time their bodies met. His hands moved over her casually, and he turned to lean down and kiss her ankles, her legs, her knees, her thighs, as he gently pushed up on the buckskin shirt. She lay back and closed her eyes. There was nothing to do but let him explore and caress and do the things that made her feel so bold and daring and wonderfully in love. She was determined not to let the despondency over leaving in the morning interfere with this present ecstasy.

His lips moved on up over her flat belly, kissing her

protruding hip bones, her stomach, inching the shirt up over her breasts and savoring their fruits.

She raised up, and he pulled off the shirt, then untied his loincloth. "Let's not waste this last night in the coolness of the cave," he told her in a husky voice.

She reached up toward him then, her golden hair cascading over bare shoulders, her blue eyes glazed with love. "I love you, Rainmaker," she said softly. "I'll be your friend forever."

The words struck him. The vision of her lying there, reaching for him, speaking the words. He felt as though someone had pierced his heart with a lance. Did it all mean this was the last time they would have such a beautiful moment?

She didn't understand the way he looked at her, why he hesitated for a moment, why his eyes teared.

"And there's the difference between making love to a woman — and truly loving one, being loved by one," he replied. "The one who truly loves you is more than . . . just a woman to lie with. She is a friend."

The vision! There it was. He could not help the fear it brought him. He loved her. He did not want to ever lose her. Yes, he loved her more than he had even realized until this moment.

He came down to her then, shuddering, embracing her. "Hold me, Cass."

She hugged him as tightly as her small arms could hug. For the first time she sensed he needed her as much as she needed him, that even Rainmaker could be vulnerable, that perhaps for all his outward strength, there was the little boy in him crying out for love and help. And she knew that just as she remembered her family's death and the fear it had brought that would never be forgotten, so must Lance Raines remember his own fears as a five-year-old boy who had lost his family and was taken in by a strange people. All his life he had been trying to make up for not being big or strong enough to help his mother. Now he had a son, who in his eyes was helpless, helpless against being raised by a kind of people who might destroy the good in him, and it deeply pained Lance Raines.

There was a difference to their lovemaking that night. Something had changed. Something had gone deeper. A new understanding developed without any words being spoken, and Cassandra Elliott was suddenly older and wiser. His every touch to her body was even more pleasing, and for the first time she touched in return, wanting to comfort, please, show her affection. She was bolder, more aggressive, awakening even more passion in the man, passions he'd not felt with any other woman.

Lance never knew that being with a woman could be this satisfying. In spite of all he'd been with, none had brought forth this aching desire in his soul, this fierce love and possessiveness, this great hunger that never seemed to be satisfied. There was so much more to intercourse with this one, such rich, rewarding pleasure, a terrible need to please her just as much as she pleased him, rather than just to feel good for the moment. This woman loved him beyond just making love. She loved all that was Lance Raines, and he knew without question that she would stay by his side through all adversities. This was the kind of woman a man needed in this land. She would never complain, never turn him away in the night, never be untrue to him. And she would love his son. If only he could get

Julien, she would love him, and they could be so happy.

He took her hungrily, almost savagely, for she responded with equal hunger, her inhibitions gone, lost to glorious ecstasy and undying love. He raised up just to look at her, to watch the beautiful young body as it arched up to him in response to his hands running along her slender thighs and around under the firm, small hips. He could not help but wonder how he fit at all, and he knew the pain was still not completely gone, but she took him anyway. Her fingers dug into his forearms as he plunged deep into her body, deep into her soul, and he came down on her then, groaning her name as his lips tasted the sweetness at her neck and his life spilled into her belly.

Yes, this was different. This was the most glorious experience he'd ever known, even with women who knew all the ways to excite a man. For this woman was different. He loved this one, and she loved him.

They went to the house first to bathe and change, and for the first time in many days, Cass could put on a real dress again. It had been a long journey back to Abilene, and they had taken little time to rest, although they had found time more than one night to share bodies again. Always it seemed they had the energy for that, in spite of their weariness. Now they did not stop to rest at all. They had to get to Kate. And on the way, there was business to settle with the sheriff.

"Those boys are in the custody of their parents," the man told them. "And from what I can tell, they'd be better off in jail. I don't think Miss Elliott needs to worry much about them any more."

389

"Have any of Farr's men been here to report a raid on their ranch?" Lance asked the man.

The sheriff looked him over and grinned wryly. "A raid? By one man?"

Cassandra had to smile. "By one man."

The sheriff rubbed his chin. "Well, I expect they'd be a little embarrassed about that. At any rate, nobody has shown up, but then, they don't really dare, do they? They'd have to answer to charges of kidnapping Miss Elliott here. Far as I'm concerned, you did what any marshal would have done, and you rescued the girl. I see no problems for you, even if you killed someone to do it. You . . . uh . . . you didn't kill anyone, did you?"

Lance shrugged. "Who knows? They shot at me, and I shot back. Far as I know, I didn't kill one man."

Their eyes held and the sheriff nodded. "Of course." He glanced at Cassandra, a sweet, pretty girl. How could he bring a man up on charges of trying to help her? In this land, law was still young, and men who helped others without the aid of the law were still needed.

"You'd best be going to see Mrs. McGee. The doctor has checked with me off and on to see if I'd heard from either one of you so he could tell her you're all right. She's very worried, and in her condition that's not good."

Lance nodded, putting out his hand. "This matter is settled then, even if Farr's men show up?"

The sheriff shook his hand and released the hold. "It's settled. And if Farr's men show up, I'll chase them right back out of town and tell them they'd better not show up in Abilene again or I'll jail then. No names

390

will be mentioned. With some luck, we can keep them off your back."

Lance took Cassandra's arm. "Before long I'll probably be leaving Abilene myself anyway," he told the man. "Miss Elliott and I are going to be married, and I think I'll head up Montana way and do a little ranching."

Cassandra's heart ached for him. He was trying to be brave, trying to tell himself that after seeing Julien once more he could go far away and forget about his son. She knew that for the boy's safety, and for his love for her, he would try. But she worried about his happiness. Would he truly come back from Denver once he saw Julien again? Was his love for her strong enough for that? Surely it was. They had shared so much together now, bodies and souls. They were one. And here he was talking about marriage and settling. Surely Rainmaker would not shatter her heart by not coming back, by changing his mind. He squeezed her arm as though reading her thoughts, and she was instantly comforted.

She was hardly aware of the rest of the conversation, too full of love for Rainmaker. Soon he was leading her out and toward the clinic, where they found Kate sitting up in bed, leaning against pillows, her eyes closed, but her color better.

"Is this all you do all day, old woman?" Lance asked, leaning over and fluffing a pillow.

Her eyes opened from a light sleep, and she sucked in her breath. "Lance!" He gave her a hug, and when she looked over his shoulder, she saw Cassandra standing there, looking tired, but smiling.

"Hi, Kate," she spoke up, tears in her eyes.

"Oh, my!" Kate looked up at Lance as he pulled

away. "You found her! Mattie told me about what those awful boys did—" She glanced at Cassandra and reached out to her. "Come here, child."

Cassandra hugged the woman, and Kate patted her back. "You poor thing. So many tragedies you've suffered. Dear God, tell me those men didn't harm you."

"No one touched me, Kate," the girl answered. "Rainmaker came before that awful rancher could make me his wife. I'm all right."

"Of course you are. I knew when Mattie said Lance went for you, everything would work out." She sniffed as Cassandra pulled away. "Oh, my, this is almost too much for me. I don't know which is worse, worry, or excitement and joy." She patted her chest as Lance wrapped his arms around Cassandra from behind, hugging her back to him with a familiarity that told Kate all she needed to know, for they had obviously been alone together for several days. Cassandra looked up at Lance, and the look they exchanged gave off almost visible sparks of passion. Cassandra Elliott had loved this man for a long time, and Lance Raines was surely not willing to wait any longer to claim the girl he'd said he owned nearly four years ago when he took her from the Cheyenne. That girl was no longer a child, and never before this moment had she looked quite so womanly. Only one thing could change a girl that way.

"I see an awful lot of happiness in those eyes, you two," she observed, watching them knowingly. "Could it be due to more than Cassandra's rescue?"

Cassandra reddened and looked down, but Lance just squeezed her tighter and laughed lightly. "It could. And I don't want any speeches out of you. Besides, you're too weak to be scolding someone bigger than you.

392

We've come to take you home with us, Kate. You're going to just lie around and get better while Cass takes care of you and I go to Denver one last time. When I come back, Cass and I will be married, and the three of us are heading north, where I intend to start a ranch. And you, dear Kate, are never going to work hard again. You'll just sit under a shade tree and knit."

He had moved from around Cass as he spoke and bent over her now. "I've already talked to the doctor, and I'm carrying you right out of here so you can go home where you belong."

She put a hand against his chest, her eyes worried. "Denver? Why are you going back there? You didn't tell me what happened the first time, Lance, why you were gone so long. What happened to you, son? You shouldn't go back there. Stay here and marry Cass right now."

He sighed and sat down on the edge of the bed, talking quietly. "I would marry her now; but she's the one who says we should wait, and she's probably right."

"Wait!" She looked at Cassandra, who moved around to the other side of the bed. "Why?"

Cassandra looked lovingly at Lance. "He's got to go, Kate." She looked at Kate again. "I'm afraid for him to go, too, but he can't leave it this way. He's got to see his son once more and decide in his heart he can do this. I can only trust God and trust in his love for me and believe he'll come back for good next time."

Kate's eyes teared, and she looked back at Lance. "You've laid your claim, Lance Raines. You do right by this girl, you hear? You come back, and don't be taking two years to do it."

He looked over at Cassandra, his eyes roving over

393

her lovingly. "One month, at the most, probably less, now that I can go there and back by train." He looked at Kate again. "That's a promise. I don't break promises, Kate. I don't want to be away from Cass any longer than necessary."

"And what in God's name will you prove to yourself by going to Denver?"

His eyes teared. "I don't know yet," he said in a near whisper. "But I have to see him, Kate. It won't keep me from coming back for Cass. I love her. I'll always love her, no matter what happens."

"Kate, it's all right," Cassandra reassured the woman. "I know in my heart he loves me. And even if something happens that he can't come back, he was my—" She reddened and looked down at the blanket. "I've . . . been with him," she finished quietly. "I wouldn't change a thing. For the rest of my life, even if I married somebody else, Rainmaker would be the only man I love. But I just know God will make it work out."

Kate took hold of each of their hands. "I hope you two know what you're doing. There's nothing I want more than to see you together, married, settled." She squeezed their hands with what strength she could muster. "I love you both. I'm some better now. When you were gone, Lance . . . and Cass disappeared . . . I almost gave it up. I guess all I can do is thank God for now that you're both here, together and unharmed. I want to hear about Denver—and about that rancher. And Cassandra, you've got to bake this poor man a pie. I think you owe him that much, I'd say. Of course, the debt's been paid in something he enjoys more than pie, no doubt."

Cassandra reddened deeply, and Lance laughed lightly

394

as Kate squeezed their hands even harder, her breathing labored. "God knows I can't blame either of you for what you've done. I suppose it had to be, and you sure look like you belong together. God have mercy on you both. Take me . . . home now, Lance. I want to go home . . . lie in my own bed . . . rest my eyes . . . on the two of you."

Chapter Twenty-three

Cassandra awoke to the feel of Lance's breath against her neck. He slept soundly, and she lay with her back to him, studying the firm muscle of the arm that embraced her, the skin darkened by the prairie sun. It seemed strange that her own small self had commanded this powerful man's love, had pleased his keen hunger for woman, had even been able to fit all of his masculinity into her small frame. Even now there were still remnants of pain, and she didn't doubt they were just tiny hints of what giving birth would be like. But she would endure both kinds of pain, for both would be for Rainmaker.

All the years of waiting and dreaming were over. She could only hope it would not begin all over again when he left for Denver; hope that this time would only be for a while, and soon he would return, riding out from the horizon like the quiet wind. Had she finally captured the wind? It supposedly could not be done. If it could not, then Rainmaker would not come back to her.

She quelled an urge to break into tears, refusing to cry in front of him. She must be strong for him, for right now he needed her to be the strong one. He was going to Denver to say good-bye to a son he'd never really known. In spite of his determination that the Françoises should not raise him, to do anything about it could only

396

mean harm to the boy. How many times had they discussed it? How many times had she worried he would do something wild and foolish and risk their own happiness just to be with the boy? He had already nearly lost his life once trying to get him. God only knew what Jessica Françoise would plot against him once she discovered he was still alive.

How she hated the woman! She'd never met her and hoped she never would. The thought of Lance lying in the woman's bed for five days wrenched at her soul painfully, yet she'd had no claim on him then, no right to be angry about it. But look at what had resulted. A son. A son by another woman. The child would probably forever come between them to some extent, pulling at Lance Raines's heart in the deep of the night, the child's angelic face and green eyes haunting him. At first Cassandra had determined she would not marry Lance Raines if the boy still existed and Lance could not have him. But she knew she could not live her life away from Lance Raines's bed. She would take the risk. If he came back from Denver and declared he was ready to go on with his life even without the boy, she would marry him and do the best she could to provide him with more children, children who would help ease the pain of that first son he might never see again after this trip. But how much danger was there in his going? She could not and would not stop him. But Jessica Françoise had already tried to kill him once. Surely she wouldn't dare try it again, but what else was she capable of doing? How long would the woman's existence come between them, preventing them from truly fulfilling their own dreams?

She turned and kissed his chin, so firm and square and handsome. "Come back to me, Rainmaker," she whispered.

He stirred and groaned, opening one eye to see her watching him. Both were pleasantly tired from a night of heated lovemaking, for today he would leave for Denver. Their eyes held and he pulled her against his chest.

"Can we stop time?" he asked.

"How I wish we could."

He kissed her hair and fingered the gold band she wore on a ribbon around her neck. "This should be on your hand, Cass."

"It will be — when you come back. I want no ties that force you to come back, Rainmaker. It has to be because you really want to, still really want me to be your wife. If that makes me bad for now, then I'll be bad. But you've bought the ring, and I'll treasure it forever and ever and always wear it next to my heart, if never on my hand."

The thought of her lying in some other man's arms made his chest burn, and he gripped her tightly, nuzzling her neck. "It will be on your hand soon — very soon. I just have to see him once more, Cass. I'll always remember how you understood. You're more woman than I thought you could be." He kissed the ring — her breasts. "If I don't make it back, don't go to another man too soon. Promise me."

"After being with you, how could I ever go with another man?"

Their eyes held then, and they ignored their sleepy morning state. This was their last morning for a while. They were warm, soft, relaxed. He nuzzled her neck again, moving on top of her.

"God, Cass," he whispered. The words seemed to say everything. She opened slender legs and gasped when he was instantly inside of her. He shuddered, and it seemed he was filled with a mountain of emotions. He moved slowly, rhythmically, expertly, building her tremendous love and desire for him, sending her into waves of ecstasy until it seemed her body exploded more forcefully than it ever had before when he worked that magic with her.

Automatically muscles deep inside her belly grasped at him, pulling, drinking him in, wanting, shuddering with rhythmic aftershocks as he responded to their beck and call by surging deep and hard, as though to claim every inch of her one last time, to the depths of her soul, before releasing his passion's life with a groaning of her name.

There had been little foreplay, and no words. It was all said in his one whisper, in hot, vibrating bodies, in giving and taking. There would be more moments like this one. There must be. He would make sure of it. Yet he could not be sure how he would feel, what he would do, when he saw Julien again, now over two years old. Julien, a part of him, his blood, his heart, his soul.

"I'm so sorry, Cass," he whispered.

"For what? For loving me?" She kissed his shoulder. "I never dreamed you'd love me this way. I'm so happy. Whatever happens now, I'll know you couldn't help it . . . that it doesn't mean you don't love me."

He sighed deeply, moving off her and lying on his back. She nestled into his shoulder. "Just promise me there won't be any other women, and that you won't touch that horrible Jessica woman unless that's the only way you can get Julien."

He kissed at the thick, golden hair. "You're all I want, Cass. You're all I've wanted for a long time, but I couldn't have you. The others just filled in, that's all. They never meant anything to me, not like you mean to me. I'm tempted not to go at all, not to let you out of my sight again. But it pulls at me, Cass. Stay close to

the house, will you? Find somebody else to run your
errands for you. Pay them if you have to."

"Abilene is more peaceful now, and those boys don't
dare come near me. But I'll be careful."

She turned then, putting her arms around his neck,
and he hugged her tightly. "Come back to me, Rainmaker," she whispered.

He could not forget the vision, and the words she
spoke when he saw it realized. "*I love you, Rainmaker. I'll
be your friend forever*." He could not decide if the vision was
a good omen, or bad. He just held her, his face buried
in her neck, and she felt a wet drop on her skin. He
held her for a very long time.

Lance waited behind a long, manicured hedge in the
garden, listening to Julien's laughter as the boy chased a
butterfly while his mother sat nearby reading a book.
Slowly but surely the butterfly led the sturdy, handsome
lad toward his real father. Lance's heart quickened. If
ever there was a more perfect boy child, he'd like to see
one. Julien Françoise ran on strong legs, his steps sure
for his age. His smile was quick and bright, his hair
dark brown and curly, his skin a lovely brown, and his
eyes matched the green gardens. He was his father's son,
and as Lance watched through the bushes, his chest
ached with love. How could he go away again and leave
this precious, perfect, beloved son behind? But what
choice did he have? And what of Cass? He missed her
fiercely in the short week he'd been gone, longed for her
in the night, needed her sweet friendship as well as her
precious love. He felt like a man torn in half.

Closer and closer the boy came!

"Don't go too far, Julien," his mother called out to him,

glancing at him and then returning to her book.

"Udderfly, Mama!" The boy giggled, almost managing to grasp the elusive bug. But it flew away again.

"Julien!" Lance whispered. "Here it is!"

The boy's smile faded, and he looked around with the wide, green eyes in confusion. "Udderfly!" he whined.

"Here, Julien. Come around here." The mountain wind, which was strong that day, helped shroud Lance's soft words from Jessica's ears. Little Julien tottered around the end of the hedge, his face brightening when he saw a man there with kind eyes and strange clothing, holding the pretty orange and black butterfly. "See?" Lance spoke up, smiling warmly, wanting to cry at the close sight of his beautiful son.

Julien put chubby hands over his mouth and giggled. "Udderfly!" He laughed again as Lance held it to the boy's cheek, keeping hold of one wing so that the other fluttered against the boy's skin. "Udderfly! Udderfly!" the boy squealed.

Lance pulled the bug back for a moment. "What's your name?"

"Joolen!" the boy answered, reaching out and touching the butterfly with a dimpled hand.

"Are you a good boy, Joolen?"

The boy stared at him, and there was a magic between them. The child did not answer right away, but was suddenly more intrigued by the strange man than by the butterfly. He moved the chubby hand to Lance's cheek, touching it, and in that moment Lance was swept with choking emotion. Perhaps he could not leave this boy after all! Julien touched the fringes of his buckskin shirt. "What dis?"

"Fringe. Buckskin fringe."

" . . . skin finge?"

Lance grinned, but his eyes were wet. "Yes, that's it." He took a bone hair-pipe necklace from around his neck, one an old Cheyenne woman had made for him when he had proven his manhood through the Sun Dance ritual. "Do you like it?"

He held it out to the boy, and the child studied it. "Pitty."

"Yes, it's pretty. I'll give it to you. A gift from me to you to keep forever." He reached around the boy's neck and tied it, and the necklace hung heavy and big on the child; but Julien just touched it and laughed. Lance found it amazing that the child warmed to him so readily. Did children his age have a sixth sense? Why did the boy so readily trust him and talk to him?

"Julien?" Jessica called out again.

Lance reached out and pulled the boy close, hugging him, his throat aching. Little Julien wrapped chubby arms with dimpled elbows around his unknown father. "Skin finge!" he giggled. "Udderfly!" He reared back and pouted then, seeing another butterfly wing away. "All gone!"

Lance could not speak. All gone. Yes, all gone. "Julien!" he whispered, hugging the boy tightly. "My God."

How easy it would be to run away with him now! He could leave and go get Sotaju below the hill and be off! Should he try?

It was too late. A black satin skirt appeared from around the bushes, and there was a terrible gasp. Lance looked up at Jessica Françoise, whose dark eyes were wide with shock, quickly being replaced by fear. She backed up as he rose. He hung on to Julien and looked at her with more hatred than he had felt for any enemy in his entire life. This woman had caused him more pain and anguish than all his enemies put together.

"Good morning, dear Jessica," he said bitterly, slightly nodding his head. He managed to swallow back his momentary grief over the impending loss of his son forever. He would not break down in front of this woman.

"You!" she gasped, staring at him as though he were a ghost.

"Sorry to disappoint you, but I'm still alive," he told her, his voice husky with hatred. Julien simply let the man hold him while the boy played with beads sewn into his father's buckskin shirt at the shoulder. He showed not the least bit fear of the big, tall, strong man who held him.

Jessica's face was utterly stricken with horror. "Please . . . give me back my baby!" she squeaked.

Lance bounced the boy on his arm, making him giggle. "Why should I?" he returned. "You've taken more from me than just a child. You cheated me out of the very seed of my loins, and then you blew my guts out and hoped I'd rot somewhere else and never be found." The words were cold, his eyes frightening. Never had he wanted to kill so badly, for revenge was in his blood. But she was a woman and more than that, she was his son's mother, much as he hated the thought of it.

She was visibly shaken, her face pale for her normally dark coloring, her whole body quivering. "I should have put that gun to your head!" she hissed. "I should have remembered wild animals don't die easily. They survive!"

He smiled. "I guess that's why you're still around."

She sucked in her breath, wanting to step forward and grab her son, but afraid of Lance. "What do you want! What are you doing here!" she squeaked. "If Claude sees you together—" She looked around nervously.

"So what if he does? I think it's very interesting how

403

much this lovely little boy here and I look alike, don't you? Look. Can you tell he's my son?" He held the boy's face close and smiled for her.

"Don't do that!" she hissed through gritted teeth. She stepped closer then. "Give him to me!"

He stared at her a moment, clinging tightly to an unconcerned Julien. Lance sobered, his whole countenance filled with rage. "What kind of a woman are you, Jessica Françoise? Is it so terrible that I want to hold my son for a few minutes?"

She blinked and eyed him warily. "Is that all you want?"

"Let me tell you how much I love him, dear Jessica. I have never wanted to kill anyone as badly as I'd like to kill you; but you're my son's mother, and even though you blew my guts out, I'll not touch you. I could go to Claude, tell him everything, expose you to the public for what you really are, although half of them probably already suspect. I could claim my son, and once people saw us together, they'd believe my story. I could call you up for attempted murder, adultery, expose your background. But I'll not endanger my son's life by doing so, and I'll not have him grow up knowing what his mother really is. I'm sure he loves you as a mother and nothing more, and because it's probably best for him, I'm leaving after a few days. I won't be back, Jessica."

She looked him over sneeringly. "I don't believe you!"

"Believe it. I'm going back to Abilene and marrying that girl I told you about once. We're heading north to ranch, and she'll give me more sons. I'll not bother you again."

"You're lying! I tried to kill you, and you'll never forget that. You're up to something."

He snickered sadly. "You don't even understand love

and forgiveness, do you, Mrs. Françoise? That's very sad." He looked at Julien, running a big hand through the boy's curly hair and over the soft skin of his angelic face. His eyes teared, and he kissed the boy's cheek. Julien just giggled again and grabbed his nose with a chubby hand. Lance moved his face up and bit at the boy's fingers, and Julien squealed. "Skin finge!" he said again, as though he thought that was Lance's name now. Lance just laughed and bounced him, then hugged him close, turning away from Jessica. He squatted down and set the boy on his feet. "Where's the butterfly?" he asked teasingly

Julien's eyes widened, and he looked around. "Udderfly!" He went toddling away looking for one. Lance watched him for a moment, then turned to Jessica, his eyes red and watery.

She was surprised at the stricken look on his face. "I spent all last winter lying paralyzed because of the bullets you put in me," he told her. It was obvious he was struggling not to break down. "The only thing that kept me going was my love for Cassandra, and my desire to see my son again. Now I've seen him." He swallowed. "Don't be alarmed if you see me here and there the next few days. I just want to look at him . . . get his face fixed in my mind. Then I'll go and that will be the end of it." His voice started to break. "Good-bye, Jessica."

He turned and walked off, not waiting for a reply. She watched after him, one side of her longing to lie in his bed one more time, the other side wanting him dead. As long as he was alive . . .

Julien came toddling up to her then. "Where skin finge?"

"Skin finge?"

"Taw man! Skin finge!"

"Tall man went away, Julien." She bent over and picked up the pouting boy. "You won't see him—ever again," she told the boy, a cold determination in her voice.

Claude Françoise opened the box for his son, taking out a perfect copy of a Denver & Rio Grande engine and train cars in miniature form and made of hand-carved wood. "There you are, son!" he laughed, rehooking some of the cars, setting the train on the floor and pulling it around. "It cost me a fortune, but here's your train. Some day maybe you'll own most of this railroad. You'll be the richest man in Colorado and you'll run Denver!"

The boy just stared at his father, pouting. He did not like the train. He wanted the pretty necklace the tall man had given him, the one his mother had taken from him and thrown far out in the bushes. He couldn't understand why she had done that; and it instilled a tiny fear in him he'd never felt around her before, for she'd looked mean and vicious when she threw away the necklace. Now his father was crawling around on the floor like a little child, making "toot-toot" sounds and pulling the train. But Julien didn't like trains very much. He liked butterflies better.

"Come now, Julien, there isn't a two-year-old alive who wouldn't love this! Come pull it."

The boy just plunked down on his rear, his lips puckered, his eyes scowling. "Skin finge!" he whined.

Françoise frowned. "Skin finge? Now, what is that new word?" He glanced at Jessica, who sat near the hearth in a plush chair, just staring at the fire. "Jessica, what is skin finge?"

She turned to look at him, but her eyes were distant.

"I haven't the faintest idea. He just suddenly started saying it today. He's been in an ornery mood, Claude. You've heard of the terrible twos."

The man looked disapprovingly at Julien. "Come now, son, what's all this grumping? You miss your nap today? You want to go sleepy?"

"No!" The boy turned to his hands and knees, then stood up and started running. "No sleepy! No sleepy! Skin finge!, Udderfly!" He ran out of the room as though looking for something. Françoise followed after, calling down the hall to the nanny.

"Suzanna, watch after Julien," he told the woman. "You might as well take him upstairs. He's in a cross mood, and I can't tolerate him when he's that way."

The man turned and came back into their private sitting room, closing the door behind him. "I'll be glad when he's old enough to appreciate things," he grumped. He stooped to pick up the train and put it back in a box. "Some day when he's bigger, I'll have a whole room added on, just to hold the giant scale model of the Denver & Rio Grande for him to play with. As soon as he can comprehend things, I'll teach him all the ways there are to make his wealth grow for him. It will be exciting watching him grow and learn, Jessica."

He closed the box and set it aside, coming over to a chair and picking up a pipe to light it. "This is the hard age. I wish we could skip these damned baby years and have him instantly fifteen or so." He puffed on the pipe, wondering why she was so quiet. "And isn't it about time you were pregnant again? I don't want Julien to be an only child, you know. We've worked hard at it lately. No progress?"

She moved her dark eyes to meet his. "I'm doing the best I can." She was tempted to tell him she and the man

407

in charge of the stables were doing the best they could. Just the night before she'd had a very exciting experience, lying in the hay with the man, whose huge, round muscles, dirty, animallike advances and grunts made for a glorious secret meeting. She had been watching him a long time, wanting him, thinking that surely his seed was good, too. But ever since Lance, there had been no one to equal the ecstacy she had known with Julien's real father. Still, the stable man was fun.

"I know you are," Claude was telling her. "Well, there's always tonight again. One nice thing about marrying a woman like you—a man never tires of bedding her. You always make it exciting, Jessica."

She smiled for him, wanting to tell him how sick she was of looking at him. "And how is the Denver & Rio Grande progressing, love?" she asked.

"Very good. Very good. We've branched through the canyons to Canon City and Coal Creek Mine."

"Out of Pueblo?"

"Yes. You should see the trestles we built into Canon City over a couple of the canyons. They're masterpieces, Jessica. Absolute masterpieces. It's amazing all that wood can hold an engine and an entire load of gold."

Jessica brightened. She needed to get away for a while, for she was afraid—afraid of Lance Raines and what he might do. Had he left Denver yet? Would she see him again?

"I'd like to see it, Claude. Why don't you give me and little Julien a ride on the train down to Pueblo and over the trestles into Canon City. Julien would love it, and it would get me out of this house for a while."

The man's eyebrows raised. "A train trip can be dirty, Jessica."

"I don't care. It would be a wonderful diversion for

408

Julien. And I've never seen one of those mining towns. And I would like to see those wonderful bridges your men have built. Please do consider it, and soon. I get bored here."

The man sighed and thought a moment. "I don't see why not. I'll be leaving late next week for Pueblo on business. The two of you could come along. I have a special car that is quite comfortable, like a plush hotel on wheels, you might say." He smiled more. "Yes, Jessica, I think it's a fine idea. Perhaps the change will help you relax more and make a difference in your getting pregnant."

"Of course!" She wanted to tell him what a fool he was to continue thinking her failure to get pregnant was her fault and not his own. But Claude Françoise was her ticket to wealth and status. "Thank you, Claude. I feel better. It will be exciting."

The man puffed his pipe. "Anything to please you and Julien. I just hope it helps cool the boy's pouting temper. Where on earth did he get that word 'skin finge'? I don't understand it."

She looked back at the flames, diverting her eyes from his own. "I can't imagine."

"Hmmm." The man puffed his pipe a moment longer. "At any rate, you'll have fun, I'm sure. We have nothing but the best working for the D&RG. The trestles may seem a little frightening, but they'll hold." He sighed. "I lost one good man a year ago, though."

Her heart quickened. "Oh?"

"Yes. That Raines fellow—the one who always dressed in buckskins and was raised by Indians. He was one of the best. Then one day he left to go marry some girl in Abilene, and he never came back. I guess the girl really got to him—must have talked him into settling someplace else. The strange part is he never got his money out of the bank here in Denver."

She swallowed. "Perhaps he had other money and will come for the rest later."

He sighed. "Perhaps. It's there for him, at any rate." He tamped out the pipe. "I guess you can't really trust a man like that—half wild and all. That kind works at one thing for a while, then wanders off to something else. Maybe he never even married that girl. Maybe he just rode on to something new. Men like that are always restless and wandering." He leaned back in his chair. "It's too bad. I liked Raines."

She did not reply.

"Hurry!" Jessica called out in a whisper to the stable man. "Get up here!"

He climbed the stairway quickly and quietly, and Jessica pushed at him a little to hurry him into her room. She closed and locked the door.

"I wasn't sure you understood me this morning at the hitching post," she told him. "Claude is in town on business, and he'll be gone for hours."

The man grinned, unbuttoning his shirt. He was poor but handsome, and he reminded Jessica of an ape in his short, squat build, his chest huge and powerful, his arms large with round muscles. He was pure animal in thought and deed, and he excited her. "Are you sure no one saw you, Sidney?"

He looked her up and down as she opened her robe, letting it drop so that she stood there naked.

"No one saw me," he replied. He threw his shirt aside and removed his pants and boots as she sauntered over to the bed, which was adorned with all pink bedding.

"Isn't this nicer than a haystack?" she asked in a whispering voice.

He rubbed a hand over his lips. "I'd say so. Taking a chance, aren't you?"

She smiled. "I often sleep late. And Julien is in the gardens with his nanny. No one will bother us." She lay back on the bed, opening her legs.

Sidney Drake walked on tight-muscled legs to the bed, jumping on it and wiggling between her legs. She laughed and pushed at him, forcing him to roll onto his back. She sat straddling him then, throwing her head back so that her long, black hair hung wild, rubbing herself over him but not allowing him to enter her.

"Keep the secret, Sidney, or I'll see you dead," she sneered, grinning wickedly.

"I don't want to die. I want to do this forever, Mrs. Françoise."

"I'm sure you do." She moved rhythmically, teasingly, deliberately building his anxiety. "But you have to do something else for me, too. I'll pay you. If you do it, I'll never turn you out of my bed."

She stretched one foot up, and he grabbed her ankle, kissing her foot. "You name it, sweet lady."

"Do you remember one of my husband's men who used to come here by the name of Lance Raines? He looked Indian—wore buckskins and all. I believe you met him at the cookout a couple of years ago."

The man frowned, rubbing her foot and leg. "I think so. It's been a long time."

"I know. But I think he's in town, Sidney. I want you to check all the hotel registers, and if you find him, I want you to follow him. When he leaves Denver, I want you to follow behind, and I want him dead." She moved up toward his face, straddling herself over it for a moment, then moving back slightly and bending down to grasp his hair, kissing him wildy. "Do you think you could shoot a man in the back for me, Sidney?"

He studied the dark eyes. To be bedding the wife of the wealthy Claude Françoise was more glorious than anything he'd ever experienced in his sorry life. He felt like a real man. She even gave him money. Some day when it was safe, he could brag about this one, all right. He kissed her breasts.

"I'd go to hell and back for you, love. I don't know why you want it done, but I'll do it, if I can find the man. What about my job here?"

"There are others to fill in for you. Just tell them you're running an errand for the lady of the house."

He grinned. "Lady?"

She threw her head back and laughed wickedly, and he sat up slightly, kissing her belly, pushing her backward so that he landed with his face against her. He made growling, animal noises, and she wrapped her legs around him.

"How much?" he asked huskily, kissing her thighs.

"Five thousand dollars," she answered. "I can get it easily."

"Done."

She stretched then and let him do what he would with her, able to relax more now that she was sure that this time Lance Raines would be out of her life for good. Sidney Drake would see to it. She gasped as he moved over her.

"Do it right, Sidney," she whispered. "He's . . . hard to kill."

He rubbed against her hips. "Don't be worrying about it. A bullet in the spine and one in the back of the head never left any man alive I ever heard of. You just get

412

that five thousand, lady, and don't ever lock the door when your husband is gone."

She smiled and breathed deeply. So what if he was the stable man? A man was a man, whether he was a Claude Françoise, or a Sidney Drake. The key was to enjoy the wealth of one, while enjoying the body of another.

Chapter Twenty-four

A lonely wind groaned through canyons and crevices, echoing the loneliness in Lance Raines's heart as he rode Sotaju through the foothills of the Rockies. There was a cold sting to the wind, for already in the peaks winter was trying to take hold, even though in the foothills and valleys it was deceivingly warm. Lance watched one dark cloud that hovered over Pikes Peak. Even from this distance, he could see that it was snowing up there. That's the way it was this time of year in the Rockies, a constant mixture of rain and snow.

Watching the barren, cold peaks and listening to the groan of the wind only accented the ache in his own lonely heart for his son. He had been so sure he could see the boy and then go. He'd come here to be alone, to pray to *Maheo* for the strength he would need to leave this land called Colorado and never come back, for here lived his blood, his son. Always the boy would call to him. Always when he looked at distant peaks and heard the wind, he would see the boy's angelic face, the soft, chubby cheeks, the wide green eyes, the soft, curly hair and bright smile. He would hear the sweet voice saying "udderfly" and "skin finge," and would feel the dimpled hand on his nose. It was amazing that he could feel so attached to a child he'd only seen and touched twice. But blood could not be denied, and even little Julien had seemed to sense something special when Lance had held him. The boy had shown no fear. They had warmed to each other as though the child had seen Lance Raines every day since his birth.

He closed his eyes against the pain of it. Julien! He had to leave. There was no other choice. Cass was waiting faithfully for him, and he'd promised her . . . and loved her. But how was he to pull himself away?

He would pray. He would offer a blood sacrifice. Perhaps if he bled, the pain would help ease the pain in his heart of never seeing his little son again. Besides, he deserved to suffer for what he'd done. His own irresponsibility had caused all of this, and a scheming woman.

Then his keen ears picked up another sound. He halted Sotaju to listen. He'd sensed another presence for quite some time, and had even felt watched before he left Denver. He turned and eyed every rock and crevice around him but saw nothing. He listened again, hearing only the wind, and the distant, lonely whistle of a Denver & Rio Grande engine that made its way south from Colorado Springs to Pueblo. Still, he could not get over the feeling that someone was close by.

He rode forward, making his way up an escarpment and into a small cove, where he dismounted to make camp. He unloaded Sotaju, remembering a time when the horse was his only care in the world. Now Kate was old and ill, the girl he loved was waiting for him in Abilene, and his son lived in Denver, with a witch of a woman who would make sure he could never have the boy. His carefree, happy days as an Indian boy were over, but life was sad now even for the Indians themselves. It seemed that with civilization, only sadness and heartache had come to this western land.

He chopped at yucca bushes and small, dead pines to use for a fire, piling them on a layer of hard-crusted earth. He would pray all night, perhaps let blood. He must forget. He must go to Cassandra and forget.

He stopped, again sensing another presence. And again as he looked around, he saw nothing. He frowned, unable to shrug off the chilly sensation. He stood up and stripped off his shirt, wearing only his leggings and moccasins. He threw the buckskin shirt aside, and his tobacco pouch fell off his belt when he did so. He looked down at a frayed rawhide tie.

"Should have got a new pouch a long time ago," he muttered, bending down to pick it up. God could not have made his timing more perfect. Just as he started to bend over, a shot rang out. A bullet ripped across the top of his right shoulder, causing little damage. It all took place in a fraction of a second. Instantly Lance was on his belly. Another ringing shot hit the dirt beside him, and he rolled and scrambled for the rocks at the outer rim of his campsite, two more shots pinging the stones around him.

He dived for the boulders, skinning his arms and back as he did so, then crouched, peeking through a crack between two rocks. He finally saw movement, guessing quickly by the spacing of the shots that only one man was after him. For what reason, he couldn't know. But the fact remained someone wanted him dead, and he had no weapon on him but his knife. His rifle still lay beside his gear, and he had not worn his handgun that day. It lay temptingly near his rifle, but he didn't dare try to get them.

All his Indian training flooded forward. He must become like the rocks and the earth. He must be quiet as a gentle morning wind. He would not sit there and become the prey. He would make his hunter the hunted.

He watched again, seeing then the glint of the sun on something shiny—a rifle barrel, no doubt. The man was headed down a thickly wooded hill toward his campsite. Lance watched him dart among aspen and pine trees. His own job of staying out of sight would be more difficult, for on his side of the little cove there were no trees, only a scattering of boulders and short bushes. Somehow he had to get behind his attacker. He scrambled on his belly to a ledge and rolled over a little drop-off of perhaps three feet, landing on rocks and a dried-up bush. He had long ago learned never to cry out in pain when an enemy was near, no matter how bad the wound. The bush poked the scar on his stomach where he'd taken Jessica's bullet, a spot that still remained tender. But he ignored the pain and made his way around the edge of the cove, moving like a cat, watching for every moment his bold attacker looked in the wrong direction. The man had come out of the trees into the cove, rifle in hand. He looked around at Lance's gear, seeing the rifle and handgun. Lance moved again while the man was not watching, working his way around toward the side of the cove where there were trees.

"Come on out, Raines!" the man called out. "You've got no weapons on you. I know you're wounded, and you can't survive without your gear."

There was no reply but the wind, and the man watched all around the cove carefully, cocking his rifle again. Lance watched, silent as the clouds above. His assailant was short and stocky, a dark, monkey-looking man who looked familiar. But Lance could not place him. The man turned away from where Lance crouched; and Lance moved again, his moccasined feet making no sound, for his keen eyes avoided stepping on anything that would snap or make stones roll. Below him Sidney Drake kept turning in a circle, watching for any movement. Drake wondered if he had perhaps hit Lance Raines more accurately than he first thought. Maybe the man was dead. But if he was not . . . The man's chest tightened. Had he become the prey rather than Lance Raines? It struck him that Raines had been raised by Indians, that scouting and spying were his specialty. Still, one of his bullets had hit its mark, he was sure.

"Raines! You're a dead man!" he called. "I just had to wait till you were far enough into the wilderness that no one would find you for a good, long time." He swallowed nervously. Five thousand dollars was a lot of money, but he should have gotten closer before firing. If only he knew for sure his bullet had hit right. He'd seen Raines go down, then head for the rocks. Was he lying there wounded right now?

Drake walked forward, rifle held tightly, ready to fire. He headed into the rocks where he'd seen Lance go, seeing blood on the ground beside one big boulder. He smiled. "I did hit him!" he muttered.

He looked around at the boulders farther above, sure that Lance Raines was a crawling dead man. He had only to follow the drops of blood. He saw one near the little drop-off and walked up to inspect it.

Suddenly a strong arm gripped him from behind with viselike strength, and a huge blade flashed in front of his eyes.

"Drop the rifle, mister!" a voice growled. "Drop it or I'll cut out your eyes!"

Drake's eyes bulged, and he threw the rifle aside. But two powerful hands grasped Lance's wrist then, pushing Lance's knife hand away from Drake. Drake was himself an extremely strong man, but Lance was taller and broader. At the moment, that was his disadvantage, for Drake yanked quickly on Lance's knife arm and bent over, flinging Lance over his head. Lance landed hard on his back, at first stunned. He realized he was still not really at full strength, and his body ached and bled from scrambling shirtless in the rocks and from the superficial wound at his right shoulder. In the quick movement, his only thought was to cling to his knife, but a foot smashed hard against his arm then, causing his hand to open.

Something grabbed the knife out of his hand, and Lance saw the apelike man bending over him. He reached up and grabbed at the man's arm, his right arm weaker now, his whole body stinging and aching. The wound Jessica had inflicted in the right side of his back had left that whole arm and shoulder still tender and weak; but this was a fight for his life, and he'd promised Cass he'd come back to her.

He pushed hard, drawing on that reserve strength few men could muster, gritting his teeth and growling like the savage he could be, keeping his attacker's arm from coming down to stab him with his own knife. Drake grabbed for Lance's hair with his free hand; but Lance's arms were longer, and he could not reach as Lance held the man's other arm away with his own two arms stretched full length.

Lance managed to bend his legs under himself and get to a squatting position, then to his feet, pushing the whole time, straining every muscle, while Drake kicked and hit at him, scratching into the skin of Lance's arm in a fruitless effort to make the taller man let go. Lance moved one hand quickly to Drake's wrist and brought a knee up, bending Drake's hand back at the wrist while the man

419

screamed as ligaments pulled and the knife fell from his hand.

Lance backhanded the man then with his right arm, mustering all the strength he could. Drake grunted and turned slightly, then landed into Lance as Lance lunged for the knife. He rammed a shoulder into Lance's tender belly, and Lance cried out as he went down against the rough earth with his bare back again, Sidney Drake on top of him. His mind spun with the question of who the man was, but it didn't matter now. The fact remained the man wanted him dead.

They rolled in the dirt until Lance ended up on top of the small but strong Drake. He landed a big left fist into the man's face twice, three times, four, then grabbed the man by the shirtfront and yanked him to his feet. Blood poured from Drake's nose and mouth.

"Who are you!" Lance roared. "Why are you after me?"

The man didn't answer at first, but coughed and sputtered, trying to keep from breathing in blood. He grabbed at Lance's wrists then, slamming his head into Lance's chest and trying to bring a knee into Lance's privates. But he was too short. Lance managed to wrench his left wrist out of Drake's grip, and he dealt the man several swift blows underneath his bent head until Drake backed away.

Lance kept swinging then, battering the man's face and belly, forcing him back toward where the knife lay. Drake tried to land his own punches; but once Lance got him moving, there was nothing he could do, for his reach could not meet Lance's body in the right places because of the difference in height and arm length. His only hope was to get Lance into a close tumble, for he was sure his strength was equal, and Lance was already weak from his wound. But Lance knew it, too, and was not about to let the man get close again.

Finally Drake stumbled backward over a boulder, hardly able to see from all the blows. Lance lunged for his knife then, his hands bleeding. He wondered if either of them was broken. He managed to grasp the knife, and he straddled Drake, who still lay on his back, groaning and spitting blood. Lance grabbed the man's hair.

"Tell me who you are!" he growled. "I'll by God scalp you!"

"Drake! Sidney Drake! I oversee the stables . . . on the Françoise estate!"

Lance's rage knew no bounds. "Jessica sent you!" he hissed.

"She . . . said she'd pay . . . five thousand dollars . . . if I killed you!"

Lance laid the knife against the man's cheek. "And you no doubt showed her a good time in bed, like the ape you are!" He slashed the knife down the man's cheek, and he cried out in horror. "I'd let you live, Drake, just because I feel sorry for any man who's been fooled by that witch! But five thousand dollars is a lot of money, and I intend to sleep well tonight!" He plunged the knife deep into the man's chest. He needed to kill. He needed to pretend it was Jessica Françoise's heart he pierced. He'd promised to walk out of her life, leave his son, and this was her gratitude—to pay a man five thousand dollars to kill him.

He yanked the knife out and stood up. "You'd have done the same to me," he said coldly. He wiped the knife off on the man's clothing and shoved it into its sheath, ignoring his pain and bleeding then as he dragged the body several yards to the little drop-off and shoved it over. He spent the next several minutes picking up large rocks and piling them on top of the body. It would be a long time before the body was found, and who was to know how it got there? Only Jessica would know the truth, and she'd never tell, for she would only implicate herself. How many more crimes would she have to cover in order to keep her prestigious position?

He looked around the hills above. The man's horse must be up there somewhere. He would leave it. It would yank itself loose eventually and wander away. The longer before anyone found it, the better.

He walked wearily back to his camp then. He would have to move it. He would not spend the night near a dead man, so he quickly loaded things loosely back onto Sotaju, then picked up the bundle of sticks and wood as best he could. "Come on, boy," he told the horse. "Let's find a better spot."

He left the cove, feeling little regret over killing Sidney Drake. He'd killed many an enemy before. His only regret was that it wasn't really Drake who needed killing. It was Jessica Françoise. It sickened him that his son would be raised by such a woman. The woman was wicked and half crazy, and it worried him. Would she get worse? Would she ever use her cruelty against her own son? After all, she could hardly look at the boy without seeing Lance Raines. Perhaps she would neglect the child to tend to her own wicked desires, letting him cry while she lay with a man.

Leaving would not be as easy as he had hoped, due to this new twist in circumstances. She was still laying with men, and still scheming to have him killed. He could not help but feel a terrible need to stay around and protect his little son, who was too sweet and beautiful to be raised by such a woman. He felt like crying. How could he make such a terrible decision? He could marry Cass and bring her to Denver; but Jessica was too crazy for that, and Cass had already refused to live in Denver. The woman would surely find a way to hurt Cass just for spite, either emotionally or physically. He wanted Cass nowhere near Jessica Françoise and hoped the girl would never even meet the woman. The decision still remained: He must either stay around Denver and leave Cass behind, or leave Julien behind and go to Cass.

He made camp a good mile from the first spot, where he found a small waterfall in which he could wash his aching wounds. His hands were scabbed and swollen, the wound at his shoulder also scabbed over. He stood under the cool water and let it rinse off sweat and dirt and blood, while his mind raced with terrible indecision. If he didn't go back to Cass, she'd understand, but her heart would be shattered. She was so young. It was like ruining the rest of her life, and he loved her dearly, needed her, wanted her, longed to bed her again, to show her tenderly and passionately how much he cared for her. He wanted his seed to grow in her, wanted sons by her, wanted to wake up every morning beside her. But someone else's life was also at stake. Little Julien. The boy was of his blood, his responsibility, no matter who actually was raising him. The fatherly instincts in his soul were too strong. To the Cheyenne, sons were all-important, and in his heart he was Cheyenne. Besides that, he'd never had the chance to know his own real father. And the fact remained that the Françoise environment was simply not a good place for any child.

He made a fire but got out no food. He would fast and pray. He must decide.

For three days there was only the wind and the call of the eagle. At times a faint sound could be heard from the distant hills, someone chanting, singing, sometimes crying out in anguish. The wind groaned along with a man's prayers. The waterfall flowed along with a man's blood from self-inflicted wounds. Rain fell twice, along with a man's tears. In his fasting he prayed for an answer. He opened his arms and threw back his head, letting the sun burn into him, crying out to *Maheo,* smoking a prayer pipe at times and offering it to the four directions and to the god of the Sky and the god of the Earth. Did the vision of Cass mean then that she was saying good-bye, that he would not return to her arms?

After three days he had no answer but his own instincts. He must have his son. If that was his answer, then it must be. Something would happen to allow to it to be so. He began eating small bits of food to get his strength back, then more and more over the next two days until he was strong enough to ride. There was only one way he could hope to have both Julien and Cassandra. He would find a way to steal Julien. Surely he could do it. He would take the boy to Canada, then wait for a long time before sending for Kate and Cass. Yes! He could do it! Claude Françoise would surely put out a tremendous manhunt. But Lance Raines knew the land, knew the mountains, the prairies, the rivers. Perhaps the Cheyenne and Sioux could help him smuggle the boy northward. It was worth the risk. The only danger was that if they were found, Françoise would know why Lance had taken the child. He didn't care that his own life would end, but what would happen to Julien? The only answer was that if they were found, he'd kill his son himself before he'd let

424

Françoise touch him. Death would be better at his own father's hands, for he would do it as quickly and painlessly as possible. He would rather kill his son than have Françoise sell the boy into some kind of slavery. And it wouldn't matter what happened to Jessica then. He didn't care about that anymore, didn't care that he'd be taking the boy from his mother. The child would be better off.

It was the only answer, his only choice. He could never live in peace knowing his son was with Jessica and Claude Françoise. Knowing Claude was ruthless and held life of little value, and knowing Jessica was still whoring with every man who crossed her path told him all he needed to know, let alone the fact that the woman was vicious, a murderess at heart.

He spent his last night in camp in prayer again, begging *Maheo* for the strength to do what he must do. Cass would understand some day when he explained it to her. He could only hope she was all right, and that Kate was better and would live long enough to come to Canada. He would worry about how to get them there when the time was right. For now he must concentrate all his thoughts and plans on getting his son away from the Françoises.

He felt stronger, as he always did after praying and fasting. He could do this. He must do it. He ate a whole rabbit for breakfast, then cleaned up camp and packed his gear, checking to be sure he left no telltale evidence behind for the day Sidney Drake was found, if he ever was.

He checked all the straps on his gear, then mounted up. He had made a decision, and he would follow through with it. He headed toward Colorado Springs. He would take the train north to Denver. It was faster. After

425

all, even if he saw someone he knew from his railroad days, what did it matter? No one knew why he was there. No one knew about Julien, where he'd been or where he was going. Jessica's own guilt kept her from ever involving him in any trouble. It made him grin to think of it. He could show himself anyplace he liked, and Jessica could do nothing about it. He was curious to see how she would look when she saw him again and realized her second attempt at murdering him had failed. Yes, he was going to get his son, and nothing would stop him.

Lance stared at the growing, busy little town of Colorado Springs. It was amazing what the railroad could do. It had been over a year ago when he had helped work on the Denver & Rio Grande, laying tracks south toward this very town, which really didn't exist then, other than one shack that held a railroad crew. Now it was a bustling little railroad stop of nearly a thousand people, with every kind of necessary business. It was obvious the D&RG was going to be a tremendous success, and already it was branching into the mountains to meet the mines and carry out their wealth for high fees. The railroad would profit tremendously, as would men like Claude Françoise. But Françoise would lose in the end. Lance would see to it.

He headed Sotaju down the street to the railroad depot, dismounting and tying the animal and walking into the little building to ask about the next train north.

"One just headed out south, mister. You just missed seeing some of the Denver & Rio Grande big-shots on their way to Pueblo. Next train north will be in two hours."

426

Lance could not help wondering. If Claude Françoise was away, his job would be even easier. "Who were the railroad men on the train to Pueblo? I used to work for one of them. Was one Claude Françoise? I haven't seen him in a long time."

"Why, yes, he was along. And he brought his wife and son this time for a little vacation."

Lance's heart quickened. "Wife and son? Isn't that unusual?"

"Yes, it is. But I guess they wanted to see the railroad for themselves. He bragged about how he was going to give them a ride on the Canon City line over them new trestles they've built. Had some other railroad men along he wanted to show off them trestles to, you know. I guess the wife and kid was along for the adventure. That Mrs. Françoise sure is one beautiful woman, and their son is a right handsome boy."

The man started to write out tickets. "Wait," Lance spoke up. "How long ago did the train leave?"

"Like I said, only an hour or so ago. I think they'll be holding up overnight in Pueblo. Why, mister?"

"I think I'll head that way myself. I'd like to see Françoise again."

The man shrugged. "Whatever. But there won't be a train for a while now."

"That's all right. I'll ride."

He mounted up again and headed south. He would follow. He would watch from the shadows. Perhaps there would be a moment when Julien Françoise was left untended. Perhaps it would be easier this way than trying to get into the Françoise mansion again. Yes. Perhaps this was his answer from God. Perhaps there was a reason the Françoises had all taken the train together, a reason he

427

had discovered it and had crossed their path this way.

He rode Sotaju hard until it was too dark to see. He made camp just a few miles north of Pueblo, then headed into town at the break of dawn. From the outskirts of town he could see a train sitting at the station and people milling about. They had not left yet. It hit him then that the best place to snatch Julien would be in Canon City, if he could get there first. It was a mining town, full of sights. And the mountains would give Lance a thousand places to hide as he smuggled the boy north. He knew the mountains, knew how to survive, even though it was getting colder. Canon City was a better bet than Pueblo, but he had to get there first, watch them disembark, see where they would stay and let them relax and visit. They would be tired then. Now they were rested, probably ready to leave. Now was not a good time. He headed Sotaju into the foothills, noticing that high up in the mountains a huge, nearly black cloud hung low, dumping a torrent of rain on the upper regions. He could see lightning in the cloud, hear the booming thunder. Here below it did not rain at all. He reminded himself he would have to watch for sudden rushing creeks. In the mountains a small stream could turn into a wild, raging river in minutes.

He rode west, following the railroad bed most of the way. He had a good start on the train itself, which still sat back at the station in Pueblo and which would probably make many scenic stops on the way into the mountains so its special guests could view the scenery and the D&RG road work. He was surprised himself at the progress that had been made since he left the railroad's employ, thanks to Jessica Françoise. He didn't doubt that within the next few years the railroad would reach into every mining city in the mountains and go over the mountains to western Colorado. It was amazing what man and money could do.

He rode for several hours, feeling suddenly happy and lighthearted. He had all his money that had been waiting for him at a bank in Denver. He had made a decision, and somehow he would follow through. It would be hard waiting for Cass; but he knew she would wait, for she loved him and trusted him. He would not betray that trust. He only regretted having to make her wait and wonder for a while, but it must be done. He must have Julien. He would have his son or die trying.

He came across the first trestle then, trying to decide how he would get across the swollen stream below it. The rain he'd seen earlier must have been one of those freak mountain rains that occasionally dump several inches of rain in minutes, creating instant, sweeping floods below. He made his way down the steep canyon wall. This particular canyon was usually dry, but already water swept through it at a deep, bubbling speed that made it impossible for him to cross with Sotaju.

He looked up at the trestle, a tremendous man-made project made up of thousands of wooden beams, crisscrossed from top to bottom to support the weight of a loaded supply train. It was an awesome sight, and he wondered how many men had died building it, falling to a crushing death on the boulders below.

His chest tightened then. The stream was swelling rapidly, roaring now through the canyon, beating at the wooden beams. Had the engineers made allowances for a sudden, rushing flood? Did they realize what the elements were like in the mountains?

He heard a train whistle then, or at least he thought he

did. The water roared so loudly he couldn't be sure. Then there came the creaking sound, and the trestle swayed slightly. His eyes widened in horror as one section broke out from the pressure of the rushing waters. There was no way with one section missing that the contraption would ever hold a train, and surely the train out of Pueblo was on its way by now. Julien! He had to stop the train or his son would die!

Chapter Twenty-five

Lance turned Sotaju, heading the animal back up the dangerously steep canyon wall they had just descended. Now it seemed the climb took forever, when it had seemed only minutes getting down. They wove back and forth, Sotaju picking his way carefully over boulders. Lance was glad for the horse's surefootedness, for this was not the time for an accident. A much worse accident lay ahead if he couldn't flag down the train.

"Come on, boy!" he urged, a train whistle in the background. How could he have seemed so far ahead of the train, only to have it be so close now?

Ever upward Sotaju climbed, the faithful animal doing its best not to falter. One leg slipped, and the animal whinnied and stumbled slightly, then kept going, wanting to please his master, sensing Lance's anxiety.

"Julien's on that train, boy. Come on! Get up there!" He cursed Claude Françoise and the railroad for not having the intelligence to go ahead first and check out the trestles. After all, there was a woman and child aboard, and hadn't they seen the cloudburst above? Anyone who knew the mountains knew what that could mean. Flooding and washouts occurred regularly in the Rockies.

To Lance's wide-eyed horror, the train was fast approaching when he reached the top. He rode his already-winded mount hard toward the train, realizing in desperation that even if he could signal it to stop, it could never stop before reaching the trestle. He waved at the engineer, pointing at the trestle ahead. The man frowned as the train flew past, then his eyes widened when he realized Lance's signal. The train went on by, only an engine and woodbox, the fancy passenger car and a caboose.

As though in a strange dream, Lance saw Jessica Françoise's face through a window, saw her eyes widen at the sight of him. Then there was the terrible sound of brakes squealing, and he knew bodies must be flying. The train rolled out onto the trestle nearly to the middle before finally stopping, and there was only a short second of odd silence before a loud cracking sound echoed through the canyon and the trestle swayed.

"God, no!" Lance groaned. He rode forward to the edge of the canyon wall, just in time to see the engine and woodbox roll off the rails, pulling the train car and caboose with them. Somehow the engine and woodbox came uncoupled partway down and thundered into the canyon and water below with a horrible boom that shook the very earth.

Lance sat frozen. He was helpless to do anything to stop it. The sound of the crashing below seemed to shake his soul as well as the earth. The fancy passenger car hung precariously on a folded trestle, while the caboose also came uncoupled and fell with a mighty crash off the other side of the trestle, splintering into what seemed millions of pieces, crashing against boulders, much of it washing away with the wild stream below.

For several seconds Lance stared at the passenger car. It hung on the collapsed trestle, swaying slightly, the trestle boards squeaking and groaning. Lance dismounted then, running to the edge where the rails jutted out into nothingness. Julien! He wanted to scream the name but couldn't find his voice. Surely the bodies inside were so tossed that none could be alive. Just then a man's body fell out of a window, and there was a loud, long scream before it hit the rocks below. Still the car hung there. And then, above the roar of the raging river below, Lance could hear it, a child crying.

"Julien!" he whispered. He had no choice. If he did not go, the child would die. If he went down and they both died, where was the loss? He wouldn't want to live anyway after standing and watching his son be crushed to death below. If his son was to die, then they would die together, or by some miracle Lance would save the boy.

He scrambled down over broken pieces of trestle, praying every inch of the way that nothing would give way beneath him, that somehow he could get to his son. The farther down he went, the louder the river roared, and Lance was sure it was getting even higher. Surely the entire trestle and the remaining car would be swept away any moment. He reached the swaying piece of trestle and climbed out onto it, his son's frantic crying stinging his ears.

He prayed for strength as he clung to wooden beams, crawling, hanging, climbing, crawling until he reached the railroad car. It lay on its side and was somehow caught on the beams. How much longer it would hang there he could not know. It didn't matter. He had to try to get to his son.

"Julien!" he screamed out, for the crying had stopped. He made his way carefully onto the side of the car, crawling slowly to a window. He hung his head inside to see several men lying sprawled and all looking lifeless.

433

One was Claude Françoise, his head appearing to be completely split open. Next to him lay Jessica, hanging partially out of a window beneath her, her eyes wide and staring. Julien came crawling out from under her skirt, blood running over his face from a cut on his forehead. His nose was running from crying, and he stared wide-eyed at Lance.

"Skin . . . finge," he whimpered.

"Julien! Give me your hand, son," Lance told the boy, reaching down to him. "Hurry! Grab my hand! We'll go find a butterfly."

The boy just stared at him, and the car shifted slightly. Julien started crying then, looking at his mother. The woman blinked, unable to speak or scream as her body slipped farther through the window, one bloody hand clinging desperately to the frame. But she was too badly injured to hang on. Julien clung to her skirts, crying for his mommy.

"No, Julien!" Lance yelled. "Let go of her!" He could see she would slip through, and the boy would go with her. He thrust himself farther through the window, a tight fit, and stretched out his arm as far as he could manage, barely able to grasp the boy's hand.

It was then he felt an odd pressure on his wrist, and a peaceful warmth spread through him momentarily, as though someone was helping him. There was no time to wonder about it, except that he was sure he heard Kate's voice. *"Grab hold of your son, and never let him go"* came the words, so distinct that he turned his head for just a moment. No one was there. Yet now he could reach the child. He got a firm grip on the boy's wrist as Jessica's body slipped through the window and fell through the air while Julien screamed, "Mommy! Mommy!" Lance could see the body through the bottom window as it landed in the water below and disappeared.

Julien cried more, staring through the window. Lance lifted, begging *Maheo* for the strength to get the boy out of the wreckage before they all went crashing to their deaths. He clung to the screaming child, crawling backward then, tugging to get out of the window, for his frame was too big for it. His entire body was outside the car, but his arm was still inside, hanging on to little Julien, who was kicking and screaming. He pulled hard, the position awkward, for he couldn't get to his knees but had to stay flat, giving him little leverage and making Julien a difficult weight in spite of his small size.

Lance pulled desperately until the boy was at the window, then was able to reach with his right hand to get a better hold. He grabbed the boy's jacket collar and pulled him out, with no choice but to drag the poor child over the window ledge, scraping his fat knees and making him cry more.

"It's all right, Julien," Lance yelled to him. "We're going to climb, son, and find a butterfly."

The words seemed to calm the child somewhat; but Lance noticed an odd looseness when he pulled at the child's arm again, and the boy began screaming all over again.

"Damn!" Lance could see he'd apparently pulled the poor child's arm right out of its socket or dislocated the shoulder. But it was better than death. He got the boy beside him then and hugged him close.

"Don't be afraid, Julien," he spoke softly into the child's ear. He lay on his side, carefully pulling his shirt up and over Julien so that the boy was tight against his bare chest and held there by the shirt. He stuffed the child's feet into the top of his leggings then so that the boy could not fall out of the shirt and so his own hands could be free to climb and grab without having to hold on to the child. The shirt was tight enough that the boy was secure against him, and the warmth and the binding seemed to calm the boy, also holding his arm so that it could not move.

"We're going to play a game, Julien. I'm going to climb way up to the top there, but you can't cry. If you don't cry, I'll find a butterfly for you when we get to the top."

The boy just sniffed and looked up at the tall man with the buckskin clothing. He liked this man, liked his warm smile. Lance's heart ached at the sight of blood on the boy's face and the knowledge that he was hurt and in pain. But Julien Françoise was really Julien Raines, and therefore a child of courage, for wasn't he Lance Raines's son?

Lance looked up at the overhanging piece of trestle. There was nothing to do but try to get up there. He crawled off the railroad car, grabbing on to the sturdiest-looking piece of beam he could find. He swung his foot across to another piece and grabbed yet another, inching his way along until he was finally off the section that hung and swayed. He clung to a crossbeam and breathed a sigh of relief, holding on to get his breath and to put his other arm around Julien, squeezing lightly.

"You're a good boy, Julien, for not crying. You're a big boy."

He panted to get his breath, forcing himself to breathe more slowly and deeply then, while Julien's head lolled against his broad chest under the buckskin shirt. The boy's eyes were closed, and he made little whimpering sounds. Lance worried about the head injury and the

436

bleeding, and he began hoisting himself again. He had to get to the top so he could help the child. Below him the broken section of trestle swayed again, making a haunting, creaking sound. Still the railroad car hung on it. Lance kept crawling his way upward, placing a hand here, a foot there, carefully, studying each beam before grabbing it. One gave way under his foot, and he hung suspended by his arms, his legs flailing in nothingness. He prayed Julien would not slip out of his clothing, as he raised his legs and searched for another beam. He found one in front of him, but then his body was stretched, and it took all the strength he could muster to let go of the beam he was holding and reach for a forward beam, his arms spread then between the two. With gritted teeth and straining muscles, he let go of the first beam and quickly grabbed the second so that his body was more straight again.

He stayed there for several seconds before reaching for the next beam, wrenching one leg up out of an awkward position and onto a beam just below him so that his whole body was in a more normal position again. He breathed deeply for a moment. He was closer now to the more secure beams he had used to climb down. He began climbing faster then. Close! He was so close to the top! He could hear Sotaju whinny. Higher and higher he climbed, his whole body bruised and cut and his hands full of splinters. But nothing mattered other than getting his son to the top where he could help him.

With one last grunt and aching pull he felt the rail of the overhanging track. It was cool to his injured hands. He pulled up, hoping that all the times he'd bumped poor Julien against beams had not injured the boy further. He hoisted up and over, then crawled along the overhanging

437

track to land, where he fell onto his back, embracing Julien and laughing out loud while at the same time crying tears of joy and relief.

"We made it, Julien!" he shouted, unable to stop his own tears. "Thank *Maheo* and Kate's Jesus and . . ." He remembered then, remembered the odd warmth, the pull on his wrist, the sound of Kate's voice. Someone, or something, had helped him grab Julien at the very moment the boy could have gone out the window with his mother. "Kate," he whispered. A cold chill swept through him, and he didn't want to think about what the incident could mean. There was only this moment, his son in his arms, safe, alive.

Below there was a groaning shudder, and then a long, drawn out cracking sound, followed by several seconds of more cracking and crashing and a thunderous boom, as the passenger car and the rest of the trestle collapsed into the rushing waters below. Lance held Julien tightly, pressing the boy's head against his chest, covering his ears.

"It's all right," he told the boy softly. "Everything will be all right now."

For a brief moment he felt some remorse over the fact that Jessica had gone down to the rocks below. The woman he'd shared bodies with for five days and then learned to hate was dead. He'd wanted her dead, yet now there was some hurt to it. She was, after all, his son's mother. She had given him this beautiful child, although unwillingly.

He eased up onto his knees then and eased Julien out from under his shirt. The boy seemed only half conscious. Lance held him in one arm and hurriedly untied a blanket from Sotaju with his other hand, spreading the blanket on the ground. He gently laid the boy down and

438

carefully removed his jacket and little shirt. The boy only whimpered as Lance tenderly felt his shoulder and arm, then cried louder as Lance moved fingers over the boy's bones expertly, feeling for the right position and pushing the shoulder into place.

"You'll be all right," he said softly. He quickly felt over the boy's entire body, removing the rest of his clothing, almost crying with joy that as far as he could tell nothing was broken. There were only bruises.

He quickly retrieved some gauze from his supplies and began wrapping Julien's arm and shoulder, winding the gauze around his chest to tie the arm against his side so it could not be moved. "There now. You won't feel so much pain if you can't move it. In a couple of weeks it will heal back in place."

He took down his canteen and poured some water onto a rag, gently washing the boy's face and happy to see that all the blood came from one cut on his forehead. He washed the cut carefully, unable to clean it really well because it had scabbed over too much. There was a large blue bruise around it, and he didn't want to press on the sore spot.

All the while he worked, Julien watched him with curious, green eyes. He was more awake now, and again he felt no fear of this tall man who touched him so gently and made him feel better.

The boy wiggled to his knees, then to his feet, when Lance turned to pick up his clothes. The child's quickness surprised him, and when he turned to dress him, the boy had already toddled closer to the canyon edge.

"Don't go too close, Julien. Come on. Let's get your clothes back on."

The boy toddled back and lifted a foot, but looked over

at the yawning canyon. "Mommy?"

A pain stabbed at Lance's chest. "Mommy went away. She'll be gone a long time, and she wants you to come with me." He buttoned the longjohns and pulled on the boy's woolen pants. "You can call me Daddy." He turned the boy and pointed to himself. "Daddy."

The boy scowled, looking over at the canyon then, pointing with a chubby finger. "Daddy there."

Lance shook his head. "No. He wasn't Daddy. I'm Daddy." He put a hand to the boy's face and leaned forward, kissing the soft cheek. "Thank God you're young enough to raise as my own. Before long you'll forget that other mommy and daddy. You have a new mommy and daddy."

The boy stared at him and frowned, putting a hand to his father's mouth. "Daddy?"

"Yes. Call me Daddy."

Julien's eyes drooped, and Lance pulled him close. His head lolled against the man's shoulder. "Daddy," he said in a tiny voice. "Skin finge."

Lance rubbed a cheek against the boy's curls. "Yes. Daddy skin finge." His throat tightened, and he gently laid the child back down, wrapping the blanket around him and carrying him to a small spot of shade provided by a lone aspen. The child seemed to be asleep, and Lance hoped it was only that and not unconsciousness.

He walked to the edge of the canyon then, looking down at the wreckage below. Part of it was completely gone, washed away by the torrent of water. It was then it hit him, the perfect answer! The wreck! The flood! He looked over at Julien, looked around the canyon and the mountains. No one knew he was here! No one even knew about the wreckage yet. And no one knew about the

440

connection between himself and Julien Françoise. He looked below again. In such accidents, it was not unusual for some bodies not to be found at all. How easy it would be for a tiny two-year-old boy to be swept away and never be found again, supposedly killed on the rocks or drowned, possibly eaten by wolves. Of course! He could take the boy to Abilene and go someplace new with Julien and Cass and Kate. No one would ever know. And when seen together, who could deny that Julien was indeed his own son? The boy would be presumed dead. He was free to take the boy now. No one would ever know the difference! He had his answer. *Maheo* had been good after all! He would leave with the boy, using the foothills and keeping to himself, avoiding all towns until he reached Abilene. It would be hours before the accident was discovered. The only logical conclusion would be that the child had been swept away and was dead. Who cared what happened to the Françoise fortune? Little Julien didn't need it. He would provide the boy with things much more important than wealth. He would give him love, teach him to hunt, to love and care for horses, teach him to love the land and the animals. The boy would have the freedom to be whatever he wished to be, without the pressures of handling money and power and property. He would grow up with a gentle mother who knew nothing of the promiscuity and viciousness of Jessica Françoise.

He raised his arms and gave out a wild cry of victory, yelling like the Indian he once was, looking to the sun and laughing in spite of his own weariness and injuries. This was a good day, the best day of his life, in spite of the terror of the accident. The gods had helped him save his son. Surely that was the best sign of all that he was to keep him! All he had to do was ride away with the boy.

He looked down at the canyon below. Mother Nature had done something he had been unable to do legally. She had killed Jessica and Claude Françoise. The only obstacles to his happiness had been removed! And the best cover for the disappearance of Julien Françoise had been provided by the accident. He simply had to go someplace where no one lived who had ever seen Julien Françoise. The joy of it overwhelmed him. He cried out again, falling to his knees. Cass! He could go to Cass now, his son in his arms. How he suddenly longed for her, ached for her. When he reached her he would hold her forever, make love to her forever, fall into her arms and invade her body and soul and never let go. Cass! Sweet, beautiful, loving Cass! He felt like a new man, free from bonds. This was the first thing that had gone right since he first rescued Cass from the Cheyenne. So many things had changed since then. He had changed. He had a woman. And he had a son!

He hurried back over to Julien, his heart swelling with love as he stood and watched the boy sleep. How perfect he was! How handsome! He stooped down and gently lifted the child, being careful of the injured arm and shoulder.

He mounted Sotaju. "I know you're tired, boy, but we've got to get away from here, farther into the hills, before anyone comes." He turned the horse and headed south, away from the tracks. Julien lay nestled in his left arm. He knew of no other way to carry the boy for now, for he didn't want to leave travois tracks, nor did he want the child to sit up yet. In his arm, the child would feel less of the jolting motion of the horse. "Take it easy, Sotaju," he warned the animal. "Julien is hurt." He headed into a thick grove of pines and away from the canyon.

He had to force himself not to laugh out loud. He didn't want to startle the child, who slept in spite of the motion of the horse. Lance looked down at the sweet face. The boy would be afraid for a while, but one day he would forget. The natural warmth between them would eliminate the boy's fear, and soon the memory would fade until he knew only his real father and Cass. For safety's sake, no one but he and Cass would know the boy was not both of theirs. They would simply surmise that Cass had married young, and one day Julien would know only Cass as "Mommy." He leaned down and kissed the soft cheek.

"Nahahan," he spoke lovingly in a whisper, calling him "our son" in Cheyenne. *"Nemehotatse."* He had never used the word to anyone else but Cass. Even the love he had for Kate was not the kind he held for Cass and his son. Never had he dreamed that a man could feel this much love. He headed for Abilene, and Cass.

Cassandra scrubbed a sheet against the washboard. Scrubbing and hanging up clothes was a wearying chore, but she did the best she could. It was a warm day for October. She straightened and wiped sweat from her brow, and it was then she saw the rider. He was easy to recognize now, for she'd seen him coming over the western horizon before, had prayed too many times that he would come.

"Rainmaker!" she whispered.

She pushed some hair behind her ear. She wanted to run and change, comb her hair, but this time she knew it wouldn't matter. All that mattered was that he was coming. He'd kept his promise. Her heart swelled with joy and love. She didn't care what she looked like. He was coming! She quickly wiped her wet hands on her apron and walked toward the rider.

The sun was setting behind him, and he was only a shadow. It was an eerie sight at first, as though he were only a ghost approaching. Heat waves rippled up from the earth to make him look hazy and more unreal.

He urged Sotaju into a faster gait when he saw her coming, and in minutes they met, both just looking at each other at first, as though to ask if she still wanted him, and if he still wanted her. Yet neither had to question it. Her eyes moved to a handsome little boy who sat in front of his father. The boy grinned, revealing tiny baby teeth, his green eyes dancing.

He spoke up. "Udderfly!" He held out a bright orange butterfly that had long since quit struggling against the firm hold the boy kept on one wing.

Cassandra's eyes teared, and she looked at Lance. "He's beautiful. But how—"

"His parents are dead," Lance told her, his eyes looking tired. "I had nothing to do with it. It was a train accident." He looked past her toward the house, and she closed her eyes and looked down, putting her hand on his knee.

"Kate's dead, too, Rainmaker. I'm so sorry."

She heard him breathing deeply, and then his hand moved over hers. "I knew it already," he said in a husky voice. "She spoke to me . . . when I was saving Julien from the accident. I just . . . I was hoping she could see him before she died."

She looked up at him, her heart aching as his jaw flexed in an effort to stay in control, and one tear slipped down his cheek. "Oh, but I'm sure she knows, Rainmaker.

She knows you have your son. And if she spoke to you, she was there. She knows just as surely as if she were standing right here, and wherever we go, she'll be with us."

He swallowed and nodded, petting Julien's hair. "This is my son. This is Julien. He was injured in the accident; but he's a brave boy, and he'll be all right. He hardly even cried."

Cassandra reached up for him.

"Be careful of his right arm. I dislocated it getting him out of the wreckage. It's wrapped to his side." Lance lifted him down by putting one arm around him and slipping a hand under his bottom. Cassandra took him, bouncing him on her right arm. She looked too tiny to even hold the chunky boy.

"Oh, he's heavy!" she exclaimed as Lance dismounted. "He's going to be as big as his daddy."

Lance put a hand on her shoulder. "I hope you can love him, Cass."

She kissed the boy's cheek as the child studied the half-dead butterfly he still clung to. "Of course I can love him. He's part of you, isn't he?"

He sighed and took the boy from her, setting him on his feet. "You'd better go find a new butterfly, Julien," he told the child. "The one you have can't even fly any more."

The boy toddled off, holding up his captured bug and throwing it, trying to make it fly again. Lance watched him for a moment, then turned to Cassandra, and in the next moment she was finally in his arms, finally breathing in the sweet scent of man and buckskins. She could not help the tears then.

"You came," she whispered, kissing his chest and hugging him around the middle.

"Of course I came. And I'm never leaving again, Cass. The accident—the train crashed into a canyon. As far as anyone is concerned, the boy died, too. Even if the body isn't found, he'll be presumed dead, swept away by the waters, maybe eaten by wolves. Everyone died. No one knows I was there at all. It was as though God said, 'Here. Take the boy. I've given you a way to keep him now.' " He kissed her hair and looked down at her. "I want to go to Montana, Cass, maybe even Canada. I don't want anyone here in Abilene to see the boy. We'll just leave, quietly, keep him hidden until we're well away. I'll find a lawyer here in town someplace to handle the sale of Kate's house, and we'll send for the money later. I have plenty anyway. I want to go someplace where no one knows us, and as far as anyone knows, the boy is ours. We'll find a way to leave Julien here, maybe while he naps, and take a few minutes to find a preacher to marry us. It's important no one sees Julien until we get someplace new. You'll still marry me, won't you? You'll go with me?"

"How can you even ask such a question!" She smiled then. "Besides, I think I might be carrying your second son."

More love could not have shown in any man's eyes at that moment. He put a big hand to her face. "Are you all right? Maybe you're too young."

"I'll be fine."

Their eyes held, and he looked her over lovingly. "God, I love you, Cass." His lips met hers then, hungrily, gratefully; tasting, needing, wanting. He had all his answers now. There would be no more roaming, no other women, only this sweet girl whom he'd claimed as his own so long

446

go and who now was branded by Lance Raines. How ould she ever belong to anyone else?

Julien laughed as he spotted another butterfly, and not ar away a Kansas-Pacific train rumbled by, its whistle rying across the Kansas plains.

ZEBRA HAS THE SUPERSTARS
OF PASSIONATE ROMANCE!